HIGH PRAISE FOR BONNIE VANAK!

THE TIGER & THE TOMB

"A rollicking, romantic adventure with an intelligent, feisty heroine and an alpha hero every woman will want to take home."

—*New York Times* Bestselling Author Bertrice Small

"Bonnie Vanak...create[s] a highly entertaining, exciting, romantic read.... You can't go wrong when you read anything by Bonnie Vanak!"

—*Romance & Friends*

"Vanak has written a totally sensually satisfying and action-packed romantic adventure."

—*Historical Romance Writers*

THE FALCON & THE DOVE

"Bonnie Vanak touches upon a fascinating period of history with charm and panache. A wonderful first novel."

—Bestselling Author Heather Graham

"Bonnie Vanak writes with humor and passion. She masterfully weaves a stunning vista of people, place and time. I truly enjoyed this unique and compelling love story."

—*Old Book Barn Gazette*

"A fast-paced tale that hooks the audience...a riveting novel."

—Harriet Klausner

THE COBRA'S KISS

He studied her in the brilliant moonlight. The moon. Her namesake. He gestured skyward. "The beauty of the full moon pales beside you, Badra."

Nervousness fraught with an odd yearning returned to her. She glanced at the web of starlight glistening in the night sky. "But nothing's as lovely as the stars. They make me feel as though I could touch them. Like glittering gems I saw once in Cairo."

"You are more beautiful than all the stars in Egypt's sky."

His husky voice was like warm velvet. Khepri lightly clasped her shoulders. Heat emanated from him like from the glowing coals of a banked campfire. "Jabari has released me of my vow not to touch you. Do...do you want me to kiss you?" he asked softly. "Badra?"

Yes, her heart cried.

The Cobra & the Concubine

BONNIE VANAK

LEISURE BOOKS NEW YORK CITY

A LEISURE BOOK®

May 2005

Published by

Dorchester Publishing Co., Inc.
200 Madison Avenue
New York, NY 10016

ISBN 0-8439-5529-5

Printed in the United States of America.

Visit us on the web at www.dorchesterpub.com.

For the Haitian guys in the dump truck who pulled us out of the water in Gonaives when everyone else passed by. I offer you this Irish blessing: "May you live as long as you want and never want as long as you live."

Special thanks to Dr. Sharon D. Cassell, for your invaluable help with behavioral issues relating to child sexual/physical abuse; author Renee Halverson and my critique partner Julie Sloan for your endless support and encouragement; my editor, Chris, for taking a risk; and my husband, Frank, my inspiration and my greatest love.

PART 1

THE COBRA
&
THE CONCUBINE

Chapter One

Eastern desert of Egypt, 1889

Someone, please help me.

The silent plea ran through Badra's mind in a frantic chant. She quivered behind the large limestone boulder just outside the peppering of black goat-hair tents. Sounds of war raged: the screams of men dying, the triumphant war whoops of their enemies gaining a stronghold. The two fiercest desert tribes in Egypt—the Al-Hajid and the Khamsin, warriors of the wind—fought each other in a bloody clash.

Peeking around the stone, Badra's friend Farah watched. The sun burned down mercilessly upon both of them. Wind drifted across the dusky sand, ruffling Farah's long black hair. At twenty, she was five years older than Badra in both experience and wisdom. She was the one who had urged this escape.

Farah turned, her face flushed with urgency. "The Khamsin are departing our camp! Now is the time."

Badra's feet remained frozen to the sand. They had fled the harem tent in the confusion and made it outside the camp. Yet if they ran, Sheikh Fareeq would find them. "You are my slave, Badra," he had snarled. "Escape to the Sinai and I will find you. I do not let slaves go free. Ever."

Farah's voice returned Badra to the present. "Please, let us flee," she pleaded.

Somewhere deep inside her, Badra found a tiny core of strength and drew on it. She and Farah ran out from behind the sheltering rocks.

Chaos erupted—a blur of movement on fast, sleek Arabian horses. The Khamsin had recovered their prized breeding stallion and were leaving the Al-Hajid behind. The beautiful white horse was tethered to the saddle of the Khamsin sheikh who now rode off toward his home.

Farah did not hesitate. She immediately darted after him, clutching Badra's hand and screaming for him to stop.

The Khamsin sheikh pulled up his mount in an expert move, the mare's nostrils flaring. He was a magnificent figure. An indigo veil draped across his lower face, shielding his features. He leaned forward, and his dark eyes flashed with fury until Farah laid a hand upon his trouser-clad thigh.

"Please," she begged, her voice frantic, "we belong to Sheikh Fareeq. Please, I beg you, sire, take us with you as your concubines. I know you are Jabari bin Tarik Hassid, sheikh of the Khamsin. I have heard you are a just and righteous leader."

Badra raised her eyes hopefully, silently imploring the man. Words fled. She could not speak. The leader's eyes crinkled in a frown, and two more warriors—one short, but

4

with a powerful build, the other taller and leaner—pulled up, effectively trapping her between the sheikh and their horses. Three veiled faces stared down with hidden menace. Badra began to shake violently, wondering if she fled a familiar horror for one yet unknown.

"Sire, what is the delay?" the more muscular warrior asked.

"These women, Nazim. They ask sanctuary as my concubines."

Nazim leaned over his mare and gave the women a cursory glance. "Then offer it," he hissed. "But let us hurry!"

Jabari looked down at Badra, then at Farah, then questioningly at the third warrior. "Khepri, my brother, what is your opinion? Is this a trap, or should I take them into my care?"

"You could do with a few concubines," the tall and lean warrior replied with amusement. "Perhaps if they keep you busy enough in bed, you will be less inclined to ride into trouble."

"Watch your tongue, lest I cut it out for you," Jabari growled, but it seemed to Badra there was a smile in his voice. "Very well," he said to the women. "I will offer you refuge in my household."

The Khamsin sheikh stared down at Farah, nodding. He reached down and scooped her into the saddle. "Khepri, take the little one," he instructed. "I am entrusting you to keep her safe for me."

"Come, little one," the warrior named Khepri called.

Badra could not move; she was too terrified. Leaving would constitute the bravest act she'd undertaken since being sold to Fareeq four years ago when she was eleven.

5

Dust rose in a thick cloud as the others rode off. Khepri motioned to her, his blue veil hiding all but his eyes.

At her continued hesitation, the warrior looked over his shoulder. Distant, angry shouts filled the air—sounds of men gathering. The Al-Hajid had recovered and would soon ride in pursuit. He slid off his mare in a graceful move and came for her, holding out his hand. Badra dragged her frightened gaze up to meet his, then recoiled. He had the same bronze coloring as those men familiar to her, but his eyes burned a fierce blue, like the Egyptian sky.

The man tore off his veil, revealing features that tore the breath from her lungs. Badra stared, awestruck. Lean, sculpted cheeks, a strong jaw and a dark-bearded chin made him appear fierce, but he offered a gentle smile and his tone was soothing and low.

"I am Khepri bin Tarik Hassid, brother to the sheikh. Have no fear, little one. You are safe with me." Those incredible blue eyes suddenly blazed with mischief. "And I promise you, Jabari is a considerate man. If you have any trouble, I will punish him most severely." He winked.

Whether it was his teasing or his gentle manner, something about this man pulled at her. Badra nodded. He hoisted her easily onto his saddle and then pulled up behind her, cradling her with his firm, warm body. Another shiver went through Badra—this time not of fear but a deeper intensity.

They rode fast through hard canyons and deep desert, finally meeting up with the others; then they rode almost ceaselessly, taking only the short breaks required by the horses. Badra did not speak. During the rest periods, some of the Khamsin warriors cast her searching glances. Sly remarks followed.

"Fareeq took our breeding stallion, so our sheikh will bed Fareeq's concubines as revenge. Jabari will prove he is the virile leader that Fareeq is not," one man commented.

Handing Badra a goatskin of water, Khepri frowned. "Must you talk around these women as if they do not exist? You have as many words as a storm has sand, Hassan, but a sandstorm is far more pleasant to the ears."

Sharp panic pinched Badra as all the men laughed. The Khamsin sheikh would bed her immediately, to prove himself to his warriors. Would he also brutalize her? She found herself terrified as she rode.

When they reached the Khamsin camp, Badra gazed around with wide-eyed curiosity. Blue-scarved women looked curiously at her. Farah came over, offering an encouraging smile. Khepri escorted them to a many-poled tent. A middle-aged woman introducing herself as Asriyah, the sheikh's aunt, welcomed them. Badra was given water for washing, a change of clothing and shown to a soft bed. She fell asleep as soon as her body touched the mattress.

The next day, Badra woke up confused and afraid. She glanced around at the low sandalwood table near her bed, the rich, thick carpets, the elegant carvings set upon a handsome wood chest. Then it all came back. The Khamsin camp. She had a new master. She touched the cotton sheets with a trembling hand. Despite the reassurances Khepri had given her last night, Badra could not believe she was safe.

Even if Jabari was kind, Fareeq would come for her. She was one of his favorites. The only time she had escaped his attention was while she was pregnant. The childless Fareeq was desperate for a son, so she'd broken the secret pact among his concubines to ensure he'd remain childless; she'd stopped taking the herbs preventing conception. Remembering her difficult pregnancy and her labor that started two weeks early, Badra swallowed a lump in her throat. Her little girl. She had held the child in her arms and marveled at the tiny, precious life. Then they had taken her away when Badra fell into an exhausted slumber. When she awoke, she'd learned Jasmine had been too little and died. Barely had she recovered when Fareeq began raping and flogging her once more. . . .

Badra clutched the sheet as the woven door to her chamber lifted. Farah entered, smiling blissfully.

"The sheikh has taken me to his bed! He is a wonderful lover and brought me to a pleasure I never imagined. He is unmarried. Perhaps he will wed me," Farah told her.

Her friend possessed a sinuous grace. Like Fareeq's other women, she had evaded the whip, using her wiles, which she'd eventually taught Badra, to lessen Fareeq's abuse. A sage look came into her dark eyes.

"He has called for you next. He is quite virile, this one."

Badra flinched, remembering Fareeq's nightly visits, the rough way he had shoved himself into her until she cried. Men did not deliver pleasure. Only pain.

Farah's expression softened. "You must go, Badra, lest you anger him. Do you want to return to Fareeq?"

Fear twisted like a loathsome snake about Badra's spine. How could she endure sharing her new master's bed? Yet she had no choice. Her mouth went dry.

Farah drifted outside, a dreamy expression on her face. Asriyah replaced her. "I am told you are called Badra," the sheikh's aunt said. "I have been instructed to bring you to

Jabari's tent as soon as you are prepared for him. Hurry," the woman said.

Badra washed, dressed and subjected herself to the woman's gentle touch as she brushed her hair. "You are quite beautiful," Asriyah commented. "My nephew will be pleased."

Badra tensed, thinking of the horrors to come.

The sheikh's aunt escorted her out to the largest tent. Badra removed her sandals. Sucking in a deep breath, she walked inside the tent's main room, her feet treading noiselessly on a thick jewel-toned carpet. Wind blew softly through the enclosure from the partly rolled-up flaps. Jabari sat cross-legged on the floor next to the warrior she'd heard called Nazim. The men ate dates from a bowl on the floor and talked and laughed. Badra studied her new master with care. He was much younger than she'd first thought, somewhere in his early twenties. Quite handsome and tall, with long black hair spilling from beneath his indigo turban. She prayed the ebony eyes would hold kindness, that he would show a little of the warmth she'd glimpsed yesterday.

Jabari glanced up. A reassuring smile touched his mouth. His manner seemed gentle.

"Nazim," he said in husky voice. "Leave us."

The warrior gave his sheikh a grin and a wink and left. Badra trembled. Jabari invited her to sit and offered her a date. She took one as he talked. His voice was deep and soothing, but she heard little. Sweat trickled down her back. Her stomach pitched as he unfolded his muscled body and stood. "Come," he told her, holding out his hand.

The sheikh led her to a back room. A massive bed stood

near one tent wall. She knew what he wanted. Her heart thudded.

"Undress for me," he instructed softly.

Moisture dampened her palms. Badra bit her lip, filled with revulsion. But if she did not obey, this man might flog her as Fareeq had. The sheikh's broad shoulders hinted at muscle that could wield a whip harder than Fareeq. She felt helpless.

Her shaking fingers tugged off her indigo *kuftan* and stripped off the underlying *kamis* shirt and wide, blousy trousers. Naked, she stood before Jabari, displaying what Fareeq had coveted since eyeing her at the Pleasure Palace, the brothel where her parents had sold her. The sheikh's jaw dropped.

"Allah," he said hoarsely. "You are lovely."

She hated this. Hated herself. Badra tried to quell the horror that the lusty gleam in his dark eyes sent through her. He put a palm upon her breast.

No! Not again! She could not. Terrified, she jerked away. Nowhere to run. Badra felt trapped. Instinct drove her into the tent corner. She crumpled on the carpet and crouched, facing the wall. Her arms wrapped about her for protection.

Maybe if she curled up very tightly and made no noise he would leave her alone. Violent shivers racked her.

"Badra, what is wrong? What are you doing?" Bewilderment filled the sheikh's voice.

Badra crawled further into the corner. She felt humiliated and ashamed. Yet she could not stop.

"Do not be afraid of me," he said.

Air brushed her naked skin as he lifted her hair. A warm

hand suddenly settled over her exposed back, upon the deepest of the scars carved there. She flinched. Badra stuffed a fist into her mouth to stifle a scream.

No noise. Noise meant he'd hit her harder.

"Allah," the sheikh said in a shocked voice. "That fat jackal of a bastard, what did he do to your back?"

Badra whimpered.

"Please, Badra, come out. I will not hurt you."

Lies. Always the lies. *Of course you say you will not hurt me. Then you do. Oh please, don't touch me. I cannot bear it.*

Jabari's words became a buzz in her ears. She peeked and saw him offer her clothing. Another trick. He would offer covering and then rip it off. And beat her. And laugh.

Finally the sheikh stood. She heard him leave. A few minutes later, he returned and she heard Farah's voice.

"She will not say a word to me. What did that bastard do to this poor girl?" Jabari said.

"Badra hasn't spoken in months to anyone. She was our master's favorite. He enjoyed . . . flogging her."

Farah crouched down. Badra stole a peek.

"Badra, stop this before the sheikh becomes angry," her friend pleaded. "He is a skillful lover, much more than our master. Why, the Khamsin sheikh's member is far larger than our master's. Like the towering obelisks of Egypt it is—"

"Thank you," the sheikh said dryly. "You may leave now. Call Nazim in."

He followed Farah out to the tent's main section. Badra heard a man's footsteps and a deep, cheerful voice.

"Do you need assistance, sire? Advice? I had thought you would need no instructions in this matter."

"Stop joking, Nazim. Badra ran into a corner and will not come out. Farah attempted to reassure her—by telling her my member is large as the obelisks of Egypt."

"Ah, very reassuring. And not true." Nazim chuckled.

"The girl is terrified. Fareeq flogged her. Come and see if you can work your famous charm to coax her out."

Badra heard them enter the bedchamber. She squeezed her eyes shut. If Jabari wanted her, he'd have to force her. No words would move her from the slim safety of the corner.

"Look, she's shivering, poor girl. I should carve my dagger into that bastard Fareeq for what he has done," Nazim said quietly.

Opening one eye, Badra saw the man lean over, heard him murmur something soothing. Compassion shone in his odd, whiskey-colored eyes, but she knew looks could deceive. He touched her bare arm.

She shrieked and huddled further into the corner.

A heavy sigh rushed from Nazim. "She has too much fear, Jabari. I advise you to be gentle with her. Give her time."

She heard him leave, then the sheikh sat nearby.

"I see we are at an impasse, Badra." Jabari said quietly. "But I am a patient man, and I will wait for you to come out. As long as it takes."

Two hours. What was Jabari doing to her?

He had counted every minute since the sheikh took the new girl Badra into his tent. Finally Khepri could take it no longer. He stood near Jabari's quarters, fashioning a new harness for a farmer's donkey. Irritated, he frowned at two warriors exchanging sly grins and glancing at the sheikh's tent. Ribald remarks about Jabari's sexual prowess followed—not all of them positive. Jabari needed to prove himself, still. He was only twenty-three and had assumed leadership barely two months ago. Bedding Fareeq's concubines would gain the warriors' respect.

"Two hours! Our sheikh is a strong man," one said.

Khepri grimaced. Seeing him, the other warrior laughed. He said to the first, "Look, his brother already is thinking how to surpass him. Always determined to be the best. I hear fathers lock their daughters away when Khepri visits the village. They have seen how his mistress cannot walk straight for days after being with him. Perhaps our sheikh will do the same to his new concubine."

Khepri's insides twisted. The little concubine called Badra had seemed terrified. Her dark eyes had begged for help. Pity and an odd protective feeling stabbed him. He too, had quivered with fear when he came to the Khamsin, his parents' death screams still ringing in his ears.

To cover his agitation, and any noise of coupling inside the sheikh's tent, he began to sing. He tried not to think about Jabari bedding Badra. She belonged to the sheikh and he was foolish to covet her. Yet he couldn't help the jealousy stinging him like a cactus needle.

Her muscles ached. Badra dared not move. The sheikh studied a sheaf of papers. Her body ached from huddling in one position so long. But here was safety.

A horrid noise sounded outside. It sounded like someone . . . singing? Somehow, Badra realized it was the man she'd ridden with. It was Khepri. He sounded worse than a braying donkey. As if to confirm her thoughts, a donkey brayed. Her lips twitched with sudden mirth.

"He sounds like a camel farting," Jabari muttered.

The warrior sang louder. The donkey made an unmistakably rude noise. Badra smothered a laugh.

"Stubborn beast! I am the fiercest warrior in Egypt. Have you no respect?" Khepri yelled. His frustration was apparent.

This time, Badra's giggle escaped. Jabari looked at her.

"He makes you laugh, does he?"

She could not help a small smile.

"Badra, if you like Khepri, I can bring him here. I would truly enjoy seeing you smile again. Would you like that?"

She gnawed on her lip, considering. Khepri seemed gentle and protective. Safer than the sheikh. Her mind worked frantically. The sheikh seemed a proud man. He would not accost her in front of Khepri. She nodded.

"If I bring him inside, you must get dressed and come out of the corner," he cajoled.

Badra hesitated, staring at the clothing the sheikh held in his outstretched hands. Was this a trick? His expression looked encouraging. She snatched the *kuftan* and tugged it on.

Her muscles screamed in protest as she stood. Her legs felt wobbly, but she cautiously followed Jabari to the tent's main room. The sheikh went to the tent door. "Khepri, come in here immediately. Your noises can be heard to the Sinai."

Then Jabari turned. The smile he gave softened the stern lines about his face. Perhaps he wasn't such a beast, Badra thought.

14

The summoned Khamsin warrior trudged inside, looking sullen.

"Apologize to my concubine for your rudeness," Jabari commanded. "Your singing has hurt her ears. It is worse than listening to your donkey pass wind."

Khepri scowled, then saw the sheikh's mocking grin. He offered Badra a charming smile.

"I apologize for the noises you heard, but the donkey is the rude one. He does not believe in the artistry of my voice, so he teases me—like my brother." He winked.

A small giggle escaped her.

"You mock my pain," he teased her. "But I assure you, Jabari sings no better. Shall I ask him to demonstrate?"

"Don't ask the singer to sing until he wishes to sing by himself," she croaked, remembering the ancient Arab proverb.

The words, the first she had spoken since losing her baby and all hope, shocked her. Her voice sounded cracked and dry. Jabari's jaw dropped. Khepri smiled.

Apprehension slid from her. She realized the sheikh had moved back, giving her much-needed space. When he told Khepri to leave and to summon Nazim, rolling up the tent flaps fully to expose the room to the outside air, she no longer felt afraid. He made no move to touch her but spoke quietly.

"Badra, I cannot change the past and what Fareeq did to you. But I promise you, it will not happen again under my care."

Nazim appeared, smiling with delight upon seeing her. The sheikh beckoned for both he and Badra to sit on the carpet near stacked camel saddles, away from listening ears. She obeyed cautiously.

"Nazim, I cannot make her my concubine. I did not, and will not bed her, seeing what Fareeq did. Farah will, ah, keep me occupied enough."

Nazim looked worried. "Sire, the men believe you are pleased with her, since she was here for two hours."

Jabari frowned. "I see you were counting the minutes."

"Every man was," Nazim said. "The entire tribe is talking of your . . . astounding skills. If you do not claim her as your concubine, you shame her." But his look said what words did not: *You will shame yourself*.

A frustrated sigh fled the sheikh. He studied her. "Then, Badra, I will call you my concubine, but in name only. You will not share my bed. You are under my protection. Do you understand? You no longer belong to Fareeq."

"You are wrong," she replied in a broken whisper. "I will always belong to Fareeq. He will never stop looking for me. You and your men are in grave danger."

Nazim put a hand on his scimitar's hilt, and spoke. "Listen to me, Badra. We have long been enemies with the Al-Hajid. They have never defeated us in battle, nor will they. I vow this, as does every warrior in this tribe."

"You cannot stop him from coming for me," she insisted.

"Then I will give you a strong warrior to watch over you, to safeguard your every step so you feel secure," Jabari assured her. "Khepri leads my *saqrs*, my falcon guards. I am appointing him as your protector. Wherever you go, he will remain with you. He is a brave warrior. I trust him absolutely and you should. You are Fareeq's slave no longer."

16

"Fareeq will never beat you again," Nazim added. His amber eyes regarded her with pity.

Shame flooded Badra. Would every tribe member look at her the same way? She could not bear it if they knew her dark secret.

"Please. Do not tell anyone else . . . what Fareeq has done to me. I beg you," she pleaded.

"I must tell Khepri, so he knows your past and how important it is to protect you," the sheikh said.

"No," she cried. "Please, I beg you. I cannot bear it."

She could not stand the disgrace if anyone else knew. They would feel repulsed and disgusted. They would blame her.

Jabari sighed. "As you wish. It shall remain within these tent walls." He turned to Nazim. "Call Khepri in."

As Nazim walked off, Jabari leaned forward. "Badra, if I give you Khepri as your protector, you must trust me. Will you trust me? Or at least try?"

"I will try," she whispered. Khepri had seemed kind.

A torrent of wild emotions swept over her when the young warrior returned. His merry blue eyes flashed with friendliness as he eyed her. She tried to smile. It felt like her face cracked in two, but she managed.

The expression did not escape Jabari's notice. A satisfied look came over him. "Do not be dismayed by his youthful appearance. Khepri is only nineteen, impetuous and reckless, but a brave warrior and fierce."

"Being impetuous is a shared trait in this family," Khepri responded, grinning impudently. "Unlike being the best warrior."

17

Nazim cuffed him in a friendly gesture. "Mind your manners, young one. Do not make assertions you cannot defend."

"Ah, my brother's guardian takes offense at me saying Jabari is a better warrior than he. I apologize for telling the truth," Khepri said in a mocking tone.

"Enough!" Jabari ordered, but a fond smile touched his mouth. Badra relaxed even more, seeing the camaraderie between the trio.

The sheikh turned serious. "I called you here to confide in you and assign you a very special duty. I did not bed Badra, and I will not. Yet this information will remain inside these tent walls. She will remain known as my concubine."

"You did not? Why? She is beautiful," Khepri blurted.

Jabari gave a stern look that indicated it was none of his business, but the warrior's puzzled frown indicated he still wanted an answer. Badra's frantic gaze sought the sheikh's.

"She is too young and frail," Jabari said carefully. "Unlike my enemy, I am more considerate of the women I take to my bed. But since the entire tribe seems to think I already took her, it is best she remains my concubine."

He shot Badra a knowing glance. Tension flowed from her body. The sheikh had told the truth without revealing her secret. Yes, perhaps she could trust this man.

Surprise and an odd relief showed in the young Khepri's wide eyes. "Of course," he said solemnly. "What do you want of me?"

"Badra will be your responsibility from this moment forward. You are assigned exclusively to be her falcon guard and to shield her from all harm. I need a warrior whom I can trust, for she is very beautiful, and many men will covet her. You will allow no man to touch her." The sheikh paused and gave him an intent look. "No man, including yourself. I am giving you this honor because I know you would fall upon your scimitar to defend her honor and her life. Do you understand?"

A look of quiet pride settled about Khepri as he drew himself up, placing a hand upon his sword hilt. "I do, sire," he stated. "I will defend Badra's honor and life to the death."

"Like your totem, the cobra, may you always strike her enemies as fiercely as you have struck mine," Jabari said in formal tones.

Their ceremonial-sounding words should have reassured her, but they did not. Badra knew Fareeq. He would come for her. And when he did, much blood would be shed. Including her own.

Night settled about the Khamsin camp with a soft sigh of the desert wind. Badra lay in bed. Asriyah had left a small oil lamp burning, but even that light gave no peace from the shadows in her mind, the tiny, winged fears beating at her.

She knew he was coming. Khepri had reassured her Fareeq would not claim her any longer, but she knew Fareeq's resolve, his unwillingness to relinquish anything belonging to him. If he could not have her, he would kill her. Of course, death would be a welcome release to the barbaric sufferings she had endured. She would almost cry with joy at the cold bite of a blade.

The night air settled around her with a chill that sank into

19

her bones. She sensed it, felt it in the air, as thick and menacing as a dark cloud of fire: He was coming for her.

Shouts filled the air, along with the sound of pounding hooves upon the hard sand. Sitting bolt upright, Badra trembled violently. The woven door of her chamber jerked to one side and Khepri stormed inside, clutching his scimitar. He lowered it and beckoned to her. She rose from the bed, her nightdress clinging to her as she ran to him.

"The Al-Hajid are raiding us in return. Jabari expected this and I am to remain at your side. Do not fear, little one. I will guard you."

Badra rocked back and forth, tears coursing down her cheeks. "Fareeq is powerful. Your people will be slaughtered."

A cocky smile touched his mouth as Khepri held his long, curved scimitar aloft. "You have apparently never seen Khamsin warriors in battle."

He'd barely finished speaking when a knife slit the tent walls. Badra screamed as two Al-Hajid warriors spilled inside, swords aloft, eyes shining with cruelty.

Khepri draped the trailing end of his indigo turban across his face. He touched his sword hilt to his heart and then his lips, then warbled a long, undulating cry Badra knew was the Khamsin war song. He stepped forward, sheltering her with his muscled body and slicing the air with his scimitar. "Tell that dirty disgusting dog of the desert, Fareeq, that Badra is no longer his. She is Khamsin now. I am the Cobra, her falcon guard, and will shed the last drop of my blood before you jackals lay a hand on her."

"Fine by us," one laughed.

"We'll see," Khepri answered calmly, lunging forward.

Badra cringed as he effortlessly dueled with the two war-

20

riors. Harsh sounds of metal against metal clanged in her ears. Shouts sounded outside the tent as other Khamsin battled the raiders. She shrank back and squeezed her eyes shut.

Silence suddenly fell. She opened her eyes. Khepri turned, wearing a look of savage satisfaction. His enemies lay dead before him. He peered out of the tent.

"The rest are fleeing, the cowards." He wiped his blade upon the robes of his enemies, then sheathed it.

He turned, his manner reassuring and gentle. "You are safe now, Badra. No man will harm you."

Badra looked at the dead men lying on the carpet and felt no ease. Fareeq would not quit. One attempt was not enough. Others would come for her, to return her to the black tent of pain. She'd allowed a bit of hope to enter her mind, but that was gone.

There remained only one choice. Salvation hung from this young Khamsin warrior's belt. The curved dagger's wicked point would spear her heart. Darting forward, she pulled it from its sheath. Khepri whirled in a move worthy of his cobra totem. Badra cried out as he wrapped his hand about the blade and yanked it away, grimaced as he tossed it aside.

Hot tears filled her eyes. Badra looked at the discarded dagger with deep shame. "Please, let me die before others come. Let me feel death's peace, for only the blade will release me from Fareeq."

"No, Badra," Khepri said softly, his eyes never leaving hers. "You are so wrong. Death is never the correct choice."

"It is for me. I cannot live as a slave any longer."

"You have a new life now, Badra," he said, stepping closer. "And a falcon guard." Resolve shimmered in his

21

deep blue eyes. "A falcon guard who has sworn an oath to his sheikh to protect you with his life. It is an oath not easily given, and one I will honor all my days."

But his words meant nothing. "You have taken away my last chance for peace," she whispered.

Compassion filled his eyes as he gazed intently at her. "No, Badra," he said. "You are free to choose your own destiny now. Fareeq holds no power over you. Trust me, there are new beginnings. I know. For I was not born Khamsin."

While his words did not sway her, his anguished look did. "Your eyes," she said suddenly.

A bitter smile touched his features. "All anyone knows of my family is that they were foreigners crossing the desert to the Red Sea. Their caravan was attacked and everyone was killed. I remember little, but Jabari's father, Tarik, told me the story so I would honor my parents, who died to keep me safe."

"What happened?" Badra asked.

"When I was barely four, the Al-Hajid raided our caravan. My parents hid me in a large basket. The Khamsin attacked the Al-Hajid after they rode off with the spoils and they took the basket. I shook with fear as the lid came off, thinking I would die like my parents, my brother, and the servants. I looked up and saw two faces staring at me, one with black eyes and one with amber. The one with black eyes said . . ."

Here he paused and smiled. He said, " 'Father, there is no treasure in this basket. I do not think there is anything of value here.' "

Badra watched Khepri's jaw tense, and he glanced away

22

as he continued the story. "Jabari's father looked into the basket and said, 'You are wrong, my son. There is something of enormous value. A little boy.' The sheikh looked at me and said the same words I said to you."

"Have no fear, little one," Badra echoed softly.

Khepri gave a solemn nod. "Tarik sent warriors to investigate the caravan, but they found only the dead. Fareeq had burned the bodies so they were unrecognizable." His eyes closed. "Jabari's father raised me as his son." He looked at her, appealingly. "There is peace here, Badra. You can make a new life. I will help you. Jabari's father named me Khepri, after the Egyptian god of the sunrise, to reflect the new dawn of my life."

Her voice wobbled. "Khepri, the god of the sunrise. And I am Badra, named after the full moon. We are opposites."

A small smile quirked his lips upwards. "It may appear so, but the sun and the moon cannot exist without each other."

She stared, wanting to trust him. He was so handsome, seemed so good. "But does the moon dare to trust the sunrise? It pushes her from the sky with its blinding light, away from the nurturing dark. The sunrise burns. It is far more powerful than the moon."

A fierce expression tightened Khepri's face, chasing away the boyish charm she'd glimpsed earlier. He now wore the hard resolve of a warrior sworn to duty. "Powerful, yes. To shield the moon so none may find her. Badra, I am your falcon guard, given to you as your protector. I am sworn to defend you unto death. I am a Khamsin, warrior of the wind, and will never let anything happen to you. I promise. Know now: You are safe from Fareeq."

Giving a reassuring smile, he gently touched her cheek and wiped away her tears with his thumb. Something warm and wet replaced the salt water coursing from her eyes. His blood?

She turned his palm over to examine it. He'd cut himself while wrestling the knife from her. "You're hurt!"

Giving a soft cry of distress, she took the sash from his belt and wrapped it around his bleeding hand. She pressed it tight, staring at Khepri. No man had ever hurt himself for her. No man had ever combated another to defend and protect her.

A twinkle lit his eyes, turning them a deeper blue. "Ah, if I had known wounding myself would have caused you to soften, I would have cut myself much earlier."

For the first time in many long years, Badra offered a genuine smile. "You are sworn to be my falcon guard and protect me, Khepri. So I suppose I had best treat your injuries. Since you have vowed to give up your life for me, it is the least I can do in return."

"Little one, it is not a great sacrifice. For seeing you smile, I would gladly surrender my life," Khepri said in hushed tones.

Badra was mesmerized by the tenderness on his face. She leaned close. Reaching up, for the first time since she'd been enslaved, she willingly touched a man. Her trembling hand caressed the softness of Khepri's dark beard.

He groaned deeply and pulled away. He closed his eyes. When he opened them, they held a distant look.

"Ah, little one," he mused, and she heard an odd note of regret in his voice. "Daggers and scimitars hold no danger for me. But you, I think, are deadly. You hold the power to enslave my heart. I could fall in love with you. God help me, I think I already have. And that will wound me much deeper than any knife ever could. To the bone. To my very bones."

Chapter Two

The war was not quite over. The two tribes who were once vicious enemies faced off their best warriors in a fierce fight to the finish—camel racing.

Watching from the crowd, Badra's heart pounded as the tawny beasts galloped in their awkward but powerful gait. Rashid, an Al-Hajid warrior, raced Khepri, her falcon guard. Indigo, yellow and white tassels adorned the blanket beneath Khepri's wood saddle. Badra had woven it herself as a birthday gift.

Warriors whooped and hollered for their favorites. The two tribes had been friendly ever since Jabari killed Fareeq. The monstrous leader of the Al-Hajid had kidnapped Elizabeth, Jabari's American-born wife, and that had been the last straw. Afterward, Elizabeth's uncle became that tribe's new sheikh. Camel racing replaced bitter bloodshed. It was a good trade.

Clouds of thick dust drove upward from the animals'

pounding hooves. Grim determination shone on Khepri's face as he urged his mount onward, edging ahead of his opponent to cross the finish line. Wild cheers rose.

Khepri slid off his camel and flashed everyone a cocky grin. Badra ran to him and collided against his hard chest. "Oh! That was magnificent!" She hugged him, relishing the smell of spices in his sweat-dampened *binish*.

His gaze went soft as he embraced her. Suddenly a crush of men gathered around, whooping and congratulating. To have won such a prestigious race meant tremendous honor. Badra eased away. Khepri flushed as Jabari slapped him on the back. "Well done, brother," the Khamsin sheikh shouted.

In black and red robes, Khepri's opponent Rashid approached. He had the grace of a large cat. Badra studied him, remembering him well from long ago. Unlike his tribesmen, this man's facial features were delicate, even foreign. He had a slim nose, high cheekbones and large eyes heavily fringed with lashes. One might almost call him pretty. One warrior had. Rashid viciously killed him in a duel over it. Then he'd sliced off the warrior's testicles, stuffing them into a bag. Into the privacy of Fareeq's tent Rashid had stormed, tossing down the bag and snapping, "You said I have none of my own because of what that bastard did to me. Can I have these?"

Sitting nearby, Badra had flinched. Fareeq had roared with laughter and replied, "You will not serve on your hands and knees like a girl any longer. I will acknowledge you as a warrior."

Rashid had been a victim, just as Badra had been.

His expression went blank upon recognizing her. She mouthed to him, "I will not tell your secret."

She saw relief flash in his dark eyes. He nodded, then went to Khepri. "Congratulations," he said graciously.

Her falcon guard rudely turned away. Jabari frowned and admonished his brother. "You should welcome Rashid. He is becoming a Khamsin warrior."

Khepri's jaw dropped. "What?" he croaked.

"My sister married your cousin," Rashid replied, his gaze courteous. "I wish to join this tribe so she has family and does not feel alone. Tomorrow I take the oath of loyalty."

Silence filled the air.

"You may call him Khamsin, but to me, he will always be Al-Hajid," Khepri said tightly. "Do not trust him, Jabari. Do not trust any of them. There may be peace between our people, but deep down, they are merciless killers of women and children."

Badra's heart ached as he stormed off. Khepri could not find it within him to forgive, nor forget, the murder of his parents and brother. In some ways, she understood. Her troubled gaze met Rashid's. The warrior's black-bearded face remained expressionless, but she glimpsed a vulnerable loneliness. Then it vanished. He murmured an excuse and went off to join his sister and her new husband.

Khepri stormed into his tent, trying to quell his raging anger. Rashid, a Khamsin warrior? Jabari might call him cousin, but he never could. He fought down fury as he gathered fresh clothing.

Going to the quarters serving as bathing facilities for males, Khepri sang off-key as he scrubbed the dust away. He thought of the shining adulation in Badra's eyes. Both outsiders, they had naturally drawn close after years of forced togetherness. Her gentle manner cloaked a fierce tenaciousness. He secretly admired her determination to become literate. She in turn encouraged him to seek his dreams. Badra believed he could do anything. With her at his side, he could. Their love was like the dawn of new creation. Each day resonated with the rich harmony of shared laughter and a melody of smoldering passion. And it all awaited the spark of their first kiss.

Yesterday he had formally asked Jabari to release him of his vow never to touch her. The sheikh agreed. But, he had added sternly, "Remember her honor. Be very gentle. And patient."

Tonight he would tenderly initiate Badra into the pleasures awaiting her in his arms. A kiss, nothing more—but oh so much. His body tingled pleasantly. He had seen her cast longing looks at the sheikh's baby. When women looked at babies that way, it usually meant they wanted one of their own.

He'd be more than happy to give her one. He grinned. They could be married by the next full moon and spend a delightful week or so conceiving their son. Or daughter.

Finishing, he dumped the dirty water into a basin where it would be taken to irrigate an herb garden. Despite the secret cave with a bubbling spring, no one wasted water in the desert.

For five years, he'd clung fast to his vow never to touch Badra. With Jabari married, tribal law required the release of his concubines. Farah had married a warrior. Khepri had immediately asked for Badra's hand, but she'd refused. Last year, he'd asked again. She'd told him she wasn't ready.

But now, surrounded by marriage and babies, surely she

must be ready. Even the womanizing Nazim, the sheikh's guardian and best friend, had surrendered his bachelorhood. He'd married and changed his name to Ramses according to guardian tradition. Now he was expecting twins with his wife, Katherine.

A patient man, Khepri had waited five years for Badra. He could wait longer, if necessary. But he hoped that after a little gentle coaxing tonight, she would say yes.

Badra sat beneath a sprawling acacia tree and sketched Elizabeth, who was nursing her son. A book lay nearby. It had arrived in a shipment from Katherine's father, Lord Smithfield. The man, a wealthy English noble, wanted to help Elizabeth teach the tribe's children. Thanks to the sheikh's wife's work, many of his tribe were literate in Arabic, and some, like Badra, in both Arabic *and* English.

"Stop sketching. Time for your lesson. Read to me in English," Elizabeth instructed.

Somewhat haltingly, Badra read. Elizabeth finished feeding baby Tarik and listened. Approaching footsteps drew their attention.

Jabari and Khepri. The sheikh crouched down, took the baby from his wife. Expertly he put the boy over his shoulder. Badra melted as Jabari cooed to his son. Khepri's blue eyes searched hers as the sheikh handed the baby back.

"He is a fine, strong boy, Jabari. Perhaps one day I, too, shall have a son," he commented, his gaze never leaving Badra's.

A hollow ache settled in her chest. As much as her heart longed for marriage to Khepri, she couldn't make babies with him. The only lullaby she would sing remained with

30

her dead daughter. Though Jabari's gentle manner had slowly healed her wounded spirit, and Khepri's protectiveness made her feel safe and cherished, physical intimacy with men was still the last thing she wanted.

The men moved off, talking quietly. Tarik grabbed a fistful of golden hair spilling from his mother's blue scarf. Badra stared. "Elizabeth, what is it like when you make babies with a man you love?" Her cheeks flamed. But she had to know.

Her friend's expression grew soft. "It's the most wonderful feeling in the world. There's a closeness of the spirit you share as well as the ecstasy."

Ecstasy? Perhaps marriage and babies with her falcon guard were not such foolish, idle dreams. She read until she again heard the tread of male footsteps. Jabari stood over her, looking at his wife.

"Elizabeth," he said, and his voice was husky.

A sparkle lit the woman's eyes. Standing, she asked Badra to watch Tarik. Taking her husband's outstretched hand, she let him lead her into their tent and rolled the flaps down.

Badra looked at the black tent. Elizabeth had confided they'd decided to give Tarik a sibling. The sheikh was quite determined to perform his duty.

Deeply curious, slightly ashamed, Badra went and asked Tarik's delighted great-aunt to watch the boy. Then she casually strolled around the sheikh's tent to the back, drawn by the low groans and soft cries inside. Elizabeth suddenly screamed. Badra stiffened. Then she realized the cry had been one of pleasure.

A distant memory returned. She was seventeen, living in

a heavily guarded building in the village of Amarna. Jabari had moved her and Farah there to keep them safe during the war between the tribes. Each time she went anywhere, Khepri accompanied her. But this day, he had been freed of his duties. A warrior named Ali had escorted her to the market.

They'd passed Najla's house. In the marketplace, Khepri had flirted with the young widow, newly arrived in town. Walking past the women's abode, sudden intuition flashed. Badra asked Ali to retrieve the wool she'd forgotten. He hesitated, but she assured him she'd be safe.

When he left, Badra crept around the side of Najla's house. She heard Khepri's deep murmurs and a woman's soft replies, and peered through a latticed window.

The room was a bedchamber with lavish furnishings and thick carpets. But it was the bed and its occupants that drew Badra's attention. Khepri and Najla, both naked, stretched out on the bed. He was kissing the woman, and her hand cupped the back of his head. Najla caressed his long, dark locks. Badra's fingers tightened on the window frame. Suddenly Khepri sat back on his haunches. She could clearly see his exposed profile. Sweat glistened on his hard muscles. He was simply beautiful, chiseled male perfection. His thick, dark hair hung past his shoulders and he shoved it impatiently away from his forehead. Badra's hungry eyes followed the flatness of his chest, the dark hair arrowing down past his waist to the thicker nest at his groin and the jutting thickness of his . . . Oh my.

Her mouth had dropped in astonishment.

Fareeq's male part had been like a wrinkled date in comparison.

Khepri slipped his hands between Najla's slender, honey-toned thighs, opening them wide and mounting her. She uttered an alarmed cry as he pressed into her, her hands digging into his shoulders. "It is too large," she gasped.

Badra winced in sympathy and silently agreed.

Khepri crooned gently, kissed Najla and then thrust deeper. Najla's fingers relaxed their tight grip and she sighed.

Unable to drag her eyes away from the sight of his taut, pumping buttocks, Badra had stared in shocked fascination. Najla arched. Badra flinched as the woman screamed, digging her fingers into the firm muscles of Khepri's back. He murmured and then kissed her. Seeing Najla's ecstatic expression, Badra realized the shriek had been one of pleasure. Then Khepri's powerful body had shuddered as he groaned, and lay still.

The act that had brought her only pain had brought Najla nothing but pleasure. Jealousy had gripped Badra. Her falcon guard was not exclusively hers. She burned to know the same powerful ecstasy Khepri coaxed from Najla, to feel his heavy weight atop hers and run her fingers over the muscled body that fought to protect her. But still, she was afraid. She'd turned him away for that very reason.

A low cough jerked her attention from the past. Whirling, she saw Khepri, hand on his scimitar hilt. His dark-bearded face regarded her with tender amusement. She blushed, knowing he'd caught her eavesdropping on Elizabeth and Jabari.

"Badra," he said softly. "Come, walk with me."

He slowed his long-legged stride to match hers. When they reached her tent, Khepri touched her cheek, barely a caress.

"My brother and his wife are eager for another baby. It is natural. Some day you will desire the same."

Flustered, Badra glanced away.

"Do you not like babies? I know of only one way to make them," he said, a twinkle in his blue eyes.

"I have work," she muttered.

As she went to duck into her tent, he lightly grasped her wrist. "Meet me at my tent when the moon climbs up into the sky," he told her. "I have something to show you. Something special."

Badra shuddered in both fear and anticipation.

A full moon spilled over the camp as Khepri greeted her much later. Gray light glossed the long, dark hair spilling from beneath his indigo turban and winked upon the steel scimitar strapped to his waist.

They walked in companionable silence, passing the dying embers of cooking fires and black tents sheltering Khamsin families inside. It was remarkably quiet, but for the brush of the wind against the sand and horses nickering at the camp's edge.

"It's very still tonight," she commented.

"You do not hear it?"

"Hear what?"

"The sound of night," he said softly. "Of passion."

She heard nothing, then her ears opened. A woman's soft cries mingled with a man's deep groans. Rustling fabric, husky whispers. Bodies slid against bodies. Something dark and living and carnal, it was an erotic dance of sound. It poured over her senses, daring her to imagine . . .

Khepri spoke quietly. "When a man and a woman take

joy in sharing their bodies, they create the music of love. It is the sweetest sound in the desert."

They passed the main group of tents and the area where the horses were kept hobbled for the night. A twist of mountain lay before them, jagged boulders whose rugged edges shone blackish-gray in the pale moonlight. Khepri kept walking.

"What did you want to show me?" Badra asked.

Khepri halted near the entrance of a narrow canyon she recognized. "In here," he gestured.

Towering limestone walls flanked them as they wound down through the canyon. Finally Khepri halted before a scattering of large boulders. "There," he said with satisfaction.

She gasped with delight. Out of one of the tall limestone rocks, Khepri had carved a waist-high Egyptian cobra. Its hooded head reared up in menacing beauty, ready to strike.

"I wanted you to see it in the moonlight." He ran a caressing hand over his creation. "When the light strikes . . ."

"It looks real," she marveled.

"It was here I received my cobra totem, so I wanted to mark the memory," he told her, leaning a slim hip against a boulder.

"Tell me," she said eagerly.

"I was on a hunt with Jabari, looking for small game. He stepped near these rocks and we heard a hiss. I saw it first. A cobra, disturbed from its rest."

"You killed it?"

"No. My father told me these cobras do not spit venom and are sacred in Egyptian history, revered as protectors of kings. If I killed it, bad luck would visit Jabari. I remembered a trick an old snake charmer once taught. I took my rifle, forced the snake to wrap around it and the snake went still. From then on I was known as Cobra, the one who acts—swift as a serpent."

She smiled, remembering how his astonishing reflexes had stayed her hand from using his dagger to kill herself. "You *are* Cobra. Your totem serves you well."

He studied her in the brilliant moonlight. The moon. Her namesake. He gestured skyward. "As does your name. Though the beauty of the full moon pales beside you, Badra."

Nervousness fraught with an odd yearning returned to her. She glanced at the web of starlight glistening in the night sky. "But nothing's as lovely as the stars. They make me feel as though I could touch them. Like glittering gems I saw once in Cairo."

"You are more beautiful than all the stars in Egypt's sky."

His husky voice was like warm velvet. Khepri lightly clasped her shoulders. Heat emanated from him like from the glowing coals of a banked campfire. "Jabari has released me of my vow not to touch you. Do . . . do you want me to kiss you?" he asked softly. "Badra?"

Yes, her heart cried. Hope rose in her breast. She regarded him in the moonlight. The way he said her name, so soft and smooth, tickled her overly sensitive skin. She shuddered and yearned, fearing and yet craving this new closeness, this heated intensity. He brushed a finger against her cheek, drifted down to her trembling lips and she nodded. *Yes. Kiss me.*

"I have waited so long for you, Badra," he murmured.

A determined, intent look came over him. Khepri cupped

her face in his strong palms and lifted her mouth up for possession. He claimed her mouth with a kiss that stole her soul and her breath away. His lips grazed hers in reverent worship, a light caress. Intrigued, she moved her mouth against his. Then he pressed his lips hard against hers, his tongue tracing her bottom lip, flicking it lightly. When Badra gave a small sound of pleasure, he slipped into her mouth. Shocked, she compressed her lips.

"Come, Badra, open for me," he coaxed. Then his lips captured hers again.

Her breath was sucked out in a whoosh as she opened her mouth. Khepri's silken tongue plunged in, tasting her, claiming and setting fire to her as she clung to him. His body pressed against hers, all hard muscles and bone. He continued his relentless assault, plundering her mouth with expert strokes. He ravished her mouth, rousing an odd fullness in her loins. The heat he created gave Badra fresh hope. Yes, perhaps this was the pleasure Elizabeth meant.

Then she felt his hard manhood grind against her. His taut arms locked about her like shackles, trapping her against the rock with his weight and strength. Khepri uttered a deep groan. His sudden intensity frightened her, made her feel powerless. Terror replaced her arousal. He would grunt and strain as he violated her body with mindless lust as Fareeq had. And she'd hate him for it. . . .

He released her, panting as he looked down. Moonlight and dark desire glinted in his eyes. "You make a man mad with your beauty. I nearly could not stop. If we were married, I would not have," he said hoarsely.

"You would not have?" she asked, deeply shaken.

37

"I'd never let you leave my bed. I would keep you too busy to take walks in the moonlight."

His words promised old horrors. Badra could not bear to see his gentle, protective manner change as desire darkened his eyes, to wrench away in panic as his powerful body covered hers and he thrust rudely inside her as Fareeq had.

She realized the horrifying truth: If they married, no pleasured cries would come from their black tent, only her screams of terror. Warriors would look on Khepri with contempt. Whispers would start. She cared too deeply for him to shame him thus. She could not bear to condemn such a virile, passionate man to a marriage as dry as sand. Or to drive him into the arms of another woman to satisfy his body's needs—as he had done in the past with Najla.

As they returned to camp, she stifled the haunted sorrow rising in her throat. This presented no real challenge; she had plenty of experience in doing so.

Khepri's past came galloping back the following day.

Humming happily, thinking of how pliant and soft Badra's lips had been beneath his, he sat before his tent, carving a new wood loom for her. At the thunder of approaching horses, he looked up. A cloud of dust rose on the horizon. Blood froze in his veins as it drew closer. A party of white-skinned English, escorted by his brethren, approached on sleek Arabians.

Jabari had warned him about the strangers coming to visit. They'd claimed Khepri might be family. Unease had gripped him, but Khepri joked no Englishman would want him. He was too stubborn, too cocky—too Egyptian to be English.

Two pale foreigners, one with light brown hair, one much older with a shock of white, dismounted. They wore the strange linen suits English archaeologists preferred. Dry-mouthed, Khepri watched Jabari greet them. The sheikh escorted the pair to Khepri's tent. With a speed surprising for one so old, the white-haired Englishman raced forward.

He halted abruptly. Wrinkles carved his face like well-worn rock. Khepri stared into a pair of eyes as blue as his own.

"Good God, it's true," the man slowly rasped in English. "It's Michael, just when he was your age."

Khepri's panicked gaze flew to Jabari, but his brother's face tightened and he looked away.

"Kenneth, I'm your grandfather. So long I've prayed to find you. I am Charles Tristan, duke of Caldwell," the man continued.

The younger Englishman, with a thick mustache and side-whiskers, his pale brown hair thinning, stepped forward. "Hullo," he said heartily. "I'm Victor Edwards. Second cousin, on your father's side. Such a relief to find you."

Khepri reeled with shock. "I have no English family," he croaked in halted English. "They were killed by an enemy tribe years ago. The Al-Hajid murdered my parents and brother."

"Yes." Sorrow came into the old man's blue eyes. "But not you. And now I've found you. Kenneth Tristan. My heir."

Heir? What was an heir?

"I am your grandfather, Kenneth," he stated again.

Grandfather? His grandfather, Nkosi, was visiting the Al-Hajid and his wife. Khepri's frantic gaze pleaded with Jabari, but the sheikh continued gazing stonily into the distance. How could this be? He was a Khamsin, warrior of the wind. Egyptian. He rode the dusky sands. He was brother to the greatest desert sheikh in Egypt. And now a strange Englishman from beyond the seas claimed him? Khepri's stomach twisted. He must drive these intruders away.

He thrust out the soles of his feet at them. "Walk away from me. I know nothing of you," he said brusquely.

Of course they would not understand how rude the gesture was. They were English. But Jabari tensed with anger.

"Khepri!" he said sharply. Then he said in a gentler tone, "You forget your manners. A Khamsin always shows courtesy to guests." He turned to the two Englishmen. *"Ahlan wa sahlan*. You are welcome to my tent."

The news spread like a sandstorm. While the Englishmen's Egyptian servants unloaded their trunks, Jabari personally welcomed the visitors with *gahwa*. The coffee ceremony was an honor the sheikh reserved for the most prestigious guests. Elizabeth, Ramses and his English-born wife, Katherine, joined them as a crowd of onlookers hovered outside, staring at the two Englishmen.

Khepri bristled with pride at the skillful way his brother roasted the green coffee beans in a pan over a tiny brazier, cooled them in a wood dish and ground them. The two Englishmen sat on the thick red carpet watching and talking quietly. He glanced at them, irritated. Did they not hear the beautiful music the pestle made as it struck the mortar? Jabari's artistry failed to impress the foreigners. Khepri folded his arms, glaring at them with indignation.

When the coffee was ready, the sheikh politely served his

two guests small, handleless cups. The priceless porcelain had been in the family for generations. The English murmured their thanks and sipped. A barely concealed grimace twisted Victor's lips. Khepri felt fresh annoyance.

When the guests were served, he sipped his coffee, enjoying the spicy pinch of cardamom. With secret glee he noticed the English sucking on dates between sips. Dates sweetened the bitter brew. These men could not be his family. They could not even drink coffee.

Khepri kept staring at the elderly man whose face was stamped with such similar features to his own. No denying the resemblance. The world tilted crazily on its axis as he listened to the man tell Jabari how important it was to have found his grandson.

When the sheikh slowly nodded, he screamed inside. No! This man was not family. Not *his*. People gaped with open curiosity at the visitors. On the crowd's fringes, he saw Rashid. Clad now in indigo, the warrior stared intently at the English visitors. Then Rashid's gaze met Khepri's. Rashid whirled and stomped off.

Confused and uncertain, Khepri's thoughts whipped to Badra. What if the strangers wanted to take him away to their land of green grass? His whole being had centered on protecting her. Watching over her. Keeping his love and desire embedded deep in his heart, his need of her a deep ache. He would not leave her.

"Khepri," Jabari said in Arabic. "Your grandfather is asking you a question."

Not *my* grandfather, he thought resentfully.

"I kept hoping you or your brother still lived," the Englishman said. "Kenneth, you are heir to one of England's

41

Bonnie Vanak

greatest titles. You'll inherit enormous wealth and property. I know how difficult this must be, but I'm asking you to return with me to England."

Heir? Title? He glanced at Jabari, who rapidly translated. Khepri felt new shock slam into him. Leave Egypt for riches? Who needed wealth? He had the richness of the open desert.

"Who asked you to come here?" he demanded, furious.

"I did," Katherine said in her soft voice. The wife of Nazim—now Ramses—looked troubled. "My father, the earl of Smithfield, was good friends with your family. I wrote my father about the blue-eyed warrior living with the Khamsin, whose family had been killed, and he immediately told your grandfather."

Jabari's guardian slid a comforting arm about his wife's waist. "Katherine meant no harm. She wanted you to find your real family."

Real family. A family far, far away, forcing him to leave. No. He would not. His land was the arid desert. The rocky canyonlands and the hot sand. Not some foreign land of water and grass. How could he leave behind the burning blue sky and yellow sun? How could he leave his beloved Egypt?

Wildly his panicked gaze whipped about the tent, searching faces. Elizabeth looked troubled. Jabari and Ramses were grim. Katherine looked pleadingly at him. "He is a good man, Khepri. You come from an honored lineage as noble as any Egyptian king's. He's your grandfather," she said.

They were letting him go. How could they? Did not fam-

42

ily mean anything to Jabari? But he was not blood. His guts twisted. Not real family.

Badra remained his only hope. If she married him, surely his brother would not abandon him to this white-haired stranger from across the sea. He needed her. How could he leave her?

Khepri calmed. Yes, surely she would marry him. All her affection, the gifts presented to him over the years, their camaraderie, and the kiss. Warmth flooded his veins as he remembered her soft lips. Badra felt the same for him as he felt for her. Marriage was the answer. Even leaving the Khamsin seemed less menacing with her by his side. He could face the land of green grass if he must.

Politely excusing himself, he left the tent, ignoring Jabari's troubled expression. He found Badra beneath an acacia tree, weaving a colorful blanket.

"I thought you were taking coffee with your grandfather." She beamed at him. "Is it not wonderful that your family found you? The entire tribe is chattering about your honored ancestry, how you will have wealth greater than the ancient kings of Egypt."

Her too? He grimaced and sat, feeling peace merely by being with her. "I don't want any part of it."

Badra's lower lip trembled. "I don't understand. You are his grandson. If I knew a child or a grandchild that I had thought dead was found alive, I would move mountains to be with them again. You are blessed. Trust me."

He hated seeing her upset. Khepri brushed a knuckle against her cheek. A tremulous smile touched her lips. Allah, he wanted to hold her in his arms. And never let go.

43

"I have something important to ask you."

She tensed as he slid down onto his knees before her.

"Marry me, Badra," Khepri said, his gaze frantic. "I did not want to ask like this, but time is short. Do not forsake me. Marry me and I will give up everything—the wealth and land awaiting me. Marry me and we will remain here, as Khamsin. Or if you wish, we will make a life in England with riches as vast as the sands of Egypt. I can face anything with you by my side."

Please, he begged with his eyes. *I cannot lose you.*

She remained silent, biting her lip. He waited in hopeful anticipation. Surely after their kiss, her feelings for him . . .

When she spoke, the words slapped him like wet cloth.

"I am sorry, Khepri. I . . . I cannot marry you. I cannot feel the same for you as you feel for me," she whispered.

For a minute he remained speechless with shock. He searched her face. *No?* She looked away. A heavy weight crushed his chest as his last hope faded. All these years, waiting. Honoring her. Hoping. Believing she cared. She didn't.

Agony fled, replaced by bitterness as thick as a sandstorm. Khepri rose and fished his dagger from his belt, the same one she had once used to try and end her life. Something inside him shriveled to dry dust.

With a deep hiss, he laced open his palm, a symbolic reminder of how he had saved her when they first met.

"This is the last time I will shed my blood for you, Badra. But you needn't tend to my injuries any longer. Take this. It's yours now. I have no use for it in England," he snapped. With a look of disgust, he threw the blade into the sand. It stuck there, wobbling.

Then he left, droplets of blood dotting the ground like a trail of red tears. But the burning pain in his palm hurt far less than his insides.

Time seemed to grind to an agonizing halt for Khepri, though several days had passed. He made up his mind. He would go to England. There was nothing for him here. Badra had rejected him. Tomorrow, he would leave.

Jabari expressed sympathy over Badra's refusal, but the sheikh seemed oblivious to Khepri's pain. Khepri savagely quashed a bitter laugh as he went to the sheikh's tent. On the way he nearly collided with Rashid. The muscled warrior blocked his path, giving a sullen stare.

"Out of my way," Khepri ordered. "I have no time to quarrel with you."

But the warrior did not move. Instead he continued staring at Khepri, his mouth twisted. His dark eyes were cold.

"If you have something to say, say it," Khepri snapped. "I must meet with my brother before I go to England."

A sneer replaced Rashid's searching look. "Your brother? No longer. Go to England. You belong to the land of the soft-bellied English and will fit in well," he taunted.

Khepri made a rude gesture. The other man smiled darkly. "You should show respect for Badra's new falcon guard."

Shock slammed into him. Rashid laughed softly at his stunned expression, then stalked off.

Khepri was still shaking when he entered Jabari's tent. The sheikh beckoned him to sit beside Ramses. He did so.

"Rashid claims he's Badra's falcon guard," he blurted.

The sheikh and his guardian exchanged glances. "That is

true. I want Badra to feel protected when you leave. I have appointed her a new falcon guard."

"She does not need one. Fareeq is long dead," he protested. Allah, he could not bear Rashid near his beloved. . . .

"There are other men who would not honor her. And Badra . . . she asked for Rashid," Ramses put in.

She'd *asked* for him? An Al-Hajid pig? Rashid would protect what was once his? Everything about Khepri was crumbling into dust. Nothing familiar was left to him, not even his own damn dignity.

"Khepri—uh, Kenneth—I asked you here for a very special reason." Jabari withdrew a beautiful jeweled dagger from its leather sheath. A look of awed respect came over Ramses.

"You are not the brother of my blood, but before you leave, I will make you so. Tonight, beneath the moon and the stars, I will bond us together in brotherhood. And I formally hand you this. The Hassid wedding dagger. It has been passed down from brother to brother. I will give it to you, for although you are not the brother of my blood, you are the brother of my heart." The sheikh held the dagger in his palms with reverence.

He looked up solemnly. "I give it to you for when you marry, so that you will always know that our kinship will never end."

Marry? A hollow feeling settled on Khepri's chest. How could Jabari be so blind? How could the man closer than a brother expect him to marry anyone but the one woman he'd wanted for years? The woman who'd broken his heart?

A wild torrent of anger and bitterness raged inside him. They were letting him go. Jabari had not even voiced a small protest. They did not want him. Badra did not want him. He would leave Egypt and never look back. And make damn sure they knew he'd never return.

He thrust aside the beautiful ruby-and-diamond-studded dagger. "No, Jabari. I don't want it."

The sheikh recoiled, astonishment filling his ebony eyes. Ramses's jaw dropped.

"You . . . refuse my sacred wedding dagger?"

Khepri's guts churned. "Keep your damn dagger. I'm not your brother. I never was and never will be," he grunted. Then he stood and left, ignoring their stunned faces.

He spent a lonely night in his tent for the last time. Unable to sleep he listened to the sound of the desert unfolding. Anguish twisted his guts. Badra had refused him. She did not love him. She never had.

A deadly quiet fell over the tribe as Khepri prepared to leave the next day. Many avoided looking at him. All his possessions went into a trunk. His stone carvings. His scimitar. Books in Arabic. A faint noise sounded outside. He threw aside the tent flap. It was *her*.

Badra moved inside, even though Khepri did not bid her entrance to his tent. Ignoring her, he tossed items into a large trunk. She had wounded him, just as he'd wounded Jabari. The sheikh still looked deeply hurt.

Sweat dampened her palms as she wrung the fringe on her lovely blue head scarf. Telling him good-bye tore her apart.

47

"So you asked Rashid to be your falcon guard," he grunted.

"He is a good, brave warrior . . ."

Her voice trailed off. When Khepri had announced his departure, she'd approached Rashid and struck a pact. Each vowed to keep secret their tormented pasts and fend off possible suitors by pretending courtship. Neither of them wanted to marry.

The secret she wanted to confess trembled on her lips. She must tell him why she refused. But his tall, muscled frame looked distant. And his eyes—oh, his eyes—were blue ice.

Courage failed her. She could not tell him.

"Khepri, I came to say good-bye and to wish you well." Her voice broke. "I will miss you . . . terribly."

His foot kicked the trunk shut. He did not look at her.

"I wish things . . . could be different," she whispered.

I wish I could be different. You'll go to England. You'll find a woman who will love you the way I cannot. And every time I think of her in your arms, I'll die inside. But I can't be with you. My past has shackled me and I'm too afraid.

"Leave, Badra. I need to finish packing," he said coldly. He used stiff but perfect English.

She left, a sob clogging her throat.

There was no ceremony bidding him good-bye. No parting hugs, save from Elizabeth. And from Katherine, who told him to seek out her father. An awkward silence fell as the Khamsin gathered at the camp's edge to watch the English depart. To watch Kenneth, the duke's heir, leave behind the only family he'd ever known.

A harsh desert wind blew across the sand, sending stinging grit in his eyes. Surely that was why they watered. Khepri mounted his horse, stole one last glance at Badra. She clutched the sheikh's hand as if to comfort him. Jabari looked stricken, as if Khepri had stabbed him in the heart.

They meant nothing to him now. He turned and rode off, following his grandfather, cousin and servants.

He did not look back.

PART 2

KENNETH
&
BADRA

Chapter One

Cairo, January 1895

My daughter lives . . . as a slave in a brothel!

Badra stared in anguish at the lovely child she thought had died. Sunlight streamed through latticework windows, playing on the girl's rosy-cheeked face. Jasmine reclined against silk cushions on a narrow divan, watching a woman paint her feet with red henna.

A decoration for a man's future pleasure. Only seven, Jasmine's training at the Pleasure Palace had begun. The brothel specialized in training girls as concubines. Most were sold and never seen again. The most beautiful girls remained prisoners at the Palace, auctioned off for a month at a time. Men purchased their contracts at exorbitant prices for the privilege of briefly owning a slave to fulfill their sexual fantasies.

As soon as she experienced her first bleeding, Jasmine would be sold. Just as Badra had been, long ago.

A calculating look came over the brothel's chief eunuch

as he watched Badra stare at Jasmine. His pockmarked face pudgy, dark brown eyes sharp and assessing, Masud ruled the Pleasure Palace. Two turbaned guards, honed scimitars strapped to their waists, stood at his side. More armed men fortified the heavily guarded building. Sour sweat of their unwashed male bodies overlaid the sweet fragrances perfuming the harem.

Thoughts collided in Badra's frantic mind. *Which is better for Jasmine? A future as a slave, beaten and raped as I was? Or to have died at birth?*

The anonymous message sent to her at the Khamsin camp had been blunt. *The daughter you bore to Sheikh Fareeq lives as a slave at the Pleasure Palace. Come to Cairo to barter for her release.* This trip to Cairo for supplies, with Rashid, Jabari, and Elizabeth, provided a perfect opportunity to investigate.

So, Fareeq had sold Jasmine at birth. Badra had a daughter with bright brown eyes and a shy smile. She wanted to trace Jasmine's oval face, count all her fingers and toes. *I can't bring back the past, but I can be here for you now*, she silently promised. *But I can't admit you are mine, little one.*

How could she confess to birthing Fareeq's child? When Fareeq died childless, the Khamsin sheikh had rejoiced. "My enemy would have lived on through his children and I would be forced to destroy them as well," Jabari had insisted.

Masud finally spoke, interrupting her ruminations. "She is a pretty child and will fetch a good price at auction."

Badra's voice wobbled. "I beg you, release her."

"Never. She is far too valuable."

Granted this miracle, Badra would do anything to rescue her child. "I have money. Surely, I may purchase her freedom."

Masud's gaze was frankly calculating. "No. The price of her freedom is not money. It's you."

Shocked, Badra reeled back on her sandaled heels. "Me?"

"Take her place and she goes free. Omar desires you back."

Badra began to see life fall into place like a pyramid's building blocks. Unable to care for her, Badra's parents sold her at age eleven. Omar, the owner, had desired her, but had sold her to Fareeq. Omar's rough hands, fingers thick and calloused, had stroked her trembling cheek. "You are too young now, but I will get you back, Badra. When you are older, I will have you in my bed, my slave forever."

Fareeq had taken the most precious thing in Badra's life and sold her, giving Omar the tool he needed. She would not submit. There must be another way.

"No. I cannot." Badra thrust out her chin.

Masud's gaze grew shrewd. "Why do you not spend some time with her and think it over? You hardly know her."

She did not trust him, but she longed to embrace her little girl. When the woman finished painting Jasmine's feet and left, Badra rushed to her child. She stroked the girl's ebony hair as Masud watched.

"I am Badra. Your . . . sister, little one," she whispered.

Jasmine smiled shyly and began asking questions. Badra hugged her and tried to provide answers.

"My tribe, the Khamsin, is an ancient one, from the

times of the Pharaoh Akhenaten. Our sheikh is courageous and noble. We raise Arabians, and our warriors ride like the wind."

"Horses?" Jasmine's face lit up. "Will you take me out of here to see them?"

Oh, how I want to more than anything in the world. "I will try," Badra whispered.

The little girl's singularly sweet smile of gratitude broke Badra's heart. Every instinct screamed to take her, to flee and never look back. Badra studied the door leading to freedom. It loomed before her, thick, impenetrable and guarded by two huge eunuchs, curved scimitars at their waists.

As they talked, she realized Jasmine had an engaging manner. The child's mind was sharp like her father's, but she displayed none of Fareeq's sadistic tendencies. When Jasmine begged for a story, Badra told one about a courageous warrior named Khepri who had once protected her with his very life.

"Did you marry Khepri?" Jasmine blurted.

"Khepri lives in England. He is a powerful English lord." She tried to change subjects. "England has many noblemen. Ramses, a warrior from our tribe, and his wife and twins will soon leave for England for a visit. They will bring her father valuable antiquities. Lord Smithfield is an English nobleman."

"Will you go with them?"

"No. Lord Smithfield gave them the fare for the voyage."

"But you must. You have to go see Khepri and marry him and have babies. That's how it has to end." Jasmine pouted.

Sudden pain stabbed her heart. Badra chose her words carefully. "I don't think he would wish to see me."

"But it's a love story. All love stories have happy endings. So he would want to see you because he loves you," Jasmine insisted.

How could she ruin her innocent daughter's shining belief in happy endings? This particular story had none. If only real life could be thus. Badra stroked her daughter's silky hair. "Perhaps," she said lightly.

Masud lumbered over, his gaze shrewd. "That is enough. Time for Jasmine to leave now for her lessons."

Badra knew the lessons he meant. Revulsion swept through her as she thought of her little girl exposed to such knowledge. Badra asked again, in a small voice, to purchase her.

"She is not for sale."

Hope withered like dry stalks of grass in the burning sun. Not for sale. He talked of her precious daughter as the Khamsin bargained over horseflesh. Perhaps she could reason with Omar. "Please," Badra whispered. "Let me speak with Omar."

Masud looked thoughtful. "Omar is not here. He lives abroad now. However, he needs a favor. Perform it and he may free the girl. Do you know of the dig at Dashur?"

En route to Cairo, Elizabeth had insisted on stopping by the excavation. Khepri, now Kenneth, sponsored it. She wondered why, when he had left with such anger in his heart. "I was there when they discovered a priceless necklace."

"Do you know the necklace's legend?"

Badra nodded with dawning dread. Two necklaces with ancient legends buried in the sands. Legend said whoever wore the necklace with Pharaoh Senusret III's cartouche was bound as a slave, much as his daughter Meret had been bound to her father's will. But the necklace with Amenemhat II's cartouche granted the wearer the power to enslave men's hearts, just as Meret had enslaved her husband's heart.

Masud produced a gleaming gold pectoral from a small velvet bag and slipped it into her hands.

"This is it. You said Ramses is leaving for England. Go with him, smuggle this to the antiquities dealer in London who needs it to make copies. He will give you money in return."

The stolen, heavy necklace seemed almost to pulse with wicked power. For a wild moment, Badra felt evil emanating from it, like unseen mist. It felt warm in her chilled palm.

"Which necklace is this?"

"The one to enslave others."

"I cannot steal," she protested.

If he discovered her crime, Khepri would not hesitate to claim revenge. For past hurts and this new one. The necklace burned her like a brand. Surely there was another way to free Jasmine. The Khamsin sheikh would storm his warriors past the army of armed guards to rescue Jasmine. But such an assault would be difficult, and she could not risk her daughter's life in a raid.

The gold winked in the sunlight streaming into the harem. An ominous foreboding seized her. If Khepri caught her with Meret's ancient necklace, would he use its power to enslave her?

"No. I cannot." She tossed the necklace onto the divan.

Anger filled Masud's corpulent face. He turned to Jasmine, who'd gone very still. "You were naughty, Jasmine.

You were told to leave the guests' horses alone, but you petted one last week. Come now, time to take your punishment."

The girl shrank back on the silken cushions. Her large dark eyes widened. "I'm sorry," she cried. "I said I wouldn't do it again. You promised not to hurt me. You promised!"

Masud fetched the *kurbash*, the crocodile hide whip, from a nearby holder. An ugly crack spilt the air as he flicked it. Jasmine curled herself into a ball. Badra stuffed a fist into her mouth to stifle a shriek. No noise. Noise meant Masud would hit harder.

"No! Please!" Jasmine begged.

Her immobilizing terror broke; Badra grabbed Masud's beefy arm. He flung her to the floor. Badra wrapped her arms around his leg, dragging on the carpet as he stalked toward her whimpering daughter. "I beg you, please, don't hurt her," Badra sobbed.

"Only one thing will keep my lash from her flesh."

From her crumpled position on the floor, Badra stared up at his unyielding face. Her teary gaze went to Jasmine, shivering on the divan. The choice seemed clear.

A few minutes later, she forced a smile for Rashid as she returned to the reception room. She had told him she wanted to purchase the freedom of a slave, so at least one girl would not suffer as Badra had in her childhood.

Her friend studied her. "Badra? Did all go well?"

"No, Rashid. It did not."

She left the brothel, her steps dull, her mind glazed. She felt cursed.

Chapter Two

London, February 1895

The new trousers were too tight in the crotch.

Breath fled his lungs in a pained whoosh as his tailor yanked up the black broadcloth. Kenneth Tristan, duke of Caldwell, wheezed as the trousers cut painfully into his nether region. He muttered an Arabic curse about the tailor being related to a female desert jackal.

"Dear, dear, I was afraid of this, Your Grace. My new assistant did not have the correct size. You are simply much larger than he indicated," the gray-haired tailor fussed. He sank to his knees and studied Kenneth's groin with the intensity of Kenneth's French cook studying a cut of beef.

"Bloody hell, get them off me before you make me a eunuch."

The tailor glanced up with a confused look. "I beg your pardon, Your Grace. I do not understand."

His English was nearly perfect, but Kenneth's thick Egyptian accent caused confusion to wrinkle many brows.

He gritted his teeth and enunciated as clearly as he could: "Take them off. The trousers do not fit."

Standing, the tailor wrung his hands. "I apologize, Your Grace. I fear my new assistant needs to learn to measure properly."

"Then send a woman to do the task. Women know how to measure properly. Trust me," he growled.

Hovering nearby, Flanders looked aghast. Before he died, Kenneth's grandfather had hired a protocol instructor to teach his grandson. He'd hoped Kenneth would quickly assimilate into English society. It hadn't quite happened. "Never a woman, Your Grace. Your peers would be appalled," Flanders commented.

Always the worry about his peers, the noblemen who looked down on him because he came from the heathen land of Arabia. Kenneth glanced down as the tailor slid the trousers off. "They also do not fit in the legs."

"Remember, Your Grace. One does not say 'leg'—nor any other body part," Flanders instructed. "Not among polite company, certainly. 'Limb' is the correct term."

Always telling him how to speak, what to say. Kenneth frowned. "Speaking of legs, why is my dining room table covered? The *legs* are hand-carved mahogany and they should be displayed."

Flanders dropped his voice. "Because the sight of a table . . . leg . . . is known to excite men. They simply are not shown."

Good God. Englishmen became aroused by table legs? Truly this was an odd culture. Humiliated from months of being poked, prodded and instructed, Kenneth strode from his dressing room to the adjacent sitting room, with its silk-lined walls and gleaming furniture. He bent over, staring at his satinwood secretary desk.

His entourage shuffled after him, like a cluster of very proper black-coated bugs. Flanders's worried voice sounded behind him. "I beg your pardon, Your Grace, but what are you doing?"

"Studying the desk legs." He straightened and glanced down at his groin. "No, doesn't quite work for me. I'm not excited."

Suppressing a grin, he returned to the dressing room, resigned to more torture. The cook's assistant strode in, looking self-important. Kenneth bit back annoyance. His French cook created heavy cream sauces he found difficult to digest. One did not entertain without a highly regarded chef, and Pomeroy came highly recommended, hired personally by his cousin Victor.

"Beg your pardon, Your Grace, Chef Pomeroy wishes to know if you desire the chicken or the beef for dinner tonight."

Kenneth locked gazes with Flanders.

"Tell him I desire the . . . breast of the chicken."

Flanders winced.

"Yes, indeed. A nice, plump, white breast. I very much desire the breast. The bigger the better."

Oblivious, the cook's assistant nodded and left.

Kenneth stood in his sumptuous dressing room, amazed at how his life was arranged into neat pieces: A butler to answer his door, an undermaid to light his fires, a chef to give him indigestion.

The tailor took out a long string. "With your permission, I shall take your correct measurements, Your Grace."

In total surrender, Kenneth removed his shirt and stood

clad only in his white silk underdrawers. He stretched out his arms, feeling like a damn fool. The tailor ran the string from the curve of his throat to his wrist. No dignity. No privacy.

"This should be a woman's job. I know the perfect one," he grumbled to the tailor. He closed his eyes.

He thought back to the black tents in the Egyptian desert where a man was allowed to indulge in the pleasure of a woman undressing him. Badra. Dark eyes sparkling like a black velvet night's blazing stars. His heart thundered as he remembered the sun kissing her cheeks. The graceful sway to her hips that made men's heads snap around in admiration as she passed. The kiss they'd shared in the cool desert moonlight . . .

Blood rushed to his lower region.

Kenneth glanced down and bit back a groan. His swelling member bobbed and nodded in reaction to his thoughts. Badra, it said. *Oh yes, yes, yes—we liked her very, very much.* Like a disobedient child, it had a mind of its own.

Flanders looked ready to drop into a horrified faint; the rosy-cheeked tailor looked impressed.

"Oh my," the tailor said faintly, putting a hand to his face. "Er, now I know the trousers will never fit."

Kenneth's cool gaze snapped to his instructor. "And what exactly is the protocol for a moment like this?" Without waiting for an answer, he waved an imperious hand. "Out! All of you! Send in my valet with clothing that fits, damn it! Then get the man an old suit of mine and take your measurements from it!"

Everyone fled with the speed of a pack of yipping dogs. Kenneth collapsed to the floor, sitting Bedouin-style. Closing his eyes, he began breathing deeply and let the tension ease from his shoulders. He was so tired since his grandfather died. And the rich, creamy foods the French chef served did not help. In the past two months, he had become very well acquainted with one particular item in the large mansion: his extremely modern, lavish "necessity."

A few minutes later, a knock on the door sounded. He called out entry and opened one eye. His new valet timidly entered, bearing clothing.

"Beg your pardon, Your Grace—are you feeling well?"

"I like sitting on the floor," Kenneth said calmly.

Blood flushed the valet's face. Kenneth stood. "You're the new valet. Hawkins, right?"

"Yes, Your Grace."

"Just don't measure me and you'll do fine," he muttered. The young man offered a hesitant smile.

Curious about the servant's background, Kenneth asked Hawkins about his roots, discovering the valet came from a large family in east London. The man chattered about them as he cleaned up the discarded clothing from the floor, then beckoned to Kenneth with a new shirt. The duke stood, turning again to the length of gilded mirror mounted to the dressing room wall. He held out his arms so Hawkins could slide on the shirt.

"That certainly is an odd marking, Your Grace."

Kenneth glanced at the muscles of his right arm. The small tattoo of an uncoiling cobra hissed in blue-inked fury. He touched it reverently, then drew his hand away as if burned.

"I've never seen the like. What does it mean?"

"It's a symbol of my past," he said briefly.

Avid curiosity shone in Hawkins's eyes as he helped Kenneth shrug on the crisp white linen.

"Your past in Egypt? I heard something of that. You lived with an Egyptian tribe of warriors?" Hawkins fastened on the strange, tight collar Kenneth still found restrictive after a year of wearing English clothing.

Familiar pain tightened his heart like a squeezing fist. Flanders's suddenly useful advice rang in his mind. Do not be familiar with servants.

"Just help me dress, Hawkins. You're not paid to ask questions," he said, his gaze meeting the valet's in the mirror.

Hawkins swallowed hard. "I . . . I apologize," he stammered.

Kenneth felt a wrench of guilt at the apprehension in the young man's eyes. Hawkins probably feared dismissal for being familiar. It was his fault Hawkins had dared ask questions. Accustomed to the casual familiarity of the Khamsin, Kenneth still found it difficult adjusting to the strict English social classes. But his natural friendliness must be curbed.

You are duke of Caldwell now. Khepri no longer.

But he was lonely. In one year, he had gone from living casually among two thousand people to living alone, with only servants for company in a massive house. His life felt purposeless—until he'd received the cables from Egypt.

Kenneth's gaze roved to the highly polished furnishings of his enormous sitting room. On the satinwood desk, two cables lay beside a brass well of India ink and a gleaming gold pen. One revealed exciting news: One of the necklaces of Princess Meret had been found.

His father's greatest dream was coming true.

For years, Kenneth's father had sought the legendary jeweled necklaces of Princess Meret. When Kenneth was four, his father sponsored a dig at Dashur, certain he would find the entrance to the pyramid and the underlying tombs. Wanting his family to be present at his moment of glory, his father had taken them to Egypt. They'd first crossed the desert to the Red Sea on a tourist jaunt to explore the ancient land.

That was when the Al-Hajid attacked. The excavation plans had died with him, along with the dream.

But two months ago Kenneth had allocated an enormous amount of money to continue his father's work. Jacques de Morgan, Egypt's Supreme Director of Antiquities, had been excavating. He'd found the entrance to the hidden tombs, and one of the necklaces. Ecstatic, Kenneth had started planning to visit Egypt to witness the dig himself. Then he'd stopped.

When he'd left last year, he'd vowed never to return. Too many bitter memories lay in sandy Egypt. Resolved to receiving news from afar, he'd ordered his trunks unpacked.

But now he'd received the other cable. It informed him someone had stolen the necklace. The news released the warrior inside him. Ancient cries handed down through two thousand years resonated through him. The Khamsin war call. His blood rode that fever, clamored for retribution.

Hawkins finished brushing down his charcoal gray coat and striped trousers. Kenneth reached down to his waist and recoiled. Habits die hard. No scimitar.

No, he was no longer Khamsin. He felt naked without weapons.

But at least his goal of finding the thief charged him with fresh purpose. England had the world's best black market for stolen antiquities. He'd quietly search the shops and look for the missing piece. He relished the challenge. Hell, he needed one.

Kenneth gave his anxious valet a smile of approval and quietly thanked him. Relief shone visibly in the man's face.

"Summon Zaid to me," Kenneth ordered, speaking slowly.

"Yes, Your Grace." The valet gave a respectful nod.

Touching the stiff cloth covering him, Kenneth stared at the stranger in the polished mirror. He had everything: wealth, title, respect.

Yet he had nothing. Emptiness pulled at him. He stiffened his spine, ignoring the hollow feeling in his chest.

"You asked for me, Your Grace?"

His secretary appeared in the mirror. Kenneth whirled, confused. He hadn't heard Zaid approach. Had he lost his legendary ability to hear a grain of sand spill to the ground? His priorities had shifted like sand on Egypt's dunes. Attuned now to English lifestyles, his warrior alertness had faded.

He studied the middle-aged man standing before him. His grandfather had met this man during a jaunt to Egypt and had rescued him from poverty. Zaid's skin was the color of rich Arabic coffee lightened with cream. Literate in English and Arabic, he possessed a controlled, intelligent manner. Zaid ran the duchy's business affairs with quiet efficiency; his grandfather had trusted him absolutely.

"I told you, Zaid—when we're alone, I'm Kenneth."

"Yes, Your Grace." A smile touched the secretary's mouth.

Kenneth brushed at his jacket lapels. "Any more wires from Egypt?"

"One arrived this morning." Zaid offered the cable.

Kenneth's chest sunk. He busied himself with adjusting his tie. "What's the latest news?"

His secretary read aloud de Morgan's report from the Dashur excavation. Kenneth's hands stilled on his cravat as he digested the information, a scrap of fabric found in the sand where the necklace had been stolen. Indigo fabric from a desert tribe called the Khamsin. De Morgan said four Khamsin had visited just before the necklace vanished. Jabari, Rashid, Elizabeth and Badra.

He held his voice steady as he dismissed Zaid. Then, lost in thought, Kenneth paced restlessly.

Could Jabari have stolen the necklace?

Perfect revenge for how he'd insulted the sheikh upon leaving Egypt. But Jabari honored ancient Egyptian ruins. This made no sense. Deeply disturbed, he reached for a china bowl filled with lemon drops. He popped one into his mouth. It was quickly gone, and hunger still pulled at him. He descended the polished staircase and headed for the kitchen. At the door he paused, remembering Flanders's instructions. Ring for anything he wanted.

To hell with the damn bell. Why couldn't he simply get a piece of fruit instead of all this pomp and ceremony? He wanted to peel an orange with his own fingers, inhale the citrusy tang, feel the juice spurt into his mouth as he bit down, not be handed it quartered into delicate pieces.

Kenneth pushed open the kitchen door and stopped cold. His French chef stood at the trestle table, glowering at a sobbing kitchen maid. A large section of raw red beef lay on the cutting board like a sacrifice. He wanted to heave. Instead, he stared at the cook, who suddenly noticed his presence. The man snapped an order and everyone else in the room bobbed their heads.

"Why are you screaming at her?" Kenneth inquired evenly.

A nervous tic showed in the cook's plump cheek. "Truly, Your Grace, it is nothing for you to be concerned over . . . a mere matter of personnel. I was dismissing the girl."

Instinctively, Kenneth assessed the matter as he spotted the girl's rounded belly. He studied the maid. Her red-rimmed gaze held his, pleadingly.

Kenneth thought of the legions of servants standing ready to do his bidding, tailors measuring his private parts, and a social secretary fussing over proper protocol for a duke. His thoughts turned to London, the frozen mist and this girl wandering those dank streets, begging for work, her feet shuffling slowly, her cheeks growing gaunt, despair in her eyes.

Anger simmered inside him. How could this society so easily dismiss a woman carrying an illegitimate child when far greater sins existed on their very front doorsteps?

"You will *not* dismiss her," he said with quiet authority.

Pomeroy's beady eyes bugged out. The little hairs of his thin mustache quivered. He sputtered like butter on a hot skillet. Kenneth watched with interest; the effect was quite comical.

"But Your G-Grace," the cook stammered.

"Simply because the poor girl is in an unfortunate circumstance, you would toss her out on the street?"

Pomeroy stuttered some more. His face grew more crimson than the beef sitting on the carving board.

Kenneth went to the maid, who scrubbed her face with her stained apron. "You're not leaving. I won't lose good help."

"Thankee, Yer Grace," she whispered, twisting her chapped hands. "'E said 'e would marry me—and then 'e run off."

"Everyone makes mistakes." Kenneth thought of Badra, his own bitterest mistake, and of her refusal of marriage.

Hot blood infused Pomeroy's face. He looked ready to explode. "Your Grace, I must insist . . . you must not allow her to remain here. It sets a poor example for the staff."

Kenneth turned to the kitchen maid. "Can you cook?"

She bobbed her head. "I cooked for me family, Yer Grace. Simple fare, but—"

"Good. Simple sounds delightful. You can start with dinner tonight. You're now the new cook." Kenneth shot the French chef a cool, calm look. "Pack up your things. You're dismissed."

Pomeroy's jaw dropped. "But, but . . . ," he spluttered.

"Today," Kenneth said in a quiet tone.

Then, feeling much more cheerful, he left a blustering Pomeroy screaming in French and escaped to the quietness of his library. There he sank into an over-stuffed wing chair and propped his chin on his fist, staring at the flames crackling in the white marble fireplace. Every room had a roaring fire. He was wealthy and could afford the coal. And yet he was so damn cold . . .

A small noise drew his attention to the doorway. Zaid stood there, a sheaf of papers in his hand. Kenneth's heart sank.

"Those need my signature?"

Zaid nodded. Kenneth motioned to the satinwood desk. He settled onto its sturdy chair and stared at the thick documents Zaid handed over. They looked official and important.

Slowly he dipped the thick gold pen into the inkwell. His hand hovered above the vellum. Kenneth steeled his spine and drew the intricate swirls and curlicues that made no sense to him. They looked very official. Zaid dusted sand over his signature to dry it.

Kenneth pulled a gold watch from his vest pocket. His friend, Landon Burton, the Earl of Smithfield, had asked to meet him at his cousin Victor's antiquities shop. He'd promised a small surprise.

"Order the carriage, Zaid. I'm late for my meeting with Lord Smithfield."

When the secretary left, Kenneth stared at the particles clinging to the black ink on the paper. Sand. Egypt. His feet longed to walk the land he once called home. But it was home no more.

Such irony. The English duke who'd sworn never to return to Egypt pining for that land more than anything else. He felt adrift, without country or culture. From the moment he'd left Egypt, he vowed to forget the woman who'd crushed his heart. Badra was in his past, when he'd ridden like the wind across dusky sands and swung a scimitar with a mighty arm. When he'd been called Khepri. The memory of her beauty beckoned like a siren's song. He had to stuff rags into his ears to shut out the melody.

God help him if he ever saw her again. God help them both.

Chapter Three

This assignment was far more dangerous than she'd ever anticipated. Badra's heart skipped a beat as she stared out the carriage window. She blew a breath on the glass, frosting it, and drew her name in English. The letters made her smile. Once she'd been illiterate. Now she could read and write in both English and Arabic. It was her greatest achievement.

Anxiety gripped her. Did she now face her worst failure?

Smuggling stolen artifacts belonging to a stranger was one thing. But a necklace belonging to Khepri? Sweat slicked her tightly clasped hands inside her fur muff.

The cold, gray land Khepri now called home chilled her blood. Badra ached for Egypt's warm sands, soft desert breezes and burning yellow sun. She shuddered at London's smells and crowds, the thick pall of black coal smoke in the air, the pitiful pleas of ragged beggar children huddled in doorways, the continual clip-clop of carriages rushing indifferently past ordure and filth in the gutters.

She glanced at Rashid, talking to Lord Smithfield,

Katherine's father. The earl had helped them secure a trust-worthy source to sell Khamsin gold artifacts. With that money, they could educate the tribe's children in England. Rashid still wore his trousers and indigo *binish*, the turban wrapped about his long, dark locks. His only concession to English style was a thick wool cloak to fend off the icy chill.

At their destination, Badra clutched her wool cloak as the wind whistled beneath it. Her clothing felt odd. She had some trouble maneuvering in the laced boots. A wood sign swung in the winter wind above the shop window. It read ANTIQUITIES.

She followed Rashid and the earl inside. A little silver bell tinkled gaily when the door opened. She hung back, pretending to admire the glistening artifacts in their glass display cases. When the proprietor invited the men to a back room to make their transaction, she held her breath.

The clerk's eyes met hers. He was the one who sold artifacts on the black market behind his employer's back.

Badra furtively withdrew the Egyptian necklace from the satchel—called a reticule, she'd learned—and laid it on the counter. Guilt assaulted her. If Jabari knew what she was doing, dishonoring their heritage to become a lowly tomb raider . . .

Brushing aside guilt, she spoke rapidly in perfect English. The clerk studied the Egyptian pectoral, which featured a design of two griffins and the vulture goddess. Lapis and carnelian winked in the light.

"Lovely," he marveled in his thick accent. "Be hard to duplicate, but it'll fetch a pretty pence when it's done."

Duplicate? So that's why Masud wanted the necklace

smuggled here. The clerk was making replicas. No matter. Her task was finished, and guaranteed Jasmine's safety. The clerk handed over a wad of pound notes to return to Masud. As she took them, Badra's hand shook. She was a transporter of stolen goods and tainted money.

Barely had she stuffed the notes into her muff when the little silver bell tinkled again. Badra turned to see the visitor. A sharp gasp escaped her lips as she stared into a pair of blazing blue eyes she thought she'd never see again.

Khepri.

Badra.

Time took a step back, just as he did.

Reeling with shock, Kenneth stared at the woman he had once loved. He could not think or breathe. Her exotic beauty enchanted him, wove him back into the familiar spell of hot Arabian nights and the secrets inside the black tents under endless starry skies. Those luminous brown eyes, delicate cheekbones and her soft, pliant mouth still made his heart pound a frantic beat. Her eyes widened as if in fear. Badra's mouth worked violently. She took a step forward, wobbled like a newborn colt, and threatened to fall.

Habit, borne from five years of protecting her from even her foot scraping a rock, caused him to rush to assist. Grabbing her elbow, he steadied her. Their gazes caught and met, dark brown to deep blue. Her heart-shaped mouth parted in a soft, "Oh!"

Kenneth realized the arm he grasped was covered in soft, gray English fabric. Convulsive shock raced through him.

Badra clad in English dress was like seeing the limestone statue of Ramses II wearing a suit and cravat.

Sublimely ridiculous.

Yet nothing could dim her beauty. Not even sackcloth.

Roping in his emotions, Kenneth straightened and laced both hands behind his back. "Hello, Badra," he said in formal English.

"Khepri," she answered, her sultry voice winding around him like a silk scarf, teasing his senses to madness.

"Kenneth," he corrected.

He picked up the muff she'd dropped and a pound note fluttered out. Kenneth offered both back, deeply curious. He raised inquiring brows.

"I . . . I don't know where to put English currency," she stammered.

His nod toward the reticule swinging from her arm indicated the correct storage place.

"It is good to see you again, Khep—I mean, Kenneth." Badra took the note and the muff. Bright rosy color stained her cheeks. Flustered as he was, she was showing it more.

"I see you are doing quite well," she added.

He stared. Quite well? When all he wanted was to gather her in his arms and kiss her senseless? When she'd cut him to the bone with her rejection? A short laugh escaped him. Viciously, he bit it back.

"What are you doing here, Badra?"

"Rashid and I are visiting Lord Smithfield."

Silently he cursed. The earl had probably thought he'd enjoy seeing people from the tribe that raised him. Not bloody likely.

"Why?" he asked bluntly.

"Ramses was to come, but Katherine is pregnant and he was worried the long journey would tax her. We came in their stead. Do you remember the artifacts stored in the tomb of Ramses's ancestor?"

At his abrupt nod, she continued. "Lord Smithfield is helping us sell some pieces. With the money, Jabari will send a few children to school in England. They need further education." She smiled. "How is your grandfather faring?"

His throat went tight. "My grandfather . . . died two months ago. A sudden illness. I am Duke of Caldwell now." He closed his eyes briefly, then opened them. "But I am fortunate we were able to have some time together before he passed on."

Sympathy filled her lovely face. "Oh, Kenneth, I am so sorry. Why did you not write and tell us?"

Tell them? He had left the tribe behind. They knew nothing of his personal life. He had longed to share with them the deep sorrow he felt after regaining old ground with his grandfather, then losing him. He had felt so damnably alone.

But he could not tell them.

Abruptly, he changed topics. "I understand you visited my exacavation at Dashur. Did you see anything you liked?"

Two bright spots of scarlet colored her cheeks. "It—it was very educational. How did you know we were there?"

"I know everything about that dig." He studied her face, her beautiful large eyes. Lost in staring, Kenneth felt the familiar desire rise. He fought it. "How is Elizabeth? Did she enjoy seeing the pyramid?"

"Very much so. She and Jabari both. It was a welcome break for them. Tarik is approaching two and is very"—a sparkle lit her eyes—"very much a boy."

A rush of homesickness for the desert sands he'd once called home engulfed him. Kenneth studied Badra. She wore a soft gray gown with sleeves edged with ecru lace. A warm felt hat covered her silken midnight hair bundled into a tight chignon. Of all the English women he'd met, and those he'd bedded in frantic attempts to forget Badra, none could match this exotic beauty.

He willed his emotions away. Never show them to the enemy, Jabari had advised. You will be slaughtered without mercy. God, the sheikh was right—only he'd never warned that the enemy could be a beautiful woman.

"Give her my regards," he told Badra crisply.

Then, with those dismissive words, he crossed to the shop's assistant. The clerk gave him a friendly smile. Kenneth braced his hands on the counter and offered a penetrating look. "Any new pieces come in? I'm particularly interested in gold Egyptian pectorals. A design with two griffins and the vulture goddess."

Chapter Four

Oh help me, God, Badra thought frantically. Her heart thudded against her chest. Her eyes sought the clerk's, who swung his even gaze back to Kenneth.

"No, Your Grace. I don't have such an item."

Relief made her shoulders slump as he discreetly closed the drawer containing the stolen necklace.

Kenneth drummed his fingers on the counter, peering down at the display case. Badra studied him, this man who once swore an oath to protect her with his life. Now he was a stranger. She might never have recognized him but for those intense blue eyes. A sweep of thick, dark brown hair brushed against the collar of his coat. Cheeks that had been covered in a close-trimmed beard were now clean-shaven. He had a square chin. The beard had hidden this feature. The smooth-shaven look accented full, sensual lips and a thin nose. If Khepri had been merely handsome, this stranger was striking in both his arresting appearance and crisply polished manner. His wool greatcoat hung in clean lines to his thighs. She glanced at his feet—no soft leather boots of blue, but highly polished black shoes.

Once, those blue eyes had held only friendliness. Now they appeared colder than the air outside. Looking a true English duke, Kenneth's broad shoulders bore a regal posture as he laced gloved hands behind his back.

He had always been alert and sharp, watchful of her every move, and she feared one look at her ragged breathing and he'd ask questions, demand answers. But he merely studied the artifacts, asking about their origins. Voices sounded as the back room door creaked open. Badra's heart skipped another beat as Rashid stepped out.

At the sound, Kenneth turned. Rashid halted. Badra's heartbeat trebled.

The two men regarded each other with a level look. Badra shuddered at the antipathy burning in Rashid's brown eyes. Loyally, he considered Kenneth a traitor to his sheikh.

Their eyes locked.

"Hello, Khepri," Rashid said in Arabic, his jaw tensing beneath his heavy black beard. "I see you are still alive and well. A shame."

Badra's chest felt hollow with panic as Kenneth narrowed his eyes and replied in the same language, "I did not think I would ever see you again, Rashid." He paused and gave a chilling smile. "A shame."

"I do believe I owe you something for how you insulted Jabari upon your departure, Khepri," Rashid snapped.

Kenneth smiled grimly. "Then give it to me, if you are man enough, for I do not want to be in debt to you."

Rashid's hand shot to his side at the same time Kenneth's did. Badra watched in amazement.

Thankfully, neither had weapons. Hostility filled their stances as they circled like snarling dogs. Both fisted their hands and raised them to their chest. Both men were about the same height, with the same muscled builds. They could easily kill each other with their bare hands.

Voices sounded as the back room door swung open again. The proprietor and Lord Smithfield stepped out. Immediately, the earl stepped forward and placed a hand on Rashid's arm.

"Let it go," the earl said quietly.

The Khamsin warrior bristled with rage, then tossed off the nobleman's arm. He backed away, giving a curt nod.

"For the sake of honoring my host, I will not spill your blood here," he told Kenneth, watching him with wariness. "But be warned, traitor. There will come a time."

"I welcome it," Kenneth answered in a dangerously soft voice. "Do not underestimate me simply because I wear English dress now. You know I can defeat you."

She breathed easier as Kenneth seemed to rein in his temper. Rashid's face was still flushed with angry color. Kenneth's expression hardened as he glanced at her.

"Your fighting skills are best saved for protecting Badra. She is your first obligation. Or did you forget what Jabari charged you with?"

Her stomach gave a sickening lurch at the violence in Rashid's dark eyes. "I have not. My first obligation is to protect her from you."

Oh, Rashid, Badra said silently, pleading with her eyes. *Please don't . . . don't hurt him any more than I already have. . . .*

80

But it was too late. Kenneth's jaw tensed as if Rashid had delivered a deadly blow with his scimitar. "You truly think I would forsake everything I honored as a Khamsin warrior and deliberately harm the woman I had sworn a blood oath to protect?"

"You are no longer Khamsin," Rashid said evenly. The words hung in the air, quivering with silent threat.

Kenneth turned to her. "Do you think that I wish revenge?"

Would you take it if the opportunity presented itself? Badra wondered. She thought of the necklace. She smiled to hide her anxiety.

"I think we're taking up too much of this good shop-keeper's time and have provided him with enough drama for one afternoon. Perhaps it's best we leave. Right now," she said.

Kenneth fell back, as if she'd slapped him.

Badra had avoided answering his direct question. Did that mean she thought he would actually hurt her? After all the years he'd spent guarding her life more carefully than his own?

Realizing his mouth hung open, Kenneth assumed a blank expression. He compressed his lips, hiding his inner turmoil. Smithfield turned to him with an apologetic look. Kenneth twisted his lips in a crooked smile.

"Nice surprise," he said.

The earl sighed. "I thought you'd like seeing the artifacts they brought with them to sell to your cousin."

Kenneth shot a look at the quiet but glowering Rashid. "Only if there is a very sharp dagger among them."

Badra stared at Victor. He stood as tall as Kenneth. Sharp

81

intelligence radiated from his brilliant blue eyes, and his features were thin and concave.

"Mr. Edwards, the proprietor . . . he's your cousin?" she asked.

"You should remember. You saw him at the Khamsin camp when he and my grandfather came to get me," Kenneth said coolly.

"I did not realize . . ." She turned to Victor. "You have no facial whiskers now, and your hair is . . ."

"Gone." Victor smoothed a hand over his nearly bald head. "And I've gained weight. Sorry to say I don't remember you, or this fellow Rashid, here, either. Met a lot of you people that day. Faces all blend together."

"Yes, we people all look alike," Rashid cut in, glowering.

Smithfield looked uncomfortable. He nodded toward his carriage. "It's best we're off now. Caldwell? Are you leaving as well?" The earl peered out the window. "Is your man here?"

"I sent him back home with instructions to return in one hour," Kenneth admitted.

He glanced outside the shop window and noted the earl's carriage. Hot blood suffused his face in sudden embarrassment. Another gaffe. English noblemen did not send their coachmen back to warm their frozen bones before a fire while their employers shopped. Noblemen made them wait in the cold. And if they were kindhearted like Smithfield, they outfitted their coachmen in warm furs and gave them small coal stoves to warm their feet.

"I'm heading back now," Smithfield cut in delicately. "Plenty of room in my coach. Care to accompany me?"

Relief flooded him at not having to brace himself for a walk in the bitter wind. Kenneth managed a brisk nod, silently thanking the man with his eyes. The widowed earl, who had married an Egyptian princess, was a friend. He was familiar with Egyptian culture. He had proven a life-saver as Kenneth struggled to adjust to English culture. How many times had the man rescued him from social disaster, coached him in the finer graces and instructed him in matters natural to wealthy Englishmen, but utterly foreign to him?

Smithfield turned to Rashid.

"I do believe I will walk," Rashid said. He gave Badra a meaningful look. "Will you walk with me?"

Badra took a step forward and wobbled.

"I doubt she could manage in that footwear," Kenneth suggested dryly. "Unless you carried her the whole way."

"Perhaps I shall," Rashid shot back.

"No, I'll be fine," she said quickly. "Rashid, I'll see you at the earl's house."

Her falcon guard stalked past and left the shop.

Inside the carriage, Badra allowed herself a tremulous sigh of relief as the conveyance pulled away. Kenneth took the seat opposite her. He folded his tall, broad-shouldered frame into a corner, silently staring out the window. Agitation shook her fragile control. Her Khepri. How she missed him! Badra wanted to lace her fingers through his, feel the tensile strength that had protected her for five years and find the warrior this new Englishman had swallowed. Perhaps she could, given time, find him again. Fate had brought them together once more. But Jasmine's sweet, innocent face swam before her. Her fists tightened inside her muff. She must return to Egypt as soon as possible to save her daughter from slavery.

Badra leaned against the velvet seat and saw Smithfield smiling at her. "Do you miss Egypt?" he asked in English.

"Yes," she admitted. "I feel I will never be warm again until I feel her sun upon my face."

"Egypt is far different from England. I sometimes wonder how Katherine is adjusting," he remarked.

"She's doing well and misses her father."

The earl smiled fondly. He touched the single gray lock on his raven hair ruefully. "Another grandchild. I'm too young to be a grandfather. But I don't worry about her. Ramses is a good husband and father."

And he fusses over Katherine, she thought. Badra had easily convinced the protective warrior that the long voyage would overtax his newly pregnant wife. She'd assured him she could deliver in his stead the gold mummy masks Earl Smithfield had wanted. Her falcon guard had balked at visiting England. Badra winced, remembering when he'd finally admitted why: the Englishman who'd visited the Al-Hajid camp long ago and abused Rashid, and who still roamed free . . .

The carriage slowed. The earl glanced out the window. "Traffic. Unusual crush this time of year."

She and Kenneth centered their attention outside, studying the frozen tableau, empty benches and trees stripped of greenery. Suddenly the tight quarters seemed too tight, too heated. Badra slid the window down, allowing a blast of fresh, icy air to infiltrate the carriage.

They pulled alongside a gleaming black conveyance emblazoned with a gold crest. The carriage rocked back and forth violently. The windows were shuttered with thick curtains.

Smithfield made an impatient sound and opened the door, stepping outside. "I'm going to see what the trouble is. I'm afraid we're rather stuck. Nothing is moving," he called back, and shut the door.

"That carriage is moving. Very much so," Kenneth observed.

Pleased he'd broken his ominous silence, Badra leaned forward and peered outside. Through their opened window she heard loud moans and cries coming from the vehicle.

Her face went scarlet. She stammered, "I—I th-thought the English only did such things behind closed doors."

"Their door is closed."

"But, they . . . are in public!"

He looked again. "Yes. My protocol instructor would have a comment or two about their choice of venue."

A sudden spark of laughter shone in his eyes. Then it vanished, replaced by a calculating look as he watched her cheeks redden. A deep chill seized her. He was relishing her humiliation. The duke of Caldwell leaned forward. His gaze snapped to the swaying carriage then back to her. His gaze dropped to her clenched thighs hidden by layers of wool. A slow, dangerous smile tilted his mouth upward.

Once, her falcon guard would never have considered such a debasing and dishonorable look. Khepri's fist would have flown into another man's chin for such lewdness.

But he was Kenneth now. No longer Khepri.

Heated anger filled her. "Is this something you do as well? It's vulgar—something I would never have expected of you."

A chill look slid over him. "Not at all. I have no need of a carriage. Several English women find my bed perfectly delightful."

Hot blood flushed her cheeks again as tendrils of jealousy tore through her. Images surfaced of a pretty, blond Englishwoman moaning as she wrapped her white thighs around Kenneth's pumping buttocks and he pressed her down into the mattress.

Another image replaced it: Sheikh Fareeq's bloated, fat body advancing toward her, his meaty fist cruelly slapping her tender, bruised skin and then throwing her on his sheepskins and forcing himself inside her. She whimpered and cried in pain . . .

Badra gulped and slid the window up with a sharp click.

Icy air blasted back into the carriage as Smithfield opened his door and climbed back inside. "Shouldn't be long now. Carriage ran into a hack. They're clearing it." His gaze flicked to the object of their attention. "That's Baron Ashbury's carriage. But he's ill, at his country estate. His wife must be in town—but she didn't get her knocker up."

"She's got someone's knocker up," Kenneth noted.

The earl's blue eyes widened as he caught sight of the rocking carriage. "Good God. She most certainly did."

Kenneth's chest rumbled with deep laughter. Badra felt her cheeks flame with hot embarrassment. Thankfully, their carriage jerked forward and they pulled away.

The earl looked apologetic. "I hope that didn't upset you, Badra."

She managed a tremulous smile, not wanting to distress

their kind-hearted host. "It's all right, Lord Smithfield. I'm just not used to seeing . . . such things."

"Of course you never have, especially not while living in a sheikh's harem," Kenneth said in a mocking tone in Arabic.

Smithfield said quietly in the same language, "I think we should speak English. Badra is anxious to practice the language and perhaps if you speak it you will act more like the civilized English gentleman you are desiring to become."

Kenneth muttered an apology in English. Heavy silence fell as he glued his attention to the window. His body went as stiff as wood. Once more Badra was reminded how her falcon guard had changed. He belonged to her world no more.

Smithfield smiled to break the tension. "You'll have plenty of opportunity to practice English at my dinner party, Badra. Caldwell, I trust you're still coming?"

The duke's face tightened. "I would not miss it for anything. I'm eagerly anticipating it."

Tension knotted Badra's muscles. A formal dinner party? She already felt strange when people glanced at her on the street. She was Egyptian. Different. Khepri had his English friends, his English traditions and culture. He blended into this society's fabric effortlessly. She stood out like a pyramid on London's dank, dirty streets.

Silence again fell in the carriage. Badra touched the money she'd received, reminding herself of her greater priority. She suppressed a shudder of dread at getting caught. Arrested, publicly shamed, dishonoring her tribe. But her daughter must be saved. No matter what the cost.

Badra stole a furtive glance at Kenneth, who stared grimly out the window.

Even the cost to herself.

Later that night Kenneth lay in his stiff, heavy, canopied bed where generations of Tristan nobility had been conceived. The opulent bed was as sweeping as Egypt's dunes, with intricate flowers carved on wood posts thick as tree trunks. He missed his simple Khamsin bed; lightweight, portable, comfortable.

Memories haunted him—cool desert nights and Badra's sultry singing. He rolled over and punched the feather pillow. He tried for sleep, for blessed forgetfulness. It did not come.

What if she had agreed to marry him and he had remained behind as a Khamsin warrior? Or what if she'd dared to leave behind her life in the desert to be his duchess? A faint dream teased him: Badra at his side as they strolled along Bond Street. Badra presiding over his dinner table with charm and ease. Badra's nude body pressed beneath him as she gave soft cries of pleasure as they conceived the next duke of Caldwell. Badra handing him their firstborn child, her glow of pride equaling his own.

Pain gripped him, as intense as a scimitar spearing his heart. Kenneth buried his face in his pillow, stifling a deep groan. He must forget her.

But how could he?

He'd shadowed her every move for five years. Now fate had dealt him a cruel blow; she was shadowing him with equal zeal.

Bloody hell—he liked that English phrase—his body still pulsed with wanting her, desiring her as madly as a man crawling in the desert craved water. He'd thought he was able to banish memories of her sweet laughter, her shy smile. He could no more erase her from his mind than he could scrub away the cobra tattoo on his right arm. Both were carved into him permanently.

Cold sweat trickled down his spine. He wanted to find the thief himself, not rely upon others. Kenneth contented himself with images of capturing the thief, watching a cell door clank closed before him.

Eventually a languid drowsiness came. He dozed off until something nudged him awake. His warrior sense of awareness, honed by years of battle, sprang to life. His gaze jerked to the open French windows leading to the terrace, overlooking the garden. A shadow fell just inside the room.

Kenneth lay perfectly still as the intruder slipped inside. The glow of the full moon shimmered on an upraised gleam of silver.

The knife descended with lightning speed, but he reacted and rolled, seizing his attacker's wrist. Pain flared briefly as the blade scraped his arm. Kenneth threw a punch directly to his assailant's middle. A low wheeze of pain was his reward, and his attacker doubled over and wrenched away. Then he fled.

Kenneth sprang off the bed and dashed after the fleeing figure, who turned and delivered a gut-grinding kick to his midsection. Kenneth wheezed, the breath knocked out of him. His attacker vaulted over the railing. By the time Kenneth made it to the terrace, the only evidence left was a dangling rope.

His breathing finally quieted as he cradled his injured arm. Incredulity raged through him, along with a deep-seated fury and growing horror.

The person fleeing into the ghostly London night remained elusive, but the clothing he wore was no mystery. A distinctive outfit, worn by desert warriors who prided themselves on their honor, duty and fierce fighting abilities. A costume he had worn with pride, now tucked away in a chest with memories best forgotten. The indigo clothing of a warrior of the wind.

One of his former brethren had just tried to murder him.

Chapter Five

Shortly after breakfast, not caring that proper visiting hours were in the afternoon, Kenneth banged a familiar knocker. The butler opened the door, surprise showing on his dour face. Without words, Kenneth removed his greatcoat, tossed it at him and strode angrily into the drawing room. The earl of Smithfield read before a crackling fire. He glanced up.

"Where's Rashid?" Kenneth demanded.

Smithfield's blue eyes widened as he set his book down. "Walking in the park. Poor fellow keeps shutting himself inside his room. I ordered him to get some fresh air. Why?"

"I'm going to wring his bloody neck."

"Calm down," Smithfield ordered. He rang for a footman and issued a crisp order for brandy. Kenneth accepted the cut-glass snifter and sipped, relishing the burn in his throat.

"Now, please explain what has you so upset, Caldwell."

When Kenneth finished recounting the attack, and his suspicions, the earl frowned. "Are you certain it's Rashid?"

"Positive," Kenneth said roughly. "He hates me."

The earl drummed long fingers on the chair's armrest. "You suspect he came here to sell your necklace as well as the tribe's gold?"

"Positive. He may not even have sold it yet." His gaze bored into his friend's. "I want your permission to search his room."

"And if you find your necklace? What then? Will you have him arrested?" The earl's voice remained oddly neutral.

"I'll decide later. Right now I need to get into his room."

"Very well. It's the third door on the left."

Kenneth stood, nodding at his empty glass. "Thanks for the refreshment. Goes better on a full stomach—the fullest it's been since I fired my cook."

"You fired Pomeroy—the finest French chef in London?"

"Had to. His dishes were upsetting my stomach."

The earl drew his black brows together as if something greatly disturbed him. "Caldwell, about your grandfather. Had he been ill before he died?"

Kenneth racked his memory. "I recall a time or two he complained about stomach ailments. Why?"

"No particular reason," Smithfield said. "Go search Rashid's room. Afraid I must leave you. I've an appointment with my solicitor. Let yourself out when you're finished. But hurry. Most likely, he'll return soon."

Rashid's room contents did not surprise Kenneth. An ornate, hand-carved oak canopied bed with a forest green silk coverlet dominated. On the jewel-toned carpet lay a small bedroll with a pillow. Rashid always slept on the ground.

With careful stealth, Kenneth opened the drawers in the polished tallboy, systematically combing through the contents. He searched the room with efficient thoroughness until at last he spied his quarry stuffed deep inside Rashid's bedroll: a colorful cloth bag. Personal items.

Kenneth tugged on the drawstring and dumped the contents onto the rug: a small bag containing English money, a pair of scissors, and a gleam of gold flashing in the light that filtered through the polished window.

Kenneth picked up the gold pendant. It was the missing necklace. Raw anger tunneled through him.

He fingered the pendant, examining the shiny perfection of ancient Egyptian craftsmanship. His father had died trying to obtain this, or treasure like it. Yet why would Rashid steal it? As revenge for Kenneth insulting Jabari? Was that why Rashid had attempted to kill him as well?

Rashid was a powerful warrior. He could have fought Kenneth last night, made him fight for his life. But instead, he'd nicked him and run. It made no sense.

No matter. He'd stolen; therefore Kenneth would order his arrest.

His conscience pricked. Rashid's arrest would dishonor Jabari and the tribe.

He owed them nothing.

He owed them everything.

Torn, he replaced the pendant. The duke of Caldwell thirsted to watch authorities drag Rashid to prison. The

Khamsin warrior he had been resisted ordering such a public disgrace.

Bloody hell, he couldn't order Rashid arrested. *I owe it to Jabari, for how I treated him when I left. Face it,* he told himself with grim humor. *I've spent a year trying to forget I am Khamsin. But deep down, I still long to ride the sands and restore friendship with them. I loathe shaming the tribe who was my family. And it would upset Badra deeply.* He winced, imagining her shock at seeing her falcon guard hauled off to prison.

But failing to arrest Rashid meant quiet Khamsin justice must prevail. Jabari must be told. Kenneth touched his cobra tattoo, guilt coursing through him. Confronting the man he once called brother would not be easy. But did he have any alternative?

Only the prisons here in England. He jammed a frustrated hand through his thick hair. There was no choice left, only to return to Egypt, to tell the sheikh what happened. To see Khamsin justice done.

But perhaps Rashid worked with others, a ring of smugglers still present at the dig. He needed more information. Kenneth decided to immediately send Zaid, his loyal secretary, to Egypt to investigate. Then he'd make plans for himself and Victor to follow. His cousin, experienced in antiquities, would prove an enormous help.

On silent feet, he left and prowled down the hallway.

Music accosted his ears. He froze. A sweet melody filled the air, so haunting it stilled his breath. Strings plucked on an exotic instrument he had not heard in more than a year. In a different time and place.

Badra's voice followed, accompanying her strumming of the rebaba's horsehair strings, and it filled him with aching want. Oh, how he remembered her dulcet tones. Enraptured, he had stood mesmerized outside her tent. Caught in her voice's silken strands, he had become ensnared in a web of torment, his maddening hunger for her forever unsated.

Never again had he imagined hearing her sing.

But the same voice now wrapped its exotic tones about him. Aching melancholy for his past wrestled with Kenneth's need. Her voice razed all English trappings. The palatial drawing rooms, stiff and resplendent in their brocaded fabrics, the polished smell of beeswax and glycerin—all shifted into the past.

The memories burned: the soft shuffle of leather boots through sand, children's ringing laughter, women chattering as they sloshed goat's milk in leather bags, the sharp rasp of warriors' blades as they honed them against a rock.

Kenneth breathed deeply, his mind recalling various sensations. Roasting lamb, the sharp hiss of fat dripping into the fire. The smell of horses. Fresh jasmine scenting a woman's soft skin, and the desert heat contained in those hidden places a warrior dared dream about, that velvet warmth clutching and surrounding him with pleasure so intense he'd burned hot as the yellow sun . . .

He touched his hidden cobra tattoo. For a full year, the simple truth had simmered below the surface. He had rejected his tribe, and himself as well, but he still longed to be called brother of Jabari. He could not shed his upbringing as easily as he shaved his beard or cut his hair.

His eyes snapped open. Badra's song became mournful,

a dirge. What coaxed such embittered words from her sweet lips? The Arabic words pulled at him.

When did you become nothing but a shadow on my heart?
My *Ieb* is aching from the weight you placed on it, for you died and left me
Alone in my grief, tears of sorrow creating a river
Deep as the Nile
So I may drown and feel no more pain, my soul that aches for
The tender smiles you once gave
You left forever, yet you still remain
Flesh and blood and bone, standing before me and yet
A ghost still.

Kenneth pressed his fingers against the wooden door. Motionless, he stood lost in past regrets. What ghosts hammered at her deep inside?

Did she ever love me at all? He did not want to know.

Kenneth quietly slipped down the sweeping staircase, eager to return to his very English home. No memories lurked there. But in the hallway, as he reached the door, it swung open.

Rashid stepped inside. His startled gaze met Kenneth's. For a minute something deep and inscrutable flickered in his dark eyes. Then it vanished, replaced with his usual hostility.

"Rashid. Good day," Kenneth said quietly.

"It was, until I saw you. Get out of my way."

Fists clenching with white-knuckled anger, Kenneth cursed. *Arrest him,* screamed Kenneth, the outraged English duke. *No,* protested Khepri, the Khamsin warrior he'd been.

A small noise sounded from the staircase. He whirled. It was Badra, standing there, regally. Distress etched her face.

Kenneth glared at Rashid a moment longer, then pushed past and went down and out into the biting cold.

Chapter Six

"That was unforgivably rude. Where are your manners?" Standing on the staircase, Badra coldly regarded her friend. Her protector. Her companion in pain.

Rashid's handsome face pinched with sudden regret. "I am sorry, Badra. I did not mean to upset you."

She descended and paced the gleaming hardwood floor. "Why do you hate him so? Because of what he did to Jabari?"

Deep sorrow reflected in his dark eyes. Then it faded. He grunted. "It is more jealousy than hate. Khepri always led a charmed life. He always had . . . advantages most others never did."

Her friend's blunt honesty startled her. "Rashid, do not torment yourself. There are always others who have advantages we are denied. Life sometimes strips us of choices and we must make the best of what we are given."

Dark torment flashed on Rashid's face. Badra recognized the look—terror, mixed with deep shame.

"You must be cordial to Khepri, especially at Lord Smithfield's dinner party tonight."

"It is not necessary. I am not attending."

"But Rashid, you promised."

"I cannot stand the English staring as if I am an artifact on display. I hate them," he said tightly. But she sensed a more compelling reason behind his refusal.

"Rashid, what happened? I know something did. I can tell."

He remained silent. A maid carrying flowers passed. Badra sensed Rashid's unease. "Let us talk in private. In my room."

Upstairs, she closed the door and watched him sink to the floor, sitting cross-legged. She waited patiently. The warrior took a deep breath, his face pale and glistening with sweat.

"While I walked in the park . . . I saw someone. He looked exactly . . ." Rashid took a long gulp of air.

"Like the Englishman who hurt you," she finished.

Head bent, he traced a line on the elegant carpet. "Badra, there is something you should know. He did not . . . force me."

Badra stared, feeling slightly sick.

"He was a visiting English nobleman, purchasing one of our Arabians. A person of great power and respect. I begged him to help me escape the man hurting me each night. He told me such a great favor came with a great price. He, he . . . wanted me. If I did not struggle . . . he would help me. When I refused, the Englishman asked what was one time with him compared to a lifetime with my tormentor? I was so desperate I agreed. When it . . . when it was over, he warned if I told anyone, he would blame me. Then he laughed and rode off. He left me there, Badra. Trapped. There was no escape."

Rashid's voice scraped across her shivering body. "This is the real reason I loathed coming to England. He is here, in London. I know it. I cannot bear seeing him again. That face, his red hair, it haunts my deepest dreams."

"How old were you?" she asked quietly.

His long black hair curtained his expression. "Old enough to know what he did. What I *allowed* him to do. I was eight."

Badra forced down the rising nausea, thinking of the little boy subjected to such horrors. For all she had suffered, Rashid had suffered double.

"Do not blame yourself. I wasted years doing so. You must learn to live with the memories. With time, they will fade." Though she tried to assure him, a hollow note rang in her voice.

He caught it. "Do they?" he asked. Doubt riddled his tone. "For years I have lived with this torment. I cannot look upon any Englishman without breaking into a cold sweat. I feel so . . . ashamed."

His haunted eyes met hers. "Tell me, Badra. Please. Tell me that it will fade, that I will be a man once more."

Her heart ripped in half. She imagined a young boy's terrified screams as Fareeq's second-in-command indulged in his evil pleasure . . . and then the boy's shame as he allowed an Englishman to do the same.

"You *are* a man, Rashid. A brave, honorable warrior. And no one ever doubts it. Your secret will remain safe with me."

He touched her hand, nodded. Some degree of control

had returned and his old, familiar look of command returned. "As will yours," he stated formally.

She squeezed his hand. For a minute they sat, lost in memory. And regret.

It was a horrible mistake, appearing at Lord Smithfield's rout. Badra realized that now. She had wanted to shut herself away and mourn her cowardice in refusing Kenneth's marriage offer last year, but conflicting emotions tore at her. Her curiosity had won. She'd wanted to experience the English society that would have become her world had she married Khepri. So Badra had summoned a maid to help her dress and then went downstairs to the dinner party.

Beneath her elegant emerald silk gown, Badra broke into a cold sweat as she glimpsed the crowd. Choking panic welled in her throat.

The swirl of elegant women in ruffled silk gowns and the gentlemen in elegant black suits was flustering as Lord Smithfield introduced her. Men gave her speculative glances and smiles. The women were cool and assessing. Badra felt like a display piece, gazed upon and examined by curious spectators.

And then a familiar face towered over the crowd. The duke of Caldwell. Her mouth went dry.

One woman in a lemon-yellow gown leaned close to Kenneth, clearly enthralled. Badra noticed several other ladies rivet their attention to him, too. His prodigious height, dark good looks and piercing blue eyes attracted females like sand to wet skin. With seeming ease, he conversed with his admirer.

Then Kenneth lifted his head. His gaze caught Badra's

and held it across the room. For a single moment his eyes burned into her, scorching her with a heat more intense than her beloved Egyptian sun. Then he fastened his attention back on his companion. His deep, rich laughter sounded as he responded to something she'd said.

Anxiety clenched Badra's stomach. She was here in his foreign, imposing world. On her own. If she committed some grave social error, he would not rescue her. Sweat dampened her palms.

As the footman announced dinner and they were ushered toward the dining room, full-fledged panic arose. She wanted to turn and run.

But her feet, and pride, would not permit flight.

An enormous table with a handwoven lace cloth featured shiny dishes, sparkling crystal and gleaming silver. The sour-faced footman stood nearby, his manner as stiff as the dark blue velvet and gold-braided uniform he wore. The relative casualness of Lord Smithfield's usual dinners did not match this cold formality. No wonder Rashid remained upstairs.

Her heart galloped as her dinner companion, Viscount Oates, gallantly held out her chair. For a long moment Badra's legs froze. How could she do this? She was a simple Bedouin woman who sat on thick carpets on the sand, ate with flat bread as utensils and drank cups of thick, rich camel's milk. A footman moved methodically down the table, pouring ruby-colored wine into glasses. She did not drink alcohol, either.

She glanced across the table at the duke, who was conversing with his pretty dinner partner. Badra swept the table with her gaze. Which fork to use? What if she spilled something? So many crystal glasses as well.

Women glanced at her with avid interest, bright eyes eager to see her fail. How could she manage this? *I cannot.*

Badra stared at Kenneth, willing him to look at her, to offer some reassurance. Studiously, it seemed, he ignored her. *Please look at me, Kenneth. Please. I'm frightened.*

Finally, he did. Badra's desperate gaze held his steady one. Helplessly, she touched the gleaming utensils near her plate. She raised her gaze to Kenneth in a wordless request.

"Watch me," he mouthed.

Servants began serving the first course. Badra studied the white liquid sitting before her in a delicate china bowl, and then at the assortment of spoons. The duke lifted the largest spoon and dipped it into the soup, slowly bringing it to his mouth. Badra attempted the same, tasting the concoction, surprised at the creamy taste. She ate more, smiling politely as Lord Oates chatted about his family's fine collection of horses.

I will not appear a savage. I can use the correct utensil.

Badra watched Kenneth carefully as footmen cleared the soup bowls and brought the next course. He picked up the heavy silver utensil, speared a white oval dotted with green shavings and brought it to his mouth. She followed suit, resisting the strong impulse to break off some thick white bread to scoop up the meal, just as she longed to push back the heavy mahogany chair and sit on the floor.

A florid-faced nobleman sitting nearby addressed Kenneth from across the table. "So, Caldwell," he boomed. "Shall we go shooting again this year at my estate? Bag a pheasant or two?"

"As long as it is pheasant and not peasant I down, Huntly.

I'm afraid the last time I nearly clipped one of your tenants instead of the bird," Kenneth joked smoothly, to the amused laughter of those listening.

A pang of jealousy twisted Badra's insides at the women's adoring glances. Khepri was gone forever, Kenneth the duke neatly sliding into his place, a polished, sophisticated nobleman who assimilated smoothly into this strange, gleaming world. She felt like a dull pebble surrounded by sparkling rubies and diamonds.

Surprising her, Lord Oates sneered. "Bagging peasants sounds well and good, but you rarely attended any of last season's balls. Are you shunning the Marriage Mart? Or is it waltzing you fear? Did they not teach you any social graces in Egypt?"

Kenneth narrowed his eyes.

"Oh, right, I forgot. That lazy heathen tribe who raised you doesn't dance. Except when poked with a British saber." Oates's laughter rang out. Badra flinched at the insult.

A sound escaped Kenneth's lips: a whisper, a familiar undulating purr from the past, a war cry Badra knew he made when confronted with male posturing. It was the call to arms his father had taught him. Not his real father, but the sheikh who'd raised him.

"What was that?!" one woman exclaimed.

Silence fell around the table like a heavy curtain. Badra bored her dark gaze into Kenneth's, thoroughly shocked but secretly gleeful. Khepri may have been swallowed by the urbane duke, but he could surface still, the Khamsin war cry undulating from his lips. The duke turned his attention toward the woman.

"That, my dear Lady Huntly, was a demonstration of the call to dance by the tribe who raised me. You are correct, Oates. The Khamsin do not dance in the traditional English sense. Their dances are fierce displays of strength before battle. The warriors strip to the waist, anoint themselves with ceremonial decorations and gather before a mighty bonfire, preparing themselves for the bloodletting to come. They dance to show to the sheikh their willingness to die."

"Are women permitted in these ceremonies?" asked one woman faintly, fanning herself. A tiny bead of perspiration rolled down her temple.

Kenneth gave Badra a meaningful glance. "No, for it is feared a lady would faint from witnessing such a spectacle." He added softly, "For women, such displays of male potency are reserved to the privacy of the black tents."

Badra felt her cheeks flame at his remark. His sapphire eyes burned into her. Heat from her cheeks spread through her body, warming it like a stoked fire—as if they were alone, and he'd dared to relay something forbidden, exotic and mysterious.

Oh, yes. He was still vaguely threatening and yet exciting. Badra's lips parted as she watched his long, elegant fingers stroke his wineglass's stem as if it were live, warm flesh. Her imagination flamed as she pictured his hands caressing a woman's soft thigh, teasing and arousing . . .

Her mental picture shifted. It was her thigh, the duke's hooded gaze lazy and meaningful as it captured hers and his fingers slid slowly upward, heat flaring in their wake. Badra hitched in a trembling breath, disturbed and aroused.

Fans fluttered wildly now as many flushed-faced women

105

sighed. Kenneth asked them with wicked glee, "Would you care for me to explain the war dance of the Khamsin warriors?"

A chorus of female voices cried out in unison. "Oh, yes!"

The duke smiled and obliged them. The women craned their necks forward to listen. A mutual sigh of their admiration undulated down the table as he sketched with his hands how the warriors tangled with each other "like wildcats" to demonstrate their prowess to their sheikh. And how they denied themselves their wives' company before battle but after victory, the warriors stalked off to their tents and demonstrated a "savage, insatiable prowess." Kenneth's suggestive look hinted at air filled with different cries—female cries of pleasure.

They all listened, clearly enthralled. And by the time he finished, every woman was flushed. Several looked faint.

The duke gave each a polite smile before riveting his attention to Badra. Her insides felt as formless as fresh yogurt. Kenneth's burning gaze pierced her.

"Well, Badra, I hope my explanation of the Khamsin rituals did not make you homesick," he said.

"It sounds like *you* are the homesick one," she noted.

His startled expression stopped the breath rising in her lungs. Sadness lingered there, twisting her emotions. In his face she saw a longing, the call of sand and sun and the warbling of warriors racing on their mares to battle. Then the look vanished like thirsty sand drinking precious raindrops.

"Why, my dear Badra," he drawled, his Egyptian accent fading, replaced by a proper British enunciation. "How can I be homesick when it's clear I am perfectly at home?"

He picked up his crystal wineglass. But the sadness she

could not forget. It reminded Badra of all she'd lost herself. His camaraderie. His fiercely protective nature. His love.

For she had become his enemy.

It was terrifying. Deep inside, Kenneth was a Khamsin warrior still, tempering his might with a veneer of urbane witticisms and genteel nobility. If he knew her crime . . . would he release the turbulent emotions raging inside him and unleash them on her?

Her heart lurched. Badra dropped her gaze, remembering her secret dream. She had become his wife and joined him in this strange, new world—a journey together, a challenge faced as one heart, one soul.

But it was a dream as elusive as mist. She was a former slave, a concubine. Now a smuggler of the duke's treasure, who belonged to a tribe that had banished Kenneth from their midst forever.

Chapter Seven

How could he have forgotten the effect Badra had on him?

It took all the restraint and control he'd learned as a warrior to keep his emotions in check. Her subtle jasmine scent teased his senses. A soft glow of the crystal chandelier reflected in the dark pools of her eyes. As the ladies rose to retire, Kenneth drew in a harsh breath, watching Badra with the keenness of a cobra eyeing prey.

God, how he still wanted her. Would the ache never cease? When he'd seen her gracefully stroll into the anteroom, he'd hid his emotions behind an expressionless mask as his Khamsin brethren had taught him. Then her woebegone expression had tugged at his heart and he'd steered her through dinner.

The women had retreated to the drawing room now, dragging Badra off, insisting on hearing her tales of Egypt. She had thrown Kenneth a panicked glance over one shoulder.

Protocol insisted he remain with the men. Kenneth swirled his brandy. A nasty suspicion rose in him. The women were going to probe details of her life. Curiosity had filled their faces. Every bone in his body urged him to rescue her. By God, he'd once vowed to rescue her from danger and here he was, leaving her in the clutches of women whose tongues were sharper than an Al-Hajid sword . . . *But it's no longer your concern,* he reminded himself.

Lord Huntly puffed on a cheroot and directed his attention toward Kenneth. "Simply amazing, Caldwell, how your grandfather found you after all these years. Quite a miracle. Seeing you were the sole survivor and now heir. If not for you, your cousin would inherit the title, is that not right?"

He offered a twisted smile. "Victor is a second cousin, but yes, I suppose you are correct. He would have inherited."

"The old Caldwell never gave up hope one of you might be still alive—either you or your brother."

Graham, the brother he vaguely remembered. Six years old when the Al-Hajid raided their caravan. Kenneth's chest tightened like wet leather as distant memories flickered. His parents frantically trying to find a place big enough to hide Graham. The look of horrific terror on his brother's face as he whipped his head around and saw the Al-Hajid galloping toward them. Their mother shoving Kenneth into the basket and closing the lid. The death screams . . .

"I say, shame about your grandfather dying so quickly. I miss the old man. We shared an adventure or two in our youth when he dragged me off to Egypt." Huntly's voice dropped. "Even visited one of those forbidden brothels in Cairo. He became quite enamored with a lovely little missy there."

Kenneth startled. "My grandfather?"

"Quite randy in his salad days." Huntly's face contorted as silence fell all around. "I do apologize, Caldwell."

Viscount Oates seized the opportunity. His knowing gaze burned into Kenneth's. "Randy as his grandson, I'm certain. Yet, look at how you've fit into society, Caldwell. Why, I daresay, one could not even guess you belonged to those ill-mannered heathens who raised you."

"No more than the ill-mannered heathens who raised you," Kenneth shot back calmly. Lord Huntly coughed out smoke and sputtered with laughter. From the corner, Smithfield quirked an eyebrow and smiled in silent amusement.

Yes, Kenneth could hold his own among those who scorned him because of his Arabic upbringing: he had learned to. But Badra? Were the women scorning her as the men had him upon his first return to England? Panic had flashed on her face as the women escorted her out.

He could ignore the impulse no longer; Kenneth murmured a polite excuse, set down his snifter and strolled to the drawing room. The door remained open. He lingered outside, listening with stealth, not all his years of training forgotten after all.

Inside, spine rigid, Badra sat on a plush crimson chaise. Women eyed her like vultures eye fresh carrion. Kenneth's alarm intensified as he spotted several former lovers. One pressed close to Badra, hazel eyes sparkling with malice. He stifled a groan. The honorable Millicent Williams, newly come out last season and not, as he had discovered, a virgin. In a frantic effort to forget Badra, he'd bedded several ladies, had been a randy Arabian stallion among a herd of willing English fillies.

Hearing of his affairs, his grandfather had gently urged a little discretion. Kenneth had rapidly disentangled himself from the liaisons, realizing he didn't need to act like his peers in the bedroom in order to assimilate into this new and odd society—a society which disdained naked table legs but not seeking pleasure between the spread naked legs of other men's wives, as long as the affairs were, like the table legs, discreetly out of sight. His lovers had pouted, but he had been firm and polite when they met during social occasions. Far more polite than they were being to Badra now. His heart twisted at her stricken look.

"Oh, but it must be so very fascinating living in Egypt. I imagine you lived in a harem. Did you wear those frightfully scandalous clothes?" one woman asked eagerly.

Badra flinched. Her delicate fingers curled tightly around her silk skirts.

Lady Millicent made a moue of prudish distaste. "I hear these tribes have women who exist only to serve men. I hear there are harems of brown-skinned, immoral women who wear practically nothing and do all sorts of wicked acts." A loathing glance cast at Badra indicated her intent.

Kenneth's rage grew. Wicked acts? He remembered Millicent's very wicked mouth around his very willing cock, teasing him to full arousal. Now those same lips spouted hypocritical moralism. Almost subconsciously, he started forward, angered by the roses rising in Badra's lovely cheeks.

But Badra gave Millicent a cool look. "The Khamsin are an honorable tribe and their women are equally honorable," she retorted.

Brava, Kenneth said silently.

The elderly, nearly deaf Mrs. Stephens leaned forward,

rapt interest sparking in her rheumy eyes. "Arabs have harems where women do all manner of disgusting things," she nearly shouted.

Badra drew back as the woman's sly eyes roved her form. The others leaned forward, their eyes bright with cruel speculation. Kenneth's former charge looked like a terrified horse ready to bolt. Silent rage filled him. He hesitated, remembering she was no longer his responsibility. Need to protect her combated with old hurts, but habits died hard.

Kenneth's frown deepened. He instinctively knew all had witnessed his aiding her during dinner and sensed a weakness, like crocodiles who would drag prey below the Nile for a kill.

The instinct arose to storm inside, scoop Badra up over his shoulder and charge out, warbling the Khamsin war cry to make those harpies shake with terror. They leaned close, slashing with the claws of their words, vultures dressed in satin, jewels dripping from their ears and necks. But Badra was holding her own, her little chin bravely thrust out. Then he saw it quiver. Kenneth steeled his spine as a warrior prepared for battle.

"Ladies? Surely this is not a conversation I would expect of well-bred women such as you."

With proud carriage, Kenneth strode into the silk-paneled drawing room. Soft, startled gasps filled the air. Badra watched with relief and pride at his entrance. Every starched spine and creaking whalebone corset shifted as the women swung their attention to him. Authority rode on his black silk-covered shoulders. The duke raked each woman with razor-sharp blue eyes and a contemptuous gaze.

"My understanding of English hospitality was one always makes a visitor in this country feel welcome. Especially a visitor who is unfamiliar with English culture. A visitor from the land, and the tribe, where I was raised.

His voice grew dangerously soft. "When you insult them—or her—you insult me. Thanks to the Khamsin, I was rescued from death. I owe them a great debt."

A flutter of female voices rose in a chorus of false protests, twined with anxious looks at Badra. Kenneth cast the women a look hard enough to cut diamonds.

"Enough of this," he said in clipped tones, his deep voice tinged with the wonderfully soothing accent that reminded all he was raised in another land. Badra's land. Her culture. He held out a hand, no longer quite so darkened from the sun. Badra took it, stiffly bidding the others good-bye.

In the foyer, she fought back an impulse to hug him. He seemed cold and distant, quietly studying her. What if he hadn't charged forward, snatching her away from danger? *I truly am alone in the world. Khepri will not always be there for me. Never again.*

"If you're quite all right, I'll be leaving now. Tell Smithfield I'll knock him up tomorrow."

He smiled briefly, touched her cheek. Then he jerked his hand back and walked out of the house. Leaving her. Distant and remote, as stony as the great pyramids they'd once both admired.

Badra raced outside, placed a gloved hand upon his arm. "Please wait a minute, Khep—I mean, Kenneth." Moisture blurred her eyes as he turned. "Thank you for what you did for me. I don't know if I could have taken another minute of those women."

Kenneth touched a tear trickling down her cheek. The glistening droplet clung to his finger. His expression softened. "They are ill-bred, despite their titles, and quick to judge what they do not understand. They preen and put on an appearance like colorful birds, but their minds are as empty as tombs." He paused and considered, arching his brows. "Actually, that's an insult to the dead."

She laughed. He continued, "They are far below you, Badra, vapid chits who never strive to improve their minds as you have. Do not give them another thought."

A tremulous smile touched her lips. "You're the same Khepri, rushing again to my rescue—only this time from a horde of women instead of enemy warriors."

"With tongues sharper than those warriors' scimitars," he quipped, and she laughed, pressing her fingers against his arm and squeezing.

"I miss you. I truly do."

He tensed and pulled away. "I must leave."

His eyes were as chill as the frosty air. Badra felt her insides twist. This was so difficult, trying to regain old ground. But she couldn't let him walk away without trying to mend the rift between them.

Her warm breath misted the air as she exhaled, struggling for words. Once, she could tell him anything. Anything except her abuse at the hands of Fareeq. Anything but her deep shame.

"Kenneth, I know this must be equally difficult for you as it is for me. I had hoped—perhaps we could mend the break between us. We could at least be friends."

He gave her a blank look. "Why?"

Badra swallowed hard. "I-I didn't mean to hurt you.

114

Truly, I did not. And I think you resent Rashid for becoming my falcon guard when you left Egypt."

His face remained expressionless. Like a Khamsin warrior still, he concealed his feelings.

"I wish you and Rashid would put aside your differences. It troubles my *Ieb*, my heart. He is my friend."

"A friend and nothing more?"

At her nonchalant shrug, his gaze sharpened. "Don't get too close to Rashid, Badra. There may be . . . trouble."

Trouble? "Is that a warning?"

"Consider it advice."

Ruminating on his cryptic words, she nodded. "I would enjoy seeing your home, Kenneth. Truly, I would. May I visit?" She paused. "I will bring Rashid. He owes you an apology for his rudeness."

He glanced away, a tic in his jaw muscle as if he fought some deep emotion. "Yes, of course. Come to tea tomorrow. English tea is served at four."

No emotion colored his voice. The cool, polite English duke overwhelmed the hot-blooded warrior beneath. Badra sighed and, remembering a gesture of Western civility, stuck out a palm.

"Thank you. I do not want tensions between us. Friends?" she inquired softly.

Kenneth silently studied her hand. Slowly he reached out and clasped her palm. She stared back at him. Then he tugged her hand and, quickly as a snake striking, yanked her toward him. His arms locked like steel bars around her. She gasped, panicked, feeling like prey in the coils of a giant anaconda she had read about in one of Lord Smithfield's books.

A slow smile stole over his face. Badra became alarmed at his hard male body pressed against her. She had forgotten how very strong he was. She had forgotten his persistence in pursuing something he wanted. She had forgotten a lot of things.

He bent his head toward her. Her insides turned to warm jelly. Fear battled with desire at the touch of his mouth.

His scent enveloped her in a warm cloud. A foreign spicy scent clinging to his smooth-shaven cheeks mixed with sandalwood soap. The latter reminded her that this was Khepri, her warrior protector. Once, his zealous devotion had eagerly assured obedience. If she'd asked him to walk off the cliffs of Amarna, he would.

No longer. Determination shone in his blue eyes. His relentless, warm grip warned her she was no longer in control. The knowledge flooded her with fresh panic.

He eased her fears as he lowered his mouth to hers in a gentle, reverent kiss. His lips feathered over hers. To her surprise, she found herself accepting the invitation. Daringly she tasted him back, intrigued by the warmth surging through her, by the new sensations pooling in her like a low, steadily burning fire.

He cupped the back of her head and angled his mouth more securely over hers, then he deepened their chaste kiss into something more. The intensity made her heart beat wildly. Badra opened her mouth wider as he tasted her, probing its inside with expert licks. His teeth nipped her lower lip. A small whimper of pleasure rose from her throat.

Then, just as suddenly, he released her. She staggered back, nearly losing her balance.

"Friends, Badra? Are you really quite so confident you want that?" he asked huskily.

She was still trembling as he stalked off. Her hand shook visibly as she twisted the brass knob and went back inside. She dashed upstairs. She needed to check on Rashid—and to tell him of Kenneth's enigmatic warning.

Badra started to rap on his door. Sounds of distress came from inside. Alarmed, she went in, turning on a lamp.

Rashid lay on his bedroll, tossing and turning, moaning in his sleep. Pitying him, Badra brushed a hand against his brow. "Rashid, wake up. You're dreaming."

He sat up with a start. Sweat trickled down his temples. His gaze met hers and he drew back. "You should not be in here, Badra."

"I must talk with you. Khepri warned me to avoid you and said there might be trouble. Why would he say such a thing?"

A long sigh escaped Rashid's lips. "It is as I thought. He found it and thinks I am the thief."

Badra went very still with panic. "Thief?"

"Someone examined my bag. The marker I placed over it was disturbed." He snorted derisively. "Khepri is not the warrior he once was. He has forgotten much."

"What is it? What does he hold over you?"

Her falcon guard reached down into his bedroll, withdrew his woven bag and dug inside. He held up the item. "This," he said soberly.

It was the gold necklace of Princess Meret.

Chapter Eight

The necklace mocked her as she rubbed her eyes in disbelief. It kept returning to her, sticking like tiny granules of evil sand she could not brush away.

So, Rashid knew she'd sold the pectoral. His dark gaze met hers.

"Why, Badra?" he asked, his words harsh in the quiet room. "Why did you steal from Khepri? Money?"

She offered a helpless shrug. "How did you get that?"

He heaved a long sigh, swinging the necklace from his fingers. "I saw you selling it. When the shop closed, I went back and broke in and took it." His face grew stern. "You will return the necklace to the tomb."

Her stomach gave a sharp twist. She remained silent.

"You will, or I will hand it over to Khepri and confess I am the thief. And take whatever punishment awaits me."

Panic welled inside her. "Please, Rashid, you must not!"

"I must. I am your falcon guard, sworn to protect you. If you do not return it, I will. Why did you take it?" His dark eyes looked troubled.

118

The words spilled from her lips. "In exchange for the freedom of a slave at the brothel in Cairo. They would not take money."

It was a glimmer of the truth—the heart of it, really.

He sighed heavily. "Trading one wrong for another will not settle the weight upon your *Ieb*, Badra."

"Please, Rashid. Do not question my heart on this."

"You are the most stubborn woman I know. But I will not see you punished as a thief."

Rashid arrested, publicly humiliated? The hurtful image haunted her: her falcon guard dragged off in chains by a grim-faced Khepri. How could she allow this?

"I will hide it in Khepri's house, then it will no longer be stolen. I asked to see his home," Badra reasoned.

As Rashid nodded, the necklace burned coldly in her hand like her past burned in her mind, enslaving her as she had once been enslaved to a man's lust. *Never again*.

The gold pectoral, sewn to the inside of her skirts, weighed Badra down like heavy shackles. She shivered, her superstitious soul hating to touch the artifact.

She and Rashid had come in Lord Smithfield's shiny black carriage for tea at Kenneth's house. She looked around with avid curiosity. Two stiff-spined men stood at rapt attention, their green-and-gold finery sparkling like the gilded hallway chairs. The mansion radiated quiet dignity, shimmered with polish and elegance. But it felt as welcoming as a cold stone tomb. Where best to place the necklace in this immense museum?

Rashid's face tightened as a footman escorted them to a formal drawing room. She shot her guard a warning glance:

Behave. Dressed in an elegant, crisp gray suit and a silk tie, Kenneth greeted them courteously. No reflection of their kiss shone in his eyes. A tiny hurt pinched Badra.

He escorted them throughout the immense house, explaining the history of how the Tristan family had become titled more than two hundred years ago. Sweat dripped down Rashid's temples. His face became a harsh mask, as if he couldn't bear the opulence. Badra's heart sank as they toured the rooms. She could not see the right hiding place.

When they returned to the drawing room, she took a seat on the large striped settee. Kenneth sat on one side of her, Rashid on the other, flanking her like two grim-faced bookends. Egypt and England. Yes, Khepri was gone, hidden by layers of stiff gray broadcloth, his black silk tie knotted neatly at his throat; the duke had absorbed her friend as sand dunes swallow skeletal remains. Her chest tightened with sadness.

An odd jangling noise sounded. A footman appeared.

"Telephone, Your Grace. It's the steward at your country estate, a matter of the accounts this month," he stated.

Kenneth sighed. He turned to Badra. "I'm afraid I must take this in private. Please, remain here. I'll be with you momentarily."

She watched him go. Now was the time.

"I'm going to look around," she whispered to Rashid.

His eyes closed and he nodded. Poor Rashid. He looked miserable at even being in the duke's house.

A hiding place, she mused, slipping into the hallway. A place where Kenneth would not immediately find the necklace. The dining room? Badra headed there and slipped inside, eyeing the imposing polished table and matching sideboards, the expensive silk-paneled walls. A polished silver tea service sat on a sideboard. Badra lifted its gleaming silver cover.

"May I help you?"

She jumped at the pompous voice behind her. Badra whirled. "Er, no thank you. I was . . . looking for the duke."

"In the teapot?"

She peered into the pot's depths and offered a smile. "You're correct. I do believe this is too tight a fit for him."

The footman stared impassively at her. Not a hint of a smile cracked his face. She sighed and walked off. These English, did they not know how to laugh? Perhaps it was prohibited among servants.

Badra hurried and returned to the drawing room, sitting just as Kenneth walked back into the room.

"Well? Shall we have tea?" he asked.

Servants set up the tea service in the drawing room, complete with lacy doilies and stiff linen napkins. There were paper-thin sandwiches with leafy greens, sugared scones and squares of dark brown cakes Kenneth explained were gingerbread.

His mouth turned downward. "My brother, Graham, loved gingerbread. Grandfather told me he used to eat it at Christmas until he got sick."

She had forgotten all his prior losses. His grandfather's recent death had probably reminded him of the tragedy of losing his other family members. "Were you close?" she asked gently, moved by the sadness in his eyes.

"I was only four. I don't remember much, except Graham was bigger." His mouth twisted in a crooked smile. "I do remember one thing. Graham used to call me 'Runt.' I called him 'Canary' because he whistled all the time, like our pet bird."

She wondered how he felt, all alone in this enormous house, only servants for company, ghosts of the past haunting his thoughts. Upset by his melancholy look, she tried to steer him toward more cheerful conversation; she asked about the house's history. The haunted look fled his face, replaced with quiet pride as he relayed how generations of Tristan nobility had entertained kings and queens inside the mansion. Badra felt the tightness inside her ease. She hated seeing Kenneth forlorn and lost. She pressed further, asking about his new life in England, desiring to coax him out of the sadness of his past.

It worked, for his charm and wit sprang to the surface as he dutifully regaled her and Rashid with stories of balls and society teas. A new sadness pulled at her; she could not see a trace of the Khamsin warrior who had protected her, who had sworn his eternal love. That man seemed to have vanished.

She reached for another scone and nibbled its edges. Rashid drank more tea and ate another gingerbread cake. Soon the sweets vanished. Conversation ground to a halt. Rashid looked ready to bolt. Badra shot him a pleading look, which Kenneth, to her dismay, intercepted.

"I'll have my man drive you back to Lord Smithfield's. Badra, you will remain here. I have something to show you. I can have my man return you a bit later."

She wondered at this new Kenneth, his seeming ease at commanding servants, the implacable set of his lips. She felt drawn to his mouth, the sensual full lower curve of his lip. His air of arrogance mixed with courteous regard intrigued her, despite her inner trembling at her continued deception.

She set her teacup down with a shaky clink. Rashid left. Kenneth leaned forward, hands on his knees.

"I did not show you the entire house. There is something rather special I think you'll like."

He stood. Badra gathered her courage and smiled. How could she plant the pendant with him hovering over her?

Lacing his hands behind his back, the duke strolled with her up the curving main staircase. Scents of lemon and beeswax hung in the air, mixing with the faint smell of his cologne. She stole a glance at him. Polished as the staircase. His black signet ring winked in the light.

How could she fool this man?

Kenneth caught her looking and raised an inquiring brow. "Are you nervous being all alone with me, Badra?"

A speculative light glimmered in his eyes. Startled by his scrutiny, she stumbled and pitched forward. Kenneth reached out. She caught hold of his steadying arms. Her fingers curled tightly around the hard muscles, and he looked down at her solemnly as she grasped him.

"Are you hurt?"

Yes, she wanted to say. I'm hurt that there is this cold distance between us, that I've done something despicable in order to achieve another end. I'm hurt that our worlds are too different to bridge the canyon between us.

"No," she said automatically. "I'm fine."

He grasped her elbow as they cleared the last step and headed down the hallway. Her cheeks grew flushed at his continued touch, the warmth searing through her wool sleeve. He steered her toward a massive set of paneled wood doors and twisted a brass knob, ushering her formally inside.

A delighted gasp fled her lips.

He stood with a quiet air of pride, his hand gesturing to the floor-to-ceiling bookshelves, forest-green carpet and carved mahogany fireplace. Tall brass lamps flanked over-sized leather armchairs. The effect was quietly masculine and yet, as she breathed in the scent of leather-bound learning, Badra had never felt more at home.

"Oh, Khepri!" She caught herself, flushed and added, "I mean, Kenneth." She turned, her eyes shining, burning with excitement and wonder. "May I?"

"But of course." He strolled over to one wood case and thumbed through the selections. He chose one and handed it over with reverence. She fingered the tome and read aloud the gold lettering on the jacket.

"*David Copperfield* by Charles Dickens. What type of book is this?"

"Some call it popular," he said, peering over her shoulder.

Badra clutched the book to her chest like a child holding a treasured toy. "May I borrow it?"

Kenneth smiled. "Of course."

Her mouth worked up and down as she stroked the calf-leather binding. No one had ever given her such a treasure.

"I never told you, Badra, but do you know how proud I was when you learned to read?"

A flush of pleasure at his compliment lit her cheeks. "Thank you," she said shyly.

The loud ringing of the telephone was followed by a soft knock at the door, breaking the tension between them. "Yes," he called out impatiently.

A white-gloved footman stepped inside. "Beg your pardon, Your Grace, but there is another telephone call."

"Very well." He glanced at her. "I'm afraid I have some pressing business I must finish. Please, enjoy yourself. I'll be back in a few minutes. If you see anything else you like, feel free to borrow it."

She thanked him, setting down Mr. Dickens. Like a starving man eyeing a banquet, Badra combed through the books, hungry for each one. Between the stacks, she would hide the pendant.

After a few minutes, something nagged her about Kenneth's collection. The books all seemed too new. None had a well-worn feeling, pages thumbed and bindings creased from frequent use as the cherished books sent by Lord Smithfield to the Khamsin camp did. Were all the titles Kenneth stocked merely for show, as one would display rare Egyptian artifacts?

She did not think him a shallow man, yet he had changed. . . .

Badra wandered over to another shelf and examined the titles. The books were all in Arabic. She chose one and thumbed the pages. It was well worn, much used. A few others showed the same signs.

She doubted any of his English friends read Arabic books. Clearly Kenneth read these. Why not the English?

125

She pursed her lips over this mystery. Perhaps the Arabic was a link to a life he seemed determined to leave behind, yet could not. Badra shrugged. A wooden ladder rested nearby. Lifting her skirts, she released the necklace from the threads holding it captive. Prize in hand, she climbed the ladder, carefully slid the pectoral between two volumes, and peered between them. Excellent. It was well-hidden.

A volume with an interesting title caught her attention. Badra retrieved it. "*The Kama Sutra of Vatsyayana*," she said aloud slowly. "Translated by Sir Richard Burton."

She skimmed the pages and nearly fell off the ladder. Her eyes widened. Oh my. A book of instruction on sexual pleasure!

Badra replaced it, selected another book with illustrations. She peered at them in shocked fascination.

Could a man and a woman really do that?

It looked difficult, like one of the daring moves Ramses made with his scimitar while performing the Dance of the Swords.

Climbing down the ladder with the book, she set it upon a small polished table and leafed through the illustrations. A blush flamed her cheeks as she encountered one in particular. The erotic image before her brought an odd surge of heat low in her belly. Did Kenneth do these things?

Badra moved on, lingering over another drawing she found particularly interesting: a nude man and woman. The woman's face was contorted not with pain, but pleasure.

Did her former falcon guard do this with English women? Did their white limbs drape over his hips, pulling him closer? Did their faces show the emotions the woman in the drawing did?

Did they cover Kenneth with their heavy scent of cloying perfume, and the musky smell of their sex?

Badra trembled. She could not digest such ideas. Still, the drawings held a fascination for her. She turned another page and stared at an illustration of a naked woman with eyes closed in apparent pleasure. The man had his face . . . Oh my. Oh my!

She had heard whispers of the pleasures a woman received from the Khamsin warrior's secret of one hundred kisses. Yet she could not imagine such a thing for herself. Her fear ran too deeply.

Still, she earmarked the page to consider the possibility and continued leafing through the book.

Footsteps sounded in the hallway. In desperation, Badra closed the book with a snap and looked around. No place to return it among the tightly packed books on the lower shelves. No time to climb the ladder and replace it.

Kenneth was returning. What would he think if he caught her with this private, very revealing book?

Panic rushed through her, but she was trapped.

Chapter Nine

She had to hide the book. Badra glanced down at her thick skirts. She just managed. Just as the door opened, they fell back into place with a swish.

Kenneth came forward. "Did you find anything you like?"

"Oh yes, indeed, I have Mr. Dickens and I am quite looking forward to indulging myself," she babbled.

He nodded. "Excellent. Why don't you read it to me?"

"Read to you?"

"I miss the sound of your voice." His warm gaze locked with hers. "When you speak, it's like hearing Egypt. Hearing you read a book in English would please me."

This simple admission moved her. The duke gestured toward the large, overstuffed striped chairs. Badra burned with embarrassment. Making herself comfortable with a heavy, leather-bound book sandwiched between her thighs? She could barely walk.

But neither could she remain standing here wearing a

silly smile. Badra swallowed, shifted her calves in an awkward walk.

Kenneth's brow wrinkled. "Are you still having trouble with those shoes? Lord Smithfield can find you another pair more comfortable."

"These are fine," she answered, taking another awkward step. She felt the leather begin to slide downward.

Badra halted.

Kenneth frowned. "You're walking as if you're in tremendous pain. Let me assist you."

She held up a hand. "No, please, I am quite . . ."

Thunk! The volume fell from between her clenched thighs with a heavy thud on the carpet.

Kenneth raised an inquiring eyebrow.

"Did you drop something?" he asked politely. Her cheeks burned as he pointedly looked at her hem.

Badra stepped back, revealing the forbidden book concealed by her skirts. Kenneth bent down, picked it up, and flipped it over, and it fell open to the page that had fascinated her—a man pressing his face deep between a woman's plump thighs.

"Interesting," he murmured, his blue eyes twinkling. "Badra, if you wish to learn more about this, I advise reading the book, not using it to ape the illustration." The teasing light in his eyes grew as he set the book down on the table.

Heat filled her cheeks. "I . . . I wanted to know your tastes." Then she blushed deeper, realizing her words.

The duke simply looked at her. Hunger filled his rich blue eyes, which shone like jewels. He reached forward.

His forefinger gently brushed her bottom lip. "My tastes have always been constant."

Badra closed her eyes, trembling at the warmth of his touch. A shard of deep yearning pierced her.

"You are so beautiful." His voice evoked shudders of need within her.

Why could she not have mustered the courage to tell him yes when he'd proposed? Would Kenneth have hurt her as her former captor had? She had no courage. She could never do the things the woman in that book did. Not willingly. Never. She had to remind herself: Kenneth deserved a woman with passion to equal his own.

If only she could dare feel a little of the desire flaring in his intense eyes. Could she? Badra yearned to try.

He moved closer, his thumb resting at her bottom lip, teasing it back and forth in a feather-light caress. His gaze locked with hers. So different. Yet so familiar. Her hand touched the firmness of his chiseled jaw, as she stared into the deep, intriguing mix of green flecks in his blue eyes, which were fringed by a sweep of long, dark lashes.

Thick, dark hair fell across his forehead. With a trembling hand, she reached up and brushed it aside. Once it had swept past his shoulders; now, it was close-cropped. She grasped for her Khepri, the man who would have given life and limb to protect her.

Kenneth took her hand, brought her finger to his lips. His eyes closed as he gently pressed a kiss there. His lips were moist and warm; then he rubbed her hand against his cheek. The intriguing brush of that masculine, clean-shaven skin unleashed a torrent of wild uncertainty in her. Badra wanted to pull back, torn with yearning and deep-seated fear at the raw hunger evident in his expression. Where would this lead?

Once, he'd sworn an oath to shed every last drop of his blood to defend her virtue. Would he now strip that very same virtue away? No longer Khamsin, he was now a powerful English duke. He was no longer governed by the same rules.

She laughed to cover her nervousness and let her hands rest upon his shoulders, feeling the hard muscle beneath the texture of his jacket. That lean, tensile steel of a warrior still existed beneath his tailored finery.

"You look so different. Yet this suits you. Like your cobra totem, you have shed your Khamsin skin for an English one and blended in perfectly."

A flicker of sadness shone in his eyes. "I am a cobra, maybe, but one uncomfortable in his new coat," he admitted. "Stuffed and shoved into a skin totally unfamiliar."

His honesty startled her. "But you have adapted well."

"I have no choice. I have obligations and duties of a vastly different sort now, Badra. Duties I must take as seriously as any I did when I was a simple warrior."

Newfound respect for him emerged. "You are one of the most honorable warriors our people have ever known, Khepri. I am certain you make an equally honorable duke."

A distant look came into his eyes. His hand cupped her cheek, his thumb drifted across it in a feathering touch.

"Am I still Khepri to you, Badra? I'm a duke with a small touch of longing for Egypt and his past. Oh, you smell like Egypt—desert flowers, sunshine, heat and hot sand," he said in a husky voice. "No matter how many layers of English clothing you wear, you will always be the desert. It's within you."

"It's within you as well. You cannot leave it behind. You are still Khepri, here, in your *Ieb*." She took his hands and clasped them together, pressing them to his heart.

He leaned closer, hunger sparking in his eyes. "Give me back my desert, Badra. Another kiss, one small memory of the home I left behind. Kiss me, Badra, and let me taste Egypt once more," he begged, his voice low and husky.

Deep within the fathomless pools of his sea-blue eyes, she glimpsed the real Kenneth: adrift and alone on an ocean of uncertainty, flooded with new duties and a new life, yet longing for the familiar, torrid heat of Egypt.

How could she deny him a kiss, a memory of the land they both loved and that he had forsaken?

Giddy with daring, Badra tilted her head up, summoning her courage. So tall. She arched up on her toes, reaching for him like a budding flower for the sun, hoping it will touch her petals and give her life.

His lips burned like the promise of passion. They reminded her of the black tents of Egypt, the subtle rubbings of flesh against flesh, the quiet cries echoing in the still desert night. They made Badra think of women pleasured by their warriors.

Oh, she wanted more.

A tiny sigh escaped her throat. Kenneth cupped her nape in one strong palm and held her still as his mouth angled more securely over hers. His touch was gentle, considerate, undemanding. Then his tongue lightly traced the seam of her closed lips, flicking as if in invitation. Intrigued, she parted her lips.

Like a snake's, his tongue darted inside, flicking and exploring as he swept into her mouth, claiming her. Badra opened her mouth, willing him to explore.

Willing to let him claim her.

Kenneth slid an arm around her waist, pulling her close. His hand swept over the curve of her hip, cupped her bottom through her thick skirts and kneaded the flesh there. She moaned and gripped his shoulders, quivering at the odd sensations racing through her. The pleasure she'd felt when he kissed her for the first time had returned. Surely, this was passion. Maybe she could overcome her fears, if he . . .

Then he tore his mouth away, panting. He stared down at her.

"No, don't stop," she protested hoarsely. "More."

She rubbed her body against his, desiring more of this closeness, needing to quench the fire in her loins. Her hands hooked around his neck, pulling him down. She kissed him.

A strangled moan arose in his throat. He gently backed her up against the large polished desk, eased her down upon it and continued kissing her. She felt the solid hardwood beneath her, the strong male body above pressing her against it.

A sense of unreality stole over Badra, as if she were watching everything unfold before her in a dream. She slipped into a favorite fantasy—Khepri proposing and her working up the courage to say yes. They married in England. Their wedding night . . .

The fantasy merged with reality in the urgent heat of Kenneth's silken mouth. His kisses were sweeter than warm honey, and his arms secure and strong, like the pillars of

Egypt's temples. His hands, capable of brute strength and of crushing an enemy with ease, were gentle as he stroked her body. He whispered sweet words of love into her ear.

His hands . . .

She became aware of the large male hands pushing at her skirts, thrusting them up. The hands were warm, and she felt them brush against her bare hips, a delicious scrape of his flesh on hers as he slid down the odd white English underdrawers, pulling them off her legs, past the soft kid slippers that did not pinch her feet.

A thumb edged her silk stockings, teasing the flesh there then working upward as Kenneth stroked the hot flesh of her thigh. She moaned into his mouth. Answering with a growl, he pushed skirts, petticoats and chemise up around her hips.

Dawning shock roused her from sleepy passion, from the sweetness of her innocent dream.

Startled, she clamped her legs shut. Wool abraded her sensitive flesh as Kenneth's knee drove between her legs. He stood between her parted thighs. Air brushed against that most private, feminine part of her. Badra felt open, vulnerable. As Kenneth tore his mouth away from hers, she opened her eyes—and saw his face, intent, looming over her.

It was a face taut with male lust, not tenderness.

Kenneth unfastened his trousers, tugging them past his narrow hips, pulled down his thin white silk drawers. His member jutted out, heavy and thick with arousal. He leaned forward, trapping her with hardness and heat.

This was her nightmare, coming true again. Trapped beneath a man's weight, slave to his needs.

134

Savage possessiveness flared in Kenneth's eyes. "You're mine, Badra. Mine alone. You always have been."

Fareeq's words blazed in her memory. *"I will never let you go, Badra. You are mine. My slave."*

Kenneth leaned over her, his hands pinning her wrists to the desk. Badra felt his hardness pushing at the soft hollow between her thighs and panicked.

She struggled in his unyielding embrace. He was a powerful English nobleman. His word here was law. Servants would ignore her cries. She was helpless in his arms, vulnerable to his passion. The enormous strength of his grip frightened her. He could crush her like a flower petal, use her body. Memories surfaced, Fareeq's bloated face gleaming with cruel victory as she lay helplessly beneath him.

Replaced now by Kenneth's.

Past memories assaulted her; Fareeq's body crushing her to the dirty sheepskins, burning pain as he shoved himself into her untried body as she screamed and struggled. . . .

Never again. Badra writhed against Kenneth's muscled weight pinning her down, turning away from his heated kisses. With every last ounce of strength, she struggled until he released her wrists. The rounded knob of his member began to push inside her. Badra shoved at his muscled chest.

"Stop, stop—get off me!" she shrieked, beating at him.

Panting, he stared down, eyes large and glazed with passion. Naked desire simmered in their depths. For a wild moment, terror seized her. He would not relent. Then Kenneth uttered a low curse in Arabic and eased off her.

Badra immediately sank to the floor on her knees, her

skirts piling around her like wilted flower petals. Scalding tears blinded her. Fear coupled with shame coursed through her.

His hard fingers curled about her wrist. "Don't touch me!" she cried. Her hand struck his cheek in a stinging slap.

Through the haze of tears she saw him step back, button his trousers, his breathing ragged. "I was trying to help you stand," he finally said.

Gulping in a trembling breath, she scrambled to her feet. Kenneth touched the faint red mark her palm had made.

"Badra, what's wrong?" Bewildered lines furrowed his brow. His concern threatened to unloose the torrent of emotions dammed inside her. She could not sob and break down . . .

Deliberately she forced disgust into her voice, disdain on her face. "This was a horrible mistake. I told you once before, Kenneth, I can't return the feelings you have for me."

A blank expression replaced his tender one. "I'll order the carriage and have my man escort you home."

Kenneth turned, presenting his back. At the doorway he paused, a hand resting on the frame, his heavy signet ring winking in the light. "Good-bye, Badra."

She knew the words meant farewell forever. His tall, dignified form moved away with stiff-shouldered resolve.

Badra blinked back scalding tears, aching and wanting. Afraid to confess her secret. For a wild moment she regretted extracting a promise from Jabari never to tell how Fareeq had flogged and raped her. But years had buried her secret like layers of sand covering Egypt's tombs. Her past was dead and buried. It was too late to expose it and face the shame, and the pity.

"I'm sorry, Khepri. How I wish it could be different," she whispered after his departing figure.

He did not hear.

Kenneth dragged himself upstairs to his bedroom. His head swam with Badra's fragrance. Hot blood pumped through his veins. His aching loins cried for release.

It had taken every ounce of restraint and control he had learned as a Khamsin warrior to pull away from her. For a minute he had thought he couldn't, so great was the urge to push inside and claim her at last. Passion and self-discipline had wrestled in him, and finally restraint had won. Kenneth ran his tongue along his lips, still tasting the honeyed sweetness of her mouth. Bewilderment raked him. The way she had responded, her lips growing rosy and soft beneath his, her eyes darkening with desire—why had she pulled away?

He paused before the door, stricken with a memory— Jabari telling him to guard her virtue. But never had his sheikh told Kenneth anything about her past. Kenneth had asked, once. Jabari had quietly told him he needed know only his duty, to protect her.

Now he wondered. What had Fareeq done to her? Badra had never displayed any interest in another man. Even now, in Rashid's company, the two acted more like friends than a courting couple.

Was Badra afraid of him? Then, he remembered her disgusted look. Her words. *"This was a horrible mistake. I told you once before, Kenneth, I can't return the feelings you have for me."*

He felt flayed, open, vulnerable. He was a cobra defanged, without a skin to protect him.

He fished a key from his pocket and went into a storage room. Dust motes danced in ghostly beams of late afternoon sunlight streaming from its round window. A brass-tipped trunk was in a corner, and Kenneth approached it with wary dread. He shut his eyes, inhaling memories.

Opening the chest, he stared down into it. His hand touched one yellowed stack of vellum tied with a frayed blue ribbon. He untied the ribbon, took the first letter and squinted in the dim light at the strange letters inked there.

The cursive, neat script eluded him.

Read to me, Badra. His words echoed mockingly in his head.

Read to me, Badra, for I cannot read for myself. Not English. Not the very language of the country where I was born.

No, but I will learn. Here, where no one will witness my shameful secret. Where no one English may look down upon me, a heathen, and laugh. Kenneth pressed a forefinger to the first word, grappling with what little he'd taught himself. He scanned the words, then stopped. He'd forgot. One read English left to right. Backward. Not like Arabic, right to left. Toward the heart. Letters so different from Arabic characters.

"M-mm-y. M-my. D-d-d-e-a-r."

In keen frustration he slammed a fist down on his thigh. Letters he could not read. He couldn't even spell his own damn name. His signature mocked him, large whorls and intricate loops that looked pompous and official and ducal, but meant nothing.

Kenneth could spell his name in Arabic. He devoured books in Arabic. He just could not read nor write English.

Literate in both languages, Jabari had helped him master reading and writing until his Arabic was as flawless as that of a native Egyptian. But Jabari had failed to teach him to read and write English. Oh, he'd meant to. But Khepri had become such a part of them, so Egyptian, so *Khamsin*, that no one had thought it necessary. Becoming a warrior, a skilled fighter like Jabari and Ramses, had taken precedence in his life. Kenneth had never bothered going back and pursuing the studies.

And he'd never regretted the lack of schooling until returning to England, until the day his grandfather told him of the letters stored in the attic trunk. Letters Kenneth's father had written on the day Kenneth was born. A journal chronicling his life. His mother's soft smile. His brother Graham's mischievous inclination to eat all the gingerbread at Christmas. His father's days at Oxford. His entire family history recorded on crisp, yellowing sheets with fading ink.

And he couldn't read one single, bloody word of it.

Kenneth carefully replaced the letter, his throat tightening. His gaze fell upon a folded swath of indigo. The indigo *binish* of a Khamsin warrior of the wind. His trembling hand stroked the cloth. Tucked against the trunk's edge was a metallic sheath holding a curved sword. Kenneth lifted it, aching to see the dull, tarnished silver handle.

He slowly withdrew the sword from its sheath and held it aloft. His eyes closed and he tried making the low, undulating cry he had been taught. It came out as a hoarse rasp.

Kenneth swallowed hard and replaced the weapon. No longer Khamsin. He was Duke of Caldwell now. The illiterate Duke of Caldwell.

He let the trunk lid slam with a sound that echoed the dull thud of his heart. He stared at the chest until a nagging thought nudged him.

Why had Badra selected a volume deliberately kept from arm's length? Had he not seen her with it, he'd never have given in to his lust.

He sped back to his library, climbed the ladder and began thumbing through volumes. His answer came quickly—the necklace of Princess Meret tumbled out from between two books.

Kenneth stared at the stolen necklace. Badra had hidden it here. Why? Had she taken it from Rashid? Gratitude to see his property returned mingled with the hundreds of questions racing through his mind.

His hand caressed the gold and semi-precious stones like a lover. But this treasure was lifeless, and he burned to hold the real prize in his arms. Badra. She had wound him about her like a snake's coils, ensuring he was her slave.

Kenneth thought of the earlier phone call from his cousin; Victor had booked passage for them. Zaid had left already on a steamship bound for Egypt. In Egypt, he would meet Badra again. He was certain of it.

Chapter Ten

Cairo. A storm of sights and smells assaulted him in fresh waves; a cacophony filled his ears. Kenneth perched on a cane-back chair on the wide terrace of the Shepherd's Hotel. Domed minarets rose above the city in graceful arches, the muezzins calling the faithful to noon prayer. Men in long shirt-like *thobes* and baggy trousers began drifting toward the mosques. Mists of steam curled into the air from the blue-veined cup before him.

Kenneth turned his attention to the street below. A snake charmer coaxed a slithering reptile from a basket. Performers with trained monkeys executed antics to the amused glee of an English boy and girl enthralled by the dark-skinned strangers. Their horrified parents appeared and hustled them away with angry admonitions.

Kenneth let a finger drift over his teacup's rim. It was still the same Egypt. Yet different. He had never glimpsed this land through the eyes of an English noble before. Two worlds colliding. Egyptians who bowed and salaamed before stiff Englishmen who passed them by with indifference. Wily dark eyes looking for opportunities, dark-skinned hands stretched out in an endless plea for baksheesh. Disapproving, pale-faced Englishmen, noses tilted in the air, radiating contempt.

Hail Britannia! Allah-hu-Akbar!

Kenneth felt comfortable in neither world now. He glanced at the tea leaves puddling at the bottom of his cup and felt a sudden stab of longing for thick, rich, bitter Arabic coffee in small, handleless cups. Large chunks of date bread with almonds, drizzled with golden honey. His mouth watered.

He took another sip and swallowed his regrets. Once he had stayed here with Ramses when the Khamsin guardian came to Cairo to negotiate a sale of Arabian horses to a wealthy buyer. Kenneth had marveled with wide-eyed fascination at the sights. The snake charmer and the monkey owner appeared enchanting and delightful then. Now, he noticed the grime dusting the hems of their long *thobes,* the careworn wrinkles carved into their sun-darkened faces, their skeletal frames.

Dirty natives, the English called them.

British imperialism. Haughty, upper-class, stiff-upper-lip contempt for the "slovenly, lazy, and stupid Egyptians."

White-bellied fish, Ramses had laughingly called the English in return, a sneer in his voice, a curl to his lip.

Yes, prejudice existed on both sides. But Ramses himself had finally admitted his English half and embraced it. He'd married the daughter of an English earl. They were deeply in love. Could Egypt and England reconcile to each other as Ramses and Katherine had? Could the imperialistic blue blood running through Kenneth's veins ever mix freely with hot-blooded sensuality learnt in the black tents?

Again, he felt like a skinned snake. Raw, inside out. Vulnerable and alone. Belonging to neither world.

"Do be careful with those trunks!"

His attention swung to a stern Englishwoman in a starched white gown with large, puffy sleeves, accompanied by three young, white-frocked girls trailing her and a dour-faced husband. Two exhausted-looking porters puffed behind the family and carted trunks up the steps of the verandah. Kenneth leaned back in his chair, watching with interest. And the English called the *Egyptians* lazy?

The matriarch paused in her ascent and surveyed the verandah like the captain of a frigate scanning a shoreline. Her gaze landed on Kenneth. She clasped her hands and burbled.

"Your Grace!"

The woman sailed toward him, skirts billowing in the wind, her charges dutifully skimming in her wake with the haggard husband. The tired porters set down the trunks with grateful sighs. She halted before him, dipped into a curtsy that made her corset stays creak, and hissed at her girls to do likewise. Rising, she beamed, showing yellowed teeth.

The Khamsin had gleaming white smiles, always chewing mint leaves to sweeten their breath and scrubbing their teeth with myrrh.

"Lady Stenson-Hines," she introduced herself. "My husband, Sir Walter Stenson-Hines. And these are my daughters, Iris, Rose and Hyacinth."

Kenneth did not stand. He accorded the woman and her English flower garden a polite nod. Lady Stenson-Hines gushed, "It is so good to see you here in Egypt! I was telling Walter the other day I absolutely could not wait to arrive at the Shepherd's and mingle with civilized people. These natives . . ." She wrinkled a bulbous nose. "Disgusting, the way they live. Greedy, unscrupulous and cowardly. Sly, lazy heathens. One must keep constant vigilance."

Sir Walter cleared his throat, looking uncomfortable. "Felicity, my dear, I think the duke was raised . . ."

Kenneth offered a thin smile. "Do not let me delay you, Lady Stenson-Hines. I'm certain you and your family are anxious to settle in—with the help of the assorted lazy heathens," he said dryly.

She gave a vigorous nod, his sarcasm soaring over her head like a flock of doves. "Perhaps later we shall see you in the lounge. Come along, girls!"

The matron and her flower garden traipsed off. The husband, twirling his waxed mustache, gave Kenneth an apologetic look and retreated.

Acid churned in Kenneth's empty stomach. He signaled for a waiter and ordered a honeyed pastry. When it arrived, he bit into the flaky treat and swallowed disappointment. It tasted mediocre and not half as excellent as Khamsin cakes.

But disappointment was an emotion he'd learned to live with these days. Kenneth brushed crumbs off the table as he spotted his cousin snaking his way through the crush.

A wet cigar stump protruded from Victor's lips, its glowing end punctuating a determined mouth. He carried a small leather valise, which he promptly set down by a chair. Kenneth stood and his cousin vigorously pumped his hand.

They settled into seats while Victor mopped his perspiring brow.

"Bloody heat," he complained. "Feels like sticking my body into an oven. Give me London's winter any day."

"Ah, yes, the yellow fog and blackened skies from the factories. I relish the smell of sulfur in the morning," Kenneth remarked dryly.

Victor's blue eyes, much like his own, searched the terrace. Kenneth's second cousin owned a prosperous antiquities shop here in Cairo as well as the London store. He had built up a successful business trading in them. He was also closely connected to Kenneth's affairs here, and the dig at Dashur.

Yet, Kenneth felt reluctant to reveal what he'd discovered. Victor exhibited some of the same prejudices many Englishmen had toward Egyptians. If he knew Rashid, an Egyptian from the tribe that had raised Kenneth, was the thief, he would insist on calling in the Cairene authorities. The Khamsin would be disgraced. Honor would be irrevocably lost. This was a battle Kenneth intended to fight on his own. He would not shame the tribe that raised him.

"So, any news from Dashur?" Victor asked.

Kenneth examined the rim of his teacup. "De Morgan assures me they are making progress each day, and he expects to find the second necklace soon—and more jewelry, making it one of the season's most spectacular hauls."

"I'm glad I can be of assistance to you," Victor commented. He gave Kenneth a steadying look. "I mean it."

"I appreciate your help, Victor. You've been invaluable."

His cousin tapped his cigar on his chair edge. Ash fell like dust onto the terrace. He reached down, fished in his valise and withdrew a thick, intimidating sheaf of papers.

145

"While you're here, I have some documents for you to sign regarding the share of your proceeds from the shops."

The shops. Kenneth's father had invested in Victor's antiquities business and taken a cut of the profits as payment. Kenneth felt his chest tighten, wishing Zaid were here to decipher the documents. But the secretary had begged off for the afternoon. He took the pen his cousin proffered, pretended to scan the papers, and signed them.

He started to hand them back, then hesitated. "If you don't mind, I'd like to have my secretary look these over, record the pertinent information. And seeing the shop in Cairo is half mine, I'd like a key," he said casually.

Victor's eyes widened, and the cigar wobbled on his lips. Hard anger appeared for a moment, then he blinked, banishing the look. Kenneth's dismay grew. What was his cousin hiding?

Victor dug into his waistcoat pocket and flipped a brass key over. "Shop's quite dusty. I had an assistant, but had to dismiss him. Couldn't quite trust him."

"Why not give me a tour right now?" Kenneth asked casually.

Color flooded Victor's cheeks. "Now?"

"No time like the present. I need to depart afterward."

"To the dig? Shall I accompany you?" Victor asked, puffing on his cigar as they scraped back their chairs.

"No. I've a small business matter to clear up first. I'll meet you at Dashur." Kenneth thought of his next destination and swallowed hard. The journey would take all his strength to complete. He dreaded returning to the Khamsin camp, and to the sheikh he'd sworn to never see again.

* * *

146

"You promised to release her!"

"I lied."

Badra gathered her dignity about her like a warm cloak as she stood in the harem at the Pleasure Palace. The trip from England to Egypt had frayed her nerves like silk threads unraveling from a Persian carpet. Intensely worried about Jasmine, she'd delayed returning to the Khamsin camp, giving Rashid the excuse that she was shopping in Cairo for a day.

"You have your money. Give her to me," Badra said.

"Something happened while you were gone. Her value has increased. There is only one way she will leave here. You must take her place," Musad grunted.

Badra's insides crumbled. She could not resort to becoming a concubine again. "Never. There must be another way."

"Perhaps. If we could get the next necklace . . . We have a worker on the site who took the first one. But they are suspicious. They will not suspect a woman. Omar made arrangements with a high official on the dig site for you to be there as an artist. Find the second necklace of Princess Meret, bring it here and your daughter will go free."

"Omar wishes me to become his thief?"

"Or his whore. It is your choice."

Impotent rage coursed through Badra. She drew in a trembling breath and glanced at Jasmine sitting quietly with a woman on a divan at the room's far end.

Musad caught her look. "I have a buyer."

Terror whipped through her. "You told me she was not to be sold! She is but seven years old!"

"Nearly eight. A European man liked her looks. He offered a good price for her contract and gave us money already. She will be sold when he returns in six weeks. As we speak, Jasmine is being instructed in her new duties to her future master."

Badra's heart twisted as she looked at her daughter. Jasmine looked confused and her wide, dark eyes held fright.

Oh, dear God. How could she abandon her baby?

Badra returned to Musad. "If I do this thing for you, and bring you the second necklace, you will immediately release her to me. If not, I will tell the duke of Caldwell exactly who is stealing from him." Her eyes hardened with resolve.

Musad's nostrils flared. "Tell him and your brat gets sold tomorrow and you will never find her again."

Fighting fear, Badra locked gazes with him. "Are you familiar with *falaka*, eunuch?" The blood drained from his face. Satisfied, she leaned forward, and pressed her advantage. "Because if you do not free her once I return the necklace, I will lay responsibility for all this at your feet. The duke of Caldwell will give you to the authorities to beat the soles of your feet to elicit a confession."

Musad grunted. "It is a bargain, then. Return with the necklace and she will be freed."

He added in a lower tone, "But if you do not bring back the necklace, you may only free her by remaining here, your contract sold each month to the highest bidder. That is a promise."

Badra drew in a trembling breath. Making such a dangerous offer to a cold-blooded reptile such as Musad was like dancing with a snake. But her love for Jasmine outweighed all the risks.

"May I have a moment alone with my daughter?" she asked.

He grunted again, but ordered the other woman to leave. Badra went to Jasmine and enfolded her in a tight hug. Twin emotions of gratitude and guilt pulled her. "I'll take care of you, precious."

"Badra, I do not understand the things that woman told me. Why would a man want to do those things?" Jasmine asked, uncertainty and fear shadowing her sweet face.

"Forget them, my darling," Badra whispered, kissing her forehead. "Let them slip from your mind and think only of pretty, pleasant matters." She rocked her child in her arms and began singing an English lullaby she'd heard Elizabeth sing to her son.

A few minutes later, a guard appeared. "Time to leave."

Badra gave her daughter one last hug. A brave smile wobbled on her trembling lips. *Never again. My daughter will never suffer as I have. Even if I must take her place. But I will not fail.*

The camel's gait soothed Kenneth as he listed from side to side. As he approached the Khamsin camp, Kenneth felt stabbing regret that he had not accepted Victor's offer to accompany him.

His cousin's shop had turned out to be a dusty storefront in a deserted alleyway. Kenneth's suspicions flared. If there were any profits coming from the store, he doubted it. He promised himself to have Zaid do a little checking into Victor.

Black tents dotted the pebbled sand. Warriors posted at the camp's edge noticed him and gave an undulating cry.

It was of warning—not of welcome.

Kenneth slid off his camel, grabbing the reins. Sweat

plastered his shirt to his drenched skin. He'd never sweated in the summer heat as much as he did now, facing the tribe he had thought to shun for good—facing the sheikh who had called him brother, but who called him brother no more.

People began gathering, whispering and nodding toward him. Since it was impolite to point in the Arab world, they simply stared. Kenneth felt naked, exposed. He returned their stares with a grim smile and halted short of the first tent. A herd of sheep bleated, running from him as if he were a wolf.

He felt like a snake slithering into Paradise. Not one face showed a welcoming smile. Two warriors scowled, holding their rifles at chest level, but not pointed at him.

Not yet, anyway.

A pretty woman in indigo, a blue scarf wrapped around her blond head, rushed forward. "Kenneth," she cried softly.

Elizabeth's two slender arms surrounded him as she hugged him tightly. Emotions washed over him as he embraced the sheikh's wife. The women were much more forgiving than the men.

"You have come back to us," she said in English. "I knew you could not forget us."

Kenneth released her, his fingers curling about her arms, hating to banish the hopeful look in her blue eyes. "Elizabeth, it is not what you think," he began.

His voice trailed off as a tight band of indigo-draped warriors marched toward him. He spotted two very familiar faces leading the pack. Once they'd been friends. No longer.

Two sets of eyes, one black as pitch, one dark as gold, burned into him. Jabari and Ramses. The sheikh and his Guardian of the Ages. There were no signs of welcome in their tight-lipped expressions. The sheikh moved near, his dark eyes blazing. He unsheathed his ivory-handled scimitar and held it to Kenneth's throat.

"Get your hands off my wife."

Chapter Eleven

His Egyptian brother had become his enemy.

The cold steel sword rested upon Kenneth's throat. He felt an odd calm settle on him, though anger radiated from the depths of the Khamsin sheikh's dark eyes. Those eyes had once expressed affection and understanding. Now a chilled blankness resided there. Kenneth did not remove his hands from Elizabeth. He could not let Jabari intimidate him, or he would incur the sheikh's contempt. Better his wrath than his scorn.

"Odd way of saying hello to a visitor, Jabari," he drawled in Arabic. "I suppose this means no welcoming cup of coffee?"

"Jabari, stop it. Right now," Elizabeth snapped.

The sheikh gave a disapproving grunt but lowered his scimitar. He did not sheath it, but kept it tightly clenched in his hand.

Elizabeth stepped back, breaking Kenneth's hold. The flare of disapproval in her blue eyes faded. She placed a sun-darkened hand on her husband's shoulder. "Jabari, Kenneth is visiting. Will you not at least show him hospitality?"

Jabari grunted again. "I suppose I must, since as sheikh I am obliged to show hospitality to visitors."

Ramses stepped forward, amber eyes flashing. "Well, I am not," he said calmly, and suddenly Kenneth felt a huge fist smash into his mouth. Elizabeth cried out. Kenneth staggered back, overcome by shocked dizziness and pain.

Righting himself, he wiped a trickle of blood from his lip, examining the crimson on his fingertips with a rueful smile. "I deserved that," he admitted. He locked gazes with his sheikh's guardian. "I deserved it for what I did when I left. Shall we call it a draw, or will you force me to return your kindness?"

Ramses's cold gaze burned into him. "A draw? I am not so certain."

"Stop it—stop it now, all of you," Elizabeth cried out. "Kenneth is your foster brother, Jabari. Why are you treating him like this? He's family!"

The normally self-possessed woman began to cry. Tears gathered in her luminous blue eyes and ran down her cheeks. "He's family, don't do this to him," she sobbed.

Instantly Jabari's expression shifted to contrition. He sheathed his sword and embraced his wife. She wept into his chest. "I am sorry, my love, for upsetting you."

"Elizabeth? Is everything all right?" Kenneth asked gently, more surprised by her shattered composure than worried by the present hostilities.

"She is emotional because of the baby. She found out just yesterday that she is with child," the sheikh explained.

A petite, dark-haired woman clad in the same manner as Elizabeth—indigo *kuftan* and a light blue scarf about her head—pushed her way through the crowd. A scar flared on her left cheek. She had deep green eyes. Katherine! Her face lit up with a delighted smile.

"Khepri!" she exclaimed, and hugged him.

With a blank expression, Ramses gently reached out and pulled his wife to his side.

Terribly uncomfortable, Kenneth offered them both a rueful smile. "Your father sends his best wishes for all of you, Katherine, and the new baby you're expecting."

Silence from the men. The women looked troubled.

Bloody hell, this was so damn difficult. He wished he'd never lashed out in anger at Jabari when he'd left. Those words had wounded deeper than any physical injury could.

He tried again, focusing on the women. "Well, I'm not surprised you're both expecting. Ramses always did brag that a man's hair length was a sign of his fertility."

He gave a pointed look to the two Khamsins, whose long locks spilled from beneath their indigo turbans. Then Kenneth touched his bare head, his waves of dark brown hair clipped and barely feathering his collar.

"Contraception?" he suggested.

The women laughed, and Ramses and Jabari both offered reluctant smiles. Kenneth turned and headed for his camel and rucksack. He withdrew a parcel and a envelope and sauntered back, handing both to Katherine.

"From your father. He sends his love."

Katherine took the items, an eager look on her face as she handed her husband the package and ripped open the envelope. "A letter from Papa. Oh my! A long one, too!"

154

Ramses unwrapped the square box and wrinkled his brow, reading the label. "English tea?"

"The best," Kenneth commented. Hell, it could have been arsenic for all he could read.

Elizabeth's red-rimmed eyes shone with pleasure. "Real English tea. What a treat!"

"Thank you." Katherine glanced up at Kenneth from scanning the pages. "It's good to see you made friends with Papa."

"He's been a tremendous help to me."

"Kenneth," Jabari said slowly. "You have returned to us."

The mood shifted like hot sand blowing upon the dunes. Kenneth met the shiekh's piercing gaze. "Not exactly. I need to discuss something of grave importance. In private. The ceremonial tent will suffice. I came here because I wished to honor the bond we once shared."

A flicker of emotion showed on the sheikh's tight-lipped face. He nodded and glanced at Ramses. "Both of us will hear what you have to say." He jerked his head sideways toward the large, black ceremonial tent where war councils and important decisions were made.

The men detached themselves from their wives and strode toward the tent. Katherine clutched the white vellum in her hands, looking at Kenneth a bit bemusedly. It wasn't a good sign. Between that and Jabari's failure to order his men to set up guest quarters, it meant they clearly did not intend for him to stay.

He hooked his thumbs into his belt and strode purposefully, following the two warriors who were once his closest friend and brother.

* * *

He sat crossed-legged on the tent's colorful carpet. The flaps had been rolled down to allow for privacy. Wind ruffled the sturdy sides. Kenneth studied the sheikh and Ramses, taking care to appear calm and unruffled himself. His breath came steady and even. No trace of anxiety showed. Yet sweat soaked the inside of his lightweight khaki trousers. After years of living with the desert heat, it was as if his body had totally forgotten how to adjust.

Once he'd worn this uniform of a tribal warrior: indigo *binish,* trousers, soft leather boots, and sharp scimitar dangling from his belt. No longer. Today his well-tailored khaki suit set him apart.

Jabari regarded him with a guarded expression. Kenneth studied the sheikh with equal care. Animosity crackled like flames leaping into the air between them. Kenneth's hand briefly touched the small cobra tattoo on his right arm as if to remember another time and place when he'd fought alongside these men.

"You indicated very clearly the day you parted for England that you did not wish to see me again," Jabari said flatly.

Kenneth rubbed the back of his neck, feeling the muscles there tense. Forging ahead immediately with the news that Rashid was a thief wasn't wise. First he must make peace with the past, with the sheikh. Deep in Jabari's dark eyes flickered the damage Kenneth had inflicted when he left. *I'm not your brother and I never was.*

That rage blazed in Jabari's eyes when he spoke again. "I considered you my brother. I gave you a position of highest honor, to be falcon guard to Badra." The sheikh paused.

156

"You know I love Badra like a sister. When you came and offered for her hand, I thought it a good match."

"But Badra turned me down." Kenneth looked away.

"I could not force her hand." Jabari laid his palms open on his knees. Kenneth remembered the gesture. It meant, *What do you want from me?* Memories arose: Badra's refusal. Her velvet soft voice cutting him to the bone.

"No, you could not force her hand," Kenneth agreed. "But you didn't even encourage her to reconsider. No, you let me walk away with my grandfather back to England. Sometimes I wonder if you ever really considered me your true brother." Bitterness dripped from his words; silence hung in the tent.

Jabari's voice thundered. "You lie!" The sheikh took a deep breath and fisted his trembling hands. "Not my brother? Not my brother, Kenneth? No, not a blood brother, a brother much closer."

Jabari glanced down at his side, at the jeweled wedding dagger strapped there. He removed the blade. In a swift move, it sailed through the air. The symbol of Hassid kinship landed inches from Kenneth's boots.

"I gave you this—the Hassid wedding dagger, handed down for hundreds of years through blood. You refused it. *You* denied *me* as your brother. Not I!"

Kenneth studied the blade that had cut him off from the tribe that raised him, from the brother who loved him. In his own way, he had rejected Jabari as cruelly as Badra had rejected him. His heart twisted as he continued staring at the dagger. It pierced the carpet like a dividing line, reminding him of the ties he'd cut with his former brethren.

Khamsin no longer.

No, the sheikh could not ever forgive such a tremendous insult. But if he knew the reasons behind the refusal . . .

"Jabari, why do you think I refused your dagger?"

The sheikh lifted his chin and squared his shoulders, facing Kenneth with an air of dignified pride. "Because you turned your back on everything Egyptian. You were turning your back on me because, when you found out you would become a wealthy English duke, you were ashamed of us. Of me as your brother."

"Ashamed of you?" Kenneth let loose a short bark of laughter. "My God, all this time . . . you thought I was some high-handed English snob?"

Ramses and Jabari stared at him as if he'd lost his wits. "What exactly is so amusing?" Ramses asked evenly.

Kenneth gulped down a breath. "Everything. You thought I was ashamed. I was—but not of you. It took all my strength to board that ship and leave behind this life, everything I had known and honored and loved." He continued to laugh.

Pure bewilderment crossed their faces. "Perhaps the desert heat has affected his brain," Ramses suggested.

Swallowing his pride, Kenneth struggled to continue. "Do you know why I said what I did?" Not waiting for an answer, he forged on, knowing only the painful truth would heal the past. Kenneth summoned every inch of his strength.

"I *was* ashamed, Jabari. But not of you. Ashamed to tell you how deeply I cared for Badra and how much her rejection hurt. You told me to keep the dagger for the day I would marry. How could I even think of marrying another? Badra was my life. For five years, I guarded her every step. I watched her every move, I cherished her. And she refused me. Your words mocked me. They were like that dagger, lacerating my heart."

Pausing, he forced out the words he had not admitted to anyone. "I *loved* her."

He continued, pouring out his confession to his foster brother. "If Elizabeth, the woman you love more than your own life, had spurned your marriage offer, and then I came to you and cheerfully handed you a symbol of marriage, what would you have done? Would you not have lashed out in anger? Wouldn't you have boarded that ship and made certain you could never go back?"

Ramses's mouth shifted as his amber eyes widened. Both he and Jabari exchanged glances. The sheikh looked guilty as he rubbed his bearded chin.

"Allah, I did not realize how deeply you cared. I thought your pursuit of her was mere determination, the same zeal you displayed with everything. Not . . . something deeper and more meaningful," Jabari finally said.

"It was," Kenneth replied. "And leaving was the hardest thing I've ever done. You were family. The desert was home. The idea of living as an English aristocrat terrified me. Hell, I didn't even know if they had good horses there. If the English could ride."

The sheikh relaxed noticeably, seemingly lost in thought. After a moment he asked, "Do you remember the riding test at your initiation?"

Kenneth chuckled. "A warrior had to ride his mare

159

through a series of intricate moves." He'd had a different experience.

Ramses grinned slyly. "How we pulled you aside and told you that the real test was a test of manhood?"

Ramses and Jabari had ushered him into the mud brick home of the village whore, an experienced woman known to initiate young warriors. They'd told him his riding test was how long he could last with the woman. He'd lost his virginity that day.

"You bragged to Father you were the only warrior who could stay on for a full fifteen minutes," Jabari recalled.

"And he said, 'My son, you must learn to ride longer. To be a warrior means riding hours upon end. You may get sore, but it is your duty. Show your mount you are the master. Be gentle but firm. Stroke her nose to gentle her. Do not dismount if she shows signs of wanting to throw you. Hang on with your knees and ride her until she tires,' " Kenneth reminisced.

"So you went back, determined to do as he said!" Jabari howled with laughter.

Kenneth grinned. "She hit me when I stroked her nose but I hung on tight as he instructed."

"I heard she could not walk for a week—but had a smile on her face for equally as long. You should have married her instead of chasing Badra." Ramses laughed, then abruptly stopped.

Jabari rubbed his bearded chin. "So, Khepri, tell us what you wanted to discuss."

Khepri. As if he'd formally restored the ties between them. The use of the Khamsin name indicated the sheikh's acceptance. A calming peace settled over Kenneth. He drew in a breath, glad for it, for what he was about to tell them would hurt. More.

"It's a matter of tomb robbery." Kenneth paused for effect, noting the men's startled looks. Ramses appeared angry. Jabari's thunderstruck expression was almost comical.

"I'm here investigating thefts from the tomb at Dashur, the excavation I've been sponsoring. A priceless gold artifact vanished from there shortly after its discovery."

Ramses growled and settled one hand on his scimitar hilt. More than any other Khamsin warrior, he despised tomb robbers.

But Jabari's face filled with disquiet. "You are not here to share information, Khepri. Why do you tell us this?"

Kenneth reached into his waistcoat and withdrew the lone piece of evidence found in the tomb. The torn strip of indigo dangled from his fingers like a noose. A sharp intake of breath escaped the sheikh. Ramses looked stricken and swore softly.

"It is no Khamsin who does this evil," the guardian denied hotly. "Someone is laying the blame at our feet."

"This means nothing," the sheikh agreed, even as his bronzed cheeks paled. "Elizabeth, Rashid and Badra were at the excavation with me. Perhaps Elizabeth tore her garment."

"Perhaps. Or perhaps someone fascinated by artifacts wanted a closer examination than accorded in the tomb. And stole it."

"You dare accuse Jabari of thievery?" Ramses exclaimed.

"No. Rashid."

Dismay tightened Jabari's face. "Are you certain?" the sheikh asked.

"I found the item in question in Rashid's bag when he was staying with your father-in-law."

There was silence. Then: "And what will you do? Turn him over to English authorities?" Grief touched Jabari's face.

"No. I will preserve Khamsin honor and not shame the tribe that raised me. I could have ordered Rashid's arrest. It would have created a public sensation in the newspapers. I did not." He drew in a laboring breath. "I came to you instead."

The sheikh looked visibly relieved. "How may we help?"

"I'm certain Rashid is working with smugglers. He'll probably use Badra to gain access to the dig. He's used her before. Don't act surprised if she requests to join the excavation, probably as an artist. I'm heading there now to catch Rashid. Once I do, I'll turn him over to you to punish as you see fit."

The three men fell silent, knowing tribal law. Rashid would be banished, stripped of his scimitar, dagger and indigo, and shunned forever.

"So be it," Jabari said slowly. "I trust you will do what you must and I hope you are wrong. Very wrong."

"I as well." But Kenneth knew Rashid was guilty.

As they stood, the sheikh clapped a hand on his shoulder. "I hope you will stay with us, at least for the evening."

"I would be honored," he replied formally.

He blinked at the sunlight as they emerged from the tent. "And how is your son, Jabari?"

As if in answer, there came a loud hooting sound. Kenneth turned his head as a brown-skinned boy, wheat-colored hair flying in the breeze, raced by on chubby legs.

"Ah, yes, my son. Tarik thinks he is a horse."

Tarik galloped circles around the trio. Stark naked.

"Poo!" he shrieked.

Jabari looked resigned. "We are trying to teach him English and Arabic. Arabic he has handled better than English. The only English word he knows is 'poo.'"

At Kenneth's inquiring look, Jabari sighed, looking more like a beleaguered father than an arrogant, proud sheikh. "He learned the word after Badra taught him to say it for the other matter of equal concern to us."

"Reading?"

"Using the latrine. Tarik uses the word for everything."

Kenneth laughed as the toddler raced around them, screaming. "Where is his clothing?" he asked.

"He threw it down the latrine again."

Ramses laughed uproariously, holding his sides. Jabari scowled. "Just you wait, my friend, until it is your turn. You have twins. Twice the trouble. I will be the one laughing then."

Kenneth glanced down at the sheikh's son. He squatted, propping his chin onto a fist. "Hello, Tarik," he said in Arabic.

The child ground to an abrupt halt and stared, his large, dark eyes holding Kenneth's. Desert wind blew his hair. He stuck a finger in his mouth and stared.

Kenneth held out a hand. Sunlight caught the gleam of his ducal onyx ring, making it gleam. Noticing Tarik's fascinated stare, he slid it from his finger and held it up.

"Pretty?" he suggested in Arabic.

The toddler took the ring with a wondering look in his

eyes. Behind him, he heard Jabari say, "Khepri, I do not think that is wise . . ."

"Poo!" shrieked Tarik. He tore away from them, Kenneth's ring in hand, heading straight for the latrines in the distance. Ramses galloped after him and swung Tarik up into his arms. He grinned as he handed Jabari back his son and Kenneth his ring.

"Your ring was headed for a most foul burial, my friend. And do not think for a minute I would have retrieved it."

Kenneth glanced at the symbol of his duchy and pocketed it. "Safer here," he murmured.

In truth it felt too heavy for his finger, too foreign. Like many things these days.

Chapter Twelve

Much later, Kenneth came to dinner at the sheikh's tent.

In a move perfected over the years, he gracefully sat on the carpet. He felt odd in English dress in this desert tent, but familiar surroundings eased his displacement: desert wind blowing across the sands, the sharp scent of cooking fires, the soft laughter of women. Hunger assaulted him as Elizabeth and Katherine set dish after dish on a small raised dais.

Jabari quirked an eyebrow at him as Kenneth stared at the platters. Roast lamb rolled in rice. Small savory pastries. Stacks of flat bread and yogurt sauce. Garlic. He could smell the fragrances wafting up from the dishes. After a year of heavy beef dishes swimming in rich cream sauces, he found his appetite returning.

"We thought you'd enjoy a few of your favorites," the sheikh commented.

A few. Kenneth's gaze met his, and he saw the former affection resting there. A lump rose in his throat. This, more than mere words, demonstrated all Jabari did not say.

Welcome back. Welcome home.

Kenneth hid his emotions as the sheikh broke off some flat bread, dipped it into the sauce and handed it to him, serving the guest first as was customary. Kenneth ate and sighed with pleasure.

Tarik sat in his mother's lap, looking wide-eyed at the food. Sitting sandwiched between Ramses and Katherine were two babies about a year old, a girl and boy identical in their ebony hair and brilliant green eyes. Fatima and Asad, their twins.

Elizabeth took a wedge of flat bread smeared with yogurt and gave it to Tarik. The child examined it with the seriousness of an archaeologist studying a pyramid, then threw it into his father's face. White goo dripped from Jabari's black beard.

"Poo!" Tarik said happily.

"Ah, yes. My son. The future leader of our people," Jabari said dryly, wiping his face with a clean cloth.

Tarik blew through his lips, and Elizabeth smirked.

"Here, let me. I remember what your father did to me. He kept telling me in Arabic to eat, and that was the first Arabic word I learned." Kenneth reached for the child. The toddler felt warm and soft in his arms as he adjusted Tarik on his knees. He felt a brief stab of longing for a baby of his own with large chocolate eyes, just like Badra's. He took a small piece of flat bread and scooped up a bit of rice.

"Eat," he said sternly in English, and repeated the word. Tarik opened his mouth. Kenneth popped the food inside. The toddler chewed the rice solemnly. Kenneth gave a smug grin. "Just have to show him who is in charge," he advised.

Tarik's parents exchanged amused glances. Then their

son spat out the rice, spraying chewed grains all over Kenneth's face.

"Eat!" he burbled in English.

Jabari and Elizabeth looked delighted. "Tarik learned a new English word! Thank you, Kenneth," Elizabeth said.

"You're most welcome," Kenneth replied, wiping away the sticky rice plastered to his cheeks.

Tarik scampered off his lap and swaggered over to the twins, who were chewing on slices of flat bread. Tarik stopped before Fatima, snatching the bread from her hands. With his father's aplomb, he plopped to the carpet and began eating it. A frown formed on Elizabeth's brow, but Jabari held up a hand.

"Wait," he said quietly. "I want to see what they will do."

The adults waited, watching the children. Fatima regarded Tarik with wide, unblinking green eyes, then babbled something unintelligible to her brother. Her little fist shot out, snaring a thick lock of Tarik's wheat-colored hair. She gave a hard yank.

Tarik dropped the bread, howling, holding his hair, but the baby girl held it fast. Her brother Asad picked up the bread, gurgled and smacked Tarik with it, then handed it back to his sister. Tarik looked so woebegone and stunned, Kenneth laughed until tears rolled down his cheeks.

"What a pair of little warriors you have, Ramses!"

Ramses smiled proudly. "They take after their mother."

Then they piled questions on Kenneth, inquiring about his new life, which he answered as diplomatically as possible. Kenneth felt a terrible nostalgia for what they had all once shared.

To his shock, he watched Jabari and Ramses clear away the meal, the proud sheikh and his guardian bringing dishes over to soak in a large basin. Katherine gave Elizabeth a rueful smile.

"Does he do the washing as well?" Kenneth asked.

Elizabeth responded, "The nights I put Tarik to bed, he washes. Jabari says washing dishes is much easier on the ears. Dishes don't scream."

A while later, when the women had returned to their tents to settle the children, Kenneth sat with Ramses and Jabari. The three studied the stars studding the night sky.

Kenneth glanced at the two men he'd considered brothers, the two he'd grown closer to than anyone else in the world. They had fought together, shed blood together, bonded as warriors in battle and the heat of death. How he wished he could recapture everything with them. Here, the responsibilities of being a duke slid off him like an old skin. Here, he could relax.

Jabari laid his palms upon his knees, face up. Ramses exchanged glances with him.

"Khepri?"

He nodded slowly. "Of course."

"Do you wish to truly be bonded to us, Khepri? As a brother? Will you accept the blood-brother ceremony?"

The sheikh's formal tone hammered home the seriousness of the question. Kenneth did not hesitate. He gave a solemn nod.

"So be it."

Bare-chested, clad only in indigo trousers, the trio sat on the pebbled sand at the Khamsin ceremonial grounds. Fire-

GET UP TO 4 FREE BOOKS!

You can have the best romance delivered to your door for less than what you'd pay in a bookstore or online. Sign up for one of our book clubs today, and we'll send you **FREE* BOOKS** just for trying it out...**with no obligation to buy, ever!**

HISTORICAL ROMANCE BOOK CLUB

Travel from the Scottish Highlands to the American West, the decadent ballrooms of Regency England to Viking ships. Your shipments will include authors such as CONNIE MASON, SANDRA HILL, CASSIE EDWARDS, JENNIFER ASHLEY, LEIGH GREENWOOD, and many, many more.

LOVE SPELL BOOK CLUB

Bring a little magic into your life with the romances of Love Spell—fun contemporaries, paranormals, time-travels, futuristics, and more. Your shipments will include authors such as LYNSAY SANDS, CJ BARRY, COLLEEN THOMPSON, NINA BANGS, MARJORIE LIU and more.

As a book club member you also receive the following special benefits:

- **30% OFF all orders through our website & telecenter!**
- **Exclusive access to special discounts!**
- **Convenient home delivery and 10 day examination period to return any books you don't want to keep.**

There is no minimum number of books to buy, and you may cancel membership at any time. See back to sign up!

*Please include $2.00 for shipping and handling.

YES!

Sign me up for the **Historical Romance Book Club** and send my TWO FREE BOOKS! If I choose to stay in the club, I will pay only $8.50* each month, a savings of $5.48!

YES!

Sign me up for the **Love Spell Book Club** and send my TWO FREE BOOKS! If I choose to stay in the club, I will pay only $8.50* each month, a savings of $5.48!

NAME: _____

ADDRESS: _____

_____

TELEPHONE: _____

E-MAIL: _____

☐ **I WANT TO PAY BY CREDIT CARD.**

☐ VISA   ☐ MasterCard   ☐ DISCOVER

ACCOUNT #: _____

EXPIRATION DATE: _____

SIGNATURE: _____

Send this card along with $2.00 shipping & handling for each club you wish to join, to:

**Romance Book Clubs
20 Academy Street
Norwalk, CT 06850-4032**

Or fax (must include credit card information!) to: 610.995.9274.
You can also sign up online at www.dorchesterpub.com.

*Plus $2.00 for shipping. Offer open to residents of the U.S. and Canada only.
Canadian residents please call 1.800.481.9191 for pricing information.
If under 18, a parent or guardian must sign. Terms, prices and conditions subject to change. Subscription subject
to acceptance. Dorchester Publishing reserves the right to reject any order or cancel any subscription.

JOIN NOW!

light cast ominous shadows on their faces, which were striped with ash from burnt wood—the ceremonial facial tattoos that warriors donned the night prior to riding into battle.

Kenneth braced himself and stared into the fire as Jabari took the ceremonial dagger and cleaned it. The sheikh raised it to the thick muscles of Kenneth's left arm.

"Are you certain?" he asked.

Kenneth swung his head around to regard him, unblinking, spine straight and proud. "I've never been more certain in my life. I want to be your blood brother."

"Very well."

They settled their palms upon their knees and the sheikh uttered words in a deep, somber voice.

"Blood to blood, brother to brother, the *ankh*, the symbol of life, binds us together for life. May courage flow through our veins; stout be our hearts and strong be our bond to each other. Even if we lie weak and shattered upon the point of death, our blood flows in each other's veins, our link of brotherhood remains strong forever."

Kenneth gritted his teeth hard as the knife dug into his flesh. He steeled himself against the pain, breathing evenly as Ramses had taught him in boyhood, to center himself. When it was finished, the sheikh wiped his arm with a cleansing cloth and passed the knife, shimmering with Kenneth's blood, to Ramses.

Ramses offered a cheerful grin, breaking the solemnity of the moment. "Ah, a first. My sheikh hands me a dagger and instructs me to shed his blood. Perhaps a tattoo is not enough. A decorative symbol? Perhaps your wife's favorite flower?"

"We could create a map of Egypt so if you become lost, you will always find your way," Kenneth offered cheerfully.

Jabari grunted. "Ramses, get on with it before I carve a permanent smile on your face." The Khamsin sheikh stared grimly into the fire as his guardian created the cut. When finished, Ramses wiped his arm and handed over the bloodied dagger.

The sheikh looked at his guardian pensively. Kenneth saw his predicament and he began to laugh. Ramses heaved a heavy sigh. "Must I receive another?" He held out his arms, each thick as tree trunks, one bearing a tattoo of a falcon, one bearing the intricate symbols signifying his marriage status. "I am running out of space," he complained.

His sheikh arched a black brow. "I can always find room on another body part," he offered helpfully.

Ramses cheerfully cursed him. Kenneth laughed, glad for the companionship and restored friendship. He felt at home at last.

Jabari settled for the space below the falcon tattoo. He finished and held up the dagger to the sky.

"May this dagger, which has shed our blood, serve as the instrument that binds us together as blood brothers, as the sacred *ankh* on our arms serves as the eternal reminder we are brothers for life."

"Brothers for life," Kenneth echoed solemnly.

"Brothers for life," Ramses repeated.

The sheikh cleaned the dagger and reverently replaced it in its cedar box. Kenneth arched his neck and stared at the sky. A sense of rightness, of wholeness that he had missed since leaving, felt restored.

Ramses nudged him and gestured at the circle on Jabari's smooth, muscled chest. The *almha:* It had been tattooed on the sheikh the night before they rode against the Al-Hajid to reclaim that sacred disk.

"Do you remember when he received that?" Ramses asked.

Kenneth gave a solemn nod. Lost in recollection of long-ago, he mused over that night the warriors sang and danced around the fire and the sheikh received the tattoo. He propped his chin upon a fist, staring off into the sand. Finally the sheikh stood. They walked back to the camp, Kenneth wondering where his quarters would be for the night.

To his shock, Jabari halted before Badra's tent, giving Kenneth an apologetic look. "She is not returning until late tomorrow. Rashid's quarters are much less comfortable. Since it is late, I thought it would be acceptable. If it makes you uncomfortable . . ."

"You can stay with us," Ramses put in.

"No, it's fine." He gave a small shrug. "Only for tonight. I'll be on my way at first light."

He bid them good-night, removed his boots and stepped inside the black tent. An oil lamp flickered on a sandalwood table. Kenneth made his way toward a bedroom curtained off from the main section and halted.

Badra's bedroom. He smelled her scent, the fresh jasmine. A silver hairbrush sat on a wood table before an oval mirror. The large, comfortable bed, neatly made with clean sheets, was piled high with silk pillows.

She always had enjoyed sleeping with many pillows.

Spellbound by memories, he closed his eyes, remember-

171

ing the first time he had saved Badra from the Al-Hajid, when he'd lost his heart to her. When he had shed his blood for her.

He lifted the tent flaps to allow a soft breeze through; then he washed, dumped the dirty water into the container used for irrigating the herb garden, and tumbled into Badra's soft bed, falling into a sleep deeper than he ever had in England. The duke of Caldwell, former Khamsin warrior, began to dream of jasmine and a shy, alluring smile.

Home at last.

Badra had pushed them at a breakneck pace back to camp, for she needed to return to Dashur as quickly as possible. Moonlight pooled silver upon the pebbled sand as she and Rashid made their way quietly through the tents.

She went into her own, heading for the bedroom, smiling at someone's thoughtfulness. They had partly rolled up the flaps, allowing moonlight and a fresh desert breeze to spill inside. Undressing in the moonlight, she did a quick wash, donned a soft cotton nightdress she'd bought in England. Badra stroked the material wistfully, feeling a small connection to Kenneth and his native land—her one concession to relishing the tiny dream that she could have been his wife. She would have worn this to her marital bed, watched Kenneth's face glow with pleasure as he gently tugged it off her and let it pool around her feet as he advanced on her, hunger flaring in his eyes. He'd trap her beneath his heavy weight, the gleam of desire turning to the madness of lust as he pinched her, pushing himself crudely inside her—

Badra shivered. She went to her bed, lifted the sheet and slid onto the mattress. A tiny sigh of regret fled her lips. Would it truly have been that revolting to share her body with Kenneth? What if she had allowed him to continue to make love to her? If only she wasn't so afraid.

The odd scent of sandalwood and soap teased her nostrils. Kenneth's scent. She was so enamored of him that her mind played tricks! But suddenly she became aware of steady, even breathing. A hard male body pressed against hers. Muscles and sinew molded themselves to her soft curves. She froze in panic, her mouth opening to cry out and summon Rashid and a horde of warriors, when a sleepy male voice spoke:

"Mmmmm. Badra."

Kenneth?

She lay perfectly still, shock replacing her fear as he snuggled against her. A warm hand skimmed her rib cage and slid upward to cup one breast. His forefinger and thumb took her nipple and gently kneaded it. An odd tingling pooled in her loins. He buried his face in her hair, his warm breath feathering her nape.

She whimpered with pleasure. He uttered a soft groan. She realized he was sleeping, dreaming of her.

She did not move one rigid muscle as he molded his body firmly against her, the hard ridge of his arousal nestling against her bottom. Memories of Fareeq surfaced. She fought them.

The feather-light caresses continued, sending fire through her veins. Caught in a quandary, Badra lay still. If she startled him into waking, he might awaken others. She did not want a scene.

173

And delicious sensations pooled through her as he gently caressed her breast, filling her with pulsing yearning. She waited, arching against his touch as he murmured sleepily.

Suddenly he rolled away. Badra slid quietly from the sheets and stood, gazing at him. Moonlight exposed the sharp edges of his profile, his sensual mouth parted slightly as he breathed. The sheet was pulled only waist high, revealing a naked chest covered with a wealth of dark hair. The cobra tattoo showed in stark blue on the sculpted bicep of his right arm.

He dreamt of holding her in his arms. She could only imagine the courage it would take to fall into his welcoming embrace. A piercing regret stabbed her as she padded out of the bedroom to sleep in the corner of the tent's main room.

Before the first gray streaks of dawn stole into the tent, Kenneth awoke, the fragrance of jasmine lingering in the air. He inhaled the scent seeming to dust his hands. Was it a dream? Had he held Badra in his arms? Had his tender caresses caused sighs of pleasure to ripple from her sweet lips?

After dressing, he looked around the bedroom in speculation. He lit a lamp and silently padded over to the curtain separating the room from the main chamber. Lifting the fabric, he knew already what he would find.

Badra lay on the floor, curled into a tight ball, fast asleep. It had been no dream, then.

He looked at her a long minute, studying the delicate curves of her cheeks, her lush lips, her long, slender neck and rounded hips. So beautiful. Then he turned and headed back to her bedroom to gather his things. Dawn crept over the horizon, promising another cloudless, brilliant blue Egyptian sky.

Kenneth saddled his camel and slipped away from the Khamsin camp as silently as his cobra totem.

Chapter Thirteen

With its nearly level surface halved by a small crater, the pyramid of Senusret III at Dashur resembled a volcano more than an Egyptian monument. Reddish brown sand stretched as far as the eye could see, marching up to the etched lines of the twelfth-dynasty structure. The pyramid's ebony bricks, fashioned from sun-dried Nile mud, rose toward the sky. Kenneth studied the pyramid's cleft, formed by previous excavations in 1839 by archaeologists attempting to discover the entrance.

Sunshine warmed his chilled blood. Glancing up at the cloudless blue day, he gauged the time as he had been taught by his Khamsin brethren. Afternoon. Kenneth squatted down, sifting the sand through his fingers. Like flour, it spilled down, blown away by the wind. Sturdy cream-colored tents dotted the area in small outcroppings—although the dig's director, Jacques de Morgan, stayed in a nearby village, some of his team elected to camp near the pyramid. Kenneth stood, dusting off his hands. Sand kicked up by his leather boots whorled at his feet as he strode down to the camp.

The gold pectoral stolen from the dig site had been found in the northern section of the pyramid, in a series of galleries containing the tombs of Senusret and the royal family. Those sarcophagi had proven empty, the royal mummies long gone; Kenneth suspected they had been buried in another tomb for safekeeping, something not uncommon among the descendents of Egyptian royals, who feared having their remains disturbed by tomb robbers. However, the magnificent pectoral had been found layered in ancient dust at the foot of the granite casket, and so there de Morgan suspected a secret chamber lay below the galleries, a chamber used for storing precious artifacts buried with the dead for comfort in their afterlife.

Kenneth had given strict instructions not to explore that theory until his arrival. He needed to be present when the underground chamber was found. If more jewelry existed, Rashid would seize the chance to steal it. Then Kenneth would catch him and bring him back to the Khamsin for justice.

Steeling his spine, he strode toward the encampment, ruminating over the trap he'd prepared.

He washed at the basin propped on an empty crate in his tent and left for luncheon. Beneath a white canopy at a portable table, Victor and Jacques de Morgan dined off china plates and sipped fruit juice from crystal goblets. Kenneth's austere soul winced at the opulence in the desert's rugged simplicity.

On the distant horizon, a small cloud kicked up and

horses' hoofbeats thundered on the sand. Dust thickened and swirled. Shading his eyes, Kenneth stared at the sight.

Two Khamsin warriors came riding into the encampment on beautiful, sleek Arabians, guiding the horses expertly with their knees instead of bridles. Seeing them sent a ripple of unease through him, though he'd expected it.

Kenneth watched Jabari and Ramses dismount.

He knew the Khamsin leader would not simply let such a grave matter as tomb raiding rest in his hands. Tribe honor was at stake, and Jabari had a fierce sense of that. Likewise with Ramses. The Khamsin guardian despised tomb robbers even more than his sheikh.

With a heavy sigh, Kenneth went to greet his friends.

Jabari's keen gaze met his. "It is as you predicted, Khepri. Badra informed us de Morgan hired her to sketch the excavation. Rashid will be here with her soon."

Unease rippled through him. Jacques de Morgan had hired her? He wondered about the French archaeologist's motivation. He nodded to de Morgan's table. "I'll introduce you."

As they approached the canopy, Kenneth caught the words, "If the necklace is stolen . . ." His cousin glanced up, looking startled. He fell silent.

After introductions were made, Victor looked at de Morgan. He said, "I need to check on a few things. I'll meet you at the dig."

Kenneth gazed after his departing cousin. What had he been discussing with de Morgan that he was so eager to hide?

The French archaeologist swept Jabari and Ramses with a curious gaze. "*Mon Dieu*, those weapons you carry!"

An air of quiet pride settled on Jabari's broad shoulders as he gripped his scimitar's ivory hilt, the symbol of his clan's leadership passed down from generation to generation.

"But pistols and rifles are so much more sophisticated," de Morgan went on, fussily patting his mustache with a linen napkin. "I suppose it is the culture. Egyptians are so simple compared to civilized societies such as the French."

Kenneth's gut twisted. Jabari's mouth tightened in anger beneath his black beard. The sheikh gave de Morgan a look of contempt and stalked off, shoulders stiff with pride.

Left alone with de Morgan and a seething Ramses, Kenneth felt the awkwardness of his two worlds colliding.

Ramses's silent gaze held his, questioning. Which are you, it asked. Duke of Caldwell? Or Khepri? Are you our brother still?

A brother would not allow such a deep insult to pass.

Oblivious of the tension in the air, de Morgan stood, went outside the little canopy and brushed crumbs off his fine linen suit. Kenneth glanced at the bowl of gleaming, imported fruit on the table. Oranges and bananas. An idea surfaced. He took a banana, tossed it to Ramses, and said softly in Arabic, "Sit. Wait until my cue and then peel this with your dagger."

Interest shone in the guardian's amber eyes. De Morgan returned and sat again as Kenneth leaned an elbow on the table.

"You say Egyptians are simple, Monsieur de Morgan. I have found living with the Khamsin that the warriors are fierce fighters, very courageous and oblivious to pain. And their weapons serve a . . . useful purpose." He gave a dramatic pause.

Ramses took out his sharp dagger and held it aloft, admiring the blade. Mirth flashed in his eyes.

"As I was saying, the warriors are fearless, ruthless fighters, trained upon reaching manhood. When the training is complete, we undergo a ritual to signify our status as men." Hiding a smile, Kenneth continued. "Circumcision," he gleefully told the Frenchman. "A painful process, but one which guarantees, ah, a certain stoicism among us warriors."

Ramses began peeling the banana very slowly and very carefully with his dagger.

"A sharp blade must be used for the process, and the warrior must stay absolutely still. One slip and . . ."

A curse in English flitted from Ramses's lips as the dagger jerked, scoring a deep notch in the banana. De Morgan blanched. Kenneth swore even the tips of his mustache paled.

"Khamsin warriors learn to endure," Kenneth added. "Women also claim it makes certain acts of love more pleasurable. *Much* more."

With a sly wink, Ramses chomped down on the peeled banana, chewing with relish. The Frenchman looked physically ill.

Ramses took another banana and offered it to de Morgan. The archaeologist mopped his brow with a handkerchief and shook his head, muttering excuses about overseeing the workers. When he bolted from his chair, Kenneth caved in and howled with laughter. Ramses joined him, holding out the extra fruit.

"Banana? Women love them." He winked.

"Only if it is peeled," he shot back, and they howled with laughter again.

* * *

Draped in her customary indigo *kuftan*, blousy trousers and blue head scarf, Badra surveyed the encampment for her contact, the digger whom Masud had told her stole the first necklace. Rashid, Jabari and Ramses busied themselves with setting up tents.

The sheikh and his guardian made her vastly uneasy. Jabari had told her Kenneth had made peace with him, and he'd decided to visit the dig site and observe the work. But the sheikh's gaze was frank and steady as he explained this to her, and that made her nervous.

Committing theft in front of them would require all her wits.

A tall, thin Egyptian in an ankle-length *thobe* with distinct blue stripes, and a white turban sitting askew on his head, spotted her and gave a small nod. Badra tensed, nodding back. This was the digger who was her contact. She must take care, or all her carefully laid plans would collapse.

Or worse, she would weave a noose out of an Egyptian necklace for Kenneth to hang her.

Badra wiped clammy hands on her *kuftan*, trying to calm her heartbeat. Gulping in a breath, she turned rapidly—and nearly collided with the one man she knew she could never really deceive. Kenneth.

His two hands shot out, steadying her. His shadow fell over her as he gazed down at her. She stared at his chest and the white shirt he wore, then craned her head up to regard him.

"Hello, Badra," he said quietly.

She gazed up at his somber face, his piercing blue gaze

holding hers, thick locks of dark brown hair hanging over his forehead. He wore a crisp shirt that showed little sign of sweat, despite the day's relative warmth. Open at the throat, the deep V showed a triangle of dark hair. She stared at his chest, spellbound, remembering how he had curled up next to her. How he had cupped her breast, making her ache and pulse with a strange yearning she lacked the courage to explore. His library in England: how his powerful body had covered hers as she shoved at him, screaming for him to stop . . .

"Why are you here?" he asked.

She gave a tremulous smile. "Jacques de Morgan invited me to sketch the excavation. What of you? Are you readying everything?"

"He's in charge. I'm not an archeologist."

Tension rose between them, thick as the shimmering heat from the dusky sand. Badra swallowed hard. "Kenneth, about what happened in England . . ." Heat flushed her face. She did not know how to speak of the matter. Deep shame and guilt filled her. His steady, intense blue eyes held hers, frankly assessing, devoid of emotion. Her voice dropped to a choked rasp. "I hope we can both forget it and move on."

"I can't. What happened, Badra? Why did you pull away?"

His expression remained impartial, as if he were still a Khamsin warrior. Or an English duke with the cool reserve of his breeding and culture. She couldn't confess her brutal past, the fears and shame she felt each time he touched her.

"What do you mean?" Her voice sounded too loud, too protesting. Badra affected surprise, though she felt certain he could hear the thunderous drum of her heart. He towered over her like a tall limestone column in one of the ancient temples, equally solid, massive and imposing.

"Badra, were you afraid of me?" His voice was gentle.

For a wild moment she wanted to confess all, to confide in the man who had sworn an oath to protect her. All her sexual fears. The truth about Jasmine. Then Badra's spirits sagged. She must do everything to protect her child. Masud had warned if she told the duke, Jasmine would be sold and vanish forever.

No, she needed to push Kenneth away. If he discovered she was here to find the necklace . . . Badra worked up the courage to utter words she knew would hurt.

"Do you remember the night under the desert stars when you kissed me?"

His gaze softened. "I will never forget."

"Well, I acted the way I did in your library because I was curious to see if you desired me as much as you did before, Kenneth. And you did. I saw for myself, then changed my mind."

Steel glinted in his eyes, cutting through any previous trace of softness. "Admit it, Badra. You wanted me equally."

She lifted a shoulder. "I'll admit I can act very well."

"Was it acting, Badra?" he asked softly.

Sweat beaded her forehead. How could she deceive this man? His gaze burned her. "Call it what you wish. I will call it what it was for me—a mistake. One I will not repeat."

"Sometimes the mistakes we make turn out to be the greatest lessons life has to offer us. And some of us must repeat the mistake over and over." To her shock, Kenneth clasped her trembling palm and pressed a kiss there. His lips were warm and firm.

"I would be most happy to help you learn your lesson, Badra," he added. His deep voice rubbed against her like velvet.

Badra gulped. "I assure you, I have no such need of any lesson from you."

"That remains to be seen," he murmured. His gaze bored into her as she stormed off.

It was no act. It couldn't be. Kenneth knew a woman's response, the signs of arousal. She had displayed all of them in his library. Why had she changed her mind? Was it because she wanted to tease him like she had when he was her falcon guard?

"This was a horrible mistake. I told you once before, Kenneth, I can't return the feelings you have for me."

Kenneth clenched his hands until the knuckles whitened. He forced a calming breath. She frustrated, angered him. Tormented him. And still he wanted her with a fierce desire that was merciless. He'd do nearly anything to have her.

A familiar voice sounded at his elbow. "Friend of yours, Your Grace?"

"Not quite." Kenneth glanced at Zaid, grateful to see him. He had given explicit instructions for his secretary to join him in Dashur, and to report to the dig. He wrinkled his nose at Zaid's beard and mustache.

"New look, Zaid? Trying to fit in with the locals?"

A look of surprise flashed in the man's dark eyes, then they regained their usual blank expression. "The women find it charming," he replied in his soft voice.

Kenneth laughed. "I'm certain they do." He cleared his throat. "I have papers I need you to look over, papers my cousin had me sign. I left them at the Shepherd's Hotel. I also have some correspondence for you to handle. And my cousin's shop to look into. I want to know all about it—what he's selling, if it's turning a profit."

"Shall I return to Cairo immediately?"

"You can remain for today if you want. The excavation promises to be a bit thrilling, if you want to watch."

Zaid considered. "It's best I return to the hotel to immediately resume work, if it's quite all right with you."

"Fine," Kenneth agreed absently, spotting Victor in the distance. "Make sure you charge any expenses to my account. And report to me as soon as you have the information I require."

Then he walked off, suddenly absorbed in the other matters consuming him as much as his desire for Badra. His cousin. Was Victor hiding something from him? And what?

Chapter Fourteen

An hour later, the tomb surrounded him.

Kenneth watched intensely as digging commenced to find the secret chamber he and de Morgan knew must exist within these ancient walls. Suffocating heat drenched the workers with sweat, which trickled down their temples as they scraped the earth. A stifling odor of bat droppings, dust and age layered the air, but it could not overpower the smell of tense excitement, sharp as Lebanon cedar shavings.

Workers piled debris into a small mound. Clad in Egyptian dress, her head covered with a blue scarf, Badra sat on a stool sketching the scene as Elizabeth had taught her. Her artistic gifts sprang to life in brilliant hues captured on her paper.

She abandoned her work, stood, gave a sinuous stretch and paced. Kenneth quietly watched her instead of the diggers. Beautiful Badra, taunting him with her lithe grace. Teasing him to madness with her seductiveness in his library, just to satisfy her curiosity, then calling for him to stop.

Suddenly a small scream from her echoed through the chamber. Forgetting all resentment, all anger, his inbred protectiveness raged to the surface. As he had so many times before, Kenneth sped toward Badra. Her wide-eyed gaze met his as he clasped her arms.

"What is it?" he asked.

"N-nothing," she stammered. "A bat. I was startled."

The workers all laughed loudly, and one remarked on the ill luck of having a woman among them. Kenneth shot him an icy look, quelling the mirth. "Return to work," he ordered.

Badra's large brown eyes met his. "Thank you, Kenneth, for your concern," she said softly.

Giving her an abrupt nod, he joined de Morgan. The archaeologist hovered over one particular section of diggers. Remembering the way his heart jumped at her scream, remembering her moans of pleasure as he kissed her and pressed her down to the desk, he shook his head. She confused the hell out of him. Work was much more logical, much less frustrating.

Badra remained standing for a minute longer. She didn't dare look down. When she was assured no one was watching her, a lowly woman, she lifted the hem of her dusty indigo *kuftan,* revealing her blousy trousers and delicate sandaled feet. Her left foot had sunk into the pile of debris at the edge of the sarcophagus. The hidden chamber. Excitement poured through her like hot water. She eased her sandal out, standing guard near the debris lest someone else sink into it.

Later tonight, when all slept, she would return. And she would dig.

* * *

Rose, lavender and gold dusted the sky as the camp prepared the evening meal. Small cooking fires lit the sands, crackling flames leaping into the falling night. The acrid stench of smoke stung Kenneth's nostrils.

Under a cream canopy, de Morgan and his team had assembled for dinner, sitting at a table with real chairs and a linen cloth spread over its surface. They had their food carted in from a nearby barge.

Kenneth riveted his gaze on his Khamsin brethren. A copper pot over a cook fire bubbled, while Badra kneaded dough. Some distance from the others, the Khamsin sheikh and his guardian sat on carpeting, absorbed in a game of chess, watched over by Rashid. The scene emphasized the cultures' stark contrast: the European overseers dining on white china, the simple Bedouin fare served on the ground.

Simple Bedouin fare sounded so appetizing. He ambled over and stood staring. "Have room for one more?" he asked.

Badra's hands stilled in their work. Rashid glanced up, scowling. Kenneth felt a strange regret at the warrior's animosity. In another world, he might have considered Rashid a friend. But he hated all Al-Hajid warriors for killing his parents and brother, and Rashid despised him for hurting Jabari. The circle of hatred never seemed to end. It would continue, Kenneth thought grimly, until they finally came to blows. But not here.

Rashid stood, muttered something about losing his appetite and stalked off. Kenneth guardedly watched him approach a worker and strike up a conversation.

The Khamsin sheikh, sitting with his long legs crossed, considered the chessboard. "There is always room for you, Khepri," he said.

"Monsieur de Morgan does not eat banana tonight," Kenneth noted.

Ramses gave a low chuckle and merrily took a pawn. Jabari scowled. "I doubt the fussy Frenchman will find the appetite to peel a banana ever again."

Kenneth grinned. "Well, he is learning. Some men are concerned only with the size of their banana, not if it is peeled or unpeeled."

Jabari scowled again as Ramses took a bishop. "You talk in riddles," he growled.

Kenneth exchanged an amused glance with Ramses. "Does Elizabeth eat bananas, Jabari?" he asked innocently.

The Khamsin sheikh grunted as he studied the chessboard. "Not since we are married."

"Pity," Kenneth said—then he and Ramses burst into laughter. Jabari looked up.

"What?"

"Never mind," Kenneth said, winking at Ramses. He walked over to watch Badra, and dropped to the sand. He propped a chin on one fist.

Khamsin women had an inbred grace about them. Even Badra possessed the sinuous elegance. She knelt, concentrating on her task, rolling out dough and pounding it. The rhythmic movements of her hands and the distant laughter and conversation from the others created twin sensations of peace and tension in Kenneth. Peace from routines so familiar. Tension from being so near her.

189

He sat cross-legged on the carpet and looked off at the silhouette of the immense pyramid. He closed his eyes, recalling the stories told around the crackling campfires at night during his youth, when Jabari's father had regaled the starry-eyed children with tales of Egypt's ancient pharaohs. The history lesson was burned into his brain.

He had so desperately wanted to please his foster father, to show him he could equal any warrior's aptitude. Kenneth had thrived on the lessons as a newborn lamb thrives on its mother's milk. But in the end, it hadn't mattered.

"It must have been an impressive pyramid in its time," he mused, opening his eyes and regarding the purple shadows descending upon the stark structure. "I suppose he never was buried there because his family wanted to keep him safe. Good reason too—not just because of tomb robbers. Senusret III was a cruel conqueror. He burnt crops, killed the men of Nubia, and enslaved women and children. He was ruthless. Destroying his mummy would have given his enemies the final victory; denying him the riches of the afterlife."

"Anyone who enslaves women and children *should* be denied the riches of the afterlife," Badra said.

The hostility in her voice stirred him out of his pensiveness. Kenneth shot her a curious glance. "True. Slavery is wrong. But it was a fact of life in ancient Egypt."

"It's a fact of life in modern Egypt." She took a wad of lumpy dough and slammed it onto the board with unusual violence.

Again, he wondered about her time with Fareeq. In all the years they spent together, Badra had never mentioned anything of her past. It remained a locked door.

One he suddenly desired more than anything to pry open.

"Fareeq was a cruel taskmaster, much as Senusret."

His casual statement, directed only to her, made her hands still. Badra remained bent over the dough, motionless. "Why do you say that?"

"He liked to flog his captives, and sometimes rape the women," Kenneth said, carefully watching her.

Her slender shoulders lifted under the indigo *kuftan* and she resumed her task.

He continued. "I know about Fareeq and his cruelties. You were his slave for four years. Did he ever . . . treat you the same?" he persisted, desperately needing to know.

Only after Elizabeth, the sheikh's wife, had been captured by Fareeq and flogged, and the tale seeped out, had Kenneth learned of Badra's former captor's abusive nature. He had asked Badra, very nonchalantly back then, if Fareeq treated all his women that way.

Now her answer came charging back to him with the force of thundering Arabians. She had *not* answered. Badra had distracted him with something else. He had forgotten to ask again. He studied her hands, which were trembling slightly as they slapped the dough.

"Look at me," he ordered softly. She dragged her large brown eyes to meet his.

"Badra?" he asked. "Did Fareeq ever beat you?"

The question burned into her soul.

Years ago, he had made the same inquiry. But Jabari had, thankfully, spotted them and approached, giving her welcome relief from the required answer.

If Kenneth knew the truth, his intense gaze would soften with pity. She could not bear his pity, or her own humiliation. She could not expose her shameful secret. Those times were gone. She dreaded the memories. Her life had flowered and she was proud of her achievements. If Kenneth showed her pity, all those wonderful achievements would crumble into dust, smashed by the hammers of her tortured past.

In all the years she had known him, Badra had never lied to Kenneth. Not even when she'd refused his hand in marriage. She had told him when he begged her to marry him, "I cannot feel the same as you feel for me, Khepri."

A stark truth. She could not demonstrate the same intense, heated passion flaring in his eyes. She could not let him hold her and equal his desire when he kissed her. Her love ran too deep to hurt him with a marriage without passion, with her heart as parched as desert sand. Where there would be no soft cries of pleasure tumbling from her lips when he took her into his black tent and made her his and claimed his prize at last. There would be only screams of fear, and struggles, as there had been in England when his big body had covered hers . . .

Badra raised her gaze and for the first time in her life, told him a direct lie.

"Did Fareeq ever beat me? No. He never did."

Kenneth leaned back, relaxed, satisfied with the directness of her look and her answer. He could not bear the idea of the bastard's whip tearing into Badra's soft skin. If he knew Fareeq had hurt her, his rage would have howled to the heavens.

But the sheikh had not, so Kenneth was satisfied. Badra

spread out the dough and began carefully cutting shapes with her small knife, rolling them into triangles.

He watched with interest. "Those look like scones."

A becoming rose tinted her cheeks. "They are. I . . . I grew accustomed to them in England. Lord Smithfield's cook was kind enough to share her recipe. I made these yesterday." Fishing one from a tin, she handed it over.

He adored scones, the one English food he truly liked. Kenneth nibbled, hesitant to hurt her feelings. A delicious taste of honey, almonds and sugar flooded his mouth. He took a large bite, chewing with genuine hunger as he consumed the pastry.

Her anxious gaze sought his. He swallowed. "An English scone with Egyptian flavor. Fascinating. And delicious!"

A soft smile touched her heart-shaped lips. Enchanted, he forgot the scone. Brown granules dusted a corner of her lip.

"You have sugar on your mouth," he said.

With one thumb, he reached up to brush it away, resting it against the delicious curve of her mouth. He rubbed, remembering the taste of her upon his lips.

Sultry awareness dawned in her eyes, darkening them to black. Her lips parted and a soft breath eased out. Heated by the signs of her arousal, Kenneth caressed the upper curve of her mouth with his thumb.

Her tongue darted out, licked away the sugar.

Desire fired his blood, along with dawning awareness. Badra had lied to him. What she had felt in England was no act. God, he wanted her. And she wanted him. He slid a hand around her nape, drawing her forward, enchanted by the hypnotic pull of her sensuality.

193

She shoved at him, lightly, but hard enough. Kenneth narrowed his eyes. He unfolded his body then stalked off to watch Jabari and Ramses play a game much less complicated than the one Badra played.

Dinner proved delicious, despite Badra's quietness. Kenneth concentrated on regaining old ground with Jabari and Ramses, who kept him entertained with stories of the ancient kings, and he regaled them with English history. Rashid said nothing throughout the meal but kept watch with a guarded look. Sparks from the campfire drifted upward, touching the velvet night, and Kenneth suddenly realized it had grown late.

He rose, thanking them politely for the meal, and indicated he would retire to his tent. As he strode off, his warrior instinct warned him to keep watch.

A worker strolled up to him, salaamed and requested a word. "I am keeping watch tonight. Should I be on guard for anything?" he asked, fingering his rifle with a self-important gesture. A white turban sat slightly askew on his head. His ankle-length *thobe* bore distinct light blue stripes.

"Just keep watch and wake me if you see anything unusual," Kenneth advised, nodding as the worker strolled off toward the tomb.

Pretending to settle into his tent, he extinguished the lamp and waited. Tonight was the night. He was certain of it.

Badra slipped from her tent with the stealth of a Khamsin warrior raiding an enemy camp, a jewel-toned bag she had woven on her loom slung around one shoulder. Descending the steps to the tomb, Badra let her eyes adjust from blackness to the dull dimness of a few scattered torches.

Her soft-soled shoes whispered as she hurried down the stairs leading to the galley where the men had worked earlier. Inside, the worker who was her contact started, then smiled.

"I will await you above," he whispered, then slipped away, silent as sand.

Guilt surged through her. Those who stole from the graves of the honored dead stole not only from the old ones, but from Egypt. Her own heritage lay within these carefully carved walls of rock.

She mustn't think of that. Even though her nature rebelled against the path she had chosen, Jasmine's welfare came first. Doubts would not help her daughter. Nor would the guilt constantly attacking her.

Covered by her indigo *kuftan* and strapped to her thigh atop the underlying Turkish trousers was a *jambiya*, a small curved dagger. It was Kenneth's dagger, the one he had cut his palm with the day she refused his marriage offer. She'd kept it, the only token of the man she secretly loved, who would have given his life to protect her.

Lifting her hem, she quickly retrieved the knife and knelt down, dagger in hand, and began digging in the sand.

The loosened mound of earth she had stepped into earlier surely hid the casket containing the jewels. A grim smile touched her mouth as she appreciated the irony—using Kenneth's dagger to find Kenneth's treasure so she could steal it.

Dirt yielded to the dagger's ruthless prying. She cupped earth and flung it aside. The inefficient means of excavation

195

would take a while, but she didn't dare cart tools below, didn't dare draw any suspicion to her quest.

Barely a few minutes later the *jambiya* made the hollow thud of striking a hidden chamber. Badra cleared the earth and peered into inky depths. The soft glow of her lamp picked up a glint.

Gold!

She felt blood drain from her face as she stared into the contents of a crumbled coffer, long eroded into fragments and dust. But the contents remained intact. Jewelry. Pieces and pieces of exquisite jewelry, precious gems, gold and silver leaf, lapis. With a trembling hand, she reached down and picked up a pectoral with a cartouche: the other necklace of Princess Meret. The necklace condemning the wearer to slavery. She dropped it in her bag like a hot coal.

Night settled over the encampment. Lying in his narrow bed, Kenneth forced patience. A soft voice called to him from the night, low and filled with urgency.

"Sahib, you must awaken."

Kenneth dressed quickly and emerged from his tent. It was the guard on duty, who salaamed, gripping his rifle.

"There is someone in the tomb."

Kenneth nodded, dismissing the man. Stars glittered like fistfuls of diamonds scattered against the dark velvet sky. A waxing moon shed a soft, silvery glow upon the sand.

Answers lay below, in the tomb itself. He lit a torch and prepared to descend.

An eerie silence draped over the tomb's interior. Sweat dripped off Badra's nose. The stench of bat droppings filled the air. Being underground, below her beloved desert, brought out all her superstitions. She made the sign against the evil eye as she had been taught in childhood. The stolen necklace made her feel slightly queasy.

She gazed around the deserted resting place of the pharaoh, whose tomb had been designed from the moment he ascended the throne. Her heart lurched again. Ancient Egyptians spent their entire lives preparing for the afterlife. By removing these items, which assured the royals would still have luxuries, she would be stripping the royals of all that ensured their happy afterlife. Such an act constituted an unpardonable sin.

Summoning her inner strength, she turned away from such thoughts of betrayal and dishonesty. Badra went to re-trieve her dagger—and heard the distinct, soft footfalls of someone in the descending corridor that connected the gallery.

Badra looked around, frantic. The open chamber lacked any hiding place. Scrambling around the coffin, she crouched down and waited. The footsteps were made with stealth. Yet the bearer had unmistakable weight. A man. A man doing his best to enter the tomb unnoticed.

If she stayed hidden long enough, perhaps the intruder would find what he sought and leave. Her damp palms clutched at the folds of her indigo *kuftan*. Another tomb robber?

Fresh sweat blossomed on her temples. She contem-plated another possibility. Whoever approached came fast. Her mind swiftly assembled a list of plausible reasons for her presence. But they sounded feeble, like a child's lies.

Remaining hidden was her best option. Badra tucked

herself deeper into the shadows. The footsteps sounded directly outside the chamber and then carried inside. She listened intently. They were quick, brisk steps, as if the man had business to complete and planned to carry on in haste.

Risking exposure, she craned her neck. She could see western trousers. No indigo trousers and soft leather boots, so no Rashid. Western clothing. Perhaps M. de Morgan himself?

The man remained silent. No noise filled the tomb but the erratic cadence of her heart. She huddled against the quartzite coffin.

A slight scrape, and the footsteps sounded again. A sigh of relief escaped her lungs in a sibilant hiss. She waited and heard the unmistakable sound of him leaving. With forced patience, she waited. Badra slowly uncurled her body, rubbing her cramped muscles. And let out a shriek that was effectively muzzled as a large hand clamped over her mouth and another seized her around the waist.

A deep male voice sounded softly in her ear. "What are you doing here, Badra?"

Chapter Fifteen

Kenneth! Icy fists of fear squeezed her heart as his implacable grip squeezed her waist. The duke of Caldwell ensnared her as firmly as a snake twisting prey in its tight coils. Panic seized her. Arms as strong as tempered steel held her firmly upright as she twisted, trying to wrench free.

"Badra." His heated whisper sounded in her ear.

"Kenneth, please release me," she begged.

"Not until you tell me why you are here."

"I . . . I . . . am here to honor my people's past."

His grip lessened and he wrenched her around to look at him. His intense blue gaze, bright as the Egyptian sky, pierced her. Kenneth cupped her chin; his touch felt heated like coals in a brazier as he stroked the underside with a thumb.

A dangerous, soft note entered his voice. "You lie, Badra."

"Kenneth, please," she protested.

His gaze fell to her feet. Kenneth kicked aside dirt and discovered what she had found. The hidden casket.

In the glow the torchlight cast on the walls, his eyes burned like two brilliant sapphires. Ruddy anger flushed his lean, sculpted cheeks. He looked as menacing as the ancient pharaoh who'd stormed and burned and pillaged and enslaved.

"Why are you here, Badra? To steal for someone?"

A wild trembling ravaged her body. He brought his face closer. A terrible beauty shone there with grim fury. She saw no escape. She saw hard determination and a warrior, one who could squeeze a confession from any enemy.

Kenneth leaned over her, pressing her against the wall. "You're a thief, Badra. You're stealing what is mine. You know what is done with thieves in Egypt."

She needed the necklace. Badra tried not to tremble as his hand brushed against her cheek.

"You want the treasure found here? Do you desire to see it glow against your soft skin?" His voice shifted, becoming low and husky. Before her startled eyes, he dug into her bag and withdrew the gleaming gold cartouche, Meret's necklace cursing the wearer to slavery.

"You tried hiding the other one in my library. Seduction covered your real purpose. Why did you return it, Badra? Because Rashid asked you? Did he know I found it in his pack?"

Dryness choked her mouth. She could barely speak.

"Kenneth, please . . ."

"What a fool I was!" A dry bark of laughter escaped him. "He's gotten you to do his dirty work for him. Of course."

She stared, bewilderment mixing with fear.

"No mind." His fingers wrapped about her trembling wrist. "I'm taking the matter to Jabari. He'll deliver justice."

"No!" Her shriek of protest echoed through the chamber.

"No Khamsin justice, Badra? I can have the authorities arrest you. Which would you prefer?"

At his narrow gaze, she thought frantically. Jabari would demand answers. A hue and cry would rise and the digger working for Masud would alert him. Jasmine would be sold to the European. Immediately.

She had no choice. She must return to the brothel and take Jasmine's place. But time had run out. Kenneth would keep her trapped here. She stared at his furious face. And the idea surfaced. How much he desired her. Lust turned men mindless.

Self-preservation gripped her. Badra sought the only course left to her, words the head eunuch had said at the Pleasure Palace echoing in her mind.

"If you do not return with the necklace, the only thing that will free your daughter from here is to take her place."

An odd calm born of desperation took over. Badra thrust out her hips, gave him a seductive smile. She licked her lips.

"I will give you an answer in your tent. And await you there. Allow me a little time to prepare."

Confusion mingled with fury. He had never seen Badra act this way, so overtly seductive. What did she plan? To beg him to reconsider talking to Jabari? It would not work.

He counted slowly to one hundred, then followed her out

of the tomb. Steeling his spine, he braced himself as if for battle. Then Kenneth strode to his tent and went inside.

A lamp on a folding table filled the interior with soft light. Badra stood, her back to the tent wall, long ebony hair spilling to her waist in a tangle of curls. She wore one of his white shirts. It draped open past naked thighs. And then she opened the shirt further, showing him what he had only dared dream about. Desire slammed into him like a gale-force wind. Spellbound, he stared.

Erotic dreams of Badra, naked and willing in his arms, paled beside her actual beauty. Her breasts were firm and gold as ripe peaches, tipped with dark rose nipples. Her body gleamed like honey in the dull lamplight. Her waist was slender and her hips rounded. A thatch of soft black curls rested above her womanly parts. Though she barely reached his chin, her legs were long, slender with a hint of muscle.

But her face—ah, the frozen, blank expression dulled her beauty. Cold and dead, lifeless like a tomb.

She stood motionless, a lustrous statue in the soft light.

This was her intent? Lovemaking?

He could not believe she would do it. Kenneth gripped her chin with one hand, forcing her to look up at him. Her warm, satiny lips met his in a soft, dreamlike cloud.

Kenneth jerked back, shocked, dropping his hold on her chin. Her kiss teased him to the edges of raw anger, wresting control from him. A wild vortex of pleasure engulfed him. He closed his eyes, caving in to the longing. His hand cradled her head as he held her steady. Hot blood rushed through his veins as he relished her mouth against his.

Sudden awareness flared.

Badra was kissing him as a distraction. Her lips pressed against his felt passive. He pulled her closer, deepened the kiss, coaxing her mouth to respond to him.

Badra whimpered against Kenneth's arousing, punishing kiss, for it sent fire through her veins. Heat pooled in her body, building to an incredibly sweet tension. *Not like this*, her mind screamed in protest. Not here. She collapsed in his embrace. He nipped her lower lip, slid his tongue along her mouth, teasing and flicking. Like an invading warrior, it plunged inside her mouth and ravaged, coaxing her to respond in kind.

Trapped against his hard body, her breath fled into his mouth, mingled and danced. His tongue stroked and explored, demanding that she surrender.

Twin forces of passion and fear pulled at her. She could not let him go too far, yet she needed to arouse his passion. Convince him she was worth it. Inflame his desire until he would follow her to the ends of the earth.

Or to a brothel in Cairo.

Badra willed herself into the age-old dance, a participant instead of an observer. She must convince him she was worth the price. Better to have her former falcon guard purchase her at the Pleasure Palace than face another cruel captor. Kenneth at least would try to be kind. And she did care for him.

The hard ridge of his erection pressed against the softness of her belly. His large, warm hands reached up beneath the shirt, softly kneaded her bottom. She yanked out of his embrace before they could wander farther, finding the twisted scar tissue covering her back.

"No," she said. "Not yet."

Kenneth cursed softly, aching with frustrated need. She was doing it to him again. Badra. His love. His curse. But soon, his alone. He wanted to possess her utterly and take her as a man took a woman, feel her warm skin soft beneath him, but she danced teasingly out of reach.

He watched warily as she donned her indigo *kuftan*, shielding her lovely nude body from his hungry gaze. She lifted her chin. "Not arrest, Kenneth. Nor justice delivered by Jabari. But I will be your concubine. That is the price I will pay for taking what belonged to you. I only ask one favor. Go to the Shepherd's Hotel in Cairo and find a little girl named Jasmine. See to her needs. Then you will find me at the Pleasure Palace, the brothel where I was first sold. They will put me up for auction. If you want me, buy me."

"What?" he blurted, wholly shocked and confused.

Sadness shone in her dark eyes. "Some things are stronger than life itself. Your mother knew this. She sacrificed her life to put you into that basket when the Al-Hajid raided. A mother's love is stronger than the Nile, more enduring than the sun. A mother who loves her child will do anything to save her."

Her sadness shifted to worry. "Will you arrest me, Khepri?"

He closed his eyes. "Never. I could never, Badra." When he opened them again, she had fled into the night.

Chapter Sixteen

Standing before the slave master at the Pleasure Palace, Badra spoke the words her soul dreaded. "I have failed to recover the necklace, and I am offering myself in my child's place."

No surprise flickered in Masud's dark eyes. They were in the brothel's front room where clients entered and transacted business. Lush scarlet-and-lapis divans and satinwood tables inlaid with mother-of-pearl softened the room's businesslike interior. An ornate, rolltop desk sat off to the side.

Her trembling legs threatened to collapse. Badra wanted to get this business over as soon as possible.

She prayed Kenneth would follow her. Though he'd be confused and furious, Khepri had a kind heart. He would see her daughter to safety. Only Jasmine mattered.

Badra thrust her chin skyward. "That was our agreement. I am offering myself in her place. Bring her to me."

Masud snapped his fingers. Within minutes Jasmine appeared in the doorway, looking scared, until her gaze lit upon Badra. Then her elfin face glowed with pleasure. Clutching a small bag, she ran to Badra. Badra bent down, enfolding her in a tight embrace. Then looking up, she glowered at the guards and Masud.

"Give me a minute alone. It's all I ask."

With a grunt, the men left.

Badra bent down, embracing Jasmine with all her love, all the hopes she nurtured in her heart. She kissed the girl and spoke softly into her ear. She glanced inside the child's bag, aching at the few possessions. A ragged change of clothing, little more. Taking her daughter's palm, she folded some money into it.

"They are going to release you. Take this money, hire a gharry and go to the Shepherd's Hotel. It is a large building, the driver will know the way. Await an Englishman named Kenneth, the duke of Caldwell. Do not let anyone stop you from trying to see him. Tell him I am here. He is kind and will protect you."

Doubt shadowed the little girl's face. Badra squeezed her hands. "Please, you must trust me," she implored. "It is the only way I can save you from here."

Jasmine looked up at her, eyes shining with innocence and goodness. In them Badra saw a flicker of her own childhood, innocent and joy-filled, until all had been stolen from her.

She must save her daughter.

"I will do it," Jasmine whispered.

Badra stood, gripping her daughter's shoulder as the men returned. "I am taking her to find transportation," she told Masud in a cold voice. "I do not trust you."

Two armed guards escorted them outside into the open courtyard ringing the building. A waxing moon hung low in the sky. Badra glanced up, hoping her namesake would guide her daughter's steps. Clutching her arms, the guards grimly bracketed her. Jasmine walked ahead, tossing anxious glances over her shoulder as they cleared the courtyard and moved outside. The brothel lay at the end of a deserted street, in a private clearing, like a pasha's secluded mansion. Badra walked toward the street's end until they reached the crossroad, a main street where pedestrian traffic became thicker. She spotted a gharry driver waiting with his horse.

"Go to that man. Do as I told you," she told Jasmine.

The child turned, uncertainty playing over her face.

"Go," Badra said, shoving her, feeling scalding tears burn her eyes. "Now! Run, Jasmine."

Her little girl scampered away, picking up the skirts of her gown. The guards watched silently as Badra uttered a low prayer.

"Go with God, little one. May He keep you safe."

Then she and the guards turned and they marched her back to the brothel.

Jabari wasted no time with questions when Kenneth told him what had happened; he insisted on accompanying the duke. Kenneth purchased first-class compartment tickets for the sheikh, himself, Rashid and Ramses. Their unity reminded him of the tight-knit bond among the Khamsin.

Worry and rage battled inside him. On the train to Cairo, his emotions choked him like a snake's tightening coils. He slid the dagger Badra had dropped at the dig site out of its sheath, staring at it.

Once he'd cut his palm with this, and tossed it at her feet. Now it had become a symbol of their past. Their present.

Badra never did anything without reason. She craved the familiar and the comfortable. Few things drove Badra, but what did, she reacted to with ruthless determination.

To return to the brothel where she had been sold equated to flinging herself into a pit of hissing snakes. It sounded self-destructive, yet Kenneth recognized the stubborn jut of her chin. It could only mean one thing. Something terribly important was at stake.

She was in deep trouble, and he had to know why. She had shut herself off, erecting barriers thicker than any pyramid walls. He had to break the barriers down, find out what she hid.

They disembarked the train in Cairo. At the Shepherd's Hotel, Kenneth led the way inside to the front desk, ignoring the puzzled stares of the genteel guests. He passed a clump of chattering Englishmen calling out greetings and halted dead as a little girl wearing a long scarlet gown embroidered with tiny yellow flowers darted in front of him.

A thin girl, her tangle of hair was dark as midnight. She looked at him beseechingly. "Please, sir, are you the Duke of Caldwell?"

A porter, striding past, spotted her. A torrent of angry Arabic filled the air. "Urchin! I told you to leave and stop begging from guests! She's been asking every single Englishman that since she arrived last night."

The dark-haired child's chin jutted out stubbornly, reminding him of Badra. She clung to Kenneth's trouser-leg like a limpet. With a regal wave, he dismissed the porter, then squatted down to face the girl.

"Are you Jasmine?" he asked in Arabic.

"Yes. I'm Badra's sister. She says she awaits you at the Pleasure Palace."

Dismay gnawed at him. Kenneth stared at the child, her woebegone expression, the brave way she thrust her chin upward. A courageous front, when her insides wanted to crumble, he guessed. Again, just like Badra. . . .

"Where did you come from, little one?" he asked gently.

Fear glittered in those huge brown eyes. "I came from the Pleasure Palace. Badra . . . said they were releasing me, but she stayed. Why?"

The words Badra had spoken slammed into him. Like a veil lifting from his eyes, he understood all. His throat constricted with emotion. "She stayed because she must love you, very, very much, honey."

Enough to trade herself for your freedom.

The Khamsin sheikh and the others gathered around in a circle. "Badra's sister?" Jabari frowned.

"Not her sister," Kenneth replied slowly in English, standing and facing the sheikh. "Her daughter. And Fareeq's."

For a comical moment he relished the shocked looks on the others' faces. Jasmine looked clearly bewildered at the strange tongue the white Englishman spoke. Kenneth drew her to his side, rested a hand atop her head. Feeling a slight trembling, he glanced down. The poor thing shook with fear. He withdrew a small wrapped oval from his pocket and removed the paper. Kenneth bent down, offering it to her.

"Do you like lemon drops?"

She took the candy with a solemn expression. "What are they?"

"Try one," he encouraged.

Her elfin face lit up with pleasure as she popped one into her mouth. Kenneth smiled.

"Don't worry, Jasmine," he told her softly. "Badra trusted me to protect you, and I will."

Her large eyes, too adult and solemn for her years, regarded him. "Badra said I should trust you." Jasmine slipped her hand into his. "I trust her, so I'll trust you."

The simple declaration tightened his chest. He beckoned to Ramses. "This is Ramses. He has a little girl, and he is a good father. He's going to take care of you for awhile."

Jasmine warily studied the muscular warrior who smiled gently at her.

"Does he have more lemon drops?"

Ramses held out his hand. Kenneth laughed. He gave the sweets to his friend. "Now he does. Go with him, honey."

He watched Ramses lead her over to a cluster of over-stuffed chairs in the lobby and do what any good father would—soothe a child who had suffered obvious trauma. Jabari stared at them, slack-jawed, clearly dazed.

"Why did Badra not tell us?" he finally managed to ask.

"I imagine she desired to keep her identity a secret because she was afraid of having borne an illegitimate child. The child of the man you hated above all others."

The sheikh looked horrified. "Does she think I would not welcome her daughter into the tribe?"

Kenneth's gaze was even but not incriminating. "Do you

remember what you once said—about how any children of Fareeq's you'd consider enemies and be forced to destroy?"

Blood drained from Jabari's face. He looked stricken.

"I said that in a rage. I would never hurt Badra's child."

Kenneth sighed. "I know. Let me go arrange rooms for all of us. I have an account in this hotel."

Jabari's gaze was as even as Kenneth's had been minutes before. "And where will you go, Khepri?"

"I'm going to get Badra back," he answered grimly.

Rashid bristled and spoke up. "That is my duty," he snapped.

"You lack the money," Kenneth replied with blunt honesty. "And they will be less suspicious of an English duke desiring a bit of exotic entertainment than of an Egyptian warrior."

"So, the wealthy English duke desires to purchase Badra. You think your money will buy anything, do you not? But it will not buy you honor," Rashid shot back.

"You dare to insult me?"

The man's dark eyes, filled with venom, met his. "I dare to tell the truth. You want to purchase Badra to finally use her as your whore."

Violent anger exploded inside Kenneth. He went to swing a fist, hesitating just in time, remembering Jasmine. He glanced at the little girl sitting next to Ramses.

"Not here," he grated through clenched teeth. "Let's take this outside."

Jabari remained silent, nodding slightly as Rashid's gaze whipped to his. With a grunt, Rashid trailed Kenneth outside. Past the elegant terrace where elderly men sipped afternoon tea, down the steps past the snake charmer entertaining tourists, on the street below they faced each other.

"Let's have it out, Rashid. You and me. Right now."

The man's dark gaze burned. "Gladly," he replied.

Kenneth did not wait. Women strolling idly with their English husbands screamed as his fist smashed into Rashid's chin. "That's for insulting me," he growled.

Rashid did not even flinch. The two men began sparring. Rashid's hard fist slammed into Kenneth's stomach. He doubled over, wheezing. Damn, the man had a hard punch.

"That is for insulting Jabari, my sheikh, when you left for England," Rashid jeered.

Dodging a follow-up blow, Kenneth managed to land a glancing punch. Rashid winced, pulling back.

This was ridiculous, squabbling like schoolboys. Kenneth grabbed Rashid by the lapels of his indigo *binish,* drawing him close. The warrior's nostrils flared.

"Listen to me," Kenneth said in a low, dangerous tone. "Badra's mine. She always was. I'll do whatever I must to save her. She gave up everything to free her little girl from slavery. I'm going in to rescue her, but I doubt I can do it alone. If you'll stop being such a pigheaded fool, you'll help me and stop wasting my time."

Rashid's lips thinned to a tight slash, but he did not raise his fists again. Instead, he glared at Kenneth.

"Always yours, Kenneth? To degrade? To use and discard? I would die before I allowed you to hurt her!"

"Good God," Kenneth shot back. "You think I would do that? I'd thrust a knife into myself first. I love her!"

Damn. He hadn't meant to confess that.

"What?" Rashid asked, knitting his brows.

"I love her," Kenneth said simply, releasing his grip. "I always have. Always will. All those years I was her falcon guard, I loved her."

A troubled frown touched Rashid's face. He seemed to sag into himself, brooding. "You love her," he repeated incredulously.

"I love her. And I would never, ever hurt her. Not deliberately. I'd do anything to assure her happiness."

A shadow passed over Rashid's features.

"Will you help me then? Let's put aside this foolish quarreling and, for once, stick together to help the woman we both seem to care about." Kenneth thrust out a hand.

For a minute he thought the warrior would refuse and push him aside in anger. But instead, Rashid shook it. "I will."

A grin found Kenneth's face. "Good. Now clean up, man. You look like hell."

"You look worse," Rashid accused as they trudged up the steps.

Kenneth found the brothel on the outskirts of Cairo after dropping a discreet word to the gharry driver, along with a few coins. The building looked like an upscale Cairene home, with its two stories and solid wood door. However, it sat on a stretch of secluded land with no immediate neighbors—no one to hear the screams of the little girls enslaved there.

Opulent furnishings greeted him as he was escorted inside. Thick jewel-toned Persian carpets laid upon the marbled floors and the tall ceilings featured corniced moldings. Kenneth discovered an auction would take place the following afternoon. Two women were being sold, one of them Badra.

He returned to his hotel, frustrated and restless. Jabari said little when he heard the news, only that he'd sent for a few more warriors to join them. Kenneth sent a hasty cable to his solicitor in London, instructing him to wire a large sum to a bank in Cairo. He would need that to purchase Badra. He found Zaid and ordered him to the dig site to explain his quick departure to de Morgan and Victor as "an urgent business matter." Kenneth told Zaid to remain there and keep an eye on Victor. He did not trust his cousin.

That night, in his lavish suite, he could not sleep. He lay in the expansive, wide bed. Mosquito netting draped about him like a shroud. His sleep was plagued with dreams of another man buying Badra, dragging her toward a dark room, the door slowly closing, her wide, terrified eyes shut away from him. Her screams pierced his ears.

He returned to the Pleasure Palace the next afternoon. Hovering in the *ka'ah*—the spacious reception room—with the other men awaiting the sale, he willed away his rage. Dozens of men sat on red cushions on the floor with straight-back pillows resting against the wall, or they milled about, sampling dates and drinking fruit juices. Kenneth sat, drumming his fingers on one knee.

When the Palace guards called the potential buyers into the adjacent room, he tightened his resolve. But nothing could prepare him for the agony of seeing who was on the raised dais. Wide dark eyes, ebony hair—she was beautiful as the desert night and its thousands of stars sparkling overhead.

Scarlet skirts clutched in one clenched fist, her chin upright and defiant, Badra stared out into the sea of men. Lust in their eyes, they made crude remarks. Instinct demanded Kenneth yank her off the platform, gather her into his sheltering arms and flee. Protecting her was his nature. He had to save her.

She was being sold as a concubine in her daughter's place, he realized. Her fierce love astounded him, humbled him. But why had she stolen the artifacts? For the same reason? He needed more answers.

His heart ached as he beheld her, fear sparkling in her dark eyes, yet she stood regally upon the dais. Badra did not tremble. A rough mixture of love and desire rushed through his heated blood as the auction master turned her around, displaying her in a way Kenneth had only dared dream about in the years Jabari entrusted him to her care.

Violence coursed through him, desire to pound the snickering auction master with his fists and show the man the might of an angered Khamsin warrior. Kenneth locked his gaze on Badra's face. He summoned all the discipline he had learned as a warrior, when his own desire had brewed inside him. When he had wanted nothing more than to tumble Badra to the sand and thrust deeply into the soft portal of her lush body and whisper words of passion in her delicate, shell-like ear. When he would have sold his soul merely to be around her.

Mine, mine, mine. The possessive chant filled him as he glared at the other men. The same craving was reflected in their greedy faces, as if Badra were a tasty dish to be consumed.

But he had never, not once in the five years he had guarded her, thought of her as something to be used and discarded. These men did not know her, could not appreciate her. Kenneth felt all the love he had restrained come pouring out like the ocean upon dry sand. He looked at Badra and silently sent a message, praying she somehow could hear.

I love you. I will not let another man use you for his lust and violate what I sought for five years to guard—your honor, your virtue. You are not goods to be bought and sold. You deserve love, a man who will cherish you as the treasure you are. You are more precious to me than gold. I would give up all the riches I own to hold you in my arms for one single night. I would sacrifice all my tomorrows for one night of your true love.

He burned hotter as he caught a glimpse of her shapely calf. The auction master had lifted the gown, leering as he did so, to show off what awaited Badra's buyer in bed. Kenneth swore silently, his hand going to his waistband. No scimitar. He had only his wits and his burning love to drive him on.

Kenneth gritted his teeth. He glanced around at the men crowding the platform. Sensing her terror, he willed a message to Badra.

Do not fear. I will not let them have you.

Her evil past was unfolding again before her eyes. Badra stared into the faceless crowd, unwilling to let them see her fear, her shame at being sold like a sheep. She'd already faced this, at age eleven, shivering and confused, fearful of the darkness in the eyes of the men staring at her with great hunger. Then she had known nothing of men. Now she knew.

Minutes passed in agonizing slowness. Badra bit hard on

her lower lip as the auction master raised her gown to midthigh.

"Look here, my good friends. Have you ever seen such a treasure? Surely this one will bring you to paradise when you take her to bed. She is not a virgin but well-versed in the arts of sensual delight."

Murmurs filled the air, cackling noises that splintered her self-possession. If they saw her fear, they would frenzy like desert jackals. Badra steeled her spine and tried to quiet her heart rate. *You are not a spectacle. You will not let these men intimidate you.*

She needed a focus, a peaceful place of serenity that would shut out the leering men and their ribald remarks.

Khepri. She did not see him in the crowd.

His image flashed in her mind. His startling blue eyes, his fierce warrior's might, his polish and urbane charm as an English duke. How much he'd changed. And yet, not at all. He was a man of honor. A man of might. Her protector. What would Khepri say to defray her fears?

He would wink and say, *"Look at them. Don't be afraid. Imagine them naked and impotent. The sagging paunches, the dimples in their overweight bottoms, their tiny little . . ."*

A bubble of hope rose. She thought of Khepri scrutinizing the portly man in the front row. *"Look at him. Have you ever seen a man with so many chins? Do you think he has three wives for each chin? Does each chin have a name?"*

Oh Khepri, she thought silently, wishing with all her heart to see him. *You once made me laugh. You always made me feel safe. Even now, when you are far away, I am surrounded by your memories and I can survive.*

217

Resolve filled her to stand upright and throw back her shoulders. Smiling, Badra kept the image of Khepri in mind, his friendly grin and breezy self-assurance, his tender concern and remarkable courage.

Khepri had been placed on a stage like this when he'd returned to England—stared at and studied like her potential bidders were doing to her now. The insight startled her. Had Kenneth felt as naked as she did? Yet he seemed to handle the role of English nobleman with charm, never once intimating he minded the quiet scrutiny of his peers, minded being weighed and measured like a commodity.

Knowing her former falcon guard had probably suffered a similar torment gave her new courage. Badra relaxed. Until the bidding began. Then she swallowed hard.

"Gentlemen! This lovely lady is available to one man, exclusively, for a month of pure pleasure. The bidding opens at five hundred pounds."

Fingers flicked, heads nodded, and the bids climbed higher and higher. Panic tightened her chest. Forced to endure a new master every month? It was worse than she'd thought. The bidding rose to one thousand pounds. Two thousand. Badra thought of Khepri's reassuring smile, his tender manner. She must not panic. Khamsin warriors never showed emotion before the enemy. Nor would she.

The man casting the last bid on her stood toward the front. His face was lean and hollow-cheeked. He had a cruel smile. Badra could not prevent a shudder from racing down her spine, nor the icy fingers of fear wrapping about her heart.

Then, "Five thousand pounds," a quiet voice said, and it held an air of arrogant assurance.

All heads swerved toward the back, toward the commanding voice that had softly dominated the airless, musty room. It sounded like Khepri's voice, but Badra could not be sure. She craned her neck to see. The auction master slapped her.

"Mind your place!" he snapped.

Dared she hope? No other offers followed. The room remained draped in awed silence.

The auction master barked, "Sold! Good sir, please retreat to the *ka'ah* to make arrangements to pay—and to collect your new concubine. She will see to all your wildest desires."

Badra was hustled off before she glimpsed the tall, dark-garbed stranger, his face shrouded in shadows. She could only pray with all her heart that her new master's manner with her did not match the tempered steel in that deep voice.

The building was fashioned like many lavish Cairene buildings, with a large inner courtyard and dark wooded lattice-work windows overlooking lush gardens. Inside, a high ceiling and elaborate tile work decorated the private apartment. Divans and heavy cushions were scattered about the room. Set into a small alcove was an obscenely large bed. Silk pillows sat atop a richly embroidered coverlet.

Two eunuchs guarded the door, granting no one but her new master access and barring her escape. Rubbing her arms, Badra paced, fighting her razor-sharp fear. You can do this, she reassured herself. You are a mature, experienced woman, not a frightened eleven-year-old virgin.

But she felt as scared as that long-ago child.

A full-length brass-edged mirror mounted on a wall caught her attention. Badra wandered over to examine her appearance. Large terrified eyes outlined in black kohl stared back at her. A silk gown of turquoise with white flounces covered her body. A sheer veil of white gauze fringed with coins hid her face. The veil served to add to the mystique of the exotic surroundings and excite her new owner, not to cover her modesty.

She wore saffron-colored slippers of soft kid leather, edged with turquoise piping and embroidered with tiny turquoise-and-white flowers. The slippers brought a shudder—too much like those she had worn when first enslaved.

Resigned, she walked over to the bed, testing it with one hand. Soft as a cloud. Knowing what would happen there shook her self-confidence. Badra sat, wrapping her arms about herself.

Who would it be? Another cruel, sadistic man who laughed and raped her until her mind grew numb? Perhaps this time she'd be fortunate and her master would rut upon her but not flay her with a whip.

She thought of Khepri, how gently he used to take her hand when they walked into the village of Amarna. How he had guided her back to Jabari's home. His fierce blue eyes had roved the streets, ever-watchful for enemies. She rested assured in his scimitar, which was always ready to slay any who dared touch her.

Khepri. Now Kenneth. So foreign she scarcely recognized him, his tall, leanly-muscled frame exuding only confident power. He belonged to a green land far across the water, this man who had once gazed at her with such love and devotion.

Footsteps pounded down the corridor. Badra tensed. Her clammy fingers plucked at the gauze of her harem trousers, and she hugged herself tighter as the wooden door opened. She heard the hard, firm click of masculine heels walk inside. Quivering, Badra stared at the floor and saw approaching brown leather boots.

She forced herself to speak. "My master, I am most willing to do whatever you wish of me. All I ask is—please, please, do not beat me." The words came out in a trembling whisper.

The bed sank with her new captor's weight. A hand caught her chin, lifted it up. With every last ounce of courage, Badra lifted her gaze. And found herself looking directly into a familiar pair of deep blue eyes.

"My dear Badra," the Duke of Caldwell said softly. "How can I make you understand? As long as I draw breath, no one will ever hurt you."

Chapter Seventeen

Stark relief slammed into her with the force of a raging wind. She closed her eyes, opened them, afraid he was a mirage. Kenneth tenderly regarded her.

"Jasmine? Is she safe?" she asked hopefully.

Kenneth laid a finger on her lips. He glanced at the eunuchs standing guard and issued a crisp command. "Leave us."

When they had left, he gave her an expectant look. A shiver of misgiving shot through her at his grave expression.

"Your daughter is safe with Jabari."

She could only stare in growing horror. Her jaw dropped as she struggled to make sense of his words.

"Your daughter, Jasmine. You did this because of her?"

"She's my sister . . . ," she argued.

Her denial died with the keen look he gave her. "No, Badra. Your daughter. She has your eyes, your stubborn little chin. And the remarks you made, about a mother's love. She's the daughter you bore to Fareeq. I know. Jabari does as well."

Panic gripped her. "He does? I was afraid to tell him. Jabari once said any children of Fareeq's he would consider his enemy and be forced to destroy."

"Jabari said that long ago in a rage. He would never, ever hurt any child of yours," he gently explained.

Kenneth's intent blue eyes found hers and he reached into his pocket. The gold pectoral of Amenemhat II's cartouche dangled from his hand. Badra's breath hitched audibly.

"Why did you try to steal this, Badra? For Rashid?" As her brow wrinkled in bewilderment, he added grimly, "Rashid tried to kill me back in London as I slept."

"Rashid would not kill you," she argued. Then she paused. She remembered how they had nearly come to blows in the antique shop.

"Perhaps he merely wanted to wound me, to see if I was still a warrior. Did he ask you to steal for him?"

"Never! He knew . . . he tried to protect me. It was Omar, the owner of the Pleasure Palace. Fareeq sold Jasmine to Omar after they told me she"—her voice hitched—"died. Omar wanted me and used Jasmine to lure me back. The price of freeing her was taking her place. The other option was stealing the cartouches. When I didn't obtain the one at Dashur, I had to trade my freedom for hers." Her voice dropped. "I'm sorry. I was desperate."

"Why didn't you tell me? I would have helped you."

"A raid, guns firing and Jasmine getting hurt? They threatened to sell her to a wealthy buyer if I told you. I would never see her again." A violent tremor shook her.

Kenneth dropped the cartouche on the table beside the bed. His palms settled on her hands, calming her. Still, de-

223

spite his courage, she knew he could not smuggle her out. The brothel had an interior courtyard, armed eunuchs standing guard. It was a fortress.

She told him this, adding softly, "I know it is impossible, for I tried as a child to escape. And failed."

Assuredness shone in his eyes. "Getting you out is going to be a bit of a challenge, that's all. A challenge."

Wild hope flared inside her, then died. "No. You can't get me out. It's too dangerous. No one can save me."

Kenneth flashed his old grin. "That's what you said when we first met, remember? Remember what I told you?"

A faint smile surfaced. "The Khamsin never fail."

"Not then and not now. I will find a way. But I'm afraid it will take time."

"You have exactly one month." She dropped her smile and sighed. "As long as Jasmine is safe. She's all that matters."

Kenneth marveled at Badra's enormous courage—and ached at the resignation in her soft voice. A knot formed in his throat. He envisioned her body huddled protectively around her daughter, her large chocolate-colored eyes scared but resolved. Fear resting inside her like a block of ice, but her rising above it, pushing it aside because of Jasmine. Badra was fierce as a predator when it came to something so important. She would have forced herself to become a slave only for Jasmine.

The depth of that love humbled him. He touched her hand gently, so as to not frighten her. God, she was scared enough as it was—and cold. So cold, like she'd been immersed in water.

Stiff as an alabaster statue, she sat on the bed, fingers

clutching her silk trousers so tightly her knuckles whitened. She stared, questions dancing in her big brown eyes. *What next?*

He knew what he wanted to do. He wanted to warm her, inside and out. To brush the panicked look off her face with a gentle kiss. To feel her lips turn moist and pliant beneath his, and then deepen the kiss. To melt away fear until all that remained was heated, intense anticipation. He wanted to make her writhe and moan in ecstasy. To cause the sweet hollow between her legs to dampen with moisture as his mouth and hands aroused her. To sink slowly into her and feel her tighten around him.

He wanted to push her until she strained against him. Until his heat poured into her and she'd never be cold again. And when at last he took her to the peak of pleasure, he wanted to swallow her cry in his mouth and start anew, loving her without mercy until she clung to him, exhausted. Only then would he allow himself release.

But he needed to discover the truth he suspected she hid: the real reason why she had pulled away from him. "Badra, undress for me. And turn around. I need to see your back."

Convulsive shock slammed into her. She would be forced to reveal the very thing she hated most about herself to the man she secretly loved. A thick lump clogged her throat.

"Please. Do not ask me to do this. I cannot."

Kenneth's expression softened as he touched her cheek. "I don't wish to hurt you, little one. But I must know."

Motionless, she watched him tug her veil down. When his fingers drifted away and slowly unlaced the satin ribbon holding closed her gossamer gown, her trembling hand caught his.

He easily shook off her grip and slipped the gown from her shoulders. It dropped free, baring her breasts. Her large, frightened eyes met his.

"Please, Khepri," she begged, her voice shaking.

Tears soaked her cheeks. Badra's heart sank as she stared into his face. His large hands felt warm on her quivering shoulders as he turned her around.

"I'm sorry," he said quietly. "But I must see for myself."

Kenneth flung her tangled mass of ebony curls over one shoulder. She jerked at his touch and tried to writhe away, but he held her steady. He laid a warm, gentle hand upon the twisted scar tissue lacing her back. Deep shame flushed her from neck to cheeks. Badra hung her head as his fingertips stroked the old wounds that still stung with shame.

"Damn him to hell," he said hoarsely. "That fat bastard."

She quivered and bit her lip, memories hurting as much as the sting of the lash. Her secret was out.

Bile rose in his throat.

Evidence of Fareeq's cruelty lay in deep white streaks carved into Badra's tender skin. The sheikh, her former master, had flogged her. Severely. Badra had lied to him. And judging from her tormented expression, *she* was the one who was ashamed.

"What else did he do, Badra? Did he rape you as well?"

A shaky nod confirmed his suspicions. Kenneth sucked in an angry breath. "How old were you?"

A sob shook her shoulders. "I w-was . . . eleven."

He swore loudly. Just a little girl. Kenneth's gut tightened as he envisioned the sweet child she must have been, wide-eyed and pretty, turning into a shallow ghost of herself, silent and tormented. Her bewildered wails of fear and pain as Fareeq forced her—

Damn it! Why hadn't he seen it? Because he hadn't wanted to, Kenneth admitted. He hadn't wanted to suspect the brutal truth.

"I'm sorry, Khepri," she said in a choking sob. "Jabari knew but I begged him to remain silent. I should have trusted you with this secret. I wish I had. You always protected me; you always safeguarded my steps. But I was too . . . ashamed."

She trembled violently. Deeply concerned, he began rubbing her naked back, trying to soothe her. He ached to see the torment pulsing inside her. *Oh Badra,* he said silently. *I vow you will never suffer such injustice again, my love.* A primitive masculine rage rose in him. He wished Fareeq alive, so he could crush her tormentor under his heel, force him to his knees before Badra to beg forgiveness. Although not one drop of Egyptian blood ran in his veins, he shared the stark, raging protectiveness the Khamsin felt toward their women.

He went to draw her into his arms, and she stiffened. When she spoke, her voice was as wooden as her body.

"So, you have purchased me. And you know the value of your purchase. I know what you've always wanted. If you will, please, get on with it."

She shrugged out of her gown and slippers. Naked, sitting on the bed, Badra looked ready to collapse. If he touched her, she'd shatter like glass. Frustrated, Kenneth jammed a hand through his hair.

When he made no move toward her, she glanced up. "Why did you buy me, Khepri?"

Why? A lifetime of wanting, dreaming, smelling her in his sleep, reaching for her in his dreams. He'd loved her for so long that she had branded herself on his heart.

He said none of these things to her, though, only stroked a line across the bed, imagining he stroked her soft cheek. "I bought you because I would do anything to keep you from being hurt. Just as I vowed long ago when I was your falcon guard."

Khamsin warriors were taught discipline and strict self-control. He needed every ounce of what he'd learned. With tenderness and gentle reassurance, he would coax Badra into his arms. He would teach her the deep pleasures awaiting her. But only when she wanted it. When she knew he loved her. When she wanted him to love her. Not now.

"Are you hungry?"

Wary hesitation showed on her face. "Yes."

"Good. Get dressed and I'll have food brought in."

He ordered a feast for a sultan. He knew her tastes after all this time. A bevy of servants marched in and out, bearing platters of Badra's favorite dishes on their outstretched palms. There was a silver salver of roast lamb on a bed of rice, a bowl of fresh oranges, grapes, dates and pomegranates, a basket of warm yeast rolls beneath a blue-and-white checked cloth, wedges of flat bread, and *Ful Mudammas*. A carafe of sugared tea followed, with cups. A small bowl of honey. A carafe of rich red wine and two crystal glasses.

They settled on soft velvet cushions on the floor on opposite sides of a low mahogany table. Kenneth popped a grape past his lips. He bit down, sweetness flooding his mouth. Badra would be like that, he decided—a heady rush upon his tongue. "I am sure you are hungry, and there is a feast here for two," he said mildly.

He could see interest flare as she stared at the food. Cautiously she reached for a date, nibbled at it with the edge of her small, white teeth.

Awareness of her pulsed through his body. He could take her; it was his right. He'd bought her, and he knew she wanted him sometimes. But that was not his way. She must come to him, warm and willing. He would simply wait. Take his time—ease her natural fears away until he broke them down, one by one. He would unlock the deep wellspring of her passion and allow it to flood all else until she obeyed her body's hunger to surrender.

Kenneth ate another grape slowly, savoring it as a servant poured tea for them both and wine for him. Badra took a long gulp and set down her glass, continuing to watch him like a trapped mouse eyeing a cobra. He dismissed the servant, who padded out as quietly as she'd entered.

He licked a drop of juice from his lips. Badra watched, clearly enthralled. He said nothing but smiled inside.

He could smell the delicate fragrance of jasmine the women had mixed into Badra's hair after they had bathed her. It stirred his senses. His blood sang in his veins and surged, hot and thick. He allowed himself to relish the anticipation, the want.

Propping his chin upon his fist, Kenneth stared at her. He wanted to indulge every sense, watch the gentle sway of her long black hair as she bent her head over her meal. He wanted to immerse his body in her welcoming warmth.

Kiss every inch of her satin skin. Bury his face in the silken mass of her long curls. Kenneth wanted to trace every inch of her with his tongue, let her know his raging passion.

No, the food had no appeal. He could only see and hear and smell her. Badra. A feast for the senses. A rare Madeira, as exquisite and sharp upon the tongue as the finest wine.

She took a long swallow of tea. Badra tasted a date next, then nibbled on a grape. Kenneth watched, enchanted, as her tiny tongue licked a pearl-like drop from her lips. He pressed his hands into his lap, not surprised at the hardness there.

Suddenly, she gazed at him with troubled eyes. "Kenneth, you are not eating. Why do you look at me like that?"

"I like watching you." He sipped his wine. French. Not bad. Her perfect rosy mouth parted. "Eat," he said softly. "You must be starving."

"I cannot eat." She hugged herself, looking about with large, troubled eyes. "This room . . . the smells."

His brow wrinkled. Kenneth set down his wineglass and sniffed. So intent had he been on studying her that he did not notice. Now the underlying odor hit him—a smell of cigarette smoke, the stale odor of old perfume, and the musky taint of sex. He stood, walked over to the latticed windows, went to open them and realized they were locked.

"They do it to prevent us from jumping. Should we be given a master who does not . . . smell so nice."

Startled, he glanced over and saw her holding her nose. Kenneth laughed, charmed. A small smile touched her rosebud mouth. That mouth, so lush and carnal—he ached to taste it. Instead, he resumed his seat, poured himself some wine and went to pour some for her as well. She held up a hand.

He raised a brow. "Just for tonight. It will help you sleep. Trust me."

The glass shook a little as her fingers curled around its stem. Badra took a long pull, then drew back, her mouth wet with wine. He wanted her as desperately as he had years ago. But he was no eager, hot-blooded youth of nineteen. He had a man's restraint and a warrior's honor. Tension crackled in the air. Badra looked away, studying the exquisite Persian tapestry covering the walls.

"Why did you turn me down when I asked to you marry me, Badra? I want the real answer this time."

Silence hung heavy in the air. Finally she sighed, the sound so forlorn it wrenched his heart. "How could I marry you, Kenneth? After all you've just learned?" Her voice dropped an octave. "I told Jabari you were a good man who deserved better. I knew I could never be the kind of wife you expected."

"The kind of wife I *expected?*"

"I could not be your wife, Kenneth," she whispered. "I am terrified of . . . the intimacy a wife and husband share."

"Oh, Badra," he said gently, reaching out to touch her hand. She recoiled and buried her face in her hands.

"I never meant to insult you or hurt you." Her voice leaked out between her trembling palms.

One year of trying to banish her from his mind, and still she remained buried deep inside him like tiny grains of sand ground deep into his heart. In those dark chocolate eyes he saw her pain and fear. Why hadn't he seen it before?

Pride, he admitted with brutal honesty. He had been humiliated that she had turned him down three times; he had not been thinking of her.

He had nothing left to lose. Kenneth reached across the table as her hands dropped. He caught her chin with a gentle grip, forcing her to look directly at him.

"So, Badra, answer me another question. Did you ever love me?"

Moisture sparkled in her eyes, making them glisten like dark gems. "How could I not?" Her broken voice shattered him. "Your kindness, your humor, the way you always put my needs before your own. Your fierce sense of honor and courage. The way your eyes looked at me with a love that would never die. And all those years that you kept your vow never to touch me, despite wanting to—and I know how you wanted to! That one kiss you wanted to steal . . . how many times I would lie in my bed at night and regret I pushed you away."

She paused. Her hands pressed against her heart. "I knew I could never tell you how I felt; I couldn't return your passion and you deserve a woman of passion. So I kept my love hidden inside like a precious jewel. I loved you the first time you made me laugh. I was dead before I met you, and you revived me. I dreamed of you taking me into your strong arms, teaching me not to be afraid. So many times my fear and my dreams would clash like Khamsin steel. The fear always won, so I turned you down. But I never stopped loving you."

Kenneth could barely breathe. All these years thinking perhaps she didn't return his affection, that she merely regarded him as a friend. He felt his dreams spark and flare into an all-consuming fire. Her love was true and as great as his. She'd tucked it away, cherishing it, and pushed him off because she thought he deserved someone better.

He saw her life, stretched out like the barren sands of the great Sahara, wanting love, fearing it. Putting up barriers to ward off his affections when he turned from being her friendly, protective guard into an ardent suitor.

With all his might he wished he could yank back the veil of time and woo her as she deserved. To demonstrate the pleasures of how a man and woman shared their bodies, and to banish her fears.

Kenneth dropped his hold on her chin to gently trace a single teardrop rolling down her cheek. With his thumb, he wiped it away.

She was frightened, like a skittish mare scenting a stallion. He must gentle her fears.

"Never again," he said hoarsely. "I promise you, little one. I will never let another man hurt you, not as long as one drop of blood runs in my veins."

Badra offered a smile that wrenched his heart. "I know you wish to help, Khepri. But there are some things beyond even your courage and might. You can't rescue me from here, try as you will."

"You haven't seen me begin," he stated grimly.

Confusion tightened her face as he stood. "Where are you going?"

"Back to the hotel. To tell Jabari you're safe." He turned. "Do not, under any circumstances, leave this room. I'll pay someone to guard you while I'm gone."

He slammed the door behind him and stalked off.

Chapter Eighteen

Kenneth stepped down the hallway, mentally noting corridors, twists, turns and accessibility. He turned a corner and found a doorway guarded by a stern bald eunuch, scimitar strapped to his side. An outside doorway?

The guard's face was impassive, though the man was polite. "If you are looking for an exit, sir, use the main entrance."

"I suppose that door won't get me to the *ka'ah*," he reasoned, watching the man's eyes.

"It only leads to the second-floor balcony."

The second-floor balcony, which had a stairwell leading to the courtyard interior. Good. Kenneth met the man's gaze. "I have need of a few things. Whom shall I ring?"

"Use the bellpull in the room, sir, and servants will bring you anything you desire."

"I need someone I can trust." Kenneth reached into his trouser pocket and withdrew a large wad of pound notes. As expected, the guard's eyes widened.

"I want someone to stand at the door to my concubine's apartments. I do not want anyone entering."

The man nodded. "I can have someone replace me here."

"Good. I'll need someone to go to the market as well. I want jasmine flowers. Fresh flowers, not perfume."

"How many, sir?"

"Enough to fill a room. But they must be fresh." Kenneth peeled off a few notes, making a show of counting them. Greed shone like diamonds in the guard's eyes. Kenneth handed over the notes.

"This is for you, for doing me this tremendous favor."

Kenneth took more bills and handed them over. "And this is for the purchases and for the person running the errand."

A small smile like the edge of his scimitar curved the guard's lips upward. Kenneth prayed the man would be loyal.

Khamsin warriors had invaded the Shepherd's Hotel.

In amused amazement, Kenneth sat on a large chair in the suite he had booked for Jabari. The sheikh sat opposite him, his dark gaze firm. All around Jabari was a sea of indigo-garbed men, curled up on bedrolls, sleeping on the floor, as they would before launching an attack upon an enemy tribe. Twelve of the tribe's best fighters. He wondered what the manager thought of the Khamsin invasion of indigo and sharp steel in this genteel European hotel.

"He protested so many of us, but when he discovered we are the duke of Caldwell's honored guests, he quieted," Jabari said.

Kenneth eyed the scimitar lying within the sheikh's reach, imagining the sight of several fierce warriors nudging the manager. That would explain his acquiescence more than any ducal status.

"They don't all have to stay with you, Jabari."

"My men will get rooms, but for tonight they wished to stay here, until we heard from you. We brought a woman with us to care for the child. Tomorrow I will send Jasmine back to our camp, where she will remain with Elizabeth. Rashid is with her, guarding her until then." The sheikh arched a black brow. "We did not require the extra room and have saved you money."

"Thank you for your consideration. I imagine the food bill will even the balance," he said dryly.

"Who can eat at a time like this?" Jabari mused.

Dressed in a comfortable white robe, with soft white cotton trousers, the sheikh had removed his turban. His inky black hair spilled past his shoulders. But despite the relaxed attire, tension knotted Kenneth's friend. Dark shadows hollowed beneath his eyes. The sheikh sat woodenly in his chair, muscles clenched as if waiting to attack.

Kenneth hadn't seen his foster brother this anxious in years, not since Elizabeth had been held captive by Fareeq. Jabari worried deeply about Badra. Kenneth hastened to give reassurance.

"Badra is well. She's mine for the time being."

"You purchased her?"

"Would you have seen her sold to someone else?"

"I would have seen her not sold at all," the sheikh said evenly. "Are you aware this is the same brothel where she was sold as a child?"

Kenneth grunted. "Yes. And I intend to get her out."

"Good. Then give us the word and we will invade."

"No, Jabari. You can't storm in there. You'll endanger Badra and the other women. Give me time to memorize the

236

harem layout, to find its weaknesses. I have a month before she'll be re-sold."

The sheikh's dark gaze sought his. "Return to us then, Khepri, when you have full knowledge of how we may best rescue her. But guard her well."

"I will honor the vow I once gave to protect her with my life," he said solemnly.

The sheikh wore a thoughtful look. "You said you loved her, Khepri. Badra needs the love of a good man. She is lovely as her namesake, the moon, but like the moon, she is surrounded by darkness."

Kenneth saw where this was leading and leaned forward, his voice earnest and low. "And your father gave me the honored name of an ancient Egyptian sun god, Khepri. The god represents sunrise, creation and new life. Do you remember, Jabari? He said I was as bright as the sun and just as intense. The moon and the sun cannot exist without each other." He paused. "But the moon is shy, female, and must be gently coaxed into opening fully. And eventually she must surrender to the sun's warming embrace."

"Khepri—the sun god who gives new life," Jabari mused. "Perhaps you will give new life to Badra." The sheikh's eyes darkened. "But know this. If you hurt her, I will not forgive you."

"I will not hurt her."

He stood, wending his way past the sleeping bodies to the doorway, then paused.

"Charge anything you require to my account. Just don't light a fire in the room and roast a lamb in the bedchamber," he advised.

The sheikh gave him an amused look. "Do you think us

barbarians, Khepri? When my men become hungry, we will roast a lamb in the dining room."

His soft laughter followed Kenneth out the door.

Hard boot heels clicking on the marble floor warned of his return. Badra immediately scuttled to the bed and dove under the sheets. Violent shudders racked her body.

Kenneth had left her alone for some time. Now, during the dark of night, he would not. She was both excited and afraid.

Curling into a ball, she lay still. The door opened with a click. An oil lamp burned on a sandalwood table. Sounds assaulted her ears, the plucking and rasping of buttons as he unfastened his shirt. The bed sagged where he sat. A dull thud echoed as his boots hit the floor. There came a muted rustle of trousers and underdrawers sliding off.

He was naked!

Cool air freshened her body as Kenneth lifted the sheet and slid into bed. Badra felt dipped into a bath of ice.

His deep voice startled her. "Jabari knows you are well. I told him I'm going to scout out every inch of this building and form a plan to get you out of here."

His words offered little reassurance. And until then? The question thickened her tongue. When she found her voice, it came out as a rasp.

"What are you going to do to me, Khepri?"

"Badra, I will not lie. I want you."

Tears came to her eyes. Heat enfolded her as he shimmied closer, until the warm hardness of his body pressed against her backside. He lay still, stroking her hair. The male hardness of him pressed against her bottom. Badra tensed. She knew, oh God, she knew what would happen next. Oh please—if he does, I cannot bear it, I swear I cannot. If he turned into a raging lusty beast and the mad look came into his eyes and he pushed himself crudely inside her, she could not bear it.

Not him. Not Khepri. Please, not him.

But he did not move; he merely lay still, stroking her hair. At last he rose and she squeezed her eyes shut, trying desperately to prepare for the inevitable, when he would become a groping beast, grunting and shoving his cock inside her, to rid himself of that hardness, to spill his seed deep into her womb. And then he'd lie back, panting, his eyes glowing with conquest.

The bed shifted, creaked. Something thick and soft fell over her. Badra's shivering ceased. She eased one eye open.

A blanket. Warm thick fleece lay atop her quivering body.

Kenneth moved noiselessly about the room, a Khamsin warrior still. She heard him give a soft sigh as he eased his tall, muscled body onto the large seat beneath the latticed window.

She waited. And waited.

Soft sounds of deep breathing eventually came from the window. He was sleeping. Badra clutched the warm blanket close to her. Relief soothed her body.

He had not touched her.

He was Khepri still. A man of honor.

Her heart beat quietly with love for him as she lay awake in the dark, tears slipping down her cheeks.

239

Chapter Nineteen

That night in her dreams, the past lived on. It approached like a herd of Arabians shaking the sand, but no beauty existed in this black tent. She was eleven, a newly purchased slave to Sheikh Fareeq. Badra lay upon the thin sheepskin bed, its fibers old and graying with dirt and dust, the stench of old sweat and something more intimate and darker ground into the bed skins.

A flimsy crimson gown of gauze covered her thin, undeveloped frame. Her veil was fashioned from the same fabric, and delicate slippers of saffron covered her tiny feet. Badra adored the slippers. They were the only thing of hers left when her parents had left her, sobbing at the brothel, and she clung to them as a child would clutch a battered, favorite doll.

The footsteps stopped outside the tent. Sunlight exploded into the darkness as her master pulled up the door flap and stomped inside. She shook with fear.

Breath stinking of onion and garlic flooded her face. A stench of old sweat. The sheikh removed his robes and unwrapped his black turban. His hair was thick, greasy and lined with threads of white age.

He stood before her, naked, his torso flabby and hairless but for a small thatch of black below the curve of his belly. A phallus the size of her fist jutted out.

She drew back, fear snaking into terror as he came toward her. The same gleam filled his gaze that had maddened the eyes of the men staring at her on the auction block. A meaty fist tore the scarlet gown from her body and ripped off her veil.

Fareeq glanced at the saffron slippers she was so proud of and laughed. "Leave them on," he ordered.

He pushed her flat on her back, against the sheepskins. He shoved at her, forcing her back into the sheepskins. He squeezed her tender young breasts, which were just beginning to show signs of approaching womanhood.

"Boyish," he grunted in disgust. "They had better ripen. You will open your thighs for me every night until my seed takes root in you and my son grows in your belly."

Then he mounted her, his strangling weight pressing her into the sweaty sheepskins. Breath wheezed out of her but she became aware of the little hard tube of flesh poking out from him, poking the soft, secret place between her legs.

With a grunt, he shoved inside her.

A scream of fright rippled from her throat. Fareeq laughed and pushed harder. Burning pain filled her as he ripped inside, pushing harder.

It was over in a minute as he grunted, straining over her. He withdrew, leaving a bloody streak upon her trembling thighs.

"Nothing like a virgin," he leered, wiping himself with

the discarded shreds of her gown. "You will be my new favorite each night, for your sheath is tight and accommodates me nicely." He then settled his bulk upon the bed and fell asleep. Loud snores filled the tent.

Badra curled into a tight ball, crying softly. Each night? She vowed he would not use her again. Tomorrow night, she would fight.

The next night Fareeq undressed as she lay on the sheepskins. "Open your legs for your new master," he ordered.

He went to mount her. Her fingers, curled into a tight fist, smacked him. Fareeq howled. Satisfaction tunneled through her at the smear of crimson on his lip.

"No man is my master." She thrust out her chin.

Panting, he jerked away, his eyes darkening. Fareeq grabbed her, jerking her upward. Terror flooded her as he positioned her between the thick tent poles, binding her naked body between them. Savage anger gleamed in his eyes as he picked up a leather whip and began snapping it.

"No, whore? I'll show you who your master is."

She shrieked as the lash tore into her flesh.

Badra gave a sobbing scream, and Kenneth sat up, startled out of deep sleep. The noise had lacerated him. He ran to the bed. Badra's slender shoulders shook. Kenneth pulled her to him.

"Shhh, it was a dream, my love," he whispered soothingly.

But she did not cease crying. The violence of her sobs alarmed him. In a low voice he began to sing a lullaby he remembered Jabari singing to Tarik as an infant.

Badra's shoulders went still. Then her body shook. She lifted her wet face. She was laughing.

"Oh please, do stop. Jabari was correct," she sputtered. "You *do* have a voice like a camel farting."

He grinned sheepishly and pursed his lips, making a low purr by blowing between them. A sound between a choked sob and a laugh caught in her throat. He pulled her tight against him.

Finally, she quieted. He fetched a cloth. As she wiped her face, Kenneth stroked her hair. "Tell me," he said softly. Badra stiffened. He repeated, "Tell me. Once you tell someone, dreams have no power over you," he assured her.

Finally, her hand squeezed his. Slowly the words spilled out. Kenneth listened, anger clenching his muscles. Damn Fareeq!

He pulled her against him, letting her take reassurance in the simple comfort of being held and cherished. Kenneth pressed a deep kiss against her forehead.

"Never again," he said softly. "I promise you, little love, never again will I allow another man to hurt you."

He eased her back onto the bed. She slept, long lashes lying against her cheeks. For a long while after, Kenneth remained on the bed gazing at her, until a soft knock at the door roused him from his watch.

Badra woke gritty-eyed and disoriented, and sat up, rubbing her eyes. An overpoweringly sweet scent flooded her nostrils. Now she was hallucinating as well! A fragrant illusion, though: the delicious smell reminded her of a flower garden and freedom.

Badra opened her eyes and gasped. The bed was awash in jasmine flowers. Sprigs and sprigs of fresh jasmine floated in bowls and filled ceramic vases throughout the room. The room no longer smelled of stale perfume, rancid smoke or sex.

"Good morning."

Kenneth's deep voice sent a small shiver down her spine. Sitting up, she clutched the sheet to her breasts.

Kenneth sat on the floor before the sandalwood table. A silver pot, two china cups and a tray were laid out. Steam misted the air. She inhaled the tangy scent of Turkish coffee and fresh yeast rolls. Kenneth nodded toward the bed. "A gift for you," he said softly.

Glancing down, she saw a puddle of red. Badra picked up the robe, which was embroidered with tiny gold stars. She stroked the Chinese silk, marveling at the sensual feel between her fingers. "Thank you," she told him.

She slipped the robe on over her yellow gown, went to the small connecting room serving as a necessity, then murmured about visiting the women's bath. Bathing each morning was a requirement for slaves here.

When she returned, he offered her an orange. Badra settled on the table's opposite side, her new robe draped about her in graceful folds. "I loathe oranges."

"How can anyone loathe oranges? It's like biting into a burst of sunshine." He popped a slice into his mouth.

Badra bit into a roll and swallowed hungrily. "You must adore oranges because of your name, Khepri, and being associated with the sun. So if I ever desire to bite into sunshine, I will just bite you," she assured him with a teasing smile. It disappeared when she realized what she had said.

Kenneth grinned and winked. "Any time, feel free to use your teeth on me. I won't bite back."

After a moment she gave in to an odd impulse. "Pity," she said, tossing her hair back.

Kenneth held her gaze in his. He selected another orange slice and gave it a long, slow caress with his tongue. "I didn't say anything about licking, though," he warned.

A furious heat rose to her cheeks. Badra's insides felt like warm yogurt. Kenneth watched her, his brilliant blue eyes never leaving her face. She picked up her coffee and considered him over the cup rim.

"I am named Badra after the full moon, Khepri. Have you ever seen the moon? It's pale and cold and distant. I think my parents chose the name for a reason."

"I have seen the full moon. Seen it as a silvery wash upon the gray sand, filling the land with a pale light. Egypt's moon is hauntingly beautiful, not cold and distant. Yet she yields to the approaching sunrise, gently allows herself to be coaxed into surrendering to the powerful embrace of Khepri the sun."

His voice was a whisper. Those intense blue eyes burned into her. Her hand shook a little as she set down her cup.

Why hadn't he taken her last night as she'd expected? She felt confused. Despite his relaxed position, Kenneth looked dangerous, a powerful man accustomed to having his way. He wanted her. She was his concubine. She'd stolen from him and left him wanting for years. Yet he had left her alone, except to offer comfort when she sobbed from her nightmare.

Slowly she dragged her gaze away and absorbed herself in eating. When she raised her eyes again, his intent look was gone, replaced by a charming smile. Kenneth gestured to a stack of books piled atop a table. "I thought you'd enjoy spending some time reading, so I had these sent over."

Eagerly she went to the books, brushing crumbs off her gown. Badra lifted one, hungering for the words inside the leather cover much as her body had hungered for food.

Such treasures! She recognized the Dickens she had left in his library and blushed, remembering what had transpired there.

"When you're finished with breakfast I thought we could begin your lessons."

"But I know how to read."

She turned and found he stood noiselessly behind her, silent as his totem, the cobra. Duke of Caldwell he might be, but a Khamsin warrior too.

"Not reading," Kenneth said, taking the book from her and setting it down. "Fighting."

She stared in bewilderment and he took her hands in his. "Defending yourself against men who would harm you, my love."

"I cannot. I'm not a warrior."

"No, but I can teach you a few valuable skills. Skills that will serve you well should another man ever attack you, Badra."

Intrigued, she studied him. "What will these skills do?"

"Badra, Rashid and I are not always around to protect you. Obviously. If you're ever alone, you'll be able to defend yourself. It's a good feeling, knowing how to do that."

"Very well, Khepri. Teach me, then."

"This is where a man is most vulnerable."

In her soft, blousy trousers and short scarlet jacket with long sleeves, she stood facing him. Kenneth took her hand and guided it between his legs.

"Kick a man here and you'll cause considerable pain—and considerable damage."

The shock of feeling her hand on his genitals collided with the brisk efficiency of his words. He wrapped his hand around hers, cupping the dangling softness of his testicles.

Letting her pull her hand away, he stepped back, eyeing her critically. "The best way is to knee him, but you're rather short."

"I am not short."

"I like you that way," he teased. "Use your whole leg."

Exasperated, she aimed. As her leg jerked upward, he maneuvered out of the way. "Again," he prompted.

She repeated the move several times, but he kept moving away, twisting and moving. Frustration built inside her.

"Too slow. Again. Put some power into it."

Sweat dripped down her temples. Badra eyed him with a calculating look. He was much larger, muscled and quick. She felt like a bird trying to kick an elephant.

A pretty bird . . . must catch a man off guard. She swung her hips and gave a flirtatious smile. Placing her hands on his chest, she moistened her lips. Then she lunged forward and with all her might, kicked toward his groin.

He caught her leg, barely.

Kenneth smiled—a slow, approving smile this time. "Excellent. Catch a man off guard, then attack."

A flush again ignited her cheeks—this time from the pleasure of his praise.

He showed her a few more moves, including the points on a body where most damage could be inflicted. Very gently, Kenneth pressed a thumb just above the hollow of her throat. "With the heel of your hand, deliver a quick, sharp blow here. This can strangle a man and kill him," he told her.

She shuddered at the knowledge warriors possessed. But it fed her confidence, as Kenneth had assured her it would.

They broke off to eat, and downed large glasses of cold, sugared tea. Badra watched Kenneth's throat work as he drained his glass. "You're not teaching me this simply to guard myself against a random attack. You're doing it for an escape."

"Yes," he said quietly. "When we finally do take you out, Badra, if I'm not there to protect you, I want you to fight your way free. Do whatever you must to escape."

She set down her glass, dismayed at the grim set of his jaw. "What do you mean, if you're not there?"

"I may be killed and unable to help you," he said simply.

He said it very gently, looking at her. She stared. Breath caught in her lungs. "Khepri, you couldn't—"

"I could. I told you, I will never again let another man hurt you as long as blood runs in my veins. But . . ."

Her mouth went dry. She drank more tea. "You are no longer my falcon guard. Why do you risk your life for me, Khepri?"

His gaze held hers intently. "Because I'm bound to you by something greater than a mere oath. I love you, Badra. I would die to keep you safe."

Her glass shook as she set it down. The simple declaration was uttered with stark honesty, and it brought to the fore all the considerations that were Khepri. His willingness to sacrifice his life for her freedom and his hard resolve. She saw the quiet determination of a man wanting to protect a woman. Not because of an oath, but because of love.

Kenneth took another orange slice, ate it, then wiped his hands with the damp towel provided with the meal. He stood, his tender look gone, the hardened warrior having returned. "Well, shall we resume our lessons?"

He left her to rest in the afternoon as he scouted the building, but Badra could not sleep. She picked up Dickens and curled into the window seat. Soon she became engrossed in another world. When Kenneth returned, he joined her in the alcove.

His smile warmed her insides. "Read to me," he told her.

Clearing her throat, she began. Kenneth leaned against the wall and closed his eyes. She read a few pages and stopped.

"I'm tired. Here, you go on." She handed him the book.

Kenneth's eyes flew open. He stared at the pages, a blank look shuttering his eyes.

"Khepri? I thought you liked the story?"

"I like hearing your voice, that's all."

She didn't understand his gruff tone. "Another book then?"

Kenneth rubbed his temple, sighing. When his gaze met hers, a look of pain surprised her.

"Badra, no more secrets between us. It's time you know something about me, as well."

Chapter Twenty

God, how could he tell her? Kenneth braced himself and flipped open the book. His muscles tightened. "I can't read."

She blinked, clearly bewildered. "But you read all the time when you lived among us. I always saw you with a book—"

"Arabic, Badra. I can't read English. I never learned."

Her mouth opened. "You . . ."

"Do you know what it's like to leave everything familiar and return to a country you don't know? Those first days it took all my strength not to turn back." A hard laugh escaped him. "I was born in England and knew nothing about my country. Not even"—he shoved a frustrated hand through his hair—"how to read an English book."

He looked away. "When I returned to England, I told no one about my inability to read. I was too ashamed. You're the only one I've ever told."

He waited. Her expression shifted, transformed from incredulity to a calm smile. Badra gently plucked the book from his hands and slid toward him until their thighs touched.

"Now we know each other's secrets, Khepri. Reading English is difficult, but I can teach you. Will you let me?"

Relief filled Khepri. She had not sneered. Not that he'd expected her to, but . . . He slowly nodded.

She opened the first page and took his finger, placing it on the crisp sheet. " 'Chapter One. I am born . . . ' "

For nearly the entire afternoon, his love taught him to read. Badra made him sound out each word. Kenneth struggled to make sense of the letters, his normal self-consciousness over his illiteracy fading under her patient tutoring. Totally absorbed in the lesson, he read aloud a sentence and earned a delighted smile.

"Thank you," he told her, something in his chest easing.

Badra had taught him. Soon it would be his turn to tutor her, to return the favor. His body tensed with delicious anticipation as he fetched another book. He cupped her cheek.

"Read to me again, Badra."

As she reached for Dickens, he stayed her hand. "*This* one."

She stared at the copy of the *Kama Sutra* he placed in her lap. He had brought it from England, a book he'd hoped would help fulfill his secret fantasy—Badra reading to him the acts he wanted to perform with her.

A dull flush lit her cheeks as she scanned the page.

"Do you truly want to embrace your dreams, Badra? Do you want to know what it's like to know passion?"

Her secret desire. She both feared and longed for it.

His deep voice slid over her like warm honey. Kenneth traced the edge of her jaw with his thumb. "Read it to me."

She dropped her gaze and began reading. His heat poured over her like his namesake, the god of the sunrise. She became aware of his thigh touching hers, his palm resting lightly on her knee. When she finished reading the page, Kenneth placed his hand on hers and squeezed.

"We don't have any betel nuts," he said softly. "But we do have dates."

Kenneth took one from the fruit bowl. His lips parted and he slid the pitted date into his mouth and held it there, then slipped it out and pressed it against her closed lips. It lay there, warm and wet from the moistness of his mouth; then he brushed her lips with it. An inner tremble seized her. She did not open her mouth. He persisted, very gently but determined, giving light pressure to penetrate her lips, his other hand resting against the small of her back. His scent teased her—sandalwood and masculinity.

The symbolism of the act became apparent with each tiny thrust, each gentle but determined push against her mouth. Kenneth bent his head and murmured reassuring words, crooning to her in Arabic all the while. Her tongue wanted the date's sweetness, tasted the wet juiciness. She reached out with her tongue to taste it, slightly parting her lips—and at that precise moment Kenneth gave one last firm, determined push and slipped it inside her mouth.

Startled, she took it in. She chewed slowly, let the fruit flavor explode in her mouth, and swallowed. Her huge eyes met his.

"That is how to eat a date, my love," he said softly, then covered her mouth with his. His kiss was deep and drugging, and he pressed her body close, devouring her mouth as she had the date. He tore away and framed her face in warm, strong hands. His deep voice flowed over her, seductive and full of promise.

"Let me fall again, Badra. Let me fall into you and drown in the full moon. Like Khepri, god of the sunrise, I want to die into you, the moon. Let the sun and the moon collide in passion and eclipse all else. I promise I will be there to catch you and I will not, ever, let your feet touch the ground. Come and dance in my light as I will dance in yours. Let me hold you in my arms and never let go."

"Khepri," she said in a choking voice. "I want to. But . . . I'm afraid."

"I know," he said soothingly. "But the best way to erase fear is to face it. What do you fear the most?"

He held her hands in his, lightly. She dredged up courage. "Being tied up, as I was in Fareeq's tent, and faced with the whip. *Being helpless,*" she whispered.

"Do you trust me?"

When she nodded, he touched her cheek again. "Then come to me, my love," he said, his soft voice husky and compelling. She felt trapped by its hypnotic tone. His heavy sensuality intoxicated her. This was Khepri—not an English duke, but her Egyptian warrior skilled in the Eastern way of men, coaxing women into their bed, seducing them with their masculinity and passion.

Badra trembled, afraid and yet longing.

"Do not fear me, little one," he said soothingly. "I will not hurt you." His voice deepened to a protective growl. "I will not allow anything to hurt you ever again."

She swallowed hard. Her pulse jumped. Every beat of her heart seemed to ring in her ears. He tugged her from the seat. Kenneth began undressing her, his fingertips grazing her skin, a soft caress. When she stood before him, fully nude, he swept her body with his gaze.

Admiration and desire shone from his eyes. Kenneth bent down, lifted her hair and nuzzled her earlobe, giving it a tiny lick. A shudder of pure pleasure raced through her.

"Trust me," he told her softly. "Do you? To do this, I must have your full and complete trust."

He brushed a finger across her cheek. "Do you give me your full and complete trust, Badra? Do you know I would not, will not, hurt you?"

Her throat tightened with emotion. She could only nod.

To her horror, he fetched the cartouche and draped it over her neck. Breath squeezed out of her. It was the cursed necklace. She was his slave now. Fully and completely. Powerless.

Clasping her tiny hand in his large one, he led her to the tall marbled columns. Two large steel hooks protruded from the stones, gleaming and dangerous. A shiver stroked her spine.

He held her very life in his hands. Never before had she felt more powerless, not even when Fareeq had beaten her, for she had clung to her soul, her *ba*, even as the whip scored her tender flesh.

Then, hatred had kept her alive. But Kenneth, her former protector, had the power to flay her with deeper wounds than Fareeq ever had inflicted.

He took her palms and pressed a kiss against each. He produced a silk cord and wound it about each wrist. Old terrors filled her as he tied the cord to the ominous steel hooks, stretching her arms apart. Enough tension existed to allow her arms slack, yet the knots were mercilessly tight.

She could not escape.

He bound her ankles the same way. Now she was stretched out, a sacrifice to his pleasure, bound naked between the two columns. It was nearly the same position Fareeq employed when he had beaten her. She could not help the violent shudders racking her body. Badra tried to summon courage.

Kenneth stood before her, tall, muscled and powerful. A leather whip hung on the far wall. With predatory grace, he strode over to it and released it from its place.

A sharp crack filled the air as he flicked the whip with expert skill.

Her body sagged against the ropes. *Please*. Her mouth formed the word, but no sound escaped. Kenneth approached, the whip in his hands, his expression tight and merciless.

Gooseflesh broke out on her naked flesh. Her body clenched, tensing in anticipation of pain. Time crawled by, minute by agonizing minute. She closed her eyes. She could not bear to watch the man who professed to love her, the warrior who'd once vowed to sacrifice his life for her, lift a whip to her skin.

"*Trust* me, Badra."

Kenneth had been a man of honor. Could she trust him to not hurt her, despite how badly she had hurt him?

Badra bit down on her wobbling lower lip and hung on to a precarious thread of hope, of love shutting out the fear. Her eyes flew open and resolve filled her.

"I trust you."

A small thud sounded on the floor. Kenneth stood before

her, the whip lying at his feet like a coiled, dead snake. His gentle kiss brushed her lips, softer than silk, like honey pouring over aching wounds.

Standing back, he studied her, and his face went soft with tenderness. His strong hands, capable of violence against his enemies, cupped her face as if he held the fragile faience dug from beneath the pyramid.

"My love," he said thickly. "Allow me to show you the passion of a Khamsin warrior's secret of one hundred kisses."

He vanished behind her. His mouth gently settled upon her scarred back, his lips feathering a trail of scorching pleasure down her sensitive skin. Kiss after kiss was chased by tiny, light flicks of his velvet tongue.

He was kissing her scars, she realized with wonder, pressing his lips to her past as if each kiss could ease all the pain she had suffered. It was a tender balm upon her soul. One after one, each light kiss, each touch of his warm mouth filled her body. Badra felt a tear trickle from her eyes. She squeezed them shut and began to count, and fresh awe spilled through her.

The secret of one hundred kisses.

This was the Khamsin warrior tradition she had heard women whisper of in their dark tents, kisses designed to arouse a woman's passion. The kisses ended at a woman's pleasure center and brought her to the height of ecstasy.

Kenneth's kisses bathed her in a warm sea of acceptance, of forgetfulness of the past, of assurances of his love. One hundred kisses to soothe away the burning flick of the whip. For each cruel stroke of the lash Fareeq had delivered, Kenneth healed it with his loving mouth and tenderness.

Kenneth reappeared before her, his intent gaze holding

hers a moment; then he began kissing her again. His mouth sought her breast, kissing the nipple, and she writhed in her bonds. Then he dropped to his knees. His arms wrapped about her waist as he pressed his mouth against her hot skin, his lips touching her belly, delving lightly into her navel with light, expert flicks. She felt a hot gush between her thighs.

And then, with powerful hands that could kill, yet were so gentle, he parted the softness between her thighs and pressed his mouth to her feminine core.

Pleasure burst inside her with each scorching kiss, then he took her flesh into his mouth and sucked gently, flicking out his tongue. Badra strained against the ropes, writhing as heat raked through her. Heat from his mouth, building a pleasure she had never known before. The tension mounted and she arched for something not quite there, just out of reach.

He stopped.

Quivering, she gasped for breath, looking at him. Aching frustration filled her as she sagged against the ropes, her body throbbing with want.

He stood and swiftly untied her, then carried her to the bed. She felt the soft mattress beneath her, his firm, warm mouth above.

When he removed his trousers, she caught sight of his thick arousal. Badra tensed and shrank back. He paused, regret in his gaze, and belted a thick black velvet robe about his body. Kenneth went to the door, paused, his hand on the knob. "I'm going to the baths. Why don't you remain here and rest?"

His tone was mild, assuring. Frustration and bemusement surged through her. Badra watched him leave. Didn't he want her? Was he just being kind?

She sat up, removing the pectoral of Amenemhat II with a vicious tug. The necklace landed on the table with a heavy clink. For too long she'd shrunk away from passion. From love. No longer. It was about time she did something about it.

Kenneth drew in a breath as he headed for the Turkish baths. It had taken every ounce of restraint not to finish what he had started. Her sweet taste still lingered in his mouth. Sensing her arousal, he'd wanted to continue until she reached her peak, but at the last minute he'd pulled back, needing to hold her in his arms as he watched her experience sexual gratification for the first time. The fear tightening her face had changed his mind.

He wanted to coax her to him, to fuel her desire until the tiny smoldering ember was ready to incinerate her. Best to leave her to ruminate over what had happened—how she'd been tied, helpless, but experienced only pleasure. Anticipation was nearly as sweet as fulfillment. Let the demons of the past battle new sensations of passion coursing through her. Eventually she would lie, warm and willing, in his arms.

Warm steam misted the air as he entered the men's bath chamber. Kenneth frowned, wishing for cold water. He glanced down at his throbbing cock. *Very* cold water.

The room was elongated, with a rectangular pool. Green-and-white mosaic tiles in an Islamic pattern adorned the floor. Two women, graceful and exotic, greeted him. He was the only occupant and he went directly into the pool. As he sank into the heated water, which rose to his waist, the shorter woman came over, bearing a large sea sponge. She dampened his shoulders and arms, and began washing him.

Kenneth closed his eyes, enjoying the soft hands soaping his shoulders, wishing they were Badra's.

A startled gasp filled the air.

He opened one eye and wanted to cheer. Accompanied by the eunuch he'd hired to guard her door, Badra stood at the pool's edge, a visible pout tugging her lovely bottom lip. She looked annoyed.

Kenneth offered a lazy smile, hiding his delight. "Hullo."

"What are you doing?"

"Taking a bath."

"With *her?*"

"Not with her," he corrected, glancing up at the maid. "She's merely washing me."

Ice shone in fractured shards in Badra's dark eyes. She said in a quiet, chill tone he'd never heard before, "Leave us," to both the women and the eunuch.

They looked to him for affirmation. He nodded. As they scrambled away, Badra narrowed her eyes.

Kenneth sat up in the shallow water, legs outstretched, arms draped over the bath's edge. "Well, Badra? I'm not yet finished bathing. Since you sent away my attendant . . ."

Kenneth's look was steady, frankly assessing and boldly challenging. Badra swallowed so hard her throat muscles clenched. He held out the sponge.

Badra knew Kenneth's question meant more than a mere bath. If she accepted, there'd be no turning back. But, for so long she had been afraid. Fear had kept her from love. No longer.

Sinking to her knees, she took the sponge, her fingers brushing his. With hesitant, jerky strokes, she began to wash him. The sponge slid over Kenneth's flesh, lathering him in foamy soap. Suds cascaded over him. Kenneth closed his eyes and released a groan.

Slightly emboldened, Badra's strokes became firmer, rubbing his broad shoulders, the powerful muscles of his back, down the thick biceps and the tattoos, the coiled cobra and the new one, the *ankh,* the symbol for life. Foam caught in the dark hairs of his muscled chest. She sponged his torso and stopped short. Kenneth's intent gaze held hers.

"All of me, my love. Wash all of me," he said.

She sensed a tremendous crossroads ahead. It was up to her to traverse it or stop. Did she have the courage to forge on? *Do you want to know passion, my love?*

His husky whisper echoed in her mind. I can do this, she assured herself. No hard lust gleamed in his eyes, only brooding patience and tender love.

Drawing a quivering breath, she dipped the sponge below the water, to the hardened length of him. He closed his eyes and shuddered as she stroked. His male flesh tightened under her trembling hand. A helpless groan rumbled from his chest.

With a start, Badra realized she had done this to him, her Khepri. Her warrior, who had vowed life and limb to protect her. His muscles tensed and clenched as if engaged in a battle. A sudden sense of her own power surfaced.

His brilliant blue eyes flashed open. "No more," he rasped, taking the sponge away. "Now it's your turn."

Water droplets sprayed out as he twisted and stood, sweeping her into his arms. Lowered into the water, Badra uttered a startled shriek. Her turquoise gown clung to her skin and she stared up with huge eyes. "I'm very wet," she breathed.

"Are you now?" he asked in a smooth, deep voice. "We need to remove your beautiful gown then."

Slowly he unfastened each tiny pearl button and parted the fabric, then slid the dress from her sloping shoulders. Badra's breath hitched as he kissed her neck. With an impatient tug, the gown dropped into the water, baring her body.

Kenneth drew her into his arms, kissing her deeply. His mouth felt like hot honey, delicious and sweet. He rained kisses to her chin, then feathered them across her neck to the deep hollow of her throat. She felt aflame. New and frightening sensations swallowed her whole.

Pulling away, Kenneth studied her, passion deepening his blue eyes to indigo. "Badra, do you want this? Do you want *me?* If you say yes . . ."

She wanted to fan the smoldering spark he'd ignited with heated kisses and tender caresses. Badra nodded slowly.

"No regrets?" he asked thickly.

"No," she managed to gasp. A tiny fear, like the pulsing of a miniature heart, fluttered. "What . . . are you going to do to me, Khepri?"

His warm hand cupped her cheek, caressing it. "I'm going to love you, Badra. Love you all over until you scream from the wanting—and the aching," he said quietly.

Then his lips descended on hers in an engulfing kiss, coaxing them apart as his tongue delved deep into her mouth, thrusting in and out.

Kenneth's hands settled on her breasts. Thumbs encircling the nipples, he began slow, steady strokes. A sweet, agonized tension arose in her. Then he broke the kiss and slid downward, kissing her as he did so until his mouth engulfed a breast's taut peak. His tongue rasped over it, flicking hard and fast. Badra whimpered, cradling his head.

"Khepri! Someone will come," she gasped.

Kenneth tore his mouth away, looking up with an intent expression. "I hope so," he said hoarsely. "*You.*"

But he led her from the pool, finding two large white linen towels nearby. Kenneth wrapped one about his waist and began drying her with the other. Caressing her with the cloth, he delved into her hollows and secret places until her hips thrust forward with each soft stroke.

A mysterious smile curved his lips as he draped his thick black robe about her. They left the baths. Anticipation and trepidation danced inside her as they returned to their rooms. Inside, Kenneth tugged off her robe and whipped the towel from his waist. Water beaded his chiseled muscles. Silver droplets gleamed in the dark hair resting above his thick arousal. Ever so gently, he lifted her and laid her upon the bed. His gaze was tender and cherishing.

"Are you certain, my love?" he asked.

"Yes," she replied, touching his face. "I love you. I want this. I want you."

His kiss was gentle, his lips warm and soft. He coaxed a giddy response from her, deepening the kiss, applying a slight pressure until her lips parted under the gentle insistence of his tongue.

Kenneth began small, intimate thrusts, licking the inside of her lips. His scent invaded her, sandalwood soap and masculine power. Badra moaned at the fire building inside, the need for him as he touched and caressed. Muscles jumped beneath his fingers. Then he drifted lower and touched intimately between her legs, stroking slowly. Badra arched in shocked pleasure.

He slid a finger deep inside her. Badra tensed, legs clenching together, but she could not escape his invasive touch. Muscles clenched around him as he stroked and pushed. He held her tightly as he penetrated deeper. She writhed, shocked beyond words as sweet tension built. Finding her intimate folds, his thumb began slow, long strokes.

"Look at me, my love," he coaxed softly. "It's your Khepri. Look into my eyes and see who is giving you this pleasure."

A whimper arose in her. Badra responded more, hips arching to meet his caresses. Her gaze locked to his. "Excellent—that's it, relax, yes, like that."

Tension blossomed, expanding as his strokes increased, and her thrusts became insistent. Badra clasped his shoulders. "Khepri," she whimpered. "I don't, ah—oh, it's, oh, Khepri!"

"Let go," his deep voice crooned. "Let go, my love."

Her body convulsed and she screamed as the pleasure tore her asunder, her hips rocking to the demands of his caress. He captured her startled cry in his mouth.

Her breath rasped out in short gasps as she slowly returned to earth. Sweat slicked her body and she clutched him as if drowning.

Fierce triumph glowed in the depths of his brilliant blue eyes, which blazed like lit sapphires. With the swiftness of his cobra totem, Kenneth rolled her onto her back and covered her. Warm, large hands pushed at her clamped thighs.

"Spread your legs for me, darling," he murmured, looking down at her. "Trust me. I will not hurt you, my love."

Trust him. He will not hurt you. Badra obeyed ancient instincts. He settled between her outstretched thighs as she opened to him like a blossoming flower. His heavy weight pressed her into the bed and she welcomed it.

A hard thickness pressed against her feminine softness. Her teeth clamped down at the insistent pressure of him beginning to push into her. Instinctively, she drew back, but his hands tightened on her hips and held her steady.

"I can't," she gasped.

"You can," he urged softly. "Take all of me, my love."

Kenneth's thick arousal filled her as he pressed forward. She felt stretched beyond compare. Whispering soft reassurances, he held her tightly to him as he continued pushing inside. Badra threw her arms around him, feeling the tautness of his back muscles. She yearned for him to claim her, for him and him alone. The first man to invade her body since her captivity by Fareeq became her anchor, her rock as he kept penetrating.

The friction from his body created a delicious tension in her loins. The tension grew as he slid over her, murmuring soothing masculine reassurances, words she didn't quite understand but moved her with their tenderness.

He pushed harder and she tensed. So unexpected was this tremendous yet delicious pressure between her legs.

"Come on, my love, don't be afraid. Relax, yes, like that, that's good, that's good," he crooned.

Relentlessly, he slowly pressed deeper. A startled breath fled her as he finally reached his hilt. Then Kenneth began thrusting, his breath whistling out in staccato rasps. His flesh slid over hers, his member pulsing deep inside. Ancient instinct urged her to move too, lifting her hips to meet his strokes. His deep voice whispered soothing words of love, urging her to be one with him. No more tears. No more terror. Just this feeling of total bonding, of acceptance and a growing fervor to merge completely with him. She had never trusted anyone so deeply before in her life. She did so now, willing herself to be a slave in his tender hands, to surrender to their mutual passion.

The hard muscles in his back tensed beneath her clenching fingers, showing how much control he exerted. Pressing her hands against him, she tilted her hips to drive him deeper inside.

He pounded ruthlessly into her, as if her response drove away all his control. Sweat rolled down his face, dampening his hair, each urgent thrust claiming her. Kenneth groaned, pulling her thighs about his hips as his powerful body slapped harder and harder against hers.

Finally, he thrust forward one last time and released a deep groan. He bucked and convulsed. Her name spilled from his lips like a prayer. She felt the hot wash of his seed.

Slowly, he rolled off as her heart thundered and gradually quieted to a more normal cadence. Kenneth drew her into his arms and kissed her brow. "Are you all right?"

She curled against him. "I feel like I've died, flown to beyond the stars and the sun and this is paradise. Is it?"

"It is, my love," he said softly, stroking her hair. "I can't imagine anywhere being sweeter than this."

His possessive gaze raked over her as she snuggled against him. He tightened his grip as if he feared she'd slip away like pale moonlight. Gradually his eyes closed. Badra

265

shifted and rolled over, and he molded himself to her sweet curves, draping an arm about her to hold her close.

They fell into blissful sleep in each other's arms. Hours later, Kenneth felt a breeze caress his bare shoulders. He stirred restlessly, a sudden chill seizing him like a forewarning of death. Jerked awake, he sat up, looking wildly about. Pale moonlight streamed through the latticed windows, scattering silvery geometric patterns on the bed. But he saw nothing.

Slowly, he settled back into the soft pillows, pulling Badra into his arms. But sleep proved fleeting. For the rest of the night, he could not erase a queer feeling someone had been standing by the bed, watching them sleep.

Chapter Twenty-one

The pectoral of Amenemhat II mysteriously vanished.

At dawn the next day, Kenneth hunted for it, moving quietly about as Badra slept. Dismay mounted. Who'd stolen it? Worse, who'd been in the apartment without his knowledge? Was it the mysterious Omar who wanted Badra?

But if the man wanted Badra so badly, why had he sold her?

Urgency compelled him to find answers directly from the slave master. Kenneth stalked down the hallway toward the *ka-ah*. Doors to various bedchambers lined the corridor. As one began to open, he froze, then ducked behind a tall, potted palm.

A man emerged, smoothing back his gray dappled hair and knotting his tie. He turned briefly. Dim light from the wall sconces allowed Kenneth to see his face. The man was his cousin, Victor.

Dread pooled inside him. Kenneth stepped out and stood directly in his path. Comic shock registered on Victor's florid face. He clutched his hat and his mouth worked violently, but no words came out.

"Hullo," Kenneth said pleasantly. "Fancy meeting you here."

"What—what are you doing here?"

"I imagine the same thing you are."

Hot blood infused Victor's cheeks. "Well, then, I shall be off. Er, I shall see you later, Kenneth."

Victor scurried down the hallway as if the hounds of hell nipped his heels. Kenneth returned to Badra's rooms—all thoughts of questioning the slave master having vanished. Why was Victor here? Why this particular brothel? A nagging feeling told him he would soon find out.

Back in the room, he stripped and slid into bed, gathering Badra tightly against him. She stirred restlessly as dawn slotted through the latticework shutters. Kenneth lay still, his beloved nestled against him. Hunger rose in him again as he brushed back a lock of hair from Badra's ear and kissed her lobe. She stirred, her bottom creating a delicious friction against his loins. He was already hard.

She blinked sleepily at him as she turned over, responding to the warm pressure of his gentle kisses feathering over her cheeks and forehead. Kenneth kissed the juncture of shoulder and collarbone, giving a delicate lick. Her skin tasted like salt and honey, and of last night's passion.

Kenneth uttered a strangled moan as he felt himself pulse, hard as steel. No other man, he vowed. No other man would *ever* have her again. She was his, and safe.

She trembled violently under his touch. He would have her. Now. Moving quick as his snake totem, he rolled her beneath him. Ah, so soft, so pliant. He kissed her neck and licked slowly, relishing her delicious taste. Passion darkened her eyes and she pulled his head down and kissed him.

Parting her thighs with a knee, he settled between the cradle of her legs and pushed into her warm, secret depths. He kept his gaze locked to hers, watching as dazed pleasure stole over her features. He slipped into a favorite dream: They were married. Could life get any sweeter than this, than being in bed with the woman you had loved for years, watching her lips part and her eyes dilate with desire like dawn stealing over the horizon? Each new day promised to be a fresh start and he silently vowed he would make them all as lovely as he could, one rolling into the next, like rich, dark wine.

For so long he'd craved her and dreamed of her, and now she was his. He'd marked her as his and there was no turning back. Kenneth bent down and nipped her soft flesh, chasing it with a soothing caress of his tongue. She wriggled beneath him, pressing him closer. Their slow, smooth strokes became intense and hard, her thrusting hips setting the rhythm as they writhed together, trying to achieve that perfect closeness, that bonding of bodies and flesh, the connection they both craved.

He finally allowed himself release as she clenched around him, sobbing out his name. Kenneth collapsed atop her for a minute, his own frantic breath circulating in the pillow as he rested his forehead against it. Mindful of his weight, he rolled off her, taking her with him.

Deeply content, he lay, stroking her hair. He could not stop touching her, assuring himself it was not a dream.

"Good morning," she murmured shyly.

"Indeed," he said, smiling.

All was right in his world. He would smuggle Badra from here with the help of his Khamsin brethren.

Kenneth yawned as she slid gracefully from bed, hips swaying with natural grace. While she went to to bathe, he dressed and rang for breakfast.

"Include plenty of oranges," he told the servant. A rueful smile touched his lips. "Although my concubine detests them, I do not."

Several minutes later, silent and efficient servants entered the rooms, changing the bed linens with fresh ones, replacing towels in the necessity and setting silver trays of food and steaming Turkish coffee upon the sandalwood table. They sped out as Badra returned, her sleek ebony hair falling in tangles to her waist. The red silk robe clung to her skin. His heart thudded wildly as he stared at her.

With a graceful move, she sat on the floor, sipped some coffee. He eyed the slices of honeyed oranges crusted with almonds. His mouth watered.

He slid an orange slice into his mouth, and an odd, fiery taste teased his tongue. Pepper on the almonds? Kenneth frowned, bit off a small portion and swallowed. He set the remaining half down, obeying a warning instinct. He sipped some tea. A few minutes later, his body suddenly tightened in agony.

Sweat poured down him in rivers. His body clenched. What was wrong? Fire flooded him. His groin burned ruthlessly. Kenneth doubled over, clutching his stomach. His heart galloped in a thundering, dangerous rhythm.

Suddenly he knew. Cantharides. An aphrodisiac in small doses. Perfect poison for a brothel, since men used it frequently in orgies. No one would suspect he'd been murdered. Authorities would assume he'd accidentally consumed too much. It coated the oranges. And only he liked them . . .

"Khepri, what is wrong?" Badra cried out.

He dashed for a nearby basin. Kenneth shoved two fingers down his throat. Gagging, he forced himself to retch.

When it was over, he still trembled, weak and incredulous. His throat burned. Cold water sounded good. He glanced up and saw Badra standing by solemnly, a glass in her hand. Kenneth nodded thanks and drank deeply.

"What happened?" she asked, her lovely brow knitting.

Kenneth managed a shaky smile. "I suppose I don't like oranges as much as I thought I did."

A little while later, the aftereffects of the cantharides tormented him mercilessly. Flames licked his groin. He had hardened to stone. Kenneth turned to Badra, who was teaching him to read. Grasping her hand, he pressed it to his lap.

His voice was rough. "Badra, I need you . . . I-I can't be gentle. Not this time."

As she gave a shaky nod, he led her to the bed. Kenneth jerked her gown off, tearing it in his haste. Trembling shook her at the fury of his passion, the hard gleam of lust in his eye.

Turning her around, he gave her a gentle but firm push to the mattress. She felt horribly vulnerable and exposed. I can do this. He needs me, she told herself. She would not allow fear to drown her like Egypt's hot sands.

"Badra, don't be afraid of me, my love," he begged. His voice was like dark chocolate melting. A fresh breeze drifted through the latticed windows. She willed her body to relax.

"No, Khepri. I am not afraid."

Air slid over her nude backside in a soft caress. Badra felt the bed sink with Kenneth's weight. Arms outstretched, she waited. She bit down on her wobbly lower lip and clung to her love for him.

He gently lifted her hips into the air. His naked flesh felt torturously hot as he settled behind her. Kenneth curled a rock-solid arm around her waist, as if to brace her for what was to come. A hard stiffness poked her feminine folds, teasing and circling. So hot, oh, she was fire, burning, needing him. Delicious anticipation inflamed in her loins.

The first thrust was deep and powerful, jolting her to the core. He felt impossibly huge as he stroked inside, thick as an iron bar. Hot breath feathered her cheek as he leaned over. Then he slid a hand beneath, fingers teasing, probing and stroking as they rasped against her. He was the sun, bright, burning hot, melting her with heat. She throbbed and squirmed against the stroking fingers until the fire exploded into an inferno.

"Khepri!" she screamed, clutching fistfuls of sheets.

Gulping in air, she collapsed against the mattress. He groaned and ruthlessly continued to drive into her. Each heavy slap of his body, each powerful thrust, created new waves of sensual heat until she arched and broke apart with furious pleasure once more. Shuddering, he convulsed and pumped his seed deep inside her as his hoarse cry filled the room.

Barely had her thundering heart resumed a normal cadence when he collapsed to the bed. Sweat slicked his body as he drew her forward, eyes fierce with passion.

"This time, you do it."

Locking Badra in his arms, he rolled onto his back so she lay atop him. "Sit up," he told her.

Positioning her over his still-hard arousal, he grasped her hips. Questions danced in her dark eyes as her fingers tightened on his shoulders.

"Now, my love, slide down," Kenneth instructed.

Slowly, she sank onto his thick length. Her mouth parted with a look of surprised delight as he impaled her fully. A groan wrenched from his chest.

Badra placed her hands on him, her head thrown back. Slowly she slid up. Down. A rapture overcame her.

Kenneth let Badra ride him, biting back his painful need to surge upward hard and fast. Instead, he concentrated on palming her breasts, teasing the nipples to hard little pearls. He rubbed and caressed as her hips pumped.

When a choked cry wrung from her lips and she tightened around him, his agonized body could wait no longer. Reversing positions, he rolled forward, pinning her beneath him. He relished the satin under his lips as he kissed her soft skin and stroked the curve of her breast. He touched his forehead to hers, aching for that intense connection. More than skin to skin, soul to soul. He wanted his heart merging with hers.

Badra flexed her hips, moving beneath him. He could hold out no longer. Kenneth surged forward in a violent thrust, touching her womb. She cried out, pressing him closer.

"You are all the stars blazing in Egypt's night to me, my love," he told her in Arabic, his voice thick with passion.

He thrust deep inside, marking her with his touch, his

heat, his body. No other man would ever touch her again. He would heal all her wounds and they would be together forever.

Upon the lovely slope of her neck he rained hot kisses, burying himself again and again in her, reveling in the tightness sliding against him so warm and exquisite. He threw back his head, his breathing ragged in the quiet room.

So long—he had wanted and waited and dreamed for this for so long.

His body quivered as he felt every sensation pool hot and heavy in his loins. Kenneth gave one last thrust, held her tightly and climaxed. His body shook and he cried out her name as he spilled himself again deep inside her.

After a moment; aware he was crushing her with his weight, he lifted up on his elbows, gazing down at her tenderly.

"Badra." Her name was a whisper. She caressed his cheek. Kenneth groaned at her touch.

So fine-boned and delicate, yet so corporeal and solid. She was fashioned from the sturdy elements of her homeland, as lasting as the great limestone blocks of the pyramids. Neither the harsh sun nor the raging winds of her slavery had worn her down; rather, they'd endowed her with a mature beauty as lasting as those great structures.

Reluctantly, he slid from her wet warmth. Then he rolled to the side, taking her with him.

"Do you know how much I love you," he asked, framing her face with his hands.

Her hands encircled his. "I love you too, Kenneth," she whispered back. "I always have."

They fell into a peaceful slumber. Sometime later, he

awoke. He loved her again, slowly this time, as if she were a fragile faience. He held her tenderly as she screamed with pleasure, her cry echoing off the ceiling of the large room. And in her arms, he found his needed surcease, the cooling release of the volcanic heat stoked inside him.

Much later that afternoon, he left her to rest as he quietly dressed and headed for the Shepherd's. He went directly to the front desk, inquiring about any messages from London. The desk clerk sorted through his slot and withdrew a yellow paper. A cable from London.

He ripped open the telegram, wishing he could read. Kenneth glanced at the clerk. "Can you read English?"

"No."

Kenneth tucked the cable into his brocade vest. Heading for the staircase, he swallowed hard. *Can't read,* a voice inside mocked him. *Can't even read your own damn cable.*

When he reached his suite, Kenneth hesitated. He had to find out what it said. He trusted only one person. Swallowing his pride, he walked to Jabari's door and knocked.

Rashid opened it. He murmured a polite greeting—polite for Rashid—and led Kenneth inside. Jabari sat on the floor, face drawn as he read over some papers. Ramses sat nearby, honing a dagger on a small stone.

They looked up with expectant hope as he dropped to the floor next to them. Kenneth nodded at Ramses.

"Getting ready to sacrifice a lamb for dinner?"

He held up his *jambiya*. "Getting ready to sacrifice a few eunuchs guarding a certain brothel." Mirth twinkled in his amber eyes. "Although I would say they have already sacrificed the two most important things."

"As you can see, we are eager to know how soon we may rescue Badra," Jabari said, setting the papers down.

Kenneth eyed the sheets. "Business?"

"Bank statements of our holdings, accounts." The sheikh rubbed his eyes. Dark shadows hovered beneath them.

Kenneth hesitated. "Jabari, I have something private to discuss with you."

Ramses glanced at Rashid, muttering something about obtaining coffee in the lounge downstairs. They left and Jabari focused his intense gaze on Kenneth.

"Is it Badra?"

"No." His gut kicked fiercely as he handed the sheikh the cable. "I need you to read this to me."

Surprise flared in Jabari's eyes. "Why?"

"Because . . . I can't read it for myself. I never learned to read English." Kenneth squared his shoulders.

The sheikh drew his dark brows together, then suddenly his face sagged. "Allah. I did not teach you . . . only Arabic. Ah, Khepri, I did not realize—"

"Never mind," he said quickly. "But please, read it."

Jabari unfolded the paper, the crinkling like thunder in the quiet room. In his deep rich voice he read:

"Did some checking on your grandfather's death. Stop. Physician admits signs of illness mimicked arsenic poisoning. Stop. More to follow. Stop. Be careful. Stop. Smithfield."

Arsenic poisoning. Kenneth's heart slammed against his ribs. Jabari lowered the cable, his lips set in a thin line.

"Khepri, what does this mean?"

Kenneth clenched his fists to control the urge to smash them against the wall. Someone had killed his grandfather. The food, the rich French food that made him ill . . . arsenic. He had been healthy enough to fight it off, but not Grandfather. Kenneth swallowed hard. The living were his prime concern now. Badra. Every minute she was linked to him but not free put her in danger. He had to get her out. He drew in a breath and looked at the sheikh.

"That's not important now. What is important is getting Badra out of there. Tomorrow morning, when everyone is still asleep, I'll return here. Gather everyone in my room now. I have a plan."

In the expansive sitting room of his suite at the Shepherd's Hotel, Kenneth sketched a plan of the brothel's interior for the Khamsin rescue team.

"Getting her out will prove difficult. All male visitors must surrender their weapons before visiting the harem. The brothel itself is a two-story building. The reception quarters are downstairs, the harem on the second floor. There is one outside door in the harem. It leads to an outdoor walkway that rings the entire building. There is one outdoor stairwell going down to the courtyard, well-protected from all angles. It is a fortress. Two guards, armed with scimitars, are posted at all times with orders to call for reinforcements."

Jabari frowned. "A raid is foolish then."

"Well, we can't go storming in there. It must be a more subtle attack." He glanced up at the warriors hovering nearby, awaiting word from their sheikh. "If you send these men in, disguised as wealthy sheikhs on holiday and desiring some excitement, then they can be inside the harem to assist me."

Rashid looked at him evenly. "A good start. However, they won't be armed. What do you suggest, Khepri?"

Kenneth hid his surprise at the newfound respect in Rashid's voice. He tapped his crudely drawn map, pointing to the room where business was transacted.

"This connecting door leads to the harem. It's guarded on the women's side but not locked. The guards will stop a man trying to get in, but not a woman. One of you, veiled as a woman and hiding weapons, can slip inside and join me—and pass out weapons to the others. I need a good fighter at my side."

The Khamsin guardian caught the expectant look of both Kenneth and his sheikh. Blood infused Ramses's face with ruddy color. "Ah, no. *No.* Absolutely not."

"You cannot expect me to be a woman. I am the Khamsin sheikh. If word leaked out I played the part, I would be laughed at from here to the Sinai," Jabari said coaxingly.

"And I look the part of a woman more?" Ramses blustered.

"You are much shorter."

"Your hair is longer than mine," Ramses argued.

"Just as my male part is."

"Ha! Mine is a towering pyramid. Yours is but a river reed," Ramses groused.

"Come now, Ramses. It is merely for one of us to gain access to the harem. I will even see to it that you will have big breasts. Larger than full moons. You will be the envy of the other girls. I will make you so desirable as a woman you will wish to seduce yourself," Jabari teased.

The man eyed him balefully and muttered a colorful oath about his sheikh and a she-camel's behind.

"Enough," Kenneth cut in. "Neither of you will make a convincing woman. Ramses is too muscular, Jabari is too—well, too Jabari. There's only one warrior who is suitable and a good enough fighter." He swallowed, hoping the warrior would go along with the plan.

Three pairs of eyes swung to Rashid. His eyes widened and he scowled. "I will not play the part of a girl," he grated.

"You're the best man for the part," Kenneth countered.

"No." Rashid glowered at him with open hostility.

Kenneth met his scowl with an even look. "Not even for Badra, the woman you vowed to protect? You're her falcon guard."

Two lines marred Rashid's brow. He seemed in great conflict. Then he released a deep sigh. "Very well. For her. If it is the only means of her escape."

Deeply relieved, Kenneth nodded. "Once the men are inside the harem, sequestered in the rooms, everyone waits for the signal indicating that Rashid and I are ready to depart with Badra."

Her falcon guard gave him a thoughtful look. "What shall the signal be? A whistle?" Rashid gave a sharp, skillful whistle. The others looked startled. Whistling was considered rude among most Arabs. A jarring feeling nudged Kenneth. He dismissed it.

"Excellent. Listen for the whistle and join us in the hallway. We'll pass out the weapons, which you'll hide under your robes. We'll hopefully have no need of them."

He frowned. "One more thing. We'll need small firearms, but no shooting upstairs in the harem. For the same reason the eunuchs don't carry guns—I don't want the women hurt by stray bullets."

"We will use only *jambiyas* and scimitars then," Jabari agreed. "The best method of fighting, for men of courage." He glanced at Rashid and grinned. "Or women of courage."

Rashid scowled.

Folding the map, Kenneth handed it to Jabari along with a wad of rolled bills. "Go to the *souk* and buy what you need for the disguises. I'll meet you back here tomorrow afternoon."

The sheikh eyed him somberly. "Keep her safe until then, Khepri. I am trusting you to do so."

"I will," he replied, thinking of the ominous words in Smithfield's cable. "With my very life."

Chapter Twenty-two

Morning broke in the Pleasure Palace with the haunting wail of the muezzin calling the faithful to prayer. Kenneth lay awake, watching Badra sleep. He stroked the gentle curve of her cheek, marveling at its smooth texture.

Her soft black eyelashes fluttered as she opened her eyes. Kenneth's body stirred and he kissed her. When he pulled away, she gave a sleepy smile and struggled to sit.

"I must leave for the baths. It is the rule for women to bathe each morning," she said.

"After," he murmured. "Let me bathe you in love first."

He leaned forward and framed Badra's face with his hands. They trembled a little from the force of his emotions as he leaned forward and kissed her.

A playful, seductive smile touched her mouth. His body tightened at the promise there. He took her mouth, relishing the taste, the teasing way she responded. She was like the sweetest honey, and Kenneth pulled away, his breathing ragged.

He moved to make love to her, surging into her body

281

with a violent thrust that took her breath away. Badra closed her eyes, holding on as he loved her hard and fast. She sensed his need to claim her. Fisting her hands against the taut muscles of his back, she angled her hips up to meet each pounding thrust. Straining in helpless abandon, she writhed, overwhelmed by the sensual pleasure threatening to swallow her whole.

"I can't take it, it's too much," she gasped.

"Yes, you can," he said darkly, weaving his hands through her hair. His eyes met hers, fierce triumph rising in their depths. "You can, and you will."

Shifting his position, he proved her wrong—teasing, stroking and caressing, coaxing more dewy moisture from her. Pressure built inside her, the heat building to an incinerating inferno, building and building as he rubbed and teased until she finally begged for quarter.

But he gave her none. No mercy, riding her hard and fast even as she fell apart, screaming and shattering. Sated.

He withdrew slowly, lay atop her, panting for breath, feeling the sweat slick both their bodies, his seed slowly seeping out. Mindful of his heavy weight, Kenneth rolled off, pulling her into his arms.

They lay quietly together, drinking in the silence like potent wine. Badra nuzzled against his muscled shoulder. Her fingers tunneled through his wealth of dark, springy chest hairs.

"My love?" she whispered. "What if I become . . . with child?"

She felt him stir, his hand gently stroking her hair. "We'd have to get married," he murmured. An audible pause followed, then his voice filled with hope. "Would you?"

Her sigh was like a thunderclap to him. "Of course I

would," she said shyly. "I have no reason to refuse now. If you still want me, that is."

"Hmmmm. Do I want you?" He raised his head, regarding his softening member. "Not right now. But maybe in a few minutes."

Laughter rumbled in his chest as she thumped him. "Not that way!"

"Which way then?" he teased.

"Any way you want," she said softly, kissing him.

She adored the way he smiled at her, slow and sexy. "So, how about marriage, then children, hmm? How many shall we have?"

"Lots and lots. A whole tribe of our own."

"A tribe of rosy-cheeked, chubby babies for Jasmine to rule over. I like the idea," Kenneth mused. He kissed her again. "Let's get started right away on number one."

"Now?" she squeaked. "But you just said that . . ."

Glancing down at his groin, he grinned. "It looks like I may have changed my mind."

Her trembling hand caressed the taut bicep of his right arm, rubbing the cobra tattoo. Kenneth closed his eyes and she felt the muscle clench as if she'd branded him with a hot iron.

She gently squeezed. "Your cobra totem serves you well."

"There is yet another reason for my name. It has to do with . . . my strength and endurance and flexibility."

"In battle?"

"No. In another area equally important to a Khamsin warrior."

"Which is?"

283

He grinned. "Let me show you."

She went into his arms as he began to demonstrate. Some time later, Badra lay back, gasping as Kenneth slid off her, sated and covered with sweat. Resting her head on his chest, her trembling limbs unable to move, she gulped in air. "I like snakes," she confessed in a shaky voice.

Laughter rumbled in his deep chest, vibrating against her ear. Content, she snuggled against him.

She liked snakes. Kenneth grinned.

Lying on his back, staring at the sunlight dancing on the intricately carved wood-paneled ceiling, he felt a slight breeze billow through the *mashrabiya* screens and cool their bodies. Peace drifted over him as he gazed at Badra, her eyes closed. She was falling asleep.

Easing her out of his arms, he slid off the bed. She gave a sleepy protest at the loss of warmth. Kenneth took several pillows, bunched them up, lined them against her as a substitute, and pulled a sheet over them. "Until I return," he said softly.

Badra flipped over on her back, opened one eye. "Hurry."

He shrugged into a robe and headed for the Turkish baths. When a female attendant offered to bathe him, he declined and briskly scrubbed himself, eager to return to breakfast and Badra. Kenneth wrung the sponge over his head, ducked and flung droplets from his wet head. He grinned. Breakfast or Badra? Which would he dine upon? Both?

He considered as he toweled off rapidly. Humming cheerfully, he headed back to Badra's room.

Quietly opening the door, Kenneth grinned, slipped inside and advanced toward the bed. Teasing Badra awake with a date pressed against her lips would—

He neared the bed and froze.

Badra lay fully awake, dark eyes wide with panic. Her breasts lowered and fell with her increased breathing. Scales shining in a beam of sunlight, a silvery brown cobra slithered toward her delicate feet. Silent but deadly, it inched closer and closer.

Calm. He forced down calm as he slowly approached. "Keep still," he whispered. "Don't move and it will not bite."

She lay stone-still, only her eyes moving as she tracked the progress of the snake. It rested against her foot, smelled her flesh with its forked tongue, then tested the air. *Hiss.*

Kenneth's gaze snapped around the room. He spotted the line of love instruments on the wall—the *kurbash*, or crocodile-hide whip; leather restraints. A wildly comic thought surfaced: slapping handcuffs on the cobra. No. Kenneth spotted a broom in a corner. With all the stealth he possessed, he snagged it and neared the bed. As the cobra slid onto Badra's bare leg, she whimpered.

"It won't spit," he whispered. "My love, trust me. Please, do not move. Lie absolutely still."

The cobra slithered past Badra's knee, reaching her thigh. Dryness filled Kenneth's mouth. Holding the broomstick's pole out, he faced the bed.

"Remember how I told you about saving Jabari from the cobra? I charmed the snake," he said softly, his eyes never leaving the serpent's.

Kenneth placed himself in direct line with the snake's black eyes, which were as dark as date pits. He slowly rotated the pole as the cobra reared up, hooding itself.

The snake hissed, but followed the pole's motion as the broom swayed near its face. Cobra and man, each eyed the other. Coaxing it, Kenneth continued the motion. The snake hissed again and slid off Badra's body, onto the sheets, toward him.

Kenneth struck, jabbing the pole at the snake. It hissed, attacked the wood and retreated. Using the pole, Kenneth picked the serpent up, forcing the cobra to wind around the wood.

Immediately, the beast went still as if caught in a trance. Kenneth seized the docile snake behind its head. Relief made his shoulders sag. He looked at Badra.

"Are you all right?"

The blood had drained from her face, but she nodded. Admiration rose in him. Badra had a warrior's spirit. Not many women could endure a deadly snake slithering up their thighs. Bloody hell, not *this* kind of snake anyway. He saw in her the spirit that had enabled her to endure so many years of cruel treatment.

"Tell me what happened."

"I don't know. I was half asleep when you left and felt a slight breeze, like a door opening. I felt something fall on the bed. I opened my eyes and saw the cobra."

Kenneth went to a low table holding glasses and a jug of water. Kneeling down, he forced the cobra's mouth open and pressed its fangs against the interior of a glass. Milky fluid trickled out.

"What are you doing?" Badra's voice sounded shaky, but she had followed him across the room.

"Ridding it of its venom. An old trick I learned," he said calmly. "Cobras are safe if you remove the venom."

"Of course you will not kill it, for killing your totem brings bad luck. You are still Khamsin, Kenneth."

Gratified to see her shaky smile, he nodded, continuing to milk the cobra of its toxin, watching the white fluid seep into the glass. Finally he released the snake, unwrapped it from the pole and grabbed its tail, twisting it to face him.

"Naughty snake, trying to take my place in bed," he admonished. He grinned at Badra. "I suppose when you agreed to play snake with me earlier, this wasn't what you meant?"

Her laughter filled the room. Badra pressed her hands to her temples, sputtering. "You are mad," she gasped.

"Quite," he agreed cheerfully.

Kenneth took the cobra and headed out of the room.

"Where are you going?"

"Dropping off a little present. Be back straightaway."

He headed down the corridor, stopping at the room of the man who'd nearly bought Badra, whom he'd seen before in the hallway with a bruised-looking concubine. Opening the door, Kenneth saw him sleeping upon his bed. Alone.

He set the cobra on the floor. "Go, my friend. Be careful. This one is a more dangerous snake than you."

Watching the cobra slither toward the bed, he grinned. Then he dashed down the hallway, his smile fading.

Inside their room, he looked at Badra, who, practical as ever, had retrieved a bowl of fruit and was sorting through it for dates.

Fresh sweat dampened his palms. What if he had lost her? Why would someone deliberately place a cobra in their bed? The snake was native to the desert. It had not wandered into the city by mistake.

A shudder raced through him as he watched Badra neatly pit a date and then slide the fruit past her parted lips. First the poison. Now a cobra?

He glanced at the bed again, the bunched-up pillows he'd placed next to her body to keep her warm while he was gone. Pillows resembling a man's body . . .

Looking around the room, he saw something suspicious. He grabbed the broomstick again and stood on the bed.

"What are you doing?" Badra sounded amused.

He put a finger to his lips, indicating silence. He glanced upward. The broomstick rose through the air, toward the ceiling. He poked around and his efforts were rewarded. A small door swung upward.

A trapdoor! Perfect for dropping unexpected surprises upon unsuspecting guests. The cobra had been dropped from the ceiling, directly onto the pillows, which resembled a man's sleeping form.

Yes, someone had tried to kill him. Again.

Chapter Twenty-three

Never again would he leave Badra alone. When she left shortly thereafter for the women's baths, he paid a eunuch to accompany her.

A soft knock sounded from outside. Kenneth sprang to his feet and swung open one of the double doors.

Masud, the head eunuch, stood in the hallway, his dark face looking worried. "I apologize for disturbing you, but I am greatly concerned. One of the guests reported a snake in his room. Have you seen anything . . . unusual?"

Kenneth narrowed his eyes. He walked out into the hall and shut the door. "Yes. Someone tried to kill *me* with a cobra. It nearly bit Badra. What the hell is going on around here?"

The man's hands shook a little. "Is she . . . well?"

"As well as can be expected considering she nearly died."

"My humble apologies. It is an escaped pet belonging to a guest. It must have gotten into the ceiling."

"A pet?" Kenneth leaned forward, getting in the man's

face. "You let poisonous pets inside this place? I don't believe you. I want answers. What the hell is a cobra doing in here?"

Masud backed off, gestured for the guards. "I assure you, sir, there is nothing wrong. Just a guest who wanted some exotic entertainment and who lost his pet."

"I'm about to lose my temper," Kenneth snapped, fury boiling inside him. "I want answers. Take me to see this brothel's owner. Right now."

"Sir, I assure you, it was an accident . . ."

Kenneth had backed Musad against the wall when, suddenly, a flash of sharp steel appeared against his chest. A guard held a scimitar point a whisper from his breastbone. Kenneth drew in a deep breath and gave the man a cold stare. "Fine. But know I'm on my guard from this moment on, in case other peoples' . . . pets . . . decide to drop in for unannounced visits."

Apologizing profusely, with repeated assurances it would not happen again, Masud salaamed and left.

Kenneth watched the man and his guards go, certain now that he had been the target and not Badra. He did not trust it not to happen again.

Someone had tried killing him, and nearly succeeded in killing his beloved instead. But who would want him dead?

He'd blamed the attack in his bedroom in London on Rashid, but now he saw a more intricate pattern appearing. Had someone tried disguising himself as Rashid, to draw blame away?

The overdose of aphrodisiac he might possibly have believed was an accident. But the cobra dropping onto the bed was not. A grim smile tightened his face as he went back into his room and stared at the dying lamplight. How poetic. To kill the Cobra with a cobra.

Unfortunately, more than one person might benefit from his death. Victor, his second cousin, would inherit all, including the title. And Victor had been inside the brothel. Then again, de Morgan also had reason. With Kenneth dead, de Morgan might claim the necklaces and the dig artifacts, making him a very wealthy man.

Kenneth's thoughts went to Badra, his first concern. He jammed a trembling hand through his dark locks. He'd nearly lost her. His plan had been to escape today, take her to the Shepherd's Hotel and formally ask for her hand in marriage. They'd already whispered of their future life and the gaggle of babies they'd have. They'd declared their love for each other. But could he marry her when an assassin lurked in the background?

No. It was too risky. He could not endanger her life.

Best to transfer her into Rashid's protection until the danger passed. His muscles tensed and Kenneth rolled a shoulder.

He could tell Badra and Jabari about the threat to his life, but Jabari would insist on remaining behind to deal with the threat. His brother would not abandon him. And Badra? Badra would insist as well. He'd seen her courage, her fearlessness. And then the assassin might use the woman he loved to try and lure him to his death.

When she returned from the bath, Kenneth left Badra with a soft kiss and a eunuch guarding her door, and he headed for the hotel. There he went to the front desk and hired a messenger to take a note to Dashur, telling Zaid to have de Morgan, Victor and the team report back to the

Shepherd's by the afternoon. When Badra was safe, he'd set his trap for a killer . . .

In the expansive sitting room of his suite at the Shepherd's Hotel, he organized the Khamsin warriors into a war party. When he was done, he stood back, admiring his work.

Ten Khamsin warriors had shed their traditional indigo for fine ivory-and-crimson silk robes, keffiyehs and blousy trousers. They looked like wealthy sheikhs, and they departed immediately for the brothel. Even Jabari and Ramses were dressed in light blue robes and white turbans instead of Khamsin indigo.

But it was Rashid who drew the most attention.

Clean-shaven, he looked remarkably different. His smooth face held classical features, good bone structure, an arrogant chin. The Khamsin warrior wore Kenneth's trousers and white shirt. Though it was tight on his more muscular body, it fit well enough. Despite his bronzed skin, in the tailored suit Rashid looked startlingly English. An odd feeling jarred Kenneth. He shrugged it away.

Kenneth handed over Khamsin clothing he'd had a seamstress alter for a small frame. Rashid secured it with a rope around his waist, then tucked daggers, pistols and swords around his body by wrapping them in cloth. He became a walking arsenal.

Ramses took fabric, padded to make a fake bosom, and attached it to Rashid's chest. Rashid slipped on a formless black *abbaya*. His chest jutted out considerably.

"My breasts are too big. They do not look real."

"They do too. I am an expert on this," Ramses advised.

When he finished, all the men looked on critically.

"The boots might give him away. But hopefully no one will look at your feet," Kenneth noted, staring at the soft leather peeping out from beneath the *abbaya*.

Rashid donned the black head-covering and veiled himself. Jabari had found cosmetics and lined his eyes with kohl and blue shadow.

Ramses studied him. "You look very pretty."

"I look like a fool," Rashid grunted.

"I would pay good money for you," Jabari teased.

Rashid's blue-shadowed eyes glowered.

"Not as much as he would pay for Ramses," Kenneth spoke up.

Ramses glowered at Kenneth.

Kenneth gave a nod. "Well then—let's be off, shall we? You go first and I'll meet you there."

When Kenneth arrived at the Pleasure Palace, he immediately sensed something was wrong. As he surrendered his pistol to Masud, he saw Rashid. The warrior stood quietly near Jabari and Ramses, head down, his look one of a woman humbled. Another visitor hovered nearby. A Turk, clad in flowing robes, staring at Rashid as if spellbound. Clearly besotted.

Kenneth muttered a low curse. He hadn't counted on any male suitors being attracted to Rashid. Jabari's frustrated gaze met his. *And what is your plan now, Khepri,* he silently asked.

He mouthed back, *I will take care of it.*

Ramses inquired in a loud voice about how much he could obtain for selling Wafa, their sister.

"She will make an excellent kitchen slave," Jabari added. "She is very obedient."

Rashid kept his head lowered, his shoulders hunched over to minimize his height.

"A kitchen slave? Such a jewel as this? I will purchase her for my bedroom," the Turk said, licking his thin lips.

Kenneth heard a very faint mumbling in English from Rashid, "*I knew the breasts were too big.*"

Masud held up a hand. "Before any transactions are made, I must inspect her body. We do not take unhealthy women."

He went toward Rashid.

"Of course," Ramses said easily, cleverly stepping before him. "But we will want to inspect your women as well. Perhaps we may work out a trade for my brother and me to spend time here, if your women are lovely enough. We like a woman who is dark, with big breasts. An Ethiopian, perhaps. Do you have any?"

Jabari nodded, looking eager.

A calculating look lit Masud's dark eyes. "I will take you to one you may be interested in." He turned to the Turk. "Look your fill of this one now. I will be back momentarily to inspect her, and we will argue a price."

He escorted Jabari and Ramses out of the room. As soon as he departed, the fat Turk came forward, giving Rashid a critical look. Kenneth hung back, watching warily.

The man smacked his lips. "If I am to purchase you for my slave, I want to see how responsive a woman you are."

He reached out and clapped a hand onto Rashid's groin. Shock dawned on his face. "What is this?"

Rashid slugged him. The Turk went down on the soft carpet. "It is called a penis, you son of a jackal," he growled.

"Was that necessary?"

"*You* deem it not necessary, next time a man lays a hand upon your private parts," Rashid muttered.

They dragged the unconscious Turk over to a corner and hid him among some crates and boxes. "He hopefully won't gain consciousness before we can leave here," Kenneth mused.

Sweat gleamed on Rashid's face.

"You're dripping," Kenneth said. Rashid blotted at the moisture with the edge of his scarf. Damn, was this going to work? He went to the door Masud had escorted Jabari and Ramses through and listened. "They are not in the corridor. Let's go."

They both took deep breaths and Kenneth opened the door leading to the harem. Two guards standing nearby shot them a suspicious look. They patted Kenneth down for weapons. He prayed they would not do the same to his companion. One of the eunuchs peered closely at Rashid's veiled face.

"You are new here?"

Rashid trembled. "I—I was just purchased." Good. His normally deep voice was high enough.

The guard frowned. "Who would want an ugly sow like you?"

"She's mine. I brought her as a servant for my concubine," Kenneth said quickly.

The guard gave Rashid a rough push. "Get out of my sight."

Rashid meekly bowed his head and shuffled along. Kenneth held his breath, praying the weapons Rashid hid would not clank together.

When they reached Badra's apartments, he slipped money to the eunuch on guard to run an errand. When they went inside, Badra rushed over. Her eyes widened as Rashid tore off his veil.

Delight and surprise shone in her eyes. "Rashid, are you here with Kenneth to help me escape?"

Grinning, he shed the veil, then wiped off the makeup with a damp cloth Kenneth provided. He removed the weapons carefully from the Khamsin clothing. Ten daggers, four scimitars and six pistols. Rashid sat on the bed, tugging free the flat-soled boots, tossing them to Badra. Then he took a pair of scissors from his pocket and handed them to Kenneth.

"Here. Cut my hair. If I am to look the part of an Englishman, my hair must be shorter."

Kenneth fought back his astonishment. He rapidly trimmed Rashid's hair to just below the jawline. Rashid then donned a pair of Kenneth's polished shoes and stood, the transformation complete.

With the short hair and English clothing, Rashid looked startlingly familiar. Kenneth could not remember who he resembled. His attention swung to Badra, who emerged from behind a silk dressing screen. They stuffed paper into her boots. She slipped them on. Kenneth wound a turban around her head and veiled her lower face with its trailing end. Even guised as a Khamsin warrior, she could not be more beautiful. Worry sluiced through him. This would never work.

It would have to.

"I will alert the others." Rashid vanished into the hallway. A minute later, a sharp whistle sounded.

Kenneth went into the hall, Badra behind him. The other

Khamsin warriors emerged and came toward them and he passed out the weapons, which the warriors hid beneath their robes. Only the one named Musaf was missing. A door opened and Musaf emerged. His robes were in disarray and his face flushed. He hastily arranged his clothing.

Kenneth grinned and wagged a finger as he passed him a dagger. "You're not here for sex," he whispered.

"The girl attacked me," Musaf protested. "I was helpless."

With the warriors leading the way, Kenneth and Rashid followed, forming a protective enclosure around Badra. Kenneth clutched a dagger, hoping they could avoid bloodshed.

Masud emerged from a room with Jabari and Ramses and saw them. Ramses's powerful punch cut off his shout of alarm, but not before eunuchs came running, scimitars flashing. Two Khamsin warriors passed scimitars to Jabari and Ramses; then armed only with daggers, they charged the attacking eunuchs to protect their sheikh. Kenneth silently saluted their bravery.

The men threw their *jambiyas* with practiced ease, downing their screaming opponents and taking their scimitars. Jabari and Ramses joined the other warriors, wielding their scimitars, and took on the largest of the next guards who appeared. Screams erupted as concubines peeped outside.

Using their bodies as shields—Rashid on Badra's left flank, Kenneth on her right—they fled down the hallway toward the escape route. The Khamsin warriors fought ahead, clearing a path for them through the corridor.

They were nearly at the passageway leading to the outside door when yells sounded from behind Kenneth. He whirled to find two eunuchs rushing from the opposite end of the corridor, scimitars aloft. He shoved Badra at Rashid.

He held out his *jambiya* in a practiced stance. "Get her out of here! I'll handle them!" he called.

A steel object sailed through the air. Kenneth caught Rashid's scimitar one-handed and faced his attackers, sword in right hand, dagger in the left. Steel clanked with steel as he fought.

Suddenly the eunuchs battling the Khamsin warriors in the front fell back, allowing the group to rush down the corridor to the outside. "Forget the others! Get the duke!" they screamed.

They converged on Kenneth like a pack of wolves. Kenneth fought in a berserk rage. His gaze swung over to see Rashid, who was pushing Badra to safety.

Had she been the bait, he the fly in this spider's web? All the recent attempts on his life flashed before him. The aphrodisiac. The attack in London. His illness, blamed on that insufferable French cook. The cobra. He would not leave here alive.

Cursing, he swung mightily, but there were too many foes. Six against one. He smiled grimly. He was going down, but damn, he'd die as a warrior. A nearby door opened a crack and a pair of dark eyes peered out. But unlike the frightened eyes of the concubines, these eyes seemed gleeful. Wicked. Satisfied.

His killer?

"Khepri!"

His name was roared like a lion, and Jabari suddenly flew to his side, accompanied by Rashid. The two joined the fracas, their swords glinting as they effortlessly engaged his attackers.

"Why are you back here, Jabari? Go, save yourself," he yelled.

"Abandon my brother who needs me? Never," Jabari shouted back.

And, together, they succeeded. They beat back the last guard and rushed for the exit, scurrying down the outside stairs as planned. In the courtyard, all hell had broken loose. More guards had emerged like a swarm of angry bees. They battled the Khamsin who tried to herd Badra toward the thick outside wooden door and freedom. Kenneth rushed to Badra's side. Habit born from years of protecting her surfaced as he leapt to her side, fighting off one foe who'd nearly reached her. He saw Jabari and Ramses surprise several eunuchs by charging their backs. The move threw the odds in his party's favor, and they gained ground toward the door.

The Turk who Rashid had punched wandered out into the courtyard from the *ka'ah*. He took one look at the melee, did an about-face and rushed back inside.

Almost there. Kenneth turned, clutching his scimitar to fend off one eunuch when another charged him with a dagger. It connected. A wild shriek filled the air as Badra flung herself at his attacker, deflecting the man's aim, throwing him to the ground. Fire burned in Kenneth's chest as he staggered back, grimacing at his slight wound. Wheezing, he went to Badra, who was ready to kick the downed eunuch between the legs.

"That's not very effective on these guys," he told her sheepishly, and flung his dagger as the man tried to lunge for him. The eunuch slumped to the ground, Kenneth's *jambiya* in his stomach.

He retrieved the dagger as Rashid and the Khamsin armed with pistols began firing. The eunuchs quickly vanished and emerged on the upstairs terrace, rifles in hand. Screams sounded from inside. The women were cloistered in rooms directly behind. One stray bullet could hit them!

Kenneth cursed. "Careful where you shoot! The women are in the rooms behind them!" he yelled.

Another sudden shout froze his blood.

"Kill the Khamsin sheikh! The master wills it. The tall one in the blue robes with the black beard!"

Ramses flung himself in front of Jabari as bullets showered dirt around their feet. They sought shelter behind an ornate fountain of a naked woman pouring water from a jar. A bullet sang through the air, shattering her breast, spraying limestone chips. Kenneth winced and moved closer to Badra.

"Give me your loaded pistols and go! I will hold them!" Rashid shouted.

They handed over their guns and raced for the courtyard door. Ramses grimaced as a bullet grazed his arm, but he herded Jabari toward the exit. Kenneth did likewise with Badra.

When they reached the door, Ramses shoved Jabari through and raced after him, true to his role as Jabari's guardian. The others followed. Kenneth started to push Badra out but she shrieked. Rashid had turned, a desperate look on his face.

He was running out of ammunition. Trapped.

"Rashid!" she cried, and twisted as if to go back.

"Take her," Kenneth yelled to Musaf, who grabbed Badra

and carted her to safety. Pausing in the doorway, Kenneth thought hard. He needed a distraction. The Khamsin were gathered in a group outside, mounted on horses and ready to depart.

"Where's Rashid?" Jabari demanded.

"Leave! I'll get him out," Kenneth yelled in reply.

He patted his pockets and withdrew their contents: a thick wad of pound notes secured with a silver money clip. He cursed. No weapon. Money couldn't buy Rashid time to escape. Then again . . . He recalled the eunuch's wide eyes when he'd doled out money in payment for errands.

Braving the bullets, Kenneth ran back. He held up the currency. "Hold your fire! Look! Money!"

Obviously startled by the crazy Englishman, the men ceased firing. Kenneth seized the advantage, running into the courtyard, tossing the pound notes skyward toward the balcony. They fluttered in the air like doves struggling to take flight.

As anticipated, the eunuchs abandoned their rifles, reaching out to grab for the currency. Kenneth dashed for the fountain and yanked on Rashid's arm.

"Let's go," he ordered hoarsely.

They ran for the door, slammed the heavy oak portal shut behind them, then mounted their horses and rode toward the hotel.

Chapter Twenty-four

Badra had the heart of a she-lion, Kenneth thought proudly. He clutched her close as they entered the Shepherd's Hotel. Grimly he wondered what the wide-eyed guests thought about the English duke with his blood-stained jacket gripped to his chest; the diminutive woman dressed as a warrior clutching him; and the injured Ramses clutching his wounded arm, blood streaking down it, supported by the somber sheikh.

He led Badra to his hotel suite, collapsed onto a chair and dropped his jacket. She tore off her turban, then opened his shirt and gasped. Scurrying to fetch a towel, she returned, pressing it against his chest wound.

"Hold it in place while I get water and bandages," she said. She vanished behind the screen and he heard the sounds of china clinking and water being poured.

"It's just a scratch. It stopped bleeding," he protested.

The door opened and the tall, dignified frame of the Khamsin sheikh filled its frame. Even clad in grubby, bloodstained robes, his turban askew, a small bruise marring his face, he radiated a regal air. Worry shadowed his expression.

"How is Ramses?" Kenneth asked.

Jabari grimaced. "He will live. The bullet nicked his arm and he's lost some blood, but he is well. Resting now." The sheikh rubbed his chin. "Khepri, what exactly happened back there? Why did they want *me* dead?"

His gut tightened. *Because you're my brother and whoever wants me dead wants to hurt the person closest to me,* he guessed. "You lead the greatest tribe in Egypt. Of course you have enemies."

Suspicion shone in the sheikh's dark eyes. "In a brothel?"

"Men die in brothels all the time," he replied lamely.

"From pleasure. Not from bullets."

Badra appeared from behind the screen. She bore a pitcher and a basin. "Give me your dagger," she told the sheikh.

Jabari arched a brow. "Why? Do you plan to finish what the eunuchs started?" At her stern look, he sheepishly handed over the dagger hidden in the folds of his robe.

Badra vanished back into the bedchamber. Sounds of ripping fabric floated out. Kenneth and Jabari exchanged looks.

"Ah, I think your hotel bill just increased, for I am certain they will want you to replace those fine sheets she is destroying."

Kenneth gave Jabari an arch look. "Maybe she can sew them back together when I'm healed."

Badra emerged with an armful of torn cotton strips and handed Jabari back his dagger. She dumped the strips on the table and began to wash Kenneth's chest. Her touch felt gentle as a cloud. She bound his chest with cotton strips.

Kenneth frowned. "Must I wear the entire bed?"

She began winding more strips about his body. "I'm turning you into a mummy," she explained.

"I'd rather be a daddy," Kenneth replied softly.

A becoming rose tinted her cheeks. Kenneth tried to crack a smile, but he felt it crumble. It was no joke. He truly did want a child. He wanted to see Badra glowing, her belly softly rounding with his child inside her. A horrid feeling overcame him. He'd nearly lost her when she'd deflected the eunuch's blow. He could not endanger her. Or Jabari. A tightness entered his chest that had nothing to do with his stab wound.

"I must check on Ramses," Jabari said, straightening. "Badra, I trust your ministrations are sufficient for Khepri?"

"He'll be fine . . . under my care." Her eyes grew soft as she looked at Kenneth.

Twin emotions of joy and grief dueled inside Kenneth like the clash of Khamsin steel. His blood cried out for her. When Jabari left, Kenneth could barely look at her, such was his need. He stood, shrugging on his bloodstained, tattered shirt.

"I'll leave you to rest, Badra."

"Please, Khepri. I bandaged your wound in the open for a reason. So Jabari would think you incapacitated and not suspect . . ."

Taking his hand, Badra steered him into the bedroom. She took his palm and placed it on her breast. "Make love to me. Here, in this place where I am free. I want to love

304

you as a woman loves a man, not as a concubine with her master."

"Badra," he said thickly as she rotated his hand slowly over her breast.

He groaned in agony. He crushed her to him, his lips moving ruthlessly over hers. In their eagerness, they both tore off clothing and tumbled to the soft bed, entwined like snakes, kissing frantically.

Badra sensed Kenneth's burning urgency and it shocked her. A horrific thought invaded her bliss. He kissed her as if this was their last time together, as if they would be forever parted.

She shoved the thought aside and eagerly opened her mouth for him, pressing closer as he cupped her nape in one strong palm and caressed her unbound hair.

His kisses burned like the hot sands of the Sahara as Kenneth covered her naked body with his. Pressing her deep into the cotton softness of the mattress, he drove ruthlessly into her. She did not shrink back, but arched to meet each demanding thrust, each furious slap of his flesh against hers. This was the joining of equals, violent as it might be, and it was good. Badra cradled Kenneth's head, lifting her hips, covering his neck and shoulders with urgent kisses. He growled as her teeth nipped him, and cupping her bottom, Kenneth lifted her legs and draped them around his pumping hips.

Tension mounted in Badra's loins. She writhed against his sweat-slicked skin, grinding her hips into his. Gripping him to her, she screamed out his name, and he joined her as the pleasure shattered them both.

Afterward, she lay in his arms, snuggled against his warmth and utterly fulfilled. Why then did she have a dreadful feeling everything was about to slip through her fingers?

Kenneth waited until she fell asleep, then eased her from his tender hold. Badra's skin was damp with perspiration from the frenzy of their lovemaking and he pressed a soft kiss to her cheek one last time.

"Good-bye, my love," he whispered.

One last kiss. He stroked Badra's silky tresses. How could he bear to leave her? She was his very life, his spirit. Leaving wrenched him in two. Yet instinct to protect her overrode all else. Until he knew she was safe, he had no choice. Someone had tried to kill him and had targeted Jabari as well.

Kenneth battled with a desire to tell her and to enlist Jabari's help. But he couldn't risk their lives. Someone wanted him dead and had nearly succeeded in killing both Badra and Jabari. He must lay a trap for his assassin alone.

"Khepri," she whispered drowsily. "I love you."

"I love you too," he whispered back, watching her surrender to sleep. *I will never stop loving you*. He traced the curves of her face with one trembling finger, memorizing each. She was his life. His heart and soul. But he could not have his enemy use her as a pawn.

"Badra, I must leave you now. If . . . if I never see you again, know this. My love for you will never die. And if our child grows inside you, tell him this story someday. About how a Khamsin warrior who became a wealthy duke found the most precious treasure of all, the woman he thought he had lost forever."

Thickness clogging his throat prevented him from saying more. Kenneth kissed her forehead lightly and struggled to leave the rumpled bed. He dressed quickly and stole one last glance. A soft smile touched her sleeping face.

He left the bedroom, quietly closing the door. In the hallway, Kenneth pressed a palm against the wood, anguish knotting his chest.

"Khepri. What are you doing?"

He whirled and saw Badra's falcon guard looking at him without his usual scowl. Without waiting for his answer, Rashid opened the door. Kenneth trailed him into the bedroom. A protest on his lips died as Rashid silently observed Badra sleeping on the bed. His gaze flicked to Kenneth's rumpled clothing.

Without words, Kenneth left the room, and the warrior followed him into the hallway. There Kenneth faced him with a defiant look. "Yes, it's true. We're lovers."

Rashid gave him a thoughtful look. "Why did the eunuchs try so hard to kill *you*, Khepri? And then focus on Jabari?"

Kenneth's shoulders lifted in a half-shrug. "I don't know."

"You do," Rashid said softly. "Someone is trying to kill you. Perhaps the same person who trapped Badra by luring her there with her daughter—and maybe even who lured you there, too. A man who ordered his men to kill the Khamsin sheikh because Jabari is your brother, the person closest to you."

Kenneth tensed. "I will deal with this, Rashid. Alone. That is what I'm—"

"No, Khepri," Rashid said quietly. "You cannot do this alone. I will help you."

Dumbstruck, Kenneth stared. "I can't risk it. I will not risk anyone's else's life but my own."

A grin stretched over Rashid's face. "You have no choice. I will stick to your side like wet sand."

"Why?" Kenneth blurted.

The smile faded. "Perhaps because you returned for me at the brothel, Khepri. Perhaps because you love Badra, and because you are not the no-good lecherous bastard I thought you were."

Kenneth studied the man. "I could use your help," he admitted. "But you must do as I say. Listen to me, carefully . . ."

Kenneth emerged onto the famous terrace of the Shepherd's where men sipped afternoon tea. He had asked Victor, de Morgan and Zaid to join him. Victor, who would have inherited all had Kenneth not been found. Had he not lived.

But did the man want him dead?

"Pull up a chair, Kenneth," Victor said, puffing away on a cigar.

De Morgan rubbed his waxed mustache. "About the excavation, Your Grace. The jewelry we found has been loaded onto a barge and is headed here now. Do you wish to store it in a museum until the contents can be fully catalogued and assessed?"

"No. I'm going to have it shipped to England for my personal collection. All of the jewelry. There will be no division of the treasure."

De Morgan's face turned beet red.

"That was not our agreement. You planned to allot me a portion of the finds," the director sputtered.

"True. However, it is my money that paid for the whole dig, so I have the right to change my mind." He added the final twist certain to puncture the archaeologist's hopes. "Upon my return to England, I will dictate a paper detailing the find for the *London Times*. I will mention you, of course. And you will receive a small bonus for helping me. In English pounds."

Daggers shot from de Morgan's eyes. *Interesting.* Kenneth quietly assessed the look, then turned to Victor. "I'll need some things from your shop before I depart for England. I'll be there in, say, half an hour?"

Victor gave an abrupt nod.

His cousin's shop was in an isolated, deserted alleyway lined with alcoves and shadows—a perfect spot for an assassin. The bait was proffered, the destination selected, and the trap set. Now all he needed to do was walk into it and face his killer.

Chapter Twenty-five

She'd lost her love, her warrior protector.

The large, expansive suite felt as welcoming as a tomb. Her tears burned as they dripped down her face. Badra sat on the soft bed, trying to understand. Kenneth had coaxed her into passion, claimed her body, loved her with the sweet intensity of a man who adored a woman, freed her from the demons of her past . . . then left. Why? The words he'd said while he thought she slept indicated he might never see her again. Ever.

"How could he leave me?" she whispered.

Perhaps the clash of their cultures had proven too much. The wealthy duke who would be forced to socialize in strictly English circles had realized he could not marry an Egyptian girl who'd once been a concubine. But she did not understand. Were the sweet words of love he had whispered, the assurances and promises, all lies?

Badra hugged herself. Her emotions battled with her confusion. After making love, Kenneth had whispered about marriage and creating lots of bouncing, chubby-cheeked babies. What had changed his heart? Kenneth, the Cobra, had slithered free of his Khamsin warrior duties into the skin of a wealthy English nobleman absorbed into a polished, sophisticated world. Had his declarations of love simply been a ploy to finally claim her body?

But he loved her for what she was, a Bedouin girl with sun-tinted skin, who drank camel's milk and lived in a tent. She believed that.

"You are all the stars blazing in Egypt's night to me, my love," his husky voice had whispered as they made passionate love, writhing and coiling together, tangling like snakes in a desperate attempt to become one.

I have lost him, she mourned. Then Badra sat up, fury and resolve replacing her despair.

No! I will not let him discard me! I deserve a better explanation. What about what I want?

Having discovered passion and fulfillment as a woman in his arms, Badra wanted more. No more meekly shrinking away from her needs. It was about time she finally seized all that life had to offer. All *love* had to offer. *I deserve it.*

If Kenneth, the arrogant duke, would not have her, she'd bargain. Khepri, the fierce warrior, she knew loved her. If the urbane duke doubted a simple Bedouin girl could fit into refined English society, she'd prove she could.

"I will not leave until he accepts me, on whatever terms," she whispered. "I love him too much to merely walk away."

She sprang off the bed and bolted to the mirror. She began brushing her hair to a glossy sheen. Her gaze fell on the *jambiya* on the dresser. Kenneth's dagger. The dagger she'd retrieved after he left it in the sand and went to England.

Badra weighed it in her hands. She would return it to him

as a symbol, cutting them free of past hurts and starting anew.

Lifting the hem of her indigo *kuftan,* she strapped the dagger to her thigh. Then, when her other preparations were finished, she slipped out of the hotel room.

Her step firm and assured, she went to Kenneth's door and knocked firmly. No answer. Surely he had not left Cairo already.

"He's not there." The voice made her jump. Badra whirled and saw Kenneth's cousin standing behind her. "I'm going to meet him at my shop. Care to come along?"

She hesitated. But time was running short and she must face Kenneth before losing all heart. Badra nodded.

The shop was a walk from the hotel, he informed her. "I'm afraid it's not in a very good section of the city, but I'm just starting out. I plan to move to a better location as soon as funds are available," he explained.

As they walked through the city, Victor asked about the sketches she had done, praising the quality of her work. They traversed thickets of people making their way to the marketplace. Cairo's labyrinth of streets and alleys became more and more confusing, and Badra tried desperately to get her bearings.

Victor turned a corner and they pressed deeper into the Old City. A faint prickling rode her spine as the area became seedy. Stains covered the facades of several buildings. Piles of rotting refuse cluttered the gutters. On a badly tilting balcony, someone had attempted to cheer the surroundings by placing a wilted geranium on the cracked concrete. A white cat sat unblinking, in an open doorway.

Cats, guardians of the afterlife, Badra thought dimly.

They arrived at a shop, its single windowpane smeared with grease. The sign in Arabic over the doorway read "Antiquities." The shop had an air of forlorn neglect.

Victor politely held open the door, ushering her inside. The air smelt of dust, disuse and age. She squinted in the gloom, taking in the dusty statues cluttering the table. A tarnished silver mirror hung on one wall. The gold had chipped on a figurine of Osiris, god of the afterlife, showing wood underneath. Even her inexperienced eye knew these antiquities were fake.

Her breath hitched. Was Victor dealing in fraudulent artifacts? Like the statue of Osiris, she suspected a sparkling layer hid the real, more ominous facade of Kenneth's cousin.

Noise sounded from the back of the shop. Kenneth emerged from the gloom, his white suit gleaming in the dimness like a sunrise. Color drained from his face as he spotted her.

"Badra, what are you doing here? Get out," he said brusquely.

Drawing herself up to her full height, she drew in a steady breath. "I came because you left me. You thought I slept, but I heard each word. What about your promises? You said you loved me." Her mouth worked violently. "I let you walk away once before because of my shame. I can't do so again. I love you."

"Oh, dear God," he whispered, his broad shoulders sagging visibly. "Your tenacity . . . You always did pursue something you wanted with all your heart—as fiercely as a Khamsin wind roars through the desert . . ."

"You lucky bastard." Victor shook his head. "I wish I had a woman who loved me this much."

The small silver bell over the doorway tinkled again. Badra and Victor turned. All thoughts fled, replaced by numb horror. It could not be.

"Omar?" Her voice came as a raspy whisper.

"Hello, my dear," he said pleasantly, then swept a mocking bow to Kenneth. "Ah, the duke of Caldwell, Kenneth Tristan. I do not think I shall address you as 'Your Grace' any longer."

"What the hell are you doing here?" Victor sputtered. "You agreed never to come here."

Badra's former captor turned to Kenneth's cousin. "I lied."

A sickening crack filled the air as he lifted the gold Osiris statue and slammed it into Victor's temple. Then his hands—oh, dear God—wrapped about Badra's neck, squeezing with enormous pressure. His thick thumb pressed just above the hollow of her throat, choking off breath.

"Don't move," Omar warned when Kenneth moved forward. "One step closer and I'll strangle her."

Chapter Twenty-six

"Zaid?" Kenneth stared at his loyal secretary, whose large, beefy hands were wrapped about Badra's throat. Mute terror shone in her dark eyes. She had called him Omar.

Omar, the slave master? The one who had sold her years before, threatening to own her again?

"Zaid Omar Fareeq *Tristan*," the man spat. "We are related, after all. Your grandfather was my father."

Kenneth fought for control, pressed back by the wild plea in Badra's eyes as his secretary pressed a thick thumb farther into her neck. Color flooded her face. She looked numb from terror.

"What the hell are you talking about?" he demanded.

"The last duke of Caldwell. He refused to acknowledge the bastard son of his Egyptian mistress, whom he visited at the Pleasure Palace every time he wintered in Egypt. Your grandfather gave my mother money to keep quiet. She used it to purchase the brothel. All those years, living among whores, never able to face English society. All I wanted was for him to acknowledge me. And he kept me hidden away like a dirty little secret while publicly proclaiming morality."

A jolt of recognition slammed into Kenneth. He stared at Zaid, seeing for the first time the hard lines of his grandfather's face. The faint resemblance.

"My father—" Kenneth began.

"Your father, the precious 'only son.' So noble, so damn English! But he played into my hands when he came to Egypt to search for Meret's necklaces. I hired myself out to take you all on a tour of the Giza pyramids and suggested he and his family tour the Red Sea coast before arriving at Dashur. At the same time, I paid my uncle the sheikh to attack a certain caravan."

"*You* killed my family," Kenneth said hoarsely, sickened.

"I had no choice! As long as your father, his precious heir, lived, Father would ignore me. After your father died, I beseeched the duke to hire me. I worked like a dog to gain his trust. He was about to publicly admit our relationship when you returned. Damn you!" Fury flushed Zaid's face.

Watching Badra, Kenneth did not move. He felt in his pocket for the *jambiya* he kept hidden there. Twisting his body slightly, he hid the movement from Zaid. "You poisoned Grandfather. And me," he guessed, wanting to keep the man talking. Almost there. Furtively he eased the blade from its sheath.

"I attacked you in your bedroom, in your home, after Victor told me you hated Rashid, who had become a Khamsin. But I failed. I knew you'd grow suspicious. I decided to kill you at the Pleasure Palace. I knew you would buy Badra if she were enslaved. I tricked her into stealing the necklace and arranged for her to fail, forcing her to take her daughter's place."

New horror stole over him. The papers he'd signed in England . . .

"What papers did you have me sign?" Kenneth demanded.

Zaid laughed. "A new will, acknowledging me as your heir and giving me the estate. You never looked long enough at documents to truly read them. I also transferred the property deed of the Pleasure Palace from Omar Fareeq, the fake name I use in Egypt, to you. So when you die, I will inherit it—legally, under my real name and as the new duke of Caldwell."

Zaid dragged Badra forward. Her skin was white where his thumb dug into her. Kenneth felt his chest sink.

Fear dawned in her dark eyes. Badra yelped as Zaid grunted and pressed deeper.

"Enough talk," he snapped. "Give me your dagger then sit."

Kenneth hesitated. "I don't have one."

"You're still Khamsin, and you'd never walk around without one."

His thumb pressed deeper into Badra's neck. A choking gasp resulted as she struggled to breathe. Kenneth threw the dagger at the man's feet and sat. Zaid snatched it. Badra wheezed for breath as he loosened his grip and held the knife to her throat.

Edging over to the table, he secured a length of rope and told Badra, "Tie him up, hands behind his back. Then his ankles, and tie him to the column."

317

Zaid pressed the knife into her back as she bound Kenneth's hands behind him, then his ankles, and tied the rope to the pole. Zaid tightened the knots.

When Zaid turned away, Badra still in his grip, Kenneth tested the knots. And then he heard words that stilled his heart with fear.

"I still want you, Badra. And I will have you now."

Badra blanched as Zaid withdrew the necklace bearing Amenemhat II's cartouche from his pocket. He draped it around her neck.

"Now you are my slave," he said, crushing her in a kiss.

Terror numbed Badra as the cursed necklace encircled her throat like a coiled snake. Zaid's cold lips descended on hers, grinding and punishing. As she had been when Fareeq raped her, she became immobilized with fear. But something inside her cried out.

She had spent her whole life being afraid. Afraid of sex, afraid of being a slave. Powerless. Captive to men. Fearful of fighting back, fearful of the pain she'd suffer.

Kenneth loved her. He'd seen past the fear and the scars and taught her to escape her inhibitions. He'd taught her pleasure and passion. He believed in her. It was about time she started believing in herself—not in cursed necklaces or myths or magic.

Something rose up from deep inside, a dull roar. She felt it erupt like a well springing forth from dry sands. Badra writhed and struggled. She raked her nails over Zaid's cheek. He gave a startled shriek and recoiled. Eyeing the vulnerable spot between his legs, she kneed him hard. Zaid

318

howled. Bright scarlet infused his face. She struck him again and he fell to the floor.

"It truly works," she commented, astounded.

Laughter filled the air. She turned and saw Kenneth's face contorted with amusement.

"I told you it would," he said.

She rushed over, grappling with the large knots binding him. But a warning from Kenneth told her Zaid had recovered.

A sharp point of cold steel pressed into her back. "Sit with your back to him," he ordered tersely.

She sat. Zaid coiled the rope about her waist and Kenneth's, binding them together. He wrapped another length of rope around her wrists, binding her arms in front of her, winding the rope down to her ankles. She and Kenneth sat back to back, immobilized. Their foe stepped back, admiring his handiwork.

"You could have lived, Badra," Zaid grunted.

"Better to die free than live as your slave," she rejoined.

Vanishing into the murky interior of the shop, Zaid emerged several moments later with sticks of dynamite, caps, a long length of fuse and a candle. He swept an arm across the table, clearing it of dusty fake artifacts. Carefully he capped the dynamite, attached the fuse, and set the sticks down on the table.

"Victor never made any money," Zaid said, "except selling dynamite to archaeologists who still like to excavate by blowing up tombs."

Zaid wound the fuse around a stubby candle. He pushed the candle halfway to the table's edge, then secured it with a few dusty books, draping the long fuse over them and back to the dynamite. Reaching into his vest pocket, he lit the candle.

"By the time this fuse is lit, I'll be long gone. No one will suspect, since Victor's shop is known to house explosives." He gave them a twisted smile. "Enjoy your last moments together."

Chapter Twenty-seven

The shop door slammed behind Zaid. Kenneth felt his chest sink as he eyed the candle dripping wax onto the floor. Easing his arms to the side as much as possible, he tried picking at the knots binding his wrists together. Sweat dampening his palms aided in loosening the rope, but it hindered him in picking apart the knots. Kenneth gritted his teeth, feeling the knots, testing them with his fingertips.

"Would a dagger help?" Badra asked.

"It might, if I could conjure one out of thin air."

"You might conjure one off my leg."

His hands stilled. "You have a dagger on your leg?"

"Strapped to my thigh. The one you threw to the ground when I refused to marry you. I . . . I was going to give it back to you as a symbol of severing our past and starting anew," she said softly.

Regret speared him. He pushed it aside. Regrets later. "Badra, you're going to have to cut yourself loose."

"How? My arms are tied to my waist."

"You can do it," he encouraged her. "Lift your legs up."

He felt her shift behind him, struggling to reach the knife, and he crooned words of encouragement. His eyes fixed on the burning candle. The wax dripped onto the floor, and the flame flickered closer, so close now, to the fuse.

"I have it!"

"Good. Cut the rope tying us to the column."

He didn't dare breathe or think. The dagger would not be well-honed. Sawing through the rope would be like using a butter knife. He closed his eyes, feeling sweat trickle down his face. Kenneth heard a small cry of distress when she obviously cut herself. But she continued on.

"It's cut!" she cried out.

"There's no time to free your ankles. Brace your feet and hands against the column, and press against my back and force your weight up. We're going to stand together and hobble over to the candle to blow it out before it lights the fuse."

"I'm ready."

Setting his feet flat against the floor, Kenneth grunted and strained to stand, pressing against Badra as she braced herself against the column. Slowly they struggled to stand. Kenneth's eyes never left the candle.

Less than an inch to spare now. An inch away from death.

"Badra, listen. I'm going to walk over there to blow out the candle. You're going to have to walk backward as I do."

He began hobbling to reach the candle, pulling at Badra, feeling her try to assist by moving her feet backward. So close, he could nearly reach it, the bright orange flame flickering near the edge of the fuse . . . burning closer and closer. He hobbled faster, life and love pressing him on.

Close enough now. He puffed out his cheeks and blew.

The candle went out.

The fuse lit.

Kenneth swore as the spark raced along the fuse. He had to put it out somehow. He spat at it. Missed. Tried again. Missed. Helplessly he watched the spark sizzle toward the dynamite.

"We're going to die," Badra whispered.

"No," he said fiercely. *I've got too much to live for.*

The shop door slammed open. His gaze snapped to the intruder. Rashid stood there, scimitar drawn.

"Cut the fuse!" Kenneth roared.

The warrior sprang forward. His scimitar snicked through the air, chopping off the fuse just before it reached the dynamite. Kenneth sagged in relief.

"You're late," he accused.

"I could not find the shop," Rashid replied.

"You can navigate the entire desert at night by consulting the stars but you cannot find a simple antiquities store in broad daylight by asking directions?" he drawled.

Rashid grimaced. "I hate asking for directions."

"Rashid, what is happening?" a familiar voice yelled.

Scimitars drawn, Jabari and Ramses ran inside. They assessed the situation and sheathed their blades. "Thank God you are all right," the sheikh breathed.

Kenneth's accusing gaze found Rashid. "You told them."

"I made him," Jabari replied. "I saw Badra leave with Victor and knew something was amiss. I am your brother, Khepri. I appreciate you trying to protect me from danger, but you forgot a man standing alone is but one warrior. When his brothers stand with him, he is an army."

"Do you not remember the vow we made beneath the stars, Khepri?" Ramses asked. "Our blood flows in each other's veins, our link of brotherhood remains strong forever. When you need us, we are there for you."

Deeply moved by their words, Kenneth could not reply. His friends withdrew their *jambiyas* to cut him loose. Jabari arched a dark brow. "I know you wanted to marry Badra, but this is a most peculiar way to tie the knot."

Kenneth groaned and the others laughed. When the ropes finally slid free, he released a grateful sigh and worked his strained muscles. Badra leaned against him, doing the same.

Their attention swung to the floor as Victor awoke with a groan, rubbing his temple. His eyes widened.

"So, coz, did *you* want to kill me, too?" Kenneth asked.

Victor looked totally abashed as he rose. "I'm sorry, Kenneth," he said brokenly. "I never wanted to hurt you. Zaid promised me the necklaces from the dig site so I could have replicas made. He said he'd return them."

Kenneth picked up the Osiris statue and flipped it into the air. "Cheap replicas you could sell as authentic to ignorant, rich Englishmen? Like these?"

A nod confirmed his suspicion. "But I swear I didn't know anything about him trying to kill you. I wouldn't have helped with that!"

"The papers you had me sign. What about them?" Familiar shame coursed through Kenneth. He steeled his spine. "Did you know I can't read English? Did you try to cheat me, as Zaid did?"

"Good God, no. The papers were telling you the losses. I

had to cover the losses at the Cairo store with profits from the London store. I was hoping you'd sign them without reading them. There simply wasn't any profit. I was desperate for funds and that's why I started making these duplicates."

Kenneth turned the statue over. "It might briefly pass for authentic, but an expert could see the differences. Tourists would not. Could you produce these in mass quantities and sell them cheap?"

"Yes, but there's no reason."

"There is now," he said, setting the statue down on a nearby table. "Visitors to Egypt can't afford real antiquities, which belong in the museum anyway. Tourists wouldn't mind paying for a duplicate of real antiquities."

Victor's brow wrinkled. "Produce fakes in Egypt to sell to tourists? What an excellent idea! I'd need plenty of labor, though. And capital to finance it."

"I will finance the expenses. We will split the profits fifty-fifty," Kenneth told him.

Relief showed on Victor's face. "I can do it. I *will* do it, by God."

Kenneth raked a hand through his hair. "Zaid will be back soon, to find out if his plan worked. We'd best leave. I'm sure he's nearby, watching."

"First let me see if the alley is clear," Rashid offered. He left the shop but quickly ducked back inside. "Someone is coming," he rasped. "Hide."

Kenneth retrieved his dagger as Ramses pushed Jabari and Badra toward the shop's shadowy back room. "In there, where you will be safe," he ordered.

"I will not hide like a girl," Jabari protested.

"I will," Victor offered, grabbing the sheikh's arm and dragging him and Badra off.

They scattered through the shop, Rashid and Ramses taking up a position in the front behind a large mummy case, Kenneth hiding behind a large stack of wood crates at the back. His half-uncle entered the room, a pistol clutched in his hand. From his vantage point, Kenneth saw Zaid advance. Sweat dampened his palm, making the *jambiya* difficult to hold.

"Kenneth? So, you escaped. I know you are still here. Come out and I promise I won't hurt you," Zaid called.

"Stay where you are, Zaid. I'm armed this time."

"Come out, Kenneth," the mocking voice whispered. "Come out and let's talk. I promise I won't shoot."

"Promises from the man who paid Fareeq to attack the caravan and murder my parents and brother? I think not," Kenneth shouted back.

Zaid fired at the crates. The bullet whistled through the air, exploding into Kenneth's hiding spot. He had one chance. He emerged partly from behind his cover. Seeing him, Zaid snarled. As the man aimed, a loud ululating sound echoed through the store. Pride filled Kenneth. The Khamsin war cry.

Zaid half-turned, shock registering on his face, swinging his gun toward the source of that terrible cry. It was Rashid, his scimitar held aloft in his right hand.

Kenneth raised his dagger. "Hello, uncle!" he sang out.

Zaid looked back for just an instant. Kenneth hurled his *jambiya*. Badra's former captor yelled as the knife sank into his back, and he dropped his gun. Rashid raised his scimitar, fury contorting his face, and he charged.

The death blow was delivered swiftly. The fury faded on

Rashid's face, replaced by an odd look of peace, as if the demons riding him had quieted at last.

Kenneth stood as Badra and Jabari rushed into the room. Kenneth grabbed Badra, hiding her face against his chest to shield her from Zaid's body. "Don't look," he whispered.

His gaze locked with Rashid's. "Thank you," he said quietly.

"I heard what you said about . . . about how he arranged to have the caravan attacked and your family killed."

Rashid's voice shook. He wiped his scimitar, sheathed it, then looked at Kenneth with a tormented expression. He unraveled his turban and shook out the fabric, covering Zaid's body with it.

"It's done now," Kenneth said.

Badra tore away from his chest. "Is he truly gone?" she asked. A tremulous note filled her voice.

"Yes, my love. He will never hurt you or me again. My uncle is dead," he assured her.

Victor finally emerged from the back room. He shuddered as he looked at the covered body. "Zaid was your uncle?"

As Kenneth explained, fury tightened Rashid's face. He kicked the body with the toe of his boot. "God rot your soul, you evil bastard. I hope you burn in hell."

The warrior's behavior perplexed Kenneth. It seemed very . . . personal. "Rashid? Are you all right?"

The man's large, dark eyes met his. "There is something you should know, Kenneth. I need to confess something. Something very important, to settle peace upon my *Ieb*." He stared at the ground. "It is about the loss of your family. You thought yourself the sole survivor. But there was one other."

Rashid spoke so quietly that Kenneth strained to hear. The delicate hairs at the nape of his neck rose as a suspicion began to assert itself. He untangled himself from Badra and stepped forward, toward the warrior he'd once thought wanted to kill him.

The warrior he'd thought hated him.

The warrior he'd thought he had nothing in common with.

"One other?"

"Your brother. Your brother who was too big for your parents to hide in a basket, but who was taken by Fareeq."

The anguish on Rashid's face twisted Kenneth's heart.

"Your brother who was raised as an Al-Hajid."

It all made sense. The gingerbread Rashid had gobbled down at his house in England. His expert whistling, when whistling was considered impolite in the Arab world.

"Oh, dear God," Kenneth rasped. "Graham. My brother."

The two men stood motionless as alabaster statues, chests heaving with the intensity of their emotions.

"Rashid is your brother?" Badra asked. Jabari and Ramses stared in open-mouthed shock. Victor made a strangled noise.

Kenneth did not respond. Suddenly he felt the pressure of his past crush him like heavy stones, and he stepped forward. Hesitated. Wanted so much to embrace him. Feared there had been too much hostility between them to reconcile.

Rashid took two steps forward. "Can you forgive me?"

"There is nothing to forgive," Kenneth replied.

The two brothers, who had been separated for years, hugged each other fiercely. Tears burned Kenneth's eyes when they finally pulled away, and he saw moisture sparkle in Rashid's. Graham's eyes. They looked just like their mother's.

"When did you find out?" he asked hoarsely.

"I did not know you survived until last year when Katherine announced she'd found our grandfather. Then I knew."

"Why?" Frustration gripped Kenneth and he slammed a fist into his thigh. "Why didn't you tell me? Why keep it a secret?"

Graham kept looking at Ramses and Jabari, who still looked shocked. He gripped the hilt of his scimitar so tightly his flesh was white. Kenneth sensed he had something deeply private to share that he could not reveal to the other warriors. He cleared his throat, but Jabari interceded.

"We will step outside, Kenneth, to give you time to become reacquainted," he said tactfully.

"Badra can stay," Graham said quickly.

Jabari did not look surprised. When he, Ramses and Victor left the shop, the white-knuckled grip Graham had on his scimitar eased. "I could not return with you to England. I knew I had to keep my identity concealed." His voice dropped to a bare whisper. "I was jealous. You survived the attack and were treated as an honored son by the Khamsin. And you could slip into the English life as easily as your totem sheds its skin. I could not."

Anguish twisted his face. He bent his head. "I could not face the shame, the scandal should someone find out . . . what had happened to me when I was taken prisoner. Taken by one of Fareeq's men, who liked boys. I was afraid others would discover . . . that I am not a man after all." He turned away, his face flaming.

"Oh, Rashid," Badra managed to say, tears streaming down her face. She turned to Kenneth. "I heard what happened to him. When you announced your departure, I told him what Fareeq did to me. We made a vow to pretend we were courting, so we could escape the scrutiny of others who inquired why neither of us wished to marry. That was why I asked him to become my falcon guard."

Kenneth felt raging, violent desire to murder Fareeq with his bare hands for the abuse his brother had suffered. And for Badra. He fervently wished the sheikh alive so he could make him suffer as the two people he loved had suffered.

"What made you come forward now?" he asked quietly.

Graham's tormented gaze flicked to Badra. "When you told me of your plan to buy Badra because you loved her, I realized what courage it had taken to trade herself for her daughter and become a slave again. And if she could have such courage to face the fears of her past, then perhaps I could as well."

Kenneth went forward, placed his hands on his brother's shoulders, forcing him to face him. "You have that courage, Graham. You survived and became an honorable, fierce warrior as well. This courage will serve you when we return to England. You must return to England and assume your rightful place."

Horror flared in his brother's dark eyes. "Never," he said tightly. "I will never return to England."

Confused, Kenneth studied him. Slowly Graham began to talk about the redheaded Englishman.

"I was eight, Khepri. I saw him and begged him to slip out a message of how I was held prisoner. I told him my name. I promised him riches, if he sent someone to rescue me. He told me delivering such a message came with a different price."

Raging anger filled Kenneth as he learned the truth. He calmed, for his brother's sake.

"Afterward, the redheaded Englishman laughed. He warned me never to tell anyone, for he would deny it and blame me. I begged him to free me. I begged and waited, hoping he would tell someone where I was. I waited. But help never arrived."

Resolve pooled inside Kenneth. He put a calming hand on Graham's shoulder. "You are no longer that little boy, Graham. You will not return to England alone. I will be with you. Our family's property in Yorkshire is remote. We'll go there instead of London. You must come with me."

Hope flared briefly in Graham's eyes. Then it faded.

"Come. Please. I will be at your side to help you. Please. Now that we've found each other, I can't bear to lose you."

Graham sought Badra's gaze. She gave a small nod. "He's right. You can do it," she said.

Graham heaved a deep sigh. Mischief suddenly danced in his eyes. "Only if you return as Badra's husband."

Kenneth glanced at her hopeful face. But before he could sink to his knees and take her hand, Badra surprised him by doing just that. She stared up at him with large, dark velvet eyes.

"I know you asked me to be your wife and I refused three times. It is my turn now. Will you marry me?" she whispered.

Pulling her to her feet, he kissed her gently. "I love you, Badra. I never stopped loving you. I would be honored."

She touched the necklace she still wore. "This means I'm your slave."

Kenneth smiled as he removed the pectoral. "No, it means the opposite. This is Amenemhat II's cartouche. That's why I placed it around your neck in your room at the Pleasure Palace. I gave you the power to enslave my heart, my love. Zaid mixed up the cartouches."

He pocketed it. "The best place for this, and all the jewelry from the excavation, is a museum."

After he called in the others and told them the news, Jabari smiled at Kenneth. "I am happy for you, Khepri, that you have a real brother. Blood relatives are most important."

"So are relatives of the heart, Jabari," Kenneth responded, glancing around. "Badra, the sister you took in when she came to you as a frightened concubine. Me, the brother your father rescued from death. That's what a real family is, Jabari. People who come together, despite the circumstances, and support each other through good times and bad. I could discover I had ten brothers I never knew about, but you'll always be one who was most important in my life, Jabari. You were there for me when I needed a family the most."

Emotion shone in the sheikh's dark eyes. "And I will continue to be, if you need me, Khepri."

Kenneth gave his old cocky grin. "I'll need you to perform a small wedding ceremony. Would you?"

The sheikh glanced at Badra's shining face. "Of course. But I doubt it will be a small ceremony, Khepri. The entire tribe will wish to attend. The Khamsin are your family."

"There's one relative I don't think will be present," Graham joked, nodding to Zaid. Kenneth grimaced.

At last, their parents' deaths were avenged. There remained only one problem. They glanced at the body.

"We cannot leave him here," Jabari mused.

The warriors eyed each other. Sand covered any trace of the bodies of their enemies in the desert.

It was over; yet one last brick to the pyramid of lies, deception and suffering remained standing. Kenneth remembered the sticks of dynamite lying on the table inside the shop. "I have an idea," he said.

That night, Khamsin warriors invaded the Pleasure Palace again. They met with little resistance after the guards were told Kenneth was the new owner. He watched proudly as Graham, bearing a new dignity, took charge and told the eunuchs and women they had a choice: the streets or a job assembling replicas of antiquities.

All agreed to the jobs. They were instructed to report to Victor's shop the next day and were ushered out. Khamsin warriors escorted the women as they departed to their quarters for the night. To the Shepherd's Hotel. At Kenneth's expense.

Kenneth hid a smile, thinking of the shocked look on the hotel manager's face as several former concubines guarded by fierce Khamsin warriors invaded his hotel.

When all had cleared the brothel, Jabari, Ramses and Graham brought in Zaid, rolled up in a fraying carpet. Badra gripped Kenneth's hand as they laid the body of the man who had owned the brothel upon a bed. Graham placed dynamite on the bed and attached a long fuse allowing enough time for them to escape. Then the trio departed, leaving Kenneth and Badra alone.

Kenneth nodded. Badra stuck the match. The flame glowed, burned with a fierce intensity. Shadows danced upon her grim face. Badra touched the flame to the fuse. It sparked, caught. Hand in hand, she and Kenneth ran out of the compound. Then they stood and waited, watching from the street.

Minutes later, loud explosions shattered the night. Orange flames leapt toward the sky. Badra watched, nestled against Kenneth's chest, his arms wrapped securely around her.

"Let it burn," she whispered. "Oh, let it burn to rubble. Never again will it house slaves. Never again."

In silence they watched the orange flames lick the air and devour the building. Shouts could be heard as people nearby caught sight of the fire. Kenneth signaled Badra to leave.

As they vanished into the shadows to a safer vantage point, he turned her to face him. The harsh glow of the fire danced across his solemn expression. "There's something I need to say. Something you may not want to hear."

"Say it, my love. You can tell me anything. I trust you."

Kenneth's gaze darkened. "It must have been hell for Zaid. Imagine spending your whole life longing for recognition from a father who ignored you and thought you were a blot on his morality. It drove him to murder. Maybe if my grandfather had acknowledged he had an illegitimate child, and maybe if Zaid had finally received the attention he craved, he would have turned out differently. I don't know."

His knuckles brushed her cheek. "I do know this. You have a beautiful little girl, Badra. Her smile. Her sweetness. You can't deny the resemblance. And if you deny Jasmine a relationship as her mother, you're denying yourself as well. Doesn't being her mother matter more than the fact that she's illegitimate?"

He added softly. "I don't care who fathered her. I only care about you. She needs a mother, Badra. Not a sister. She needs you. She hasn't had you for years. Shouldn't you start making up for lost time?"

Emotion clogged Badra's throat. Jasmine did deserve truth and recognition as her daughter. She'd wanted to protect the child from the humiliation of being a bastard, but the greater crime was not acknowledging her.

"Jasmine can weather being an outcast from society, being born out of wedlock," Badra mused softly.

"She has her mother's courage. And she won't be an outcast. She'll have you. And me. I'm going to legally adopt her as my daughter as soon as we return to England."

Warmth rushed through her at his declaration of support. With his love shielding them from rigid English society, she and Jasmine would never be alone.

But what of Khamsin society? Facing the tribe's scrutiny, the tribe that had been her only family all these years, would be harder by far.

Chapter Twenty-eight

Two days later, Badra, Kenneth and Graham departed for the Khamsin camp in the eastern desert. Jabari and the others had gone ahead, giving Kenneth time to clear up his business at Dashur.

The harsh yellow sun began to set as they approached the camp on their camels. Badra did not voice her fears. Would the tribe, knowing Jasmine was Fareeq's daughter, deny her? She did not care. All that mattered was Jasmine. She would proudly acknowledge the child as her daughter.

Graham let loose a low, shrill whistle as the outcropping of black tents appeared on the horizon. He grinned. "Now they're certain to know who it is. I'm the only one so rude."

A flurry of activity took place; small indigo figures rushed about like ants carpeting the sand. As they approached the camp's edge, Badra saw a sight immediately warming her heart: Beneath the sprawling shade of a thorn tree, Jasmine stood between Elizabeth and Jabari, clutching their hands.

Badra pulled her camel to a halt and forced the beast to

its knees. Jumping off, she cautiously approached her daughter. Jasmine looked up at her. Recognition dawned on the girl's elfin face. So many changes, so many new people. Yet her daughter displayed courage and fortitude facing each.

"Jabari formally welcomed Jasmine into the tribe as the daughter of his heart. The people have accepted his edict and Jasmine as well," Elizabeth told her in English.

The sheikh's steady gaze met Badra's. She smiled in thanks. His welcome put Jasmine under his protection and assured that no one would dare shun her when they discovered Fareeq was her father.

Badra knelt down, her body trembling so hard she could barely wrap her arms around her daughter's thin frame. She hugged the child with all the intensity of years lost and hope found. Slowly she pulled away, brushing a lock of silky black hair from the little girl's eyes.

"Jasmine, I have something to share with you," she whispered. "I am your mother. Not your sister."

Those solemn brown eyes blinked, then a delighted smile touched the girl's lips. It was like watching the sun burst from sheltering clouds. "You're my mother? They said my mother died!"

"They were wrong," Badra answered in a choked voice. "You were taken away from me when you were born. But that's not important now. This is: I promise, I will never, ever, let you go again."

A warm hand settled on Badra's shoulder. She glanced up to see Kenneth. He squatted down, gently taking Jasmine's small hands in his large ones. He gave a reassuring smile.

"And we have more news for you, honey. I'm marrying your mother, so that means you'll have a new father as well. Is that all right with you?"

Jasmine studied him with large, solemn eyes. "I think so," she said seriously. "I do like you. You have lemon drops."

He laughed and produced one from his pocket. She held it in her small palm and went into his arms for a hug, resting her cheek against his. Jasmine pulled away. With a grave, adultlike expression, she ran a hand over his face. "I like it here, but I think I'll like living with you as my father more. The sheikh's face is all scratchy when he hugs me."

"Ah, I am rejected in favor of the less hairy Englishman," Jabari mocked as he fingered his close-cropped beard.

"She has good taste," Kenneth said smugly.

The girl unwrapped the candy, popped it into her mouth and snuggled against him. Judging from his assured way with her daughter, Kenneth would make a good father, Badra thought with pride.

Hands thrust awkwardly into the pockets of his new English trousers, Graham greeted Jabari and Elizabeth and conversed briefly with them. Then the sheikh and his wife walked back to the camp, arms around each other. Kenneth released Jasmine and introduced Graham as her soon-to-be-uncle.

Immediately her daughter looked up with shining eyes.

"I have a family now," she said happily.

Badra swallowed a lump clogging her throat. Kenneth winked as he rested a protective hand on Jasmine's shoulder. "And your mother and I will have to see about getting you a brother or sister to play with, honey."

Jasmine looked hopeful. "How soon? Tomorrow?"

Graham grinned. Kenneth cleared his throat.

"Ah, no, I think it will take a little longer than that."

A charming frown knit the little girl's brow. "Why is it going to take so long? Can't you do it any faster?"

"I promise, I'll try to do it as fast as I can." Kenneth bit back a laugh as Badra blushed.

His expression turned serious when he turned to Graham. "I do want to return to England as soon as Badra and I are married, though."

Graham fingered the tan broadcloth of his trousers. "These feel very restrictive. Must I always wear English clothing?"

"You'll get used to it," Kenneth assured him. "We'll just make sure the tailor measures you properly and you'll be fine."

He glanced at Badra. "There are many adjustments ahead, for all of us. I can't promise it will be trouble free."

"I'm not afraid," she told him.

And she wasn't. The veil of terror had been lifted from her eyes. She could face English society, gossip and stares. She stood at the beginning of her life, ready to make the journey with Kenneth, wherever it might lead. Her gaze fell to Graham, who stood silently beside her. A new beginning, for all of them. She clasped Graham's hand, then Kenneth's, drawing close to her the two most important men in her life.

Linked together, like the family they were, they stood absorbed in the enchanting brushstrokes of color sweeping the sky—deep rose, violet and peach. The brilliant orb of a full pale moon hung low in the darkening sky, having chased the sun from its lofty perch.

"Look," Kenneth said softly. "The full moon. This is your time, Badra. The moon reveals her shy face, flooding the night with her soft light." He glanced at Graham, who studied the moonrise with a face rapt with fresh hope.

"Sometimes, there are secrets too painful to reveal in the harshness of the sun. Only under the moon's gentle, coaxing beams can they come to light, and finally vanquish the darkness," Graham mused.

Kenneth silently mouthed "thank you" to Badra. Her chest tightened with the tremendous joy flooding her. Graham faced many difficult struggles ahead, but he did not face them alone. He was free at last of the terrible secret burdening him. Free to embrace the brother he thought he had lost, and the life he was destined for, just as Kenneth's love had set her free from her cruel past.

Freedom called to them all in the hush of desert wind sweeping across the dusky sands. They walked back toward the Khamsin camp, listening to the promise in its sweet song.

Author's Note

The necklaces of Princess Meret, along with other fantastic finds of jewelry, were actually discovered at the pyramid of Senusret III by Jacques de Morgan during the 1894–1895 digging season in Egypt. I used artistic license to weave a legend about the two necklaces and their power to enslave.

Unfortunately, the basis for Badra's slavery is all too real. Slavery still exists in the modern world. In the Sudan, women and children are frequently sold into slavery. I became personally acquainted with the horrors of slavery while traveling in Haiti and meeting former restavèks. Restavèks are Haitian children who become enslaved when they are given by an impoverished parent to a family who promises to care for the child with food, clothing and schooling, in exchange for domestic labor. Few of those promises are fulfilled and frequently the restavèk child works long hours and is subject to beatings and sometimes sexual abuse.

Human trafficking even exists today in the United States.

341

A 2004 report by the U.S. Department of Justice said more than 17,000 people are brought illegally to the United States annually to work in sweatshops, in domestic servitude or as prostitutes.

CONNIE MASON

The Last Rogue

All London is stunned by Lucas, Viscount Westmore's vow to give up the fair sex and exile himself to St. Ives. The infamous rake is known for his love of luxury and his way with the ladies, just as the rugged Cornish coast is known for its savagery, its fearsome gales and its smugglers.

But Luc is determined to turn away from the seduction of white thighs and perfumed flesh that had once ended in tragedy. He never guessed the stormy nights of Cornwall would bring unlooked-for danger, the thrill of the chase, and a long-legged beauty who tempts him like no other. As illicit cargo changes hands, as her flashing green eyes challenge his very masculinity, he longs for nothing so much as to lose himself in . . . *Bliss*.
